THE DOÑA

The Doña

For information contact: Shalako Press
P.O. Box 371, Oakdale, CA 95361-0371
http://www.shalakopress.com

ISBN: 978-0-9798898-8-2

Cover Artist: Karen Borrelli
Editor: Judith Mitchell
Cover photograph of Erika Costa taken by Judith Mitchell
Miss Costa's costume provided by Costume Corner,
Modesto, CA

PRINTED IN THE UNITED STATES OF AMERICA

To my brother Jerry

Acknowledgments

This book is a combined effort of many people. I would first like to thank my brother Jerry for allowing me the privilege of writing The Doña. It was in his fertile mind that the idea for this story was born.

I would also like to thank Anna Collier for correcting my *gringo* Spanish.

Thanks to Erika Costa for posing for our cover.

Thanks to Jamie Hood for her input and ideas.

Thanks to Josie Costa for helping correct my mistakes.

And most of all hugs and kisses to my wife, Judy, whose expert editing always turns my hieroglyphics into something readable. Thanks Kid.

The original title of this book was *Here Hangs Rudolfo Garcia*.

Chapter 1

It was about ten o'clock in the morning when he decided to kill him. Now he had to settle on the best way of going about it. Under normal circumstances it would be simple enough, but Henry Baines frowned as he tamped the tobacco tightly in his pipe. The man he was thinking about always seemed to be surrounded by a small army of vaqueros and he'd be tough to get to. And, he'd have to make it look nice and legal, because folks in Dogtown wouldn't like it if they knew their judge had participated in a murder. He raised his eyebrows and sighed as he shoved the pipestem between his teeth. It would be tough to pull off, but it still had to be done. Besides, Henry took pride in doing the impossible. He struck a match on the bottom of his chair only to have the breeze blow it out. He cursed lightly and struck another, this time cupping the flame with his hand. Drawing deeply, he smiled with satisfaction as small clouds of smoke appeared and the taste and aroma of the tobacco filled his mouth and nose.

The chair creaked as he leaned his heavy frame back and viewed the scenery from his vantage point on the porch of the sheriff's office. Dogtown wasn't much to look at, but it was his. He could see most of the buildings from where he was seated alongside the one and only road running through the small settlement. It looked much like the beginnings of any other mining town he had seen. There were three saloons, one general store, a barber shop, two eating establishments and one hotel (if you could call it that), and a brothel district located conveniently behind the largest of the three saloons. The buildings were a combination of canvas and boards, thrown up in a hurry to attract the miners and get a portion of the gold they were starting to pull out of the ground. The hotel was a series of tents with a wash-basin and dirty towel hanging on a board across two barrels. The jail was the sturdiest of the lot, made of stone and adobe with a plank roof. But even it wasn't much. The roof leaked and a man could simply walk away if he wanted to escape. The townspeople had deemed the metal bars more valuable for digging gold, than for keeping drunks or petty thieves locked up.

"Here they come, right on time." He checked his pocket watch as the parade of prancing horses entered the street at the other end of town. It was Rudolfo Garcia making his weekly visit from his rancho.

"Dammit." The Sheriff's voice floated through the open door with the clatter of the coffee pot on the wood-burning stove.

"Use a rag or towel," Henry said. "And bring me one too."

He propped his feet up on the railing, savoring his pipe. Pod Randell wasn't too bright, but he had been Henry's choice for sheriff. It took some doing to get the townspeople to agree that they needed any form of law and order, let alone both a judge and sheriff. But Henry was a grand speaker, and after buying a couple of rounds of drinks in the Rusty Rail, he stood on a chair and gave his speech.

"You don't want the same lawlessness and thievery happening here that's taking place at every other camp, do you? This town is going to grow. And with it will come every kind of evil you can imagine. They will steal you blind. They will empty your tent or cabin while you're working your claim. Or they will jump your claim and take it away from you. They might even shoot you in the back, and who's going to protect you? Let me be your judge, and I'll appoint a tough and uncompromising sheriff. It will only cost you the time to build a jail and five dollars for each miner per month. You'll spend more than that in one night at the bar."

Five dollars a month was a small sum indeed to have someone look after your safety. And while they all agreed, no one had taken time to do the math. There were almost five hundred miners, store keepers and laborers in and around Dogtown and it was still growing. It wouldn't take long until Henry Baines would be a rich man.

"Thank you Pod." He took the steaming cup offered to him. "Hurt yourself?" He glanced toward the sheriff's smooth, delicate hand. He had mistaken the little man with smooth skin and long blond hair for a young girl dressed in a man's clothes when he first met him. But he had turned out to be just what Henry wanted. A deadly gunfighter who was not threatening to look at.

"Na, just a hot handle."

"Well, take care of that gun hand. Never know when you might need to use it." The jail was now three months old, and the only use they'd had for it was to let a couple of drunken miners who couldn't find their cabin sleep there.

"I can use the other one just as easily."

"No doubt you can, my boy. No doubt you can."

Pod tossed off the remnants of his cup and spat as he watched several of the shop owners wave friendly greetings to the Mexicans as they passed their places of business.

"You'd think they'd never seen 'em come to town before," he said bitterly, folding his arms and leaning against a post. "They act like it's some damn celebration."

"That's because he spends a lot of money in their stores." Henry propped his feet back on the railing and folded his hands behind his head. "You'd like it too if he'd give you some of his gold. Now, wouldn't you?"

Pod didn't answer right away. The silver trappings on the saddles and bridles jingled with the clatter of hooves as the prancing horses passed. They stopped at Carpenter's General Store, one building down on the opposite side of the street. Not too many of the large land grant owners had cash money. They bartered hides and tallow with the ships on the coast for what they needed. But Rudolfo Garcia was smart and Henry liked that. He not only sold hides and tallow to the trading companies, but he had seen a chance of making a fortune by selling beef to the mining camps. His vaqueros delivered fat cattle on the hoof to miners all over the Mother Lode, and were paid top dollar for them. And now he stood to make even more money as rumors persisted of a war between the states. The Army would pay almost as much as the miners for healthy stock, and Rudolfo had plenty of them roaming freely on his vast rancho.

"I see he brought Leonida with him today," Henry said, watching dust settle in his cup as a gust of wind sent a tumble weed racing down the street. "We don't get to see much of her, but I'd keep her under lock and key too, if she belonged to me."

"Don't know why you'd bother with that. She's just another woman. And you can't trust any of them, can you?"

"No, I don't guess you can." He tossed the coffee into the dirty roadway and leaned back in the chair stroking his gray goatee. Opening his tobacco pouch, he began re-packing his pipe. "But men have been eating out of women's hands ever since Eve gave Adam the apple." He watched intently as Rudolfo took the reins from his wife's small, gloved hand. "She is the most extraordinary woman I've ever seen."

The clouds hanging over the hills held a promise of rain for the San Joaquin Valley, but Henry didn't know which he hated worse, the dust, or the mud the rain would bring. He struck another match on the bottom his chair.

"Heard someone say he bought her down in Mexico." Pod shifted his feet as he spoke.

"No, it was arranged by her parents. You know, like they do in the old country. She was born in Mexico City, but her parents are from Madrid, Spain. She's true Spanish."

"How come you know so much about her?" His tone was hard, and Henry wondered what happened to make this young man hate women so.

"I ask questions, Pod. That way I can learn and know the people around me. That's how a person grows rich. You don't see either of us sloshing around in that cold creek and shoveling rock, do you?"

The sheriff didn't answer and Henry turned his attention back to the lady across the street. He watched as her husband held the horse steady while she dismounted. She removed her hat and beat the dust from her riding skirt, then shook her head and ran a gloved hand through her honey-colored hair.

"They say she's about thirteen years younger than Rudolfo," he said thoughtfully. "If he's thirty-three, that'd make her about twenty."

"Well, at that age, she should be married. She oughta be home having kids instead of ridin' into town like this."

"A woman can't stay home all the time."

Her golden-brown skin glistened in the sun and Henry almost felt hypnotized as she looked his way. He could see her perfectly shaped lips slightly parted, and the brilliant flash of green eyes from across the narrow street. Her expression then broke into a smile as her husband said something to her in Spanish. She answered him, placing the palms of her hands on his vest and looking up into his face as she spoke. Henry listened, not understanding a word, and cursing himself for not learning another language besides English. She turned quickly, offering her husband her arm, and entered the store.

"She is rather strikingly beautiful, isn't she?" Henry struck another match and re-lit his pipe as he spoke.

"They were talking about us." Pod tossed his empty cup through the door and listened as it rattled on the board floor.

"I doubt that. But, what if they were? What difference

does it make?"

"No Mexican should ever be allowed to laugh at a white. Besides, it ain't fair. It just ain't fair."

"What isn't fair?"

"That Mexican. He's got all that land. Close to 50,000 acres the way I calculate. And he's got all that money. No Mexican should be that rich."

"And he's got the girl." Henry hoped his smile would calm the boy down. "Well, he earned it. The money part of it, anyway. I guess Governor Pico gave his father the land for doing some great deed in the Mexican Army, but Garcia made most of the money himself."

"Well, no one should have that much land. It ain't right."

"Who says they shouldn't? I'd like to have that much, and more. And you'd like it too. Now, wouldn't you?"

He didn't answer, so Henry continued talking.

"You see, Pod, the difference between you and me is, I'm honest with myself. I'd like to have everything Garcia's got. I'd love to have his money, his land *and* his woman. But you, on the other hand, never gave Garcia's land or money another thought until he got that wife a few months ago. Then you got madder' a wet hen, and you've been festerin' ever since. It's the girl that's got you angry, not his money or his land."

"Just never thought much about him before, that's all. He never hardly came to town, 'til she come along. And that big weddin' party. You were there. He musta' spent a fortune. And the way he's spendin' money on her, she'll probably ruin him before long." He took a seat beside Henry and tried leaning back like the judge, but his feet wouldn't reach the rail.

"And another thing. Most anyone could buy a good-lookin' woman like her if he had that kind of money, and that's what she's after. His money. And she probably don't even care about the land."

"Yes, I can see your point. I'd really forgotten you're a woman hater."

"I don't hate women. I just don't trust 'em. They all cheat. They say they like you and laugh at you behind your back. They'll marry you and take your money and run off with another man."

Henry raised his eye brows. His pipe had gone out so he struck another match. He knew the girls at the Rusty Rail laughed about "the little man with the big star" behind Pod's back, but he'd never thought about Pod being a jilted lover before.

"What if I told you, you could have it all, Pod? The money, the land, well, maybe not the girl, but the land and the money. What would you say to that?"

Pod just stared at him.

"I've been thinking about this for awhile. There's going to be some changes taking place real quick-like, and it's only those who know how to think that are going to get rich."

"We're making pretty good money right now, and not havin' to work very hard to get it."

"Yes, I know. But there's no law that says we can't make even more, is there?" He turned to face his wide-eyed sheriff. "In fact, I believe we still can keep our present positions and own that land of his if we use our heads.

"I don't know how. He won't sell any of that land, and he don't even use it all."

"Yes, my dear boy, I've heard all that too. But I also know that sooner or later old Zachary Taylor is going to make this another State of the Union, and Garcia's title will be challenged in court, along with those of all the other ranchos here in California. They'll look at the Treaty of Guadalupe Hidalgo and examine the titles to the land grants and try to decide who really owns the land and who doesn't. And that's going to take years and a lot of money. Money that most of these land owners (with the exception of maybe Garcia himself) don't have. So, they'll wind up losing their land. Yes sir, in a

couple more years, say by '52, things will really change around here. The key is," he paused and drew deeply on his pipe, "to get hold of his rancho before it hits the courts. Because very few judges will ever question whether another white man has legal title to a ranch, especially if the claimant happens to be another judge and his partner is a sheriff. Now will they?"

"No, don't reckon they would. But, how do you propose to do it when he ain't gonna sell? And even if he did sell, we ain't got that kinda' money put together. And even then, you'd still need more money to hire punchers to run your cattle."

"Who said anything about buying his land? In fact, who said anything about running his ranch. That's a lot of hard work, the type that I don't think either one of us is up to doing. No, I just want his rancho long enough to sell it. Little by little."

The judge knocked the ashes out of his pipe and started re-packing it with fresh tobacco. Pod sat quietly as he lit another match and pulled deeply on his pipe.

"No, I don't expect that we'll have to buy that land at all. So, you can just keep your money hid in that sock under your mattress. He's going to give us the land."

"Give us all that land? He's not crazy. And I know you're not drunk. What makes you think he's just going to give it all to us?"

"Because no one's ever asked him the right way, that's why."

"And what's the right way to ask him? He's already run a couple of dozen nesters off his place that I know of."

"Well, you just leave that to me. I've never let you down yet, have I?"

"No, but I don't see how you're gonna do it. No one's stupid enough to give away his land and his money."

"You let me worry about the *how*. I'm the judge, remember? I'll let you in on the details as you need to know them. But what I need you to do right now is to find me a couple of good men. Hard men that will do what we tell them to, and won't ask too many questions."

"What do you need other men for? I can do most

anything you want done."

"Yes, and you've been a real help. But I don't want you involved in what I'm going to ask them to do."

They paused to watch Rudolfo come out of the store carrying a few small packages, and help his bride onto her horse.

"Why won't you tell me what you're gonna do?"

"When the time comes, my boy. When the time comes," he said absently as the fancy-clad riders trotted their horses down the street.

A long moment passed in which Pod sat contemplating his hat-band which he turned time and time again. Henry sighed deeply, waiting patiently for their conversation to take root in the sheriff's mind, which he was positive didn't work all the time. It was hard for him to understand how a man could be so competent in a few things, and not be able to grasp the rest of the world as it went by. Pod started to chuckle as the plan began to register. The chuckle grew into raucous laughter.

"I wonder what them miners would say if they could hear us now?" he said after calming himself. "The protectors of Law And Order talkin' like this."

"Well, if we don't help ourselves to a little extra, someone else will. And you know me, Pod. I'm not one to sit around and let someone else take what could be mine." The judge stretched his heavy frame. "What'dya say? Do you want to sit here on the porch of this rickety office and watch them come in here every week? Or, take his ranch and his money?"

"Ok, I'll get the men." Pod was still laughing as he strode toward the Rusty Rail.

Henry drew on his pipe and blew a cloud of smoke in the air as the riders disappeared over the next rise. Watching the two of them together in front of the store had placed the missing link into his plan. It really was too bad though, that he was going to have to use Leonida that way. He kind of liked her.

Chapter 2

Leonida stood in the doorway in her riding gear, smiling as she watched her husband poring over the ledger lying open on his walnut desk. Hardly any, none that she knew, of the large land owners in California knew how to read. But Rudolfo not only knew how to read and write, he was good with figures also. His father had the foresight to send his eldest son to Mexico City to be educated, and that was where they happened to meet. She was only a child of thirteen then, but she still remembered the tall handsome man standing in the doorway of the school asking the priest where he should go to learn how to read and write. She could still hear all the snickers and giggles of the girls at the thought of a man coming to a school for girls asking such a question, not realizing that the man standing before them was not able to read the sign on the front gate. They saw each other daily after that from a distance. He would smile at her on his way to the school for boys located on the opposite side of the church. She would smile back and then put up with the comments and teasing of the other girls saying she was in love with a grown man. But she didn't even know his name, and several weeks would pass before they even spoke to each other. She had gone to the marketplace with her mother. They had their baskets filled with fresh breads, tortillas, fruit and a chicken, and were on their way home when Leonida stopped at a flower stand to pick out a bouquet to decorate the table. She was intent on making the right choice, when she heard her mother mention her name. She turned to see her mother talking with the same young man who smiled at her every morning at the school yard.

He came to visit at their home weekly after that. He would sit and talk to her parents and older brothers for hours, describing his life on *Rancho Manantial Escondido*, the ranch of hidden springs where he grew up. Leonida listened intently to the conversations while she busied herself with housework or studies.

"There are many springs on the rancho that flow year round, but you'd have to look hard to find them. That is, unless you have one of the Indian *vaqueros* with you. They seem to know every inch of the land. My father built the main house directly over the top of two of the best springs. One feeds the fountain in the courtyard, and the other is located right outside our kitchen door, so the maid doesn't have to haul water very far."

She began to feel she knew his family personally. He had no sisters and his mother had died giving birth to his only brother sixteen years earlier. His father, who was in poor health, had never remarried. He described the daring vaqueros on their horses and the maidens in their colorful dresses. He told of fiestas with music and dancing that lasted for days. But they seldom spoke directly to each other. And when they did, it was mostly a simple greeting when he arrived, or to wish each other God's speed as he left. Rudolfo and her father were fast becoming good friends. But the lack of communication he had for her personally, caused her to believe he was not interested in her at all. Then one day, not long after her fourteenth birthday, she was called into the living room where he sat with her parents and older brothers. They asked her to sit down, and her father spoke to her gravely.

"As you know, Rudolfo is finishing his studies and will be returning to California shortly."

She nodded.

"He has asked for your hand in marriage and I have agreed. Your mother and brothers also agree."

She tried to speak but words failed her, so she looked around the room, opened-mouthed, at the smiling faces of her mother and two brothers. She barely heard her father as he continued.

"Of course, this marriage cannot take place until you have finished school and a proper time of courtship has passed. Perhaps in three years. You'll be seventeen then, and that will give Rudolfo time to establish himself in his position at the California rancho."

She stared at the man who was to become her husband, and he smiled at her. She thought it rather smug this time. She did not know whether she liked the idea of becoming the bride of Rudolfo Garcia or not, but she didn't really have a choice. Her father and brothers had spoken and that was the way things were done.

Two weeks later she stood with her family beside the carriage waiting to take Rudolfo back to California. It was one of the few times he actually spoke to her.

"Goodbye, Leonida. I will write to you as often as I can, and I will send for you as soon as the proper time arrives. I promise on my mother's grave, that I will do my best to make you happy."

Six years would pass before she would see the beautiful rancho bordering the Mokelumne River. When she was seventeen, word came that Rudolfo's father had been taken gravely ill and their plans had to be postponed for a while. Word came several months later with an apology from Rudolfo, saying that Señor Garcia had passed away and they would have to wait until he could get things in order at the Rancho. Then much sadness began to plague her own family. Her mother became ill, and with her death something began to die inside her father. When word came that her two older brothers had both been killed during a siege on the Texas border in the war of 1846, General Flores resigned his military position and sat at home, a wounded and broken man. Their wedding date was pushed back even further until it seemed her betrothal to this strange man from California was only a dream.

But Rodolfo was true to his word and continued to write her faithfully, several letters at a time. He wrote of the loneliness felt by everyone after his father's death, and how he wished she could be there to comfort him. There were several letters pouring out his heart to her after her mother died, filled with prayers for her comfort. He also bragged how his brother, Carlo, had grown into a fine young man, and how the señoritas constantly ran after him. Later on, there were those that told of troubles surrounding the Rancho, causing him worry. There were people he called "squatters" who were constantly claiming parts of the Rancho as their own. These people did not even offer to pay for the land they wanted, they simply tried to take it. He also wrote of a quaint village with the strange name of Dogtown. And while most of the people living there were hard-working miners and were friendly to Rudolfo and his people, others had arrived lately who seemed to hate Mexicans for no apparent reason. But mostly his letters were filled with his love, and told her how he yearned for the day she could join him. She kept every one of them, tied in a crimson ribbon, hid under her nightgown in a trunk at the foot of her bed.

The mail service from California to Mexico City was spasmodic at best. First, he would send her the letters by official government couriers who were carrying correspondence from California to Mexico City. Then came the period when she received no mail at all while the two governments fought over who owned California. After the war, mail service to Mexico was virtually cut off and Rudolfo sent his own man, a trusted vaquero named Paco, back and forth between the rancho and her home in Mexico with his precious letters of love.

Finally, the day came when she was able to exit the carriage with her father and stood looking at the vast hacienda that was now her home. It was actually a small village, with cottages and stables. The main house and church were separated by a brick patio and the fountain. A wall with heavy wooden gates surrounded the main house, church and courtyard for added safety. A small boy began ringing the church bell in proclamation of their arrival as they were ushered inside by a portly maid who seemingly talked without breathing. She told them how happy they were that the woman of the house had finally arrived and how Don Rudolfo had been longing for her presence. She told her that she herself was in charge of the hacienda and would serve as a personal maid to the Doña. She paused at a large oak door and smiled.

"You will bring much happiness Señorita. I have been praying for this moment when I can see you for myself. He talks about you much, but he did not say you were so beautiful."

"Thank you," Leonida gave the woman a small curtsy. "I'm sorry, I must have not been listening when you gave me your name."

"Oh, *perdon mi, Señorita*," she said with a laugh. "I forget to tell you. I am Maria Elena Sanchez. But come, there is time for us to get acquainted later." She opened the door to reveal a tall, well-built man with a mustache and flecks of gray above his temples standing in the middle of the room. She was embarrassed to admit later on that she had not recognized him. But as he took her hands in his and smiled she knew she was looking into the face of her Rudolfo. He looked much older than she had remembered. While she had grown into a beautiful woman, the hard life on the rancho had aged him. There were thin lines of worry imbedded in his brow that matched the gray in his hair. The one thing that had not changed was his smile and the tenderness in his eyes as he looked at her.

Their wedding was quite an affair, with the celebration lasting for three days. Everyone was invited from all the neighboring settlements and ranchos. She was amused to see the roughly clad miners from the strange village of Dogtown. Most of them were nice and polite, and joined in festivities with everyone else. There was one, though, who made her feel uneasy. A small man with cold, hard eyes who kept staring at her. Carlo told her he was the local lawman so, assuming his demeanor to be part of his profession, she soon forgot about him and joined in the party herself. Several beef and goats were cooked over open pits in the courtyard, wine flowed like water, and the music was non-stop. When one group of musicians would tire, another group with equal talent would take their place. She watched in amazement at the agility of the maidens as they danced their favorite dances. The *Fandango*, the *Jota*, the *Borrego*, the *Jarabe*, and the *Contradanza*.

One group of girls grabbed Leonida and drug her, protesting, to the center and attempted to teach her a dance called the *Bamba*. It was quite simple, they explained. All she had to do was constantly tap the stone patio with her feet, keeping time with the music, step into a silken hobble and raise it to her knees, lower it again and give two or three whirls. It sounded simple enough, so Leonida told the musicians to start. She started tapping her feet to the beat of a swift strumming guitar when one of the girls stopped her. "We forgot to tell you," she explained, holding a full glass of wine in her hand. "You have to do it balancing this glass on your head."

"You're jesting, aren't you?" Leonida glanced toward Rudolfo, who simply tilted his head to one side and shrugged as he puffed his cigar. The crowd was cheering her on, so she took the glass and balanced it on her head.

"Stop. Wait." The protest came from Maria Elena Sanchez, who had taken it upon herself to look after Leonida like one of her own daughters. She found this amusing, as Maria already had eight girls and no boys. "You want her to ruin her wedding dress? This should be passed on to the eldest daughter she will eventually give Rudolfo."

Leonida began to feel relieved, when Maria took the glass from her, but her chin dropped as she handed her one filled with water. "Here, this won't stain your dress." She downed the wine, giggled and disappeared into the crowd.

Leonida carefully placed the glass on her head and told the musicians to start. Her own mother had taught her to dance the folk dances in Mexico, so while these dances might be a little different, they were by no means strange to her. She tapped her feet to the beat of the guitar, softly at first, then louder as the crowd urged her on. She stepped into the hobble and, keeping her back and head rigid, lowered herself and raised it to her knees, always making sure she had at least one foot tapping to the music. She lowered the hobble and stepped out, feeling rather smug as the crowd cheered loudly. The guitarist picked up the tempo as she began to twirl around, and that was when the glass fell, drenching her with the water. Pandemonium broke out as everyone began shouting and dancing. Several of the young men and girls gathered around her and whirled her this way and that, teaching her the steps. She swept the damp hair from her forehead and joined in, laughing and dancing just as hard as they were. Finally, the music stopped and she made her way to a table and picked up a glass of wine for herself.

"You're rather good." Carlo handed her his handkerchief to wipe her damp brow. "You're one of them now; they accept you."

"Thank you for the compliment, but I didn't really know it was a test."

"It was, sort of. They wanted to find out if you were going to be a stuffy Señora who kept to herself, or if you were willing to rub elbows with the peasants. I think you proved yourself to them."

"I never really thought of them as peasants, and I hope you don't either."

"I don't. But there are those who would."

"Well, let's forget about them right now. This is my wedding day." She set her glass on the table and grabbed him by the arm, dragging him to the center of the patio. Carlo proved to be a proficient dancer and she found dancing with him a pleasure. But he was soon carted off by a young maid with dark eyes and Leonida found herself dancing with a miner from Dogtown who was willing, but rather clumsy in his work boots. Halfway through the dance another miner tapped her partner on the shoulder, and another miner took his place shortly after that. Her heart almost stopped as she looked in the direction from which her new partner had come, and saw a huge line of men all hoping for a chance to get to dance with the bride. She smiled and kept on dancing. It seemed an eternity had passed before Rudolfo came to her rescue and led her away amid the protests of those who had not gotten their turn.

She sat on a bench and took the glass of water Maria handed her. Her dress was dirty and soaked with perspiration. The evening breeze was cool and she tilted her head back and took a deep breath, trying to fill her lungs with its richness. Her hair hung in a matted mass across her cheeks and clung to her damp back. Her ankles and feet were bruised and blistered from being stepped on and her leg muscles were starting to cramp. After draining the glass, she looked at her husband who was gazing intently at her.

"You are the most beautiful woman in the world."

"And you, my dear husband, are drunk."

"Ah, but not too drunk to carry my bride to our chambers." He scooped her into his arms and carried her toward the house amid the hoots and cheers of the crowd.

~   ~   ~

Her feet and legs hurt too much for her to join in much of the dancing on the second day, so she satisfied herself by talking to the guests and watching the games. There were horse races and a rodeo. The miners were no match for Rudolfo's vaqueros, who put on a brilliant display of horsemanship. Rudolfo laughed as she squealed with glee and clapped her hands, watching them race around the arena. The only Americano who was any challenge for the vaqueros was a young man from Texas they simply called "Tex", but even he was eventually beaten in a roping contest.

There was also gambling, cockfighting, and a bull and bear baiting contest which Leonida did not like at all. She had enjoyed the bullfights in Mexico City, but to sit and watch a bear and bull maul each other was cruel, and she left before the contest was over. She was sitting under the shade of an oak tree in the patio sipping a glass of wine with Rudolfo when the young Texas cowboy passed by with a girl who was not much more than a child, and tipped his hat toward her.

"Who are they? I only hear him called 'Tex.' Doesn't he have another name?"

"I'm sure he does." Rudolfo laughed with his rich voice. "But I really don't think anyone knows it. I believe he is a gunfighter and would rather everyone didn't know about his past. As for Rosa, she's a, shall we say ...." He stopped and took a deep breath. "She works at a saloon in Dogtown called The Rusty Rail."

"She's a prostitute."

"Yes." He looked surprised at her frankness.

"She looks so young."

"Most of them are."

The party broke up by the evening of the third day, which Leonida thought was good. She had enjoyed the fiesta, but she was tired and had begun to worry about the guests. Even Father Franco was acting a little intoxicated.

"Aren't they worried about their own homes? Their families? Don't some of these men work for other men?" She had asked earlier.

"*Muy poco tiempo*," Rudolfo said, lighting a cigar. "Too little time. They believe there's not enough time today to do anything that could be done tomorrow."

"*Muy poco tiempo*." The saying that had seemed so strange to her at the time, now had become part of her life. The people had taught her to enjoy life to its fullest each and every day and not to even think about tomorrow. "You might not be here tomorrow," Maria explained, "so any trouble that might happen tomorrow shouldn't concern you anyway." Maria refused to let the Señora do any housework, so singing and playing with the children in the village and daily horseback rides by the river, and spending time with her husband had become routine for her. Anything else was not important and she did not care to concern herself with something that could wait until tomorrow.

~　　~　　~

"Going for a ride?" Rudolfo's voice interrupted her daydreaming.

"Yes." She smiled. "Care to go with me today?"

"I'd love to, but I can't. I have to get some cattle ready to sell to the miners in Volcano."

"*Muy poco tiempo?*"

"Not this time," he said with a laugh. "Gringos don't understand *muy poco tiempo*, especially when it comes to finding gold. They want it completed today. You have fun anyway."

She kissed him and left the house. Her pony was eager and ready to run, so she let him have his rein and enjoyed the wind whipping her face. Normally, she only saw Rudolfo's cattle or an occasional vaquero on her rides, so she was taken by surprise at seeing the horse standing beside the man lying on the ground. Stopping her horse beside the fallen man, she looked around for another rider, but the brush beside the river was thick and made it difficult to see. She dismounted and knelt beside him to see how badly hurt he might be, and had only touched his shoulder when he jumped up and grabbed her arm in an iron grip.

"Hey, Jake. I'm shore gonna enjoy this." Her assailant laughed, eyeing her with wild eyes. She tried vainly to free herself as another man appeared from the bushes.

"Boy, she's shore enough a looker. Get her in here and I'll get the horses before anyone else comes along." The men dragged Leonida, begging and pleading, into the thick brush that bordered the Mokelumne River.

Chapter 3

Sean Kilkenney turned from the small child he was examining to glare at Father Franco. The old priest had brought him to the Garcia Rancho to see if he could determine what was ailing some of the children living there.

"We don't know what is bothering them," he explained in broken English. "They eat, but they are sick."

Sean was new to the area and unfamiliar with many of the customs and problems people living on these large ranches faced daily. It was by accident that he had arrived in Dogtown in the first place. After receiving an offer of a position in a clinic in San Francisco, Sean had packed his medical diploma and what few belongings he had and left New York. Not having enough money to buy passage aboard a ship sailing around the horn, he decided to travel overland, and perhaps earn part of his keep working with a pack train carrying supplies. He knew God must have been smiling down on him when he happened to meet some men in St. Louis who were traveling to the California gold fields. Two months later he stood staring at the dusty streets of Dogtown.

Where's San Francisco? That's where I wanted to go."

"Frisco? Shoulda' said somethin'." Bear, a large burly man, scratched his thick beard. "That's where Charlie and Frank headed two days ago. Don't know where Hanky went."

"I did. I told all of you I was a going to San Francisco to work as a doctor."

"Well, we all thought you was joshin'. You ain't really a saw-bones now, are you?"

Sean nodded.

"Well, I'll be damned."

"I was under the impression everyone coming to California went to San Francisco."

Bear laughed so hard he almost choked on his chew and had to stop and spit. "California's a big hunk of land, boy, and 'Frisco's just a small seaport. What'd make you want to go there anyway? Right here's the gold." He motioned toward the countryside. "One of the latest strikes. That's why I come here. You'd be better off layin' aside them books you been readin' all the way from St. Louie and foller me 'round. They claim people's just pickin' nuggets up offin the ground out here."

"Thanks, but I've gotta get to San Francisco. I've a job there."

"Well, let's see. It's about a hundret miles or so off in that direction." He pointed toward the West. "Give or take some. I don't rightly know, 'cause I ain't never been there myself.

"Good luck son." He slapped Sean on the arm and headed toward a large tent with a wooden sign nailed to a post that read "The Rusty Rail."

Sean checked into the hotel and was shown a small, dirty military tent set among several others and was told it was his room. The towel at the community wash basin was so dirty, he returned to his tent and dug one of his own out of his bag to use. Then, feeling hungry, he started looking for a place to eat and wondered if he should bring a clean plate with him. A crowd and excited voices in front of a tent-building with a sign that read "Barber Shop" caught his attention.

"I ain't touching no greasers." The large man who was wrapped in an apron glared at the child lying at his feet. From the conversation taking place, Sean was able to determine that the boy had fallen from a hay loft at the local livery stable where the father was working. Sean knelt beside the excited father and examined the boy.

"Where's the doctor?" he said, rising to his feet.

"George here is." One of the bystanders indicated the barber. "When he ain't cuttin' hair, he pulls teeth and wraps cuts and burns."

"The boy has a broken leg."

"So?" The barber spit tobacco on the sidewalk beside the crying child.

"You'd let the lad lie there and suffer? Do something for him, man." The Irish brogue he tried hard to mask became more pronounced as his temper flared. Having been a victim of prejudice most of his life, he had little patience in dealing with men who harbored such feelings. He had worked beside his father when he was nothing but a child while they scratched out a living, because jobs weren't too plentiful for "them Irish immigrants" in New York. And his heart broke daily as he watched his mother work herself to an early grave scrubbing floors and doing laundry for the wealthy. If it had not been for the compassion of an Army doctor who wrote letters and opened doors for him, he would certainly not have been allowed into medical school.

"Don't see it's any of your business. But like I done said, I ain't touching no greaser."

The blow sent the barber sprawling through the door of his own shop where he lay, not moving.

"Bring the boy and follow me." He led the way to his tent, where he set the boy's leg and refused the father's offer of payment.

~   ~   ~

Dirty Ben's was a crowded tent with one item on its

menu that served for all three daily meals. Beef and beans with hard biscuits. Being hungry as he was, Sean accepted the fair and ignored the dirty plate it was put on. Seating himself in an empty spot at a table between two miners, he found the food surprisingly tasty.

"I saw you deck George over at the barber shop." The man seated directly across from him spoke. "You fixed that boy's leg, didn't you? You some kind of doctor or something?"

Sean nodded, chewing his food.

"That's good, 'cause we need one 'round here."

"Well, I'm not staying. I'm on my way to San Francisco to work in a clinic."

"That's probably just as good, 'cause you ain't gonna be none too popular 'round here," the one seated at his right informed him. "Old George was one of the first ones here, and he's the only doctor we got, ifin' you can call him that."

"Yeah, but no one's got much use for him. I know I ain't. I fix my own hurts and cut my own hair best I can." Sean studied the man seated across from him for the first time and wanted to laugh.

"Perhaps you should give up trying to cut your hair and let it grow. It couldn't look any worse." The man's face reddened as everyone seated around the table laughed. "But what I'd like to know is, how can you stand by and allow him to treat human beings the way he was treating that boy today. The lad was in deep pain."

"Well, we ain't got no choice. Most of us are just trying to scrape out a livin' outa that creek, and we just take what we can get." The man with the unruly hair let his eyes drop to his plate when he spoke.

~   ~   ~

Sean was asleep the instant he lay his head on the dusty pillow provided by the clerk at the hotel, but his sleep was not a restful one. His dreams were filled with crying children plagued with different illnesses and broken bones, and he woke early, feeling almost as tired as when he went to bed. Finding a pen and paper, he sat at a wooden crate and wrote a letter to the director of the medical clinic. He addressed the envelope and handed it to the postman, thinking he had gone completely mad. The letter thanked the director for the offer, but explained the situation at this mining camp, and told of his decision to stay and open his own practice.

~   ~   ~

"There's nothing wrong with these children that some good, nourishing food wouldn't cure." The tone of his voice made the mother gasp. He had almost yelled at the priest.

"They eat good." Father Franco was growing impatient with the young doctor's insistence that the children of *Rancho Manantial Escondido* were starving to death.

"Aye, but what do they eat? Tell me that Father. What do these children eat?"

"Beef, cows." He waved an arm toward the cattle grazing lazily in the sun.

"Aye, I agree. They eat beef for breakfast, dinner and supper. That's all they eat. When do they ever eat any vegetables, or fruit, or fish, or anything else?"

He bent over the watering trough and splashed cold water on his face in an effort to calm himself. He knew it wasn't really Father Franco's fault that the diet on these ranchos was so poor. In fact, the priest hadn't been in California much longer than Sean himself. Perhaps only a year or two. After the missions disintegrated, there had been virtually no manufacturing of any kind taking place. Shoes and other leather products were made of California hides in New England, and then shipped back to California at a huge cost to the consumer. Even the simple processes of making soap and candles out of the tallow from California beef was done in Chile or Peru. The missions themselves had grown a variety of grains, vegetables and fruits, but all these skills had disappeared after secularization. The Mission Indians had been the ones trained in agriculture, and most of them had drifted back to their villages. Now, the diet of the rancheros and their families consisted largely of fresh or dried beef. No one seemed to know how to produce milk, or butter, or flour. He found that even such ordinary articles as brooms had to be imported.

"I'm sorry, Father, but it's so frustrating. These children need a better diet. They are suffering right now from scurvy, and their parents aren't much better. I think the only thing that's saving you adults, is what little good you get from the amount of wine you drink. I just can't believe that no one on this rancho knows how to milk a cow."

"No self-respecting *vaquero* would be caught dead milking a cow." The voice came from the shade of a tree where a young vaquero had been sitting, supposedly disinterested in the angry doctor's tirade.

"Well now, look who it 'tis speaking the King's English." Sean put his hands on his hips and studied the young man. "Who are you, and where, might I ask, did you learn to speak like that? Your English is better than mine or the Father's here."

"My name is Carlo Garcia. My family owns this land, and I made it my business to learn English. I have friends who taught me."

"His friend kills people." Father Franco's eyes flamed with anger as he pointed his finger as though he were shooting a gun.

"The padre is referring to my friendship with Tex. He doesn't like the idea of one of his parishioners being friendly with a known gunfighter."

"And this here Tex, he taught you such good English?"

"Yes, he and a few others." Sean noted the revolver tucked in Carlo's waistband as he rose to his feet.

"And did he teach you about the use of the gun in your belt, now?"

"A little. But I'm not near as good as he is."

"Well, let's be hoping that I won't have to be digging

bullets out of you one of these days." Sean found himself liking this young man with the warm smile. "But would you tell me now, why is it that a self-respecting *vaquero* like yourself wouldn't milk a cow?"

"We make it our business to never do anything that can't be done from the back of a horse. That's the way it has always been."

"Ahhhh, I suppose it would be hard to milk a cow from horseback, now wouldn't it? But what about the women? Is there some sort of law preventing them from milking or planting a garden?"

"No," Carlo said as he pursed his lips thoughtfully. "Not that I know of. I just suppose no one's taught them, or ever thought of it before."

"Thought of it? My God, man, haven't you ever hankered for the taste of a potato, or a carrot, or cabbage before? And what about your children? No one's ever thought enough of them to want to give them some milk?"

"No." His answer frustrated Sean. He opened his mouth to reply but words failed him. And when the young vaquero started laughing, it only angered him further.

"No? That's all you've got to say? No? What kind of man are you? No?"

"You wanted an honest answer, didn't you? My answer is no. No one's ever thought much about it before you came. Oh, my brother did mentioned it a time or two after he returned from Mexico, but our father's illness and his business dealings with the cattle took precedence, and we just sort of forgot about it."

"Perhaps that is why God sends you here. To teach such things to this people." The padre looked heavenward as he spoke.

"Aye, that might be Father, but I'm a doctor, not a farmer. I'm sure if God wanted someone to teach them how to be farmers, He would send a farmer to do the teachin'."

Their attention was turned toward frantic yells coming from an approaching oxcart. Sean watched with amazement as the young lad driving the *carreta* bounced up and down on the plank seat of the springless wooden box, always seeming to land in the exact same spot without being ejected. He had seen many of these spine-jarring contraptions with the large wooden wheels since arriving in California and wondered how many of the people who rode in them had serious back injuries.

The cart ground to a halt in front of them, the lad jabbering frantically and motioning wildly. "*Madre de Dios,*" Father Franco said, crossing himself.

Sean snapped his medical kit closed and grabbed the reins of his mule. "What seems to be the problem? Is it something that I can help with?"

"Leonida, my brother's wife. She's been hurt, real bad." Carlo's hand shook as he reached for the reins of his horse. "Yes, you'd better come. Follow me."

The miner who had sold him Cathy had promised the mule was faster than most horses and twice as durable, but Sean had doubted such claims up to now. Father Franco and his burro were left far behind as Carlo spurred his black mustang faster. The vaquero was a fine horseman, and the mount he was riding was magnificent, but Cathy wanted to race and stayed right at the mustang's heels. By the time the rambling ranch home drew into sight, Sean had begun to believe the mule could indeed outrun the mustang if they were in a real race and he were not keeping her in check.

Children and dogs dove for cover as the horsemen clattered at a full gallop into the courtyard in front of the Garcia hacienda. Carlo dismounted in one flying motion before his mustang came to a stop and was climbing the stone steps before Sean could bring Cathy to a full halt. He heard Carlo saying something in Spanish through the open door as he was untying his bag, and a portly woman appeared who evidently thought he could understand Spanish, for she kept talking insistently as she led him up the stairs and to a room at the end of a long hallway. Sean entered the crowded room to find Carlo standing over a bed surrounded by several maidens, all crying, and several of them praying.

This woman wasn't hurt in some accident, he thought. Sean removed his coat as he studied the figure in front of him at a distance. *Someone's beat the hell out of her.* He took a deep breath as he felt his jaw muscles tighten.

"Can you tell me how this happened?"

Carlo glanced up and addressed the others in the room in Spanish. A large magnificent man who had been sitting on the edge of the bed rose to face him.

"I need to know what happened to her in order to help."

"I am Rudolfo Garcia, Leonida's husband," he said, taking Sean's hand in a strong grip. "We don't know how this happened. One of the *vaqueros* found her wandering aimlessly by the river. Her clothes had been torn away," he shook his head as his voice broke. "She hasn't told us anything yet."

Sean glanced at the old man bent over the bed.

"That is Jose Flores, Leonida's father. Can you help my wife, Doctor?"

"I'll see what I can do." The man in front of him was dressed in the finest Mexican costume Sean had ever seen, and carried himself with grace like a true noble, but it was the eyes that held his attention. *Aye, there is fear there for the young woman lying on the bed. You love her deeply, don't you, my friend?* But there was much more there also. If given the chance, this man would tear the ones who did this limb from limb. *And deservedly so*, he thought glancing at the figure in the bed. No man should be allowed to beat a woman for any cause. But he was also sure whoever did this act certainly did more than beat her.

"My brother and I speak good English. One of us will have to interpret for you," Carlo said.

Sean stepped toward the bed and the young woman made the sound of a frightened animal and scooted toward the headboard, curling herself in a tight ball.

"Tell her who I am, and that I only want to help her."

Sean sat on the edge of the bed and placed his bag on a chair where the frightened girl could see it while Carlo talked soothingly to her. He then took her hand and held it while he gently brushed her tousled hair back and looked at her bruised face. She was extraordinarily beautiful and Sean had to fight to keep from being captivated by her eyes.

"I compliment you, Mr. Garcia, on your choice of women. I have not seen such beauty since I left Ireland."

"I thank you, doctor. How is she?"

"I won't know until I have completed my examination. Give me a few more minutes."

Sean rubbed salve on her cut and bruised lips, and on some other minor cuts on her cheeks and arms. He smiled at her assuringly and rose to face the anxious bystanders as an exhausted Father Franco entered the room.

"Outside of a few minor cuts and bruises I can't find anything wrong with her on the surface. But I do need to look at her entire body to determine what other damage these beasts might have done." Rudolfo stiffened at the mention of Leonida's body, so Sean turned toward Carlo as he continued speaking.

"Tell the young lady here, this is something I don't really wish to do, but I have to. It's for her own good. They might have done some damage that will cause her great difficulty later on."

He waited until Carlo did the explaining, then began removing everyone except Maria and Carlo. All three men began to protest, saying it wasn't right that Carlo should remain and her husband be removed.

"She's my brother's wife, and I shouldn't see anymore of her than is proper. Let Rudolfo stay."

"Rudolfo's too emotionally involved and will probably get in my way. Besides, you can stand with your back to her, can't you? I only need your voice, not your eyes." With that, Sean closed the door on Rudolfo and the rest, then sat on the edge of the bed and looked at the frightened girl.

Carlo positioned himself in a chair with his back toward the bed and cleared his throat. "Ok, Doctor, go ahead."

"Explain to the young lady that this is much more embarrassing for me than her. I've never really done anything like this before and I'll never be able to look her or her husband in the face ever again." A crimson hue rushed to the girl's cheeks and she turned her face to the pillow as Maria chuckled and patted her hand, letting her know it was okay.

"Oh, I know what a woman's body looks like, sort of," he said as he worked, mostly to keep his mind occupied with the task at hand. "I've seen drawings in the books I got in school, you know. And I've seen plenty of children, both boys and girls. But what I mean is, I've never really seen a full grown woman in this way before, and I never hope to do so again. Well, what I mean is, not under these circumstances, anyhow."

~   ~   ~

Sean allowed the girl's father to return to the room as he joined the others in the downstairs study. After accepting the brandy offered him, he turned to face the grave-looking husband standing beside the desk.

"Outside of those cuts and bruises I mentioned earlier, I can't find any lasting damage at this moment. But that doesn't mean there isn't any. There's always the chance of something the human eye can't see. Disease, for instance, which we can't know about until much later. Then, there's the chance she might be pregnant, and we won't know that until later also." Rudolfo uttered a curse in Spanish at the mention of pregnancy and turned toward the wall.

"But I'm afraid that the real damage might be something else, that only you and God might be able to help her with." Rudolfo turned back to stare as he continued speaking. "It's in her head. She's scared to death, and rightfully so. It will take some time getting over this, you know."

"What are you suggesting, Doctor? That my wife has gone insane?"

"No, nothing of the sort." Sean set his glass on the table. "It's just that, how can I say this? She's scared, really scared. And it might be, just might, mind you, that she won't want anyone touching her for quite a while, if you get my drift."

"Yes, I get your drift, doctor, and I am a patient man. We were engaged six years before we got married. I can wait a while longer before I make love to my wife again." Rudolfo slammed his own glass down in anger, spilling its contents across the table.

"Yes, that's a long engagement indeed. But that's not quite what I mean. She might not even want you touching her at all, not even a hug. What would you do then, Mr. Garcia?"

Rudolfo's jaws tightened as he glared at him.

"I don't mean to frighten you, sir, but I do need to mention it because I've heard of strange things happening when people have trauma in their lives. Sometimes, they get over it quickly and go on as best they can. And sometimes they don't ever get over it at all." Sean took another sip of brandy and continued. "I heard of one young lady that was misused by some Indians, and all she ever did was sit and look out a window. They couldn't even get her to talk. Now, if that happened to your wife, what would you do then, Mr. Garcia?"

"Damn you." His voice was almost a whisper as he turned away. "Damn you for even telling me this."

"I'm sorry. I shouldn't be saying such things, but she's a frightened girl. Every time I touched her during the examination she would pull away as though my hands were made of fire. I'm only warning you to be real careful, and patient."

"Thank you for your concern. I'll be understanding, and patient with her."

Sean finished his brandy and picked up his bag as Father Franco came from the bedroom looking both pale and tired. He smiled as the old priest waved a silent good-bye and plopped into a chair. Carlo opened the door while Sean took one last look at the back of a broken husband.

"What do we owe you? I'm sorry, I don't even know your name."

"Kilkenney, Sean Kilkenney." He shook the young

man's hand. "We'll discuss the fees when I come back in a day or two to see the young lady again ...." Sean's voice trailed off as he watched Rudolfo take two dueling pistols from their walnut case and start loading them.

"Now, what would you be doing with those cannons, my good man?" He dropped the bag and walked to the table where the angry man stood.

"What in the hell does it look like I'm doing?" He stuck one of the guns in his belt and began loading the second. Father Franco, seeing what was happening, leaped from his chair and grabbed Rudolfo's arm, urging him to stop. The angry man pulled away, addressing the priest harshly in Spanish.

"Man, I understand how you feel, and I'd think less of you if you didn't want to kill the bastard who did this to your woman, but just stop and think for a moment."

"No, you don't know how I feel. She's not your wife." He stuffed the second gun in his belt and grabbed his hat. "Now, if you'll excuse me...."

"No, I won't excuse you." Sean stood firmly between the landowner and the door. "Just who are you going to kill? Do you know what fool did this to her? I asked her, and she wouldn't answer." Rudolfo stared blankly for a moment, so Sean continued.

"I'll tell you what's going to happen. You'll get your fool head shot off and we'll have to tell that poor girl in there her husband's dead. Then, she'll probably never recover. There's a sheriff in town, isn't there? Let the law handle this one for now. If we find out who did this, I'll help you take care of him later on myself. But, for now, you need to be here for her. To hold her and give her the feeling she's being protected. Come on, give me the guns." He held out his hand.

"I hate to tell you this, but I agree with the doctor." Carlo shut the door and leaned against it. "I know Pod Randell isn't much of a lawman, but we really don't know who hurt Leonida. Better wait until we can find out."

"Give me the guns." Sean repeated his command and Rudolfo obeyed weakly before breaking into huge sobs. Sean led him to a chair and handed him another glass of brandy after he calmed down.

"Like I said earlier, I don't blame you one little bit. I'd probably be doing the same myself." He studied one of the pistols with its smooth walnut grip.

"Mighty fine weapon you have here." He cocked the goose-neck hammer and pointed it toward the fireplace. Then, blowing the powder out of the flash-pan, he eased the hammer back down again and studied the weapon some more. "Fifty-eight caliber Coutty. Tapered brass barrel. Smooth bore. About two pounds, maybe a little less."

"Know something about guns, Doc?" Carlo spoke through a cloud of smoke from the cigar he had just lit.

"A little. I spent three years in the Army. Mostly in the Medical Corps, though. We did get to handle guns once in a while. But nothing quite so fine as this." He rolled his wrist back and forth as he studied the pistol. "A fine weapon indeed."

Chapter 4

Rudolfo lay awake all night listening to his wife whimper as she tossed and turned in her restless slumber. Several times she woke screaming and he held her tightly, stroking her head and assuring her everything was all right. The first time this happened, she fought him off, hitting, scratching and biting. It wasn't until he had suffered several wounds to his right cheek that he was able to get her attention and let her know she was safe. The last of these fearful spells came just before dawn, and Rudolfo lay holding a weeping Leonida in his arms as he watched the sun top the distant hills. He swore by Almighty God that the person responsible for this unholy act would pay with his life if it was the last thing he ever did.

He dressed and called for Maria who came in an instant, as she had not slept either. Going to the kitchen, he built a fire in the wood stove and made coffee. Carlo came only moments later and upon pouring himself a cup, sat at the table and silently studied his brother's haggard face.

"I want you to ride into Dogtown this morning and bring Pod Randell back here. Tell him only what you have to.

Do you understand? I don't want the whole town to know about this unless it's necessary. But I want that son-of-a-bitch caught and hung, even if I have to sell this whole damned ranch to do it."

Carlo finished his coffee, set the empty cup on the sinkboard and left without saying a word. Rudolfo watched as the black horse and rider pranced out of the courtyard and broke into a full run when they reached the open trail. He returned to the bedroom door and looked in on his wife, who was tossing fitfully in the bed, then went back to the kitchen to pour himself another cup of coffee. This time, though, he added a little brandy to his cup and took it to his office. He tried passing the time by working at his ledger, but that only held his attention momentarily, so he returned to the bedroom and looked in on Leonida again. She was still the same. About mid-morning Ike Carpenter arrived with the wagonload of supplies he had ordered from the store in town. They chatted a few minutes then Ike offered his condolences and left, promising to keep an eye and ear open for anything that would help find whoever hurt Leonida. That was followed by two more cups of coffee and brandy and two more trips to the bedroom door. The ledger was still open on his desk, but his heart was not in it. He took the walnut case from his desk drawer and opened it. The .58 caliber Couttys were still fully loaded. He re-primed the weapons, laid them on the desk, and waited.

~   ~   ~

Carlo had to beg Pod Randell to ride out to the hacienda, and was sure it was only because Judge Baines ordered him to that he finally came at all.

"Now, Pod, you get yourself out there and find out what went on. We're paid to represent all the community, and one of our fine citizens has been molested. You find the person responsible, and I'll see to it he pays."

He now stood defiantly in Rudolfo's parlor with his hands on his hips. "Hell, I don't know what you want me to do.

How can I arrest someone iffin' I don't know who to arrest? You don't know who done it, and she ain't sayin' nothin' either." He pointed toward the bedroom.

"Can't you at least look at the place where my *vaquero* found her wandering around?"

"We done that on the way in. The boy and me did." He nodded toward Carlo. "And all we seen was a bunch of horse tracks and broken down brush. Outside of some pieces of her clothes, ain't got nothin' to go on. I knew this would be a waste of time. I didn't want to come in the first place."

Carlo gave a tight-lipped smile. He had indeed taken the sheriff to the spot on the river where Leonida had been attacked, but the lawman had refused to get off his horse and look around. There was plenty of evidence left at the scene, such as the silver concho Carlo had found lying on the ground and put in his pocket.

"Besides," the sheriff continued, "I doubt very much that one of your own men done this thing. Not unless they're just plain crazy. So, we'd never find them here, now would we? Now, iffin' she ever starts talkin', just bring her into town and I'll line up every man I can get my hands on, and she can point to the ones that done it, and I'll arrest them. Up to now, there's not much I can do, so I'll see you in town."

Carlo watched Pod Randell ride off as he lit a cigar and turned to face his angry brother.

"Now, how do you suppose he knew there was more than one person? He didn't even get down and look."

"There were more? How many?"

"At least two that I know of."

"How do you know this? We all thought there was only one."

"Well, Pedro didn't take much time looking around. He just knew Leonida was hurt, so he brought her here, and all hell broke loose. And last night, when some of us went back to look around, we couldn't see much. But I had everyone keep the horses away from the area, and this morning I could see the tracks of at least four horses. Pedro's, Leonida's pony, and two more. It also looked like that little wife of yours put up one hell of a fight. There was some blood on the ground that I'm sure wasn't hers. Someone else's face more than likely has the same type of scratches you do."

Rudolfo thoughtfully put a hand to his cheek.

"I also found this." He tossed the concho to his brother. "Off someone's clothing, and I don't think it belongs to Leonida. I've never seen it before."

"I know it's getting late, but want to take another ride into town?" Rudolfo put the concho into his vest pocket and began tucking the twin Couttys into his belt. "I've never been in the Rusty Rail before, and I think I might want to go there and have a drink. How about you?"

"Sure." Carlo checked the loads in his revolver.

Chapter 5

Tex was seated with Rosa at a corner table having a drink when the two vaqueros entered the bar. He watched them closely as they stood in the doorway surveying the grimy tent-building and its patrons. He waited until he was sure that Carlo recognized him, then he nodded his head, letting them know he understood their intentions. The news had traveled fast. He had been there when Carlo rode into Dogtown earlier in the day, to take a protesting Pod Randell out to the rancho. Fifteen minutes hadn't passed between their departure and when Judge Baines had entered the Rusty Rail, bought a drink, and let it slip out that someone had attacked Leonida Garcia and violated her. Two hours later the whole town was ablaze with the news. He patted Rosa on the arm. "Stay put, and if there's any trouble, get under the table and lie flat on the floor." He made his way to the door and took a position against the wall where he could hear the two men talking.

"Look at that one there, next to the fat man." Carlo was lighting a cigar as he spoke softly in Spanish. "He's got scratches on his face and a silver concho missing from his vest.

Want me to go get acquainted with him?"

"No, thank you, little brother. You stay here and keep an eye on my back. I think I'll find this conversation quite interesting."

Sean Kilkenney came in for a pint of ale as Rudolfo was making his way toward the bar, and Tex grabbed his arm and pulled him to the wall.

"Say, man, what's the meaning of this?"

"Hush," Tex ordered and nodded toward the crowded bar. Sean melted against the wall as he watched the scene unfolding before him.

Rudolfo nudged his way between the fat man and the man with the missing concho and ordered a drink. "Hey, quit pushin'." The fat man snarled irritably as he turned to see who pushed him in the back.

"Say, ain't you the Mex that's got the wife who got herself raped?"

Rudolfo nodded and the bar became noticeably quieter.

"Hey, we was all real sorry to hear what happened. A lot of us met her at that big wing ding out at your place when you two got hitched, and we really like her. She shore is a fine lady, and I hope they catch the one what did this to her."

"Thank you, but how did you know what happened? We didn't tell anyone except Señor Randell, and he promised to keep it quiet."

"Well, the judge told us all. Right here in this room right after Pod rode out to your place."

"That's strange indeed." Rudolfo sipped his drink. "We didn't tell Señor Randell she had been raped, only that she had been beaten."

"Well, like I said, I hope they catch whoever hurt her."

"*Gracias*, but I don't think finding the *gringo* will be too difficult." Rudolfo tossed off his drink and turned to face the man with the missing concho as Pod Randell entered the saloon and made his way to an angle not five feet from the two men.

"It seems, Señor, that we have matching scars on our

cheeks. Who gave you yours?"

"None of your damn business, Mex."

The fat man and several others moved away from the bar as Rosa scooted her chair back to make an easier dive to the floor.

"Oh, but I think it is. You see, I received mine from my wife."

"You oughta beat the hell out of her then." The man laughed and took a step backward.

"*Si*, but someone has already done that. In fact, they not only beat her, but they did things to her that shouldn't happen to a dog." Rudolfo ran his fingers along the scratches on his cheek. "She did this last night while she was sleeping. She was still fighting the *gringos* in her dreams. I had a very hard time calming her down." He placed the glass on the bar and took a step toward the center of the room.

"What's that got to do with me?"

Tex watched as a third man positioned himself about ten feet from the vaquero, somewhere opposite Pod Randell and the man being confronted. He also took note of the guns in Rudolfo's belt. Flintlock-muzzle loaders. They were probably fine guns, but he only had two shots, and was now facing at least two men, one of which he more than likely didn't know about.

"Well, you see, Señor, we saw the place where she was attacked, and my Leonida, she fought like *el oso,* the bear." Rudolfo bent the fingers of his right hand and raked the air. "She did some scratching like she did on my face, and yours."

"Mine?" The man facing Rudolfo removed the leather thong holding his gun in its holster, and Tex did the same.

"*Si*, I'm afraid so. You see, we also found this lying on the ground where she was attacked." He pulled the concho from his pocket, tossed it high in the air, caught it and returned it to his pocket. "Are you missing a concho, Señor?"

"What are you saying? That I'm the one who raped your wife?"

Pod Randell removed the leather thong on his holster

and took a position to the right and slightly behind Rudolfo. Tex grabbed Carlo's arm, hissing orders through clenched teeth.

"Get him the hell outa' here. There's a skunk in the woodpile somewheres."

Carlo started weaving his way between tables toward the two men, when Sean began blurting out an Irish ballad in a loud voice and staggering like a drunken sailor.

"Ahhhh, Rudolfo Garcia, I'm happy to run into you." He threw an arm around the vaquero and pulled him away from the bar toward the center of the room and closer to the door. "Now, how's that little lady of yours? I'm terribly sorry I couldn't make it out there today, but you see, Father Franco kept me busy lookin' after the children."

"Not now! Can't you see...." Rudolfo tried in vain to pull away. Carlo stood between his brother and the man with the missing concho, backing toward the door as the doctor pulled his brother that way.

"But you know, I've been reading in my books, and I think she's going to be fine."

"I'll take that concho, Rudolfo." Pod stopped them at the door. "That's evidence, and you've been withholding it. I could put you in jail."

"Put me in jail?" Rudolfo struggled against the doctor's steel grasp. "That man raped and beat my wife. Arrest him and put him in jail."

"You heard him." The accused man was yelling now. "I've killed men for less than that."

"You're the one that's going to die, because I'm going to kill you myself." Rudolfo tried to draw one of the pistols, but Sean spun him around and thorough the door quickly this time. "I'll kill you. I'll kill you."

"I need that concho for evidence." Pod started toward the door, but Tex stepped in front of him and shook his head as he lit a cigarette.

"Wouldn't do that if I was you. He's mighty riled right now, and someone's liable to get hurt. Let him cool down and talk to him later."

Pod smiled knowingly as Carlo made his way past them through the door. "Ya know Tex, some day you and me's gonna see just who's the fastest."

"Could be, but not right now. Too much is happenin', and they might need a Sheriff 'round here."

Tex sat back down beside Rosa and poured himself another drink. He could still hear Rudolfo's voice fading down the dusty street leading out of town.

"He's the one who hurt Leonida. I'll kill him. I'll kill him."

Chapter 6

Pod Randell paced the floor nervously. He hated facing the judge after things went wrong. *But it wasn't my fault.* He had carried out the plans exactly the way Henry said to. He had taken great pains seeing every little detail had been taken care of. How was he to know that new doctor would mess things up? He jumped as the door to his office banged open. Henry Baines slammed the door shut again and glared angrily as Pod seated himself.

"Well, tell me about it. What went wrong? Why aren't Rudolfo Garcia and his brother dead?"

"It was that doctor's fault. The new one. I had it all set up just like you said. He was ready to draw down on Jake and shore woulda got hisself bored. And Waylon was ready to nail his brother the instant he pulled his iron. But that doctor, Sean Kilkenney? He comes in drunker'n a skunk, singing, and grabs the Mex in a hug and pulls him out through the door. There weren't nothing we could do."

"Wasn't anything you could do?" Henry shook his head mockingly. "You really thought the doctor was drunk? I just saw him not five minutes ago standing on the street talking to Tex, and he's more sober than I am, and I haven't had a drink since this afternoon."

"He shore looked it, that's all I got to say."

"What else happened?"

"Well, that Mex, it looks like he's got Jake dead to rights. He found one of Jake's conchos lying on the ground where they got the girl. And he was claimin' that it was his wife that put them scratches on Jake's face. He was yellin' like Jake was the devil hisself, and sayin' he was gonna kill him, 'cause he was the one that raped her."

"They found a concho? Why didn't you take it away?"

"I tried, but Tex stopped me. I'd have had to kill him to get at the Mex."

"So, Tex has sided with them."

"Seems that way."

"Well, it may not be as bad as it seems." Henry sat in the extra chair and began packing his pipe. "He threatened to kill Jake?"

Pod nodded.

"And everybody in The Rusty Rail heard him?"

"If they didn't, they're shore enough deaf."

"Interesting. This might call for a slight change in plans. How'd you like to take care of another little job for me? Tomorrow's soon enough."

~   ~   ~

Rudolfo lay in the dark beside his wife, listening to her fitful slumber and cursing himself for not being able to avenge her. Why had they stopped him? Why had Sean Kilkenney grabbed him like that and pulled him through the door? He was almost there. He had accused the man in front of everyone in the bar, and he was ready to draw. Leonida turn in her sleep, touching him, and awoke with a gasp.

"Shhhhhh, 'Nida. It's me. You're safe now. No one's ever going to hurt you again." He caressed her honey-colored locks, and her body seemed to relax. She scooted closer and held his hand to her bruised cheek and fell back asleep.

Carlo said there was another man standing off to his right that looked like he was ready to draw his gun if the fight proceeded, but he hadn't noticed. He'd been too occupied with the man he was confronting. That was the guilty one, and Rudolfo knew it. He felt it deep inside, in every bone in his body. That man was the one who had attacked his wife. The doctor said he should let the law handle the situation. Rudolfo had to catch himself to keep from laughing out loud and disturbing Leonida. What law? Pod Randell had been there the whole time and had done nothing. This was something that he would have to take care of himself.

But what if Carlo was right and there were two men? What if that man in the bar was the other man? No matter if there were ten men. He would find them all, one by one, and then he'd kill them.

~   ~   ~

It was still pitch black outside when Jake Teel rolled out of bed, feeling hung-over and in a sour mood. Everyone in The Rusty Rail had avoided him like the plague after Rudolfo Garcia left. Now he wanted to kill that Mexican real bad. He needed money, and the two hundred dollars Pod said he'd get was a lot to him. But now everyone believed he'd been involved in raping that girl. They had even refused to stand next to him at the bar the rest of the evening. And that damned Waylon Sunday had avoided him also. He was his pard and was in on this too. He was gonna get two hundred just like Jake, just as soon as the Mex was dead. But after that doctor drug the Mex out the door, and everyone started acting funny, Waylon stayed away from him too. *Wouldn't look right, me hangin' 'round with a rapist, now would it?* was what he'd said later when they met at the stable where they were sleeping. Jake almost pulled his iron and bored him right there.

"You're in on this too. You had your fun."

"Yeah, but no one knows about me, 'cause I didn't get myself all scratched up in a cat-fight with her, and didn't lose no concho for them Mexicans to find, now did I?"

Jake could still not understand what was causing all the ill feeling of the townspeople toward him. After all, Mexicans weren't the same as white folk in his book. Their women were there to use, but you didn't have to treat them like a white woman. He'd been there on that Fourth of July celebration in Downieville when a bunch of men got drunk and broke into Juanita's cabin. In fact, he was one of them, only he didn't make it inside. Lucky, too, 'cause she was both a looker and a fighter, just like Leonida. But somehow Juanita got hold of a knife and stuck Joe Cannon right in the gizzard, and he croaked. Well, those town folks understood how things should be, and it didn't take but two or three hours until they'd both tried and hung her.

"Hell, what's ever'one so worked up about? She's just a Mex."

"I don't think so." Waylon leaned back in his chair and rolled a cigarette. "If she were just another Mexican, Pod and whoever else wants those folks dead would just shoot her and her husband, now, wouldn't they?"

He had to agree.

"Ever wonder why he's willing to pay us four hundred dollars to draw this guy out and plug him?"

"Never thought about it much. I guess he doesn't wanna get his own hands dirty."

"Pod Randell? Hell. He couldn't clean his hands with lye-water." Waylon blew a cloud of smoke into the air and laughed. "No, dummy. It's 'cause they're not just a bunch of Mexicans. They're rich and spend lots of money in this town. It's 'cause she's pretty and treats all these miners like they're family. You wasn't at that weddin' party of hers, was you?"

Jake shook his head.

"Well, I was. And I'll tell you right now, it was one hell of a wing ding. Lasted for three days. She danced with all them dirty gold-hunters, and the most of them are in love with her.

That's why you ain't popular 'round here. It's a wonder one of them didn't plug you for Rudolfo Garcia and save him some trouble."

"Well, what are we gonna do?"

"It ain't 'what are we gonna do?' It's what are you gonna do?"

Jake scowled as Waylon continued.

"I just saw Pod out there on the street a few minutes ago, and he wants it done now. And no more mistakes. So here's what's gonna happen. First thing in the morning, we're gonna ride out to his place and hide somewheres where we can see that big house of his. And you're gonna plug him with that buffalo gun of your'n."

~   ~   ~

It had rained sometime during the night and the ground was wet. Jake cursed and kicked at the leaves, trying to find a dry spot to lay on wet ground. He had complained at just about everything that morning. He grumbled when Waylon woke him around four o'clock, and made him ride out in the wind and the rain. He wanted coffee, but they couldn't stop and make any. Waylon didn't say anything when Jake took a drink from the bottle he had in his saddlebag. He even let him take another for good measure. It wouldn't matter in a few minutes anyway.

Waylon watched Jake load the heavy .50 caliber Sharps and take a position between two trees where he could view the heavy wooden gate of the Garcia hacienda. He removed his hat to sight the gun in and a breeze blew droplets of water from the leaves in one of the oak trees down the back of his neck.

"Dammit," he said, slapping at the water. "Come on, let's get this over with. I wanna get my money and leave this stinkin' hole. Let's go to Sacramento or San Francisco."

"You sure you're close enough?" Waylon asked for the third time as he adjusted his saddle.

"Hell yes, I'm close enough. I've already told you a hundret times."

They were only three hundred yards from the house and Waylon knew he himself could hit a target the size of a man from twice that far with that gun. He'd heard of men hitting man-size targets nearly a mile away with a Sharps, but he'd only counted them as rumors. Still, it made him wonder. Maybe he'd try it some day, when the wind wasn't blowing and he was sober.

"All right, be ready now. I'm goin' down there and draw him out. Make sure who you're shootin', and don't get me."

"Don't worry 'bout it. Just get him to come to the gate and I'll take care of the rest."

Waylon climbed into the saddle as Jake turned to pick up his bottle. He had his back to him when Waylon pulled his gun from it's holster. The bullet took Jake directly between the shoulder blades and knocked him flat to the ground. A groan issued from deep inside his throat as he turned his head to look at his smiling partner holding the smoking gun.

"Sorry, Pard. But you've made too many mistakes. You've become what Pod and the judge call a *liability*. Well, hey now, don't look so shocked. You'd have done the same for me, now wouldn't ya?"

Jake coughed up blood as he tried to speak. He reached for his gun, but was too weak to hold the heavy rifle.

"Oh, yeah, I forgot. You never knowed it was Judge Baines who's Pod's silent partner, did you? Anyway, they said you drank and talked too much, and the way you messed up with the Mex lady, they was scared you'd ruin the whole deal. But they kinda figure you can die for a purpose. They're gonna blame Rudolfo for shooting you in the back."

Waylon glanced in the direction of the Garcia hacienda as faint noises drifted their way on the breeze. Several men were standing in the courtyard looking, while another pointed toward the clump of trees they were hiding behind. He watched as a vaquero entered the courtyard leading several horses.

"Well, Pard, I'm gonna have to rustle. Looks like we're gonna have company here in a minute or two. But I hate leavin ya like this. Are ya gonna go ahead and die, or am I gonna have to plug you again?"

Jake coughed and clawed at the blades of grass with his fingers. Then, expelling his breath with a deep groan, he dropped his head to the ground and lay still, his eyes staring blankly at the grass clutched tightly in his left hand.

The sound of hoof beats caused Waylon to turn back toward the hacienda where mounted riders where headed his way. He slid his gun back into its holster as he took one last look at his partner lying on the ground. "See ya 'round, pard. Hope ol' Saul don't make ya stoke them furnaces too hot." With a laugh he spurred his horse and galloped away from the oncoming riders.

~　　　~　　　~

Henry Baines sat in his favorite chair watching the line of riders make their way down the street. Their leader was Rudolfo Garcia, and one of the horses, he knew, carried the body of Jake Teel draped over its saddle. "Pod, better get out here. We got company."

Pod stepped to the porch buckling his gunbelt as the horses halted in front of the jail.

"Mornin' Rudolfo." Henry rose from his seat. "Looks like you brought us some trouble."

"*Si*, Señor Baines." He slid gracefully from his saddle while the others remained on horseback. "Paco," he motioned toward one of the riders, "heard a shot early this morning, and we found this man lying on the ground with his rifle." The young vaquero named Paco tossed the gun to Pod from horseback. "We found other horse tracks around his body, but have no idea who shot him, or why."

"Jake Teel." Pod held Jake's head up by his hair and looked into his blank stare. "Ain't this the same man you threatened to kill in The Rusty Rail night before last?"

"*Si, si*. But I did not get the pleasure, Señor. I was home sleeping in bed with my wife."

"How're we supposed to know that? That woman of your'n couldn't even talk last time I seen her. Got any other witnesses to where you was?"

"Señor," Rudolfo laughed as he moved his arm in a wide arch, "I have my whole rancho."

"Yeah, and I'm sure ever one of them Mexicans would lie for you."

Rudolfo's expression changed instantly as Pod spoke.

"Gentlemen, please," Henry stepped forward. By now, half the town had gathered around the little building, so he raised his voice for all to hear. "I'm sure Mr. Garcia is telling us the truth. And we thank you, Rudolfo, for taking the time to bring Jake's body all the way here, and report this unfortunate incident directly to us. But I would like you to do us a favor, if you would, and stay in town while we clear this mess up. A lot of people happened to hear you threaten Mr. Teel, and you know how folks can make things up. Your men can leave if they have something else to do. This shouldn't take too long."

"*Muy bien*," Rudolfo said with a nod. He dismissed everyone but Paco, to whom he handed the reins of his horse. "Now, señors, if you will excuse me, we will go get something to eat while you make up your minds what you are going to do."

"Pod," Henry spoke softly as they watched the Don and his vaquero walk toward Dirty Ben's. "Take Jake's body to The Rusty Rail and get hold of George and tell him to bring his bag with him. We'll need a doctor's opinion at the inquest. Let's get this over as quickly as possible. Mr. Garcia's a busy man. We're all busy."

Chapter 7

Sean Kilkenney had spent most of the night delivering the eighth Gonzales son and was on his way back to Dogtown when he brought Cathy to a stop. It was not an unusual sight to see a vaquero racing a fleet-footed horse across the rolling hills, but the way Paco passed him, leaning forward in his saddle with his head lying against the horse's neck, told him something was drastically wrong. He started to turn Cathy around in an effort to catch the vaquero, but decided against it as he disappeared over the next rise.

"Suppose someone will tell us what's bothering him when we get to town," he said as the mule trotted gingerly onward. He had just come into sight of the livery stable when he pulled up short.

"What the hell....?" The sight of a man hanging from the hay loft chilled him to the bone. He could tell from the loud voices coming from the crowd milling around that quite a few were unhappy at what had just taken place. He drew closer, then stopped as he recognized the dead man.

"Jesus, Almighty God." It was Rudolfo Garcia. He

climbed down and walked slowly toward the crowd leading Cathy by the reins.

"Told them there was a skunk in the woodpile." Tex was leaning against the corral fence rolling a cigarette. He looked almost as pale as his faded shirt. "Shoulda stayed away from this flea-bitten town, but he wouldn't listen." Sean was still speechless, so Tex lit his smoke and continued.

"He found that guy that raped his wife out on his ranch this morning. Someone had plugged him in the back. They heered the shot, but never seen no one. So, he brings him in this mornin', like a good citizen, and the judge asks him to hang around while they figured things out. So, Rudolfo tells his men to go back to work while he waits 'round town. Well, the judge and Pod Randell figured things out alright. They charge him with murder and hold court over in The Rusty Rail. The judge, he gets a dozen or so guys no one's ever seen before to act as jurors, and they find him guilty. Whole thing took only about an hour or so before they got him hung."

Tex threw the half-smoked butt on the ground and crushed it with the toe of his boot. "Just got here myself. Been ridin' night watch for old Ben Johnson. Them Mormons who run the Three Mile Mine are fit to be tied."

Sean put a hand on Tex's shoulder, then turned toward Pod Randell who had been standing beside several men at the edge of the circle. "What's the meaning of this? Why did you let this happen?"

"He had a trial. All we done was hang a murderer."

"No, this is murder. This man never killed anyone in his life, and you know it." Sean's angry voice silenced the crowd who turned to listen.

"You're a little late to be showing up as a witness, aren't you, Mr. Kilkenney?" Henry Baines stepped from the crowd to confront the doctor. "Do you have some information we should have had at the trial? Were you with Mr. Garcia last night?"

"No, I was delivering a baby."

"Oh, but you know for certain that Mr. Garcia did not

shoot Mr. Teel in the back."

"Yes, I am certain that he didn't do it. He couldn't have. He wasn't that kind of a person."

"Oh, but I'm afraid you're a poor judge of character, Doctor. We heard the testimony of at least a dozen men at the trial that they personally heard Mr. Garcia threaten to kill Mr. Teel. And, if I'm not mistaken, Doctor, you heard the same threats, didn't you?"

"Yes, I did. But he was angry. He...."

"He shot and killed Jake Teel." Henry's voice was loud enough for everyone to hear. "I'm afraid, Doctor, that your presence at the trial would not have added anything. You were delivering a baby last night, so you know nothing of Rudolfo Garcia's movements. You couldn't truthfully say he did, or did not shoot Jake Teel in the back, now could you? And, at your own admission, you yourself heard him threaten to kill Mr. Teel."

"Tex said that Rudolfo brought the body in. What was he doing on the Garcia Rancho in the first place?" The question wiped the smile from the judge's face and made Sean wonder if anyone had sense enough to ask it at the trial.

"Huntin'." The man who had positioned himself opposite Rudolfo in The Rusty Rail spat chewing tobacco into the dust at his feet before continuing. "He told me early this mornin' he was going huntin', so's I reckon that's where he was."

"Hunting what? Cows? That's all that's out there."

"Hell, I don't know. That was his business."

"Look, gentlemen, this isn't going to get us anywhere." Henry held up his hands. "All these questions are going to do is get everyone more upset than they already are. I suggest, Doctor, if you have any more questions or comments, that you come over to the Sheriff's office later on, and I'll be happy to listen to you."

"Cut him down," the judge said and walked away. Pod Randell looked directly into Sean's face and smirked, then followed the portly judge toward the jail. Sean had to fight a sudden urge to smash his pretty face but turned his attention to the limp body being lowered from the beam instead.

"The bastards didn't even hang him correctly," he said, studying the contorted face with its swollen tongue. "His wife will ask to see him. Damn them to hell anyway. This will drive her insane."

"Maybe." Tex plucked a straw from a nearby haystack and began chewing on it. "I had me a young filly once't that surprised me. A cougar come outa the hills one night and scratched her all to hell. I heered the ruckus and run him off, then patched her up best I could. A couple of days later he comes back and kills her colt. Well, that musta done it, 'cause she broke loose and stomped the daylights outa him. I mean she kilt him deader'n a door-nail. There wasn't enough left to skin."

"How was the filly?"

"Oh, she got clawed and chewed up enough where she finally died."

"That's what I'm afraid of."

"The point is, I never knew up 'til then a horse could kill a cat. Now, I'll admit, that cougar was kinda old and bunged-up in the first place, but a horse will run from one if it can. But when he kilt her colt, she got over being scared and got mad enough to fight back. And she done it by herself too. Now, the filly you're talkin about ain't by herself. She's got some help."

Sean followed as they carried the body to the jail and laid it in the one and only cell beside Jake's corpse.

"Fittin' end, wouldn't you say, Doc? The body of the man who committed the murder beside the man he killed?" Henry propped his feet on Pod's desk and lit his pipe.

"May I?" Sean motioned toward the bodies.

"Suit yourself, but why?"

"I'm a man of science." Sean removed his coat and began examining Jake Teel's body. "And you can learn a lot about life by studying a person after they're dead."

"I can tell you about Jake. He died because he got a

hole blowed in his back." Pod laughed at his own joke.

Sean removed Jake Teel's shirt and felt the small hard lump just under the skin on the left side of his chest. Turning the body on its side and eyeing the hole where the bullet entered, he laid the body back down and removed a scalpel from his bag.

"Hey, what's that for? What'er ya gonna do?" Pod stood over Sean smoking a cigarette.

"I'm going to remove the bullet that no one's thought important up to this point. And I would appreciate it if you didn't drop your ashes into my bag."

Pod stepped back as the doctor made a small slit and removed the bullet. He wiped it off and held it up to examine it in the sunlight filtering in through the window.

"A little flat on one side from the impact, but still in pretty good shape. I'm surprised that you didn't remove it before now."

"Like you said, we didn't think it was important. Jake Teel's dead and we caught his killer. That's what's important." Henry sounded angry as he knocked the ashes from his pipe.

"Yes, I suppose you're right." Sean put the slug in his vest pocket. "But it might have told you what type of gun he was killed with."

"By the way," he said as an after-thought, closing his bag and rising to his feet. "Why do you suppose Rudolfo would shoot this man in the back and then bring his body into town? Doesn't that seem kind of strange to you?"

"People do crazy things, Doc. You should know that, dealing with them the way you do."

"Yes, Judge, I'm afraid you're probably right." He stopped at the door to study the diploma hanging on the wall. "Yours?" He glanced at Henry.

"Yes, why?"

"Just wondering, that's all. Harvard's a mighty fine school."

"Yes it is. Did you study medicine there?"

"No," Sean said with a laugh. "I wish I could have gone

to such a fine school as that. I read medicine under an army surgeon stationed in Minnesota, and later finished my last year at Yale, which is a fine school indeed. But I was never able to go full-time to any university. I wish I had. Lucky man you are, Your Honor."

"Yes, I guess I am at that."

Sean doffed his hat and left while the judge was still smiling smugly. He walked swiftly toward his tent, ignoring the angry crowd still milling about the livery stable. *I wonder why a man would hang a bachelor of arts diploma on the wall, and tell everyone it's a law degree? Guess none of these miners can read Latin.* It was a beautiful document, but it didn't qualify him to practice law any more than the sign on the barber shop qualified George Bidwell to practice medicine.

He fingered the bullet in his vest pocket. *There's a skunk in the woodpile, just like Tex says there is. But I swear on your grave, Rudolfo, I'll find out what's going on.*

Chapter 8

He heard them before they reached the edge of town. The rhythm of the hooves beating on the hard-packed earth rolled like thunder. Sean had been lying on his bunk watching the canvas above him wave with the wind. Every time he closed his eyes he saw Rudolfo's ghastly death-mask and decided he would probably never sleep peacefully again until his killers had been brought to justice. Rudolfo was not a murderer. He knew that for certain. Crawling from his cot, he put his hat on and stepped into the warm afternoon breeze. Shading his eyes, he could see them silhouetted against the setting sun. Eleven mounted riders leading a buckboard, with Carlo in the lead. *They came for his body.* A chill swept over Sean as he ran toward the livery stable. Tex was leaning against the same railing as earlier in the day chewing on a straw.

"There's going to be hell to pay." Tex bit off a piece and spit. "I count twelve all total."

"The Sheriff will kill that boy. They'll be taking two bodies back in that wagon."

"Shore he will, if we let him. Just got to keep them apart, that's all."

The riders stopped and dismounted. Carlo nodded curtly and started walking toward the center of town with ten of his vaqueros in tow, leaving the youngest to tend the horses.

"Dammit," Tex said, throwing his straw on the ground. "Carlo, hold up a bit."

Sean could see Pod Randell and several men waiting at the end of the street armed with shotguns. He had to run in order to catch up with Tex and Carlo. It was Tex who caught Carlo by the shirt sleeve to bring him to a halt.

"They killed my brother."

"Shore they did. And they'll kill you too."

He pulled away from Tex's grasp. "I've got eleven men with me. They can't kill us all."

"Maybe not. But most of these men are married and have children. How do you want me to explain their death?" Sean said, stepping in front of the angry Mexican. "And what am I supposed to tell your sister-in-law when I bring back both bodies, her husband's and yours?"

"Get out of my way." He tried pushing his way past, but Sean wouldn't let him.

"I'm just as angry as you are, but this isn't the answer."

Carlo's right hand came quick and hard, but Sean was able to duck the blow and land one of his own just under the rib-cage. Carlo's breath left him in one gasp as he doubled over. Sean's next blow was a short upper-cut to the chin, and the young man fell in a heap at his feet. The sound of ten pistols being cocked in unison made Sean jump. He stifled a cry as the vaqueros pointed the weapons at him. Tex held his palms toward the men and began talking rapidly in Spanish.

"You'd better come with us," he said to Sean as they helped Carlo to his feet. "I told them you were on our side, and you only did this to keep Carlo alive."

"I am. I did. But I just got back from their rancho, why do I have to go there again?"

"Because if you don't, they'll probably think I lied to

them, and that might not be healthy for either of us."

"Here, take care of him." Tex pushed the semi-conscious Carlo into Sean's arms and stepped forward to meet Pod and his men as they approached.

"What's going on, Tex? These men looking for trouble?"

"Not at all, Sheriff. They just come to get Rudolfo's body, that's all."

"Then, why'd Doc here bash the boy?"

"Don't rightly know. Why don't you ask him?"

"He welched on a bet," Sean said over his shoulder as he helped Paco put Carlo on his horse. "I wagered a twenty-dollar gold piece that Cathy could beat this black of his, and now he won't pay up."

"You expect me to believe that mule of yours beat his stallion?"

"She surely did. And she'll beat that flea-bag you call a horse, too." Pod's face grew dark as the men with him started to laugh.

"You'd better get that twenty dollars ready, 'cause I'll run my mare against that mule right now."

"Oh, I'm afraid we can't race them today, Sheriff. You see, I've got to help take Mr. Garcia's remains back to the rancho and be there when the news is broken to the little lady. But we'll race them soon enough when I get back. Perhaps in a day or two. That way both animals will be rested."

"Alright, Doc. Just keep that money right handy where I can get at it."

"Right here." Sean pulled a gold piece from his pocket and held it high. "Now, tell me Sheriff, when can we get Mr. Garcia's body?"

"Anytime you want. You know where he is. We already stuck Jake in the ground while you was taking a nap."

"We'll be right over."

Sean watched the Sheriff and his men amble toward the jail before letting Cathy out of her stall.

"That was some of the slickest talkin' I ever heard, and

believe me, I've heard a lot of bull in my days." Tex pulled another straw from the stack and began chewing on it. "He had every intention of opening the ball with them scatter-guns before you told him this mule of yourn could beat his mare. Shore as shootin' someone would have died."

"That's what I was afraid of, but it wasn't a lot of bull either." Sean threw his saddle across the mule's back. "Cathy kept up with Carlo's black at a full run, and she'll beat the Sheriff's horse when we race."

"You really mean you're gonna race him?"

"Why not?" He patted Cathy's neck and looked defiantly at the Texan.

"Well, not that the mule couldn't beat his nag, but it might not be too healthy to take his money."

"Oh, I plan on taking much more that his money, my friend. Much more."

Chapter 9

"The coffin's compliments of the court. You can tell Mrs. Garcia there's no charge." Sean watched as they loaded the crudely built pine crate in the wagon, then glared at the smiling face of Judge Baines in disgust. *May God have mercy on your soul, if you have one.* Biting his tongue, he started Cathy behind the slow-moving procession through the crowded street. Better than half of the hardened miners removed their hats as they passed.

"Does Mrs. Garcia know what happened?" he asked as Tex joined his side.

"Don't know," he shrugged his shoulders. "I'll find out, though." Tex spurred his sorrel to the front of the line as they were approaching the outskirts of town. Sean groaned when he saw Carlo shake his head. Tex brought his horse to a stop and removed his hat. He sat wiping the sweatband with his scarf as Sean caught up.

"He says no. Hell, ain't it? What are you gonna tell her?"

"God only knows."

~   ~   ~

Sean's hand shook as he accepted the glass of brandy from Jose Flores. The mournful wail drifting downstairs was chilling.

"Don't take it too personal, Doctor. None of this was your fault."

Sean jerked up with a start. "I thought you couldn't speak English. At least that was what Carlo told me the day...."

Carlo glared at him from his seat across the room.

"That is what I wanted. I find it safer that way." He poured himself a glass of brandy and held it up. "To Rudolfo. May his murderers burn in hell." He sipped the amber liquid and set the glass on the table.

"Actually, my daughter and I both speak and understand several languages very well. But we have found that many people in this country feel threatened by our education and, shall we say, our difference?"

"We're all different, Mr. Flores." Sean rolled his glass back and forth in his palms. "My family came from Ireland. Yours came from Spain. We all came from somewhere. And we'll all end up in the same place, so what difference does it make?" He looked up as Carlo cursed in Spanish and rose to his feet.

"If there's a God at all, I'll never end up in the same place as the sheriff and that judge."

Father Franco overheard the curses and descended the stairs mumbling a prayer.

"I didn't mean it that way. I only meant that we'll all die, someday. Where we go after that is up to God himself."

"I would have sent Pod Randell to hell this afternoon, if it hadn't been for you." He kicked the chair he'd been sitting in.

"All you'd have done was get your fool head shot off." Tex licked the cigarette he'd been rolling. "You ain't fast enough."

"You said I was fast."

"You still ain't fast enough." He lit his smoke and threw the match in the fireplace. "Show me. Go ahead and pull your iron."

Carlo looked puzzled.

"You don't gotta shoot. Go ahead and pull. Show me how fast you are."

Carlo grabbed for his holster but stopped as Tex cocked the hammer on the Colt he was pointing at him. Sean had been watching both men, but could not remember seeing Tex draw the weapon.

"See?" He eased the hammer back down and returned the gun to its holster. "You didn't even clear your belt. Now, I don't know, but some say that Pod's faster than me. But even if he ain't, you would have still lost a fistful of brains either way. Doc was right punchin' your lights out."

"He was my brother. It's my duty to avenge him."

"Aye, my good man, but do it some other way." Sean tried to put a hand on his shoulder, but Carlo pushed it off and grabbed for the door latch.

"It's my duty." He slammed the door as he left.

"Perhaps I should take him back to Mexico with us," Jose Flores said, shaking his head.

"You're going back? Why?" Tex threw his smoke in the fireplace.

"My son-in-law is dead. There's nothing left for us here."

"Nothing left for you here?" Sean's voice broke as he choked on his brandy. "Seventy-five square miles of prime land, and there's nothing left?"

Jose stared at him blankly.

"True, Rudolfo Garcia is dead, but who do you think he'd want this ranch to go to more than his wife and family? Tell me that, if you can, Mr. Flores."

"He has a brother."

"Aye, and a fine lad he is. But he is young and rash, and would need someone such as yourself to guide him, wouldn't he? And besides that, your daughter was married to the man who owned all this, wasn't she?"

Jose raised his eyebrows.

"And now you're thinking of moving off and leaving this fine ranch to the men who murdered your son-in-law. Tell me, Mr. Flores. When you're gone, what's to become of Carlo, Paco, Maria, Father Franco, and the many others who depend on this ranch for their living? What do you think Rudolfo would say to that?"

"I don't know. I hadn't thought too much about that. It's just that so many bad things have happened."

"I know. But I would be damned, (excuse me, Father)," Sean nodded toward the priest, "if I would let those men step one foot on this property. I would stay here and fight until my last breath. It would be the greater sin not to."

"Perhaps you're right, Doctor." He nodded thoughtfully. "Perhaps you're right. But, if you'll excuse me, I'll go sit with my daughter for a while."

"Damn fine speech." Tex leaned back in a chair and propped his long legs on the table.

"Just the gift of blarney," Sean said, watching Jose close his daughter's door behind him. Then, reaching into his vest pocket, he removed the bullet that killed Jake Teel, and held it in the lamplight.

"By the way, what do you make of this?" He said, tossing it to Tex.

"Kinda flat on one side. Where'd you get it from?"

"I took it from Jake Teel's body earlier today. I'm no expert, but I know it didn't come from one of Rudolfo's Coutties. They're .58 caliber."

"Forty-four?" Tex tossed the ball and caught it thoughtfully several times. "Don't think so." He took a ball from his own pouch and placed it on the table beside the one that killed Jake Teel.

"Mine's .44 caliber. This one here's flat, but you can see it's a mite smaller. If we had some scales...."

"Coming right up." Sean opened his bag and removed a

small set of scales, and began to assemble them on the table. "I'm afraid to leave anything back at my tent," he said with a grin. "I don't have much as it is."

He placed the ball taken from Jake's body in one tray and the .44 caliber ball in the other. The scale immediately tipped toward the side with Tex's bullet.

"Right you are. This came from a smaller gun."

He then placed small weights on the scale until they balanced perfectly.

"I won't know until I have something similar to compare it with, but I'd guess this is a .31 or .36 caliber bullet. I doubt if it's even .38."

"I take note of the iron a man totes, and there's a few .36's and couple of .38's, but most around here carry .44's or .45's. Some even heavier. Now, I don't know every one, and there's probably a few more of them around I ain't seen. But I know one man that totes a Navy .31. I ain't got no use for him either. Waylon Sunday. He hangs around with Pod Randell, and he'd shoot his own mother if he thought he'd make a profit."

Sean placed his palms on either side of the scales and studied Tex. "We don't know for sure. This isn't much to go on."

"It's something, right? What if I get one of his bullets? Would that help?"

"As long as I don't have to dig it out of you."

"Don't worry 'bout that." Tex smiled and started rolling another cigarette.

Chapter 10

Sean wasn't superstitious by any means, but the raven crying in the oak tree bothered him. *Perhaps he's only mourning Rudolfo like every one else,* he told himself as he watched the coffin being lowered into the earth. The soft wailing of the women and children drifted heavenward as the black-clad figure took a handful of dirt and tossed it on the box containing her husband. He shuddered and turned away, not able to watch any longer.

"We got a war on our hands, Pard," Tex said as Sean joined him under the oak. "Seen the look in their eyes?"

Sean glanced at Carlo with his vaqueros standing opposite the grave.

"You ain't gonna be able to stop him next time either. That is, unless you can whip all of them at the same time." The Texan plucked a long stem of grass and began chewing on the end. "Yep, we'll be diggin' another grave right beside that one real soon."

"Damn," Sean said. "You're an uplifting character to be around."

"Just telling you what's gonna happen. Get them tools of yourn ready, 'cause you're gonna be pullin' lead outa a lot of men here real soon."

With one final cry, the raven took flight and Sean lost sight of it in the sun.

~   ~   ~

Jose Flores had given Sean one of the guest rooms for the evening, but sleep fled him although he was totally exhausted. He heard the crying of the raven mingled with those of the women and children every time he closed his eyes, and saw the black-clad figure tossing a handful of dirt into the grave. He slipped on his trousers and boots and sat in one of the leather-slung chairs on the patio to smoke his pipe. He took his time packing the bowl and was just about to strike the match when he heard the door at the top of the stairs creak. He could see her through the open window as she slowly descended the staircase and tip-toed to her husband's office. She wore a black riding skirt and jacket, but no mourner's veil. The black sombrero drawn tightly on her head failed to hide the blond hair sparkling in the moonlight that filtered through the window. He leaned into the shadows listening, as she carefully pulled one of the desk drawers open. *Now, what the hell is she up to?* She fumbled with something for a second or two, then stopped to blow her nose. He heard the snapping of a wooden lid and the closing of a drawer, followed by the soft clicking of small leather boots as she headed his way. He almost dropped the pipe when Leonida stepped quietly into the patio stuffing one of Rudolfo's dueling pistols into her waistband.

She was halfway to the stables before Sean laid his pipe on the bricks and rose from his chair. He might have thought the sight down-right comical, this small woman shoving the .58 caliber Coutty into her belt. But a vision of him standing over her lifeless body chilled him and caused him to quicken his steps. She already had the black Arabian out and was attempting to mount him bareback when Sean entered the gate.

"Would you be going for a ride this time of night, Mrs. Garcia?"

"Oh," she said, backing away.

"You don't have to be afraid of me, ma'am. It's just that I think you've got it in that pretty head of yours to do something downright foolish, and I'd like to talk you out of it if I could."

"*Dejame sola,*" she said, pointing the gun at him.

"Begging your pardon, ma'am, but you know I don't speak Spanish. If you want me to do something for you, you'll have to speak English." He acted as though he hadn't seen the gun.

"*Alto.*" She almost shouted and shoved the gun toward his face.

"Now, Mrs. Garcia, that really isn't very ladylike, is it? Here I am being a guest of your father's, and you go pointing your husband's pistol at me. I might get my feelings hurt if you keep that up." He started rubbing the horse's neck. "Mighty fine animal you have here. I'll bet he's fast, real fast."

"*Sacate, pronto.*" She motioned toward the gate with the gun barrel.

"I told you that I can't understand what you're saying when you speak Spanish. But I believe you're being down right rude, and I shall have to tell your father if you don't stop," he said as he took a step toward her.

"*Dejame sola, gringo cerdo.*" She cocked the hammer back.

"Well, now. I don't know exactly what you said, but I think you just called me some sort of a name. You're beginning to make me lose my temper. I've got a mind to turn you over my knee and paddle your behind." Her lips set in a thin line and her green eyes flashed as she leveled the gun only inches from his face.

"Now, you've made several mistakes. First of all, never point a gun at someone when you're not going to use it. You might have thought I'm crazy standing here talking blarney the way I am, but I'm not really that brave, and I'm not a fool either. I know you're not going to shoot me, because I removed the prime from both of those guns myself before I put them back in the case." Her mouth dropped open as her eyes darted toward the weapon then back to Sean.

"Next thing you've done wrong is, you're pointing it toward my head. When you're going to shoot someone, point the gun toward the largest part of his body." He gently took her hand and lowered the gun toward his chest. "That way you stand less of a chance of missing. And finally, you're standing way too close. The person you're trying to kill can simply reach out and take the gun away from you like this." He grabbed the Coutty and twisted it from her grasp. "See?" Sean's knees almost buckled as the gun went off with a thunderclap.

"*Bruto*," she said and hit him with a resounding slap.

"Here, now cut that out," he said trying to ward off the attack coming at him from all angles. He grabbed her left wrist only to get scratched by the nails on her right hand as she kicked his shins with her boots. "Damn," he said, grabbing both wrists. She kicked him harder and sunk her teeth into his arm. "God Almighty, you little devil, stop it." He slapped her across the cheek and instantly received a blow on the back of his head which drove him to his knees.

"*Alto*, Ildefonso, *alto*." Carlo's voice seemed to be coming from inside a cave as Sean struggled to regain his senses. He rolled to his back just in time to see the fierce-looking Indian raise the lance high in the air. "*Un momento, por favor, un momento*," Carlo said, stepping between them. The discussion that followed was heated and much too fast for Sean to understand what was being said. But one thing was clear to him. If Carlo had not happened on the scene, he would have been dead that very moment. Carlo tried to put his arm around the Señora and lead her away, but she pulled free long enough to kick dried horse dung in Sean's face and spit at him.

"Sorry, Doctor. But she's angry at you for stopping her," he said grabbing hold of her arm again and pulling her from the corral. The Indian glared at him as he closed the gate, and disappeared into the blackness. Sean sat on the ground for a moment, watching Carlo drag the furious widow to the house.

"You'd better get out of there, Señor, before her horse kicks you too." Sean turned to see Paco watching him over the railing. "The horse might be angry at you like the Doña, no?"

"There isn't a horse on this ranch that could be any worse than facing that little hell-cat's kicking and scratching, Paco." Sean scooped the pistol from the dirt before he climbed through the railing. "She almost killed me," he handed the weapon to Paco. "Rudolfo must have reloaded it after I left and she almost killed me." His voice rose in pitch as he swatted at the dust clinging to his clothes. "Who in the hell was that Indian, and where'd he come from?"

"Baca? Who knows where Baca comes from? He's here, he's there. He comes and goes however Baca chooses." Paco dipped a bucket of water from the trough and set it on a bench, then handed Sean his scarf. "You're bleeding, Señor. A cat scratches your face, and the back of the head bleeds too."

"Carlo called him something else."

"Ildefonso. That is his first name. Ildefonso Baca. He is what you gringos call half-breed. His father is Basque, and his mother is Chemehuevi Indian. They are Paiutes from Arizona, but Baca likes it here sometimes, when the weather is good. He also likes the Doña very much. You should never hit her in front of him. You are lucky to be alive, Señor." Sean held the wet scarf to his wounded head.

"I don't remember hitting any woman in my life before, Paco, and I don't think I will ever do it again. I wouldn't have slapped her then, except she was beating the hell out of me."

"Better that, than to die, Señor."

"Yes, but if I'd left her alone, she would have gone to town looking for Judge Baines and got herself killed."

"Perhaps, but she would not have been alone. Baca would have followed. You see, Carlo has asked Baca to watch the Doña and see no harm comes to her again. Baca does his job very well. Perhaps the judge would have died."

"Maybe. Of course, there's always the chance she

would have gotten him cornered by herself and scratched him to death," Sean said, dabbing his cheek with the damp scarf.

"Just remember, Baca likes Doña Leonida very much, and the Indians who work here like Baca. You hurt Doña Leonida and they will kill you."

"I never wanted to hurt her, Paco, I like her too. Too damned much. Tell Baca I was trying to keep her from getting hurt again."

"I will. You may keep the scarf, Señor. I have another."

"Thank you. Perhaps I'll see you tomorrow."

~   ~   ~

Maria served Sean his coffee on the patio and returned to the kitchen, only to poke her head out the door to look at him and grin as she bared her fingernails and clawed the air. "Damned witch," he said sullenly as he sipped the steaming liquid. General Flores paused at the door before sitting in the chair next to him and lighting a cigar.

"I'm afraid I must apologize for my daughter, Doctor. Carlo told me what happened last night, and Leonida acted most inappropriately."

"I can understand her passion, Sir. I think I might have done the same thing, given the same circumstances. It was Baca who scared the devil out of me."

"And you had every right to be frightened. But I will do my best to see that nothing like that ever happens again."

"I appreciate that, General. But I would also suggest you do your best in keeping your daughter right here on these grounds until this whole thing is settled. She could have gotten herself killed last night."

"*Si*, Doctor, and I'm sure my daughter is just as sorry for what happened as I am. We are not a violent people, Señor."

"Not violent? What do you call last night? I think I can understand your daughter acting that way, but that Indian is definitely a violent person."

"Yes, Baca is different. He is a warrior, much as I am, or was," he said, looking away sadly. "But Baca lives to fight. He rode with Don Andres against General Kearny at San Pascual in 1846. I know Kearny's report said he won that battle, but practically all the casualties were on the American side. It only took Andres' men 10 minutes to kill 22 men, including several officers. They wounded another 16, including General Kearny himself. They did that, Doctor, armed with Californian lances much like the one you faced last night. Baca rides a horse like a demon and fights like the devil himself. That is why Carlo and I agree that he should be the one to protect Leonida. You will never see him, but he will be there. So be careful Doctor. I hope you understand."

"I understand, General. I just hope you understand that I will not be spending many nights here at this rancho. And I also hope you understand when I refuse to stop her if I see her trying to sneak off and get herself killed again. Now, if you'll excuse me, I need to go pack my things."

"You are leaving us?"

"Yes, I do have a practice of sorts back in town."

Sean handed the empty cup to Maria in the hallway and nodded curtly toward the Señora seated at the dining room table. He ascended the stairs two steps at a time and closed the door to the guest room behind him with a bang. Packing his things consisted of stuffing the shirt and pants he had on last night into a bag and grabbing his medical kit. He tipped his hat to the maid, mumbled a thank you at the bottom of the stairs and reached the open door in four strides before stopping. It was Ildefonso Baca. He stood blocking the doorway with the lance in his left hand and a ferocious look on his face while Paco talked with Jose Flores on the patio.

"Excuse me," Sean said, trying to step around him, but the Indian moved just enough to block his way. "I said, excuse me." He tried going the other way, but was met with the same resistance.

"Baca," Jose said, and the Indian smiled slightly as he took a half of a step backward to let him pass.

Oh, what the hell? Sean let go of his bags as he hooked his left foot behind Baca's heel and gave the Indian a quick shove. The lance rattled free as he fell hard on the bricks. Sean grabbed the lance and shoved the blunt end hard into Paco's stomach as the vaquero leaped from his chair and rushed toward him. The vaquero folded in a heap gasping for air as Baca started to rise, but Sean drove his head back to the pavement hard with his boot and raised the lance high in the air.

"No, Doctor, *por favor*," Leonida said from the doorway. The Indian showed no emotion as he lay watching the sharp point poised above him.

"Tell him he's not the only warrior here. Tell him my people have been warriors for many years too."

She was silent.

"Now!" Sean listened as she interpreted quickly in Spanish.

"Tell him I will not tolerate being shoved or treated disrespectfully any longer. Tell him if he ever threatens me again, I shall take this lance away again and kill him with his own weapon."

"But, Señor I...."

"Tell him!" He waited until she finished before throwing the weapon up onto the roof.

"Damned barbarians." He glared at the wide-eyed Doña and picked up his bags. He would have sworn that Baca was actually smiling as she interpreted his last threat. He brushed past General Flores without speaking and pushed his way through the crowd of spectators on his way toward the stables.

"*Que* señor *macho*." It sounded like Baca's voice, but he wasn't sure. *What does it matter anyway,* Sean shrugged. He had no way of knowing what the Indian said even if it was him. *Let him say what he wants.* He threw his saddle on Cathy knowing he'd just worn out his welcome and would probably never come here again.

Chapter 11

"Andar, caballos." Arturo Horeno shook the reins and urged the team onward at a fast trot. Alice Carpenter smiled at the boy as the wagon creaked and groaned over the rough trail leading toward the Garcia Rancho. The leg that had been broken in the fall from the loft was healing nicely and he hobbled around, using the crutch more as a stick to strike or poke at things, than a walking aid. The doctor had finally given up telling him to stay off his feet, and instructed his parents in how to repair the splint when it became damaged by his activity.

"Oh," she said, grabbing the seat as the wagon hit a rock. Arturo laughed and smiled at her, flashing gleaming white teeth. As Rudolfo and his family rode horses everywhere and had not bothered to maintain the road for use by wagons, the trip was always a slow, tedious one for her. The only wagon that Alice could ever remember seeing on the ranch outside of hers or the crude *carretas*, was the fancy carriage that had brought Leonida and her father from Mexico. The vaqueros had promptly parked it in a shed and it had not been touched since. Well, she cocked an eyebrow in thought, there was the buckboard they brought to get Mr. Garcia's body in. But she'd never seen it before, and had no idea where it might be at this minute.

All the Mexicans were expert riders, including the small children. Seeing the little children almost too small to walk riding on the backs of the huge beasts was something Alice had never quite become comfortable with. On her first trip to the rancho she actually screamed in terror as a three-year-old girl jump from the top rail of a fence onto the back of a brown and white pony and raced it out of the courtyard and across a meadow. Maria Sanchez, the household maid, had put her arms around her and assured her it was alright, because Angelica had been riding the animal for quite a while. But the sight of the frail-looking child with brown legs and small arms clinging to the back of the pony as her black hair whipped in the wind still stuck in her mind.

She closed her eyes and held her breath as Arturo guided the wagon over the narrow bridge spanning the swift waters of the Mokelumne River. Arturo knew how to handle the team as well as any other young Mexican, and maybe better than most, since his father ran the stables in Dogtown. But she was frightened that the bridge would collapse with her on top and she would be swept all the way to the San Francisco Bay. Ike always laughed at her, saying she would only make it to the mouth of the river at the Delta if it did happen, which was not likely. She gripped tighter on the seat as the bridge cracked under the weight of the wagon and Arturo yelled at the horses. Then the wagon gave a lunge as the wheels found hard-packed earth again, and Alice released her grip with an expulsion of breath.

She wished Ike had come with them today. She hated going anywhere without him. But with the trouble brewing in town, and the horrible hanging of Rudolfo, he thought it would be better for her to make the trip with Arturo this time and spend time visiting with Leonida. No one had been to town to order supplies from the store and this was simply a visit they knew needed to happen. In the short time they had known them, they had learned to love and respect the Garcias. They were fine people, regardless of how much money they spent in town, or how much land they owned. It was no one else's business. And she couldn't, for the life of her, understand how one human could treat another as these folks had been treated. She felt ashamed of her own race as she thought about it. Besides, she knew as well as anybody else that the only reason for the existence of Dogtown in the first place was greed. Everybody there was hoping to get rich, either by finding gold, selling supplies to the prospectors as did she and her husband, or through evil practices like the saloons and gambling halls. The Garcias were being persecuted because they were already rich.

But then, it wasn't everybody who felt that way either. The Mormons who ran the Three Mile Mine were just as angry as her and Ike. So were many other people. But most seemed afraid to do or say anything against Judge Baines or Pod Randell. Alice found herself wishing that the Texas gunfighter who had been hanging around town would get angry enough to shoot them both, or at least run them out of the area before it was too late.

Arturo stopped the wagon at the stables and helped her down. He handed her one of the baskets of home-made jelly and bread and was reaching for the other when Maria came running to greet them.

"Señora Carpenter, *buenos dias*." She threw her arms around her and Alice's small frame became buried in the woman's ample breasts. "It is good to see you. Where is your husband? He did not come?"

"No, Maria, he thought he'd better stay close to the store, because of all the trouble in town."

"Ah, *si*. *El Diablo* himself is living there now. May he go to Hades where he belongs. *Dios* forgive me," she said looking up toward the sky and crossing her breast.

"It's okay, Maria. A lot of other people would agree with you, and I'm sure God Himself feels the same way."

Alice handed Maria her basket and accepted the other one from Arturo. "How is Mrs. Garcia feeling?"

"Doña Leonida will not eat. She only sits and looks out her window."

"That's understandable. I'm surprised that she even does that." She took hold of the maid's arm and walked toward the house as Arturo unhitched the team and led them to the watering trough. "I'm afraid I would have simply given up and died if half those things had happened to me. Won't she talk to anyone?"

"Oh, she talks a little to me. And she talks a whole lot to Señor Kilkenney, but not very nice I'm afraid."

"Really? Tell me about it." She stopped on the steps and held Maria's hand as the maid told her about Leonida's attempt to slip away several nights ago and kill Henry Baines. She giggled when hearing about the Doña fighting with the doctor in the corral, but caught her breath at the part about Ildefonso Baca and the lance.

"Oh, my God, did he hurt Doctor Kilkenney?"

"No, just a little bump on the head," Maria said pointing to the back of her head. "The next morning, Señor Kilkenney knocks Baca down and takes his lance away and points it at his chest right here on the steps. He then makes Doña Leonida tell Baca if he ever treats him badly again, he will kill him."

"He took Baca's lance from him? What did Baca do?"

"Nothing," Maria said, tilting her head to one side and raising her eyebrows. "He says the doctor is *muy hombre*. He likes him because he is strong like Baca himself."

Alice broke into laughter. "I've only met Baca once when he came into our store with Mr. Garcia. It frightened the dickens out of me just looking at him. But he sounds like most men I've known. The tougher and more stupid one acts, the better the rest like him."

"Si, Señora, they are all *loco en la cabeza*," she said twirling her index finger around her ear. "That is why my husband, Francisco, is buried behind the church. He tries *la corrida de toros.*" She paused to take a deep breath. "It is a game they play. They think they are brave if they throw the *serape* over the bull's face. But *el toro,* he does not fear Francisco's *serape* and he sticks my husband with the horn. Si, Franciso died a brave man, but he still is dead."

"I'm sorry, Maria. I never asked, and I didn't know you were a widow." Alice pulled Maria close and held on to her.

"It is okay, Señora. He is dead a long time now. It is time to cry for Doña Leonida. She has many sorrows. Come, we go see her."

They placed the baskets on the kitchen table and ascended the stairs silently. Maria tapped lightly on the door and waited. "Doña?" She tapped again. "Doña? Doña Leonida?"

"Si?" The voice inside sounded weak and distant.

"There is someone to see you. May I come in?" There was a moment of silence. "Doña Leonida?"

"*Si, entra.*"

Maria opened the door and Alice was surprised at how well the room was lighted. She had expected to see all the drapes drawn tight and the lamps and candles doused, with the frail girl lying in bed covered with black sheets. Leonida was indeed dressed in mourner's clothing including the black veil covering her gold hair. But she was seated at the window with all the curtains pulled back, watching the children play below. She looked up at Alice from the rumpled shirt she held in her hands.

"*Hola, Señora* Carpenter. It is good to see your face again."

Now that Alice was here, she didn't know what to say to the stricken young girl sitting in front of her. All the words of comfort and wisdom she had rehearsed in the wagon seemed to flee.

"Rudolfo," Leonida said holding up the shirt. "Come, smell," she said, sniffing the garment and holding it out to her. "It's my Rudolfo's scent."

Alice stepped forward, kneeling in front of Leonida and

sniffed the odor of cigar and sweet cologne from the shirt.

"See? It's Rudolfo. I remember him well."

"Oh God, I'm so sorry," Alice said as she fell into Leonida's arms weeping. Maria closed the door quietly behind them, and they clung to each other until they both stopped crying.

"Oh, look. I got your dress all wet," Alice said, digging in her bag for a handkerchief. "I really didn't mean for that to happen. I really meant to try and...." She stopped and looked up. "I don't know. What do you suppose we try to do in moments like this? I came to see you, but I can't give you back your husband."

"No, Señora, you can't give me back Rudolfo, but you gave me all you could. You gave me your heart, and I thank you." She took Alice by the hands and kissed her cheek. "I know now that you loved my husband, and that you love me right now. That means much to someone whose heart has been broken."

Alice stared into the dark green eyes and knew that it was true. She did love this girl deeply. There was a tiny scar to the left side of her mouth and another one at the corner of her left eye. She touched the cheek with her fingers. *I'm glad the man who did this to you is dead.*

"I brought you some jelly and fruit. It's down in the kitchen."

"Si? Let's go see." Leonida jumped to her feet with a smile and grabbing her hand like a child, pulled her toward the door. When they reached the kitchen table, Maria already had the baskets unpacked and was starting to put the items away.

"Ooooo, *pan*," Leonida held a loaf of bread to her nose and inhaled deeply. "And peaches." She put the bread back on the table and picking up a quart jar, held it up like a trophy. "Olga will love them."

"Doña Leonida," Maria said, shaking a finger at her mistress. "Remember what your papa says."

"Oh Papa, poohey." She made a pouty-face as she placed the jar back on the table. "Papa won't know unless you tell him."

"She gives all the fruits and *pan* to the children," the maid said leaning across the table. "Señor Flores tells her to stop. There is nothing here to eat but *carne*."

"But you've heard Doctor Kilkenney say that is why the children suffer. They also have nothing to eat but meat. So I give them a little treat now and then. What does it hurt?"

"You mean to tell me she gave all the canned goods my husband bought out last week to the children?"

"Si, she give it to the children, and her papa and Carlo are angry. They say I should stop her, but how do I stop such an angel? She smiles at me and my heart fills with love. I can't stay angry." She grinned proudly at the mistress, then tried to feign anger again by pointing her finger at the girl. "But your papa will spank you." They both laughed as Leonida hugged her.

"Thank you for coming, Señora," Maria said as the girl turned her attention back to the table. "It is good to hear Doña Leonida laugh again. You are good for her."

"Si, you are an angel, Señora," Leonida said, leaning over the table to smell the bread's aroma again. "Doctor Kilkenney will be sad he was not here to eat your bread. But, we shall eat it all tonight without him."

"It will serve him right. He is nothing but a crazy *gringo,*" Maria said setting three cups on the table. "He says Maria is no good cook." She poured hot water from the kettle in the cups and began to fill fobs with dry tea. "He wants me to cook what I do not have, like I am *Jesus Cristo*. I can make *tortillas* or *mole' con pollo* if I have corn and chocolate. But I have none." She waved her arms around the room. "*El gringo es un burro loco.*"

Alice broke into laughter. "I thought you liked Doctor Kilkenney. I think he's a very nice man."

"He is, but he drives us crazy," Leonida said stirring her tea. "He's very head-strong and says what ever pops into his head. He argues with Maria and Father Franco all the time about the children's health. That is one reason I give them the food from our kitchen."

"You have a lot of children on this ranch, my child. I'm afraid it would take more than what you can store in this tiny kitchen to feed them. You should think about growing your own vegetables. You have more than enough land."

"Si, and we have been planning to do so. But, then this happened." The smile left her face and she gazed silently into the tea before continuing.

"Señor Kilkenney is much like Rudolfo and that is why he makes me so angry."

"I thought you loved your husband," Alice said, dropping her spoon and glancing from the girl to the maid and back again.

"Si, I loved my husband very much. But he still made me angry. He was stubborn like a *burro*. He wanted everything his way. I loved my wedding very much, but it was really his wedding. He planned the *fiesta* and *rodeo*. When we would go to town to shop at your store, he chose what to buy. I was only allowed to pick out one little thing for myself, but he bought everything for the rancho. I was the Doña Leonida, and should not be bothered with such things. He would not even allow me to work around the house. I was only to look pretty, ride the horses, and keep his bed warm."

"Well, I know of a few women who would have traded places with you in one second," Alice said with a laugh.

"Si, and like I said, I loved Rudolfo with my whole heart, but he still made me angry, sometimes." She set her cup down and studied Alice intently. "You don't understand, Señora. Your husband allows you to work in your store."

"Makes me, is more like it. I have to, because it takes us both to keep it going."

"But you still get to. I went to school in Mexico City, Señora. I know numbers, and speak three languages. I can read books. But I was not even allowed to look at his ledger to see how much money or cattle we have. My father is much the same way, and Señor Kilkenney treats me like a little child."

"Don Rudolfo was smart, like a king, but Señor

Kilkenney is stupid like *poste*," Maria said with a scowl.

"No, Señor Kilkenney is not a stump," Leonida said with a laugh. "He is rather stubborn though. He thinks his way is right, and that everyone should agree with him. Like Rudolfo."

"Well, is he?" Alice watched Leonida over her cup of tea.

"Is he what?"

"Right about most things."

"Si, but he could be more gentle in how he says it."

"I've seen him with children in town, and I've always thought he was very gentle. I know for certain he was gentle while setting Arturo's leg. I was there. Was he rough with you when you were hurt?"

Leonida's eyes darted from Alice to Maria and back to Alice before finally settling on her cup. "No he was extremely gentle. I could not have asked for a kinder more compassionate doctor. But he is still stubborn."

Alice laughed again as she patted the girl's arm. "I didn't mean to make you uncomfortable, my dear. I only wanted you to see that we sometimes mistake good judgment and common sense for stubbornness. Oh, I know from experience that men can be stubborn at times, at least Ike certainly can. But they can have a little God-given wisdom at times also. I'm positive he used it the other evening when you tried to slip off to town with your husband's gun."

Leonida's jaw dropped open as she set the cup down hard, spilling some of its contents. "How did you....? Is he telling everyone in town?"

"No, he hasn't told a soul that I know of. In fact, he told my husband an out-and-out lie when Ike asked about the scratches on his face. He said that one of the girls at The Rusty Rail gave them to him. I knew it was a lie right then, because he's not the kind of a man who would consort with such women. Then, Gloria came into the store later that day to buy some sugar, and I asked her. She said she hadn't seen the Doctor in over a week."

"Then, how did you find out?"

Alice simple shrugged and stirred her tea. Maria went to the sink-board and retrieved a towel to mop up the spill.

"Maria Elena Sanchez?"

"Si, I tell her."

"*Por que?*"

"She was only worried about you, the same as I. Don't be angry with her."

"Oh, I'm not angry because she told you, Señora. You understand. I just don't want everyone to know that I tried such a thing. I'm afraid that they will be saying, *poor, poor, Doña Leonida. She lost her husband, and now she's tonta.*"

"I wouldn't be too concerned about what they might or might not say in Dogtown. The people who love you are going to love you no matter what. And the rest? Who cares? It might be better if they did think you were a little crazy. They might leave you alone."

"Si, they are crazy *gringos*, Señora. You should be happy if they leave you alone." Maria glanced at Alice with sheepish eyes. "*Perdoname, por favor.*"

"That's alright, Maria, I'm afraid there are a few *gringos* who are indeed quite mad." Alice stood up from the table. "Well, I hate to leave on that note, but I must get back to town before it gets dark."

The two women walked her to the wagon. Arturo had the team hitched and ready, and stood talking to a young vaquero. Leonida took Alice by the hands and kissed her on both cheeks.

"*Via con Dios, mi companera.* I am so glad you came. You are welcome at my *hacienda* whenever you wish."

"Thank you. And I wish I could say the same, but while you are more than welcome in my home, I'm afraid it might not be too safe for you and your family in town. Do be careful, my child."

"Si, I will. And I will not be coming to Dogtown anytime soon, unless it is to see the graves of Henry Baines and Pod Randell." She turned briskly to the vaquero. "Juan? Help the Señora up to her seat in the wagon."

"Si."

That's strange, Alice thought as she turned to wave. Leonida was feeding several crows grain from the bin and they had gathered at her feet as though they were pets. *There's a whole passal of dogs around here, and she chooses those noisy birds. Oh, well. To each his own.*

Chapter 12

He fell on his cot exhausted. Sean didn't know when he had felt this tired before. It had been three weeks since the funeral and the look on Carlo's face and the crying of the raven still haunted him every time he closed his eyes. He'd also spent many a sleepless night thinking of Mrs. Garcia's black-clad figure tossing dirt on her husband's lifeless body. He would wake up every time the wind shook the canvas of his tent, thinking it was the sound of dirt hitting the pine box. But he could not have kept his eyes open this evening if he had wanted to. He fell into a troubled sleep almost immediately with dreams of gunshots, dead men, beautiful women dressed in black who turned into skeletons, while giant ravens screamed and beat at him with their wings. His nightmare turned to loud gunshots mingled with the frantic yells of running men when he awoke. But it wasn't a dream. It was pitch black inside his tent, and someone had been shaking him. He could hear loud voices drifting from the center of town.

"Damn, where's that lantern?" The tent lit up as Tex struck a match.

"What's going on out there?" Sean said, trying to clear the fog inside his head.

"Told you there'd be hell to pay." He closed the globe and adjusted the wick on the hurricane lamp. "Pull your boots on and rustle."

Sean had trouble keeping pace with the long stride of the Texan as they approached the milling crowd of noisy men. "Here now," the Texan began pushing his way through. "Let the doctor through."

"Ain't no need for another doctor, we already got one. Besides they're both dead anyway." Sean glanced at the smiling face of Pod Randell, then turned toward the two prostrate figures lying in the dirt.

"Yep, deader'n a mackerel." George Bidwell straightened his massive frame and spit his chew, almost hitting Sean's boots. "Ain't no doubt what kilt 'em either. Got holes blowed in 'em you could drive a team through."

Sean knelt beside the man lying closest and recognized him as Waylon Sunday, the man Tex wanted to get the bullet from. *No need of that now. You can't hang a dead man for killing someone else.* Sean looked at the wound.

"This man's been shot in the back."

"Yep, by that man over yonder." Pod pointed toward the dark figure about six feet to his left. "Then, I shot him 'cause he wouldn't put his gun down."

There was something strangely familiar about the dark-clad body as Sean rose and walked to where it was lying. "Holy Mother of Christ," Sean crossed himself as he knelt by the body. It was Carlo Garcia, and he had been shot twice through the heart.

"Jesus, man, why'd you have to kill him?"

"Like I said, he wouldn't put his gun down when I told him to."

Sean rose to his feet and looked at Tex who was silent up to this point.

"Maybe my hearin' ain't so good like it used to be, but I come outa The Rusty Rail when it all come down, and I didn't hear you say nothin'." Tex calmly rolled a cigarette as he talked.

"You callin' me a liar?"

"Nope, nothing of the kind. Just said I didn't hear or see nothin' a'tall. Only heered the shots."

"Don't know what everyone's all het up about anyway," George Bidwell said with a hearty laugh. "Just one less greaser dirtyin' up our land." Sean's blow sent him sprawling in the dirt.

Two men grabbed his arms and held him back as George rose to his feet, wiping blood from his mouth.

"That's the second time you done that. Now I'm gonna beat the hell outa' your hide." He stopped in mid-stride as Tex shoved the muzzle of his gun against his nose.

"Don't think I'd do that. Not tonight. Doc and me's got a long ride ahead of us takin' this here man back to his ranch, and I don't want him all busted up for the funeral."

"That's probably for the best," Henry Baines said, pushing his way through the crowd. "There's been enough violence for the evening. Everybody go home."

"Alright, you heard the judge. Break it up and go home," Pod said, sticking his thumbs in his gunbelt and turning in a circle.

"Well, Doctor," Henry said with a wry smile. "Nearly every time I see you, you're in some sort of trouble. I could lock you up for assaulting a citizen, but I'll be generous tonight because of your emotional attachment for the Garcia family."

"That's very kind of you Judge." Sean adjusted his coat and retrieved his bag.

"You may examine the bodies at the jail at your convenience if you wish, and take Carlo back to his ranch." The judge paused as he turned to leave.

"And make sure you give my regards to Mrs. Garcia, will you."

Sean remained silent as he watched them leave. Four of the miners present carried the limp bodies toward the jail as the sun began to light the Eastern sky with a pink glow. A large bearded man approached and held out his hand.

"I'm Woodrow Black, doctor, owner of the Three Mile Mine. I don't like what's been happening around here a'tall."

"You're the one who discovered the gold in the creek, aren't you?" Sean took the hand.

"Yes, me and some of my people. Now, I'm sorry we did."

"You can't blame yourself for this, Mr. Black. Not unless you've had a hand in it."

"We didn't. You see, doctor, we're Mormons, and know what its like to be discriminated against, just because we're a little different. We found the gold and didn't say anything when others came and started building a town. But I had no idea anything like this was ever going to happen. We're a peace-loving people, and don't wish anyone any harm. I hope you understand that."

"Yes, I can understand your feelings, Mr. Black. The one thing I can't understand is why you and the rest of the people of this town are willing to stand by and do nothing about it."

"Like I said, we're peaceful and don't want any trouble. Besides, most of us have families to consider."

"Aye, and so did Mr. Garcia. Good day, Mr. Black. Hope you have a good day." Sean tipped his hat as a strange, familiar cry drew his attention to the livery stable where, perched on the very beam that Rudolfo had been hung from, sat a huge black bird. *Have you come to laugh, you old devil? Or maybe you're here to sing the mourner's hymn.*

Chapter 13

"What does that mean?" Jose Flores studied the small lead balls Sean laid on the table.

Sean waited silently as Maria led a weeping Leonida to her room. She turned and glanced at the men below before entering and closing the door. *She's still the most extraordinary woman I've ever seen*, he thought. He shook his head and took a sip of brandy before speaking.

"That's the bullet I took from Rudolfo's gun." He pointed with a letter opener as he spoke. "This is the one I removed from Jake Teel's body, and this is one of Pod Randell's bullets that killed Carlo. I couldn't find the second. It passed completely through his body.

"And this one," he opened a small envelope and let a lead ball roll across the table. "Came from Waylon's ammunition pouch. It matches the one that killed Teel. But here's the kicker," he opened another envelope and carefully placed another bullet on the table.

"This one came from Waylon Sunday. Now, look closely. Which ones seem to match?"

"Bet them two are the same," Tex said, pointing.

"And right you are," Sean said as he placed them on his scales. "Waylon Sunday shot Jake Teel in the back." He placed the two bullets back into their marked envelopes.

"But there are two more bullets that match perfectly. Can you guess which?"

"Those two?" Jose Flores pointed.

Sean silently placed the two bullets in the scales and watched them balance before speaking.

"Pod Randell killed both Carlo and Waylon Sunday. Now why would he do that?"

"Dead men don't talk too good," Tex said, striking a match on his boot. "Once't you start drivin' the devil's herd, it's kinda hard to turn 'em around and head the other way."

"What do you mean?" Jose said, pouring more brandy.

"What I mean is, they wanted Rudolfo and Carlo both outa the way awful bad. Who knows why? Maybe they want all this land and figure it's a way of gettin' it. Ya couldn't of hung neither of the Garcia boys for nothing illegal-like, 'cause you couldn't a found a cleaner livin' pair of boys nowheres you looked. Ain't too many men who got their own church and a priest livin' right on their property that I know of." He threw his cigarette into the fireplace.

"Anyways, they got to rustle up some bad mavericks. So they hurt his wife, and that gets him real riled. But Doc, here, stops them from shootin' Rudolfo in the bar. So they kill one of their own men and hang him for the murder. Now they know Carlo's hot headed, so he's easy."

"Maybe not," Sean placed the envelopes in the desk drawer and locked it, handing Jose the key. "Perhaps Carlo only went to town to ask questions, and that's why Pod killed him."

"Hell, why didn't I think of that? Did anyone ever think to check and see if Carlo even fired his gun?"

The three men stared at each other silently for a moment before Jose went to Carlo's room and returned with the Colt and handed it to Tex. The Texan checked and spun the cylinder, then worked the action several times as he admired the weapon. He sniffed the barrel and spun the gun on his trigger-finger before handing it back to Jose butt-first.

"Nope, ain't been shot for at least a week."

"Are you sure?" Sean said.

"I know guns."

"It's all very interesting, but what can you do about it?" Jose held a cigar under his nose, and inhaled deeply before continuing. "If the law itself is doing this, how are you ever going to stop them?"

"I can." Tex patted his gun.

"No," Sean said thoughtfully. "That would make you just as bad as they are. There has to be another way."

"Hell, who says I ain't that bad? Besides, if it's the land they're after, there's only one other person who's standing in their way. They'll kill the girl next."

Jose Flores stiffened. "Perhaps I should take my daughter back to Mexico before anything happens."

"No, no, no," Sean held up his hand. "Let's think about this for a day or two. You've already got Baca watching her. Post a couple more vaqueros outside the house if you want to. But you can't take Mrs. Garcia back to Mexico. That would be letting them win."

"The vaqueros aren't gunmen, Señor." Jose lit the cigar. "They only know how to take care of cattle. The men they will be trying to stop are killers."

"I'll stay," Tex said firmly. "Carlo was my friend. I'd like them to try and get her while I'm around."

A noise at the window made the men turn.

"Don't you ever sleep, you black devil?" Sean said as the raven cawed.

~   ~   ~

"Hey, Doc. You awake? Better hurry. It's an emergency."

Sean didn't recognize the voice, but it was after

midnight when he'd finally gotten back to town, and he wasn't sure that he'd recognize his own mother's voice at this hour. He rolled out of his cot and pulled his boots on.

"Gotta hurry, Doc."

"Be right there."

He pulled his coat on, grabbed his bag and stepped into the night air. The blow sent him sprawling in the dirt. He could taste blood as two strong men pulled him to his feet and held him by the arms.

"Well, how do you like it, you little bastard?" George Bidwell said as he swung a huge right hand that landed on Sean's cheekbone with a thud.

Sean tried kicking his assailant, but a blow to his midsection knocked the wind out of him. Then the blows came in a succession until he lost consciousness.

Chapter 14

The voice seemed to be coming from far away. Everything was black. *I must be dreaming*, he thought. He tried moving, but his entire body seemed to hurt. Something cold and wet was placed over his eyes and he rolled his head.

"Stop that. Hold still."

The wet cloth was removed and Sean recognized the sound of water in a basin. The cloth was gently placed over his eyes again. He reached up and grabbed hold of a soft hand and wrist.

"You're not a very good patient, Doctor. I told you to hold still."

The cloth was removed and he opened his right eye just a little. The light from the window cast a halo around the black-clad figure before him. Her long, honey-colored hair peeked out from beneath the lace scarf covering her head. *She's an angel, and I'm dead.*

"Shore took one hell of a beating, is all I can say." He recognized Tex's drawl. He wasn't dead, unless Tex had died also.

"How is he, daughter?"

"I don't know." The angel pulled her hand away and began rinsing the cloth in a pan of water. "He's the doctor. He should answer that question." She leaned closer as she spoke and gently wiped his swollen face.

It was Leonida. And she was the most beautiful angel he had ever seen, although he couldn't recall ever seeing a real angel before. On an impulse, he reached out to touch her face.

"Won't you listen to me?" She gently took his hand from her cheek and held it while she continued wiping his face with the cloth. "If you don't hold still, I'll have Paco tie you to the bedpost with his lasso.

"Is there any of that salve that he put on my cuts in his bag?" She turned away as she spoke.

"Don't know. What it'd look like?" Tex said.

Sean heard rumbling and clinking as things were dumped on the hardwood floor.

"Boys what brung him in this mornin' said the guys that done this had tore, stomped and scattered everything from here to Hades and beyond."

"Is this it?" Jose handed his daughter a small jar.

"Yes, I think it is. Could you please open it for me? It seems the doctor won't let go of my hand."

"Huh, never tried that before on a pretty girl," Tex said as he stood behind her. "There's much easier ways of gettin' to hold someone's hand."

"Sorry, ma'am," he said as Leonida glared at him.

She began applying the salve to his wounds and Sean swore that he immediately felt better. He was attributing the feeling to the touch of her hands until she started pushing and probing on his rib cage and he yelled out in pain.

"I think he has some broken ribs, right here on the left side. Help me take his shirt off so we can wrap him."

"No, not now," Sean said, shaking his head.

"Hush," Leonida said as though she were talking to a child. She began unbuttoning his shirt.

"Oh, God," he said as Jose and Tex pulled him to a

sitting position so she could remove his shirt. He tried biting his lip while they helped her wrap his rib cage, but it was too sore, so he held his breath instead.

"Jesus, just let me die," he said as they helped him back to the pillow.

"I'm afraid our Lord won't answer that prayer, just yet." The sunlight cast its halo again as she moved in front of the window, and he felt a tingling sensation in the pit of his stomach.

"And why not?"

"You still have work to do." A faint smile crossed her lips as she left the room.

Chapter 15

Ike finished packing the canned goods and carefully placed four eggs wrapped in a cloth on top before handing the basket to Susanna Black. "Be carefully of those now, they're more valuable than that gold your husband's been dredging out of the creek. I have to fight the gang at Dirty Ben's for every egg that comes to town as it is."

"I will. How much do I owe you?"

"Let's see," he said, scratching on a pad of paper with his pencil. "One dollar an egg, and the other things. How does ten dollars sound?"

"All right, but it's not enough," she said handing him the money. "You're too honest to be running a store in a mining camp, Mr. Carpenter. One of my husband's men just got back from Bodie last night, and he said there is a Chinese laundry there that gets fifty-five dollars for cleaning one shirt."

"Well, let's hope to God it never happens here. I also heard that the owners of the Bodie Mine got cheated out of their profits by the men working for them. Is that true?"

"Yes, it is. They never told the owners that they'd

found a new vein and allowed the men to sell their stock for twenty-five cents a share. Some of the miners bought a bunch of the stock themselves before bringing the gold up to the surface. Of course, the stock went sky-high immediately. Last word we got was the stock is going for fifty-five dollars a share now. Those miners are making about eight-hundred-eighty dollars a day, according to my husband."

"I hope you have more honest men working for you."

"We do," she said with a smile. "They're Mormons like us. Besides, we're dredging gold out of the stream, and Woodrow is right there to see what's happening."

"You can thank God for that."

"We do every day. Thank you."

"You too, Mrs. Black. And tell your husband hello for me."

Susanna paused at the door and frowned as she shook her head. "It was too bad about that new doctor, wasn't it?"

Ike dropped his pencil as his wife came from the back room.

"I'm sorry, I couldn't help overhearing. What happened?"Alice said.

"You didn't hear?"

"No." Alice wadded the apron in her hands and laid it on the counter.

"He got beaten very badly last night."

"How is he?" Ike had a sick feeling in his stomach.

"I don't rightly know. He was alive when that miner called Bear took him out to the Garcia place. But he's hurt pretty bad according to some of the men who saw him."

"Who in the world would do such a thing? He's such a nice young man," Alice said, as she grabbed the apron and gave it a twist.

"No one seems to be saying, but Woodrow and some of the men think it was George Bidwell. They never got along too well, and the doctor did hit him when he refused to fix Arturo's leg."

"And he deserved it, too," Ike said. "I only wish he'd

run him out of town. He isn't a real doctor anymore than Henry Baines is a judge."

"Ike," Alice said.

"Well, I don't care. Too many people's been too quiet long enough. Someone's gonna have to do something real soon, or we will turn out to be like Bodie. You know, they actually had three shootings and two stage holdups in one day? Then, they turned around and had six killings a week later. Is that what we want around here?"

"No, I was just afraid...."

"That's just the trouble. Everyone's afraid. They're scared that the judge or sheriff might hear someone say something they don't like. Well, let 'em. I'm tired of being frightened. And I'm tired of seeing all the good and decent people around here either getting killed or hurt."

"You sound like my husband," Susanna said, glancing quickly over her shoulder. "He came home the other night talking the same way after the sheriff shot Carlo. It seems the young doctor gave him a tongue-lashing for standing quietly by and allowing this to happen. But my husband's a peaceful man who loves God deeply. He wouldn't know how to begin to stop someone like Sheriff Randell. That man's a killer, and I'm afraid he would simply kill Woodrow. I agree with Alice, you need to be careful."

"Have you ever considered he just might kill your husband anyway? There is absolutely nothing stopping him from walking through that door right now and shooting me, or Alice, for that matter."

"But for what reason? Why would he want to kill Woodrow? He doesn't pose as any threat to him or the judge."

"What kind of a threat did Rudolfo Garcia pose?" Ike said, fishing a piece of candy from a jar and popping into his mouth. "They would kill you folks for the same reason they are trying to kill every Garcia in the country. Money. He had plenty of it. And your husband has the richest claim in the area. Please, Mrs. Black, don't either of you forget it." Susanna nodded and slowly closed the door behind her.

"Was it really necessary to talk so roughly, Ike? I'm afraid you frightened that poor woman nearly to death."

"It's better than having her wind up like Leonida Garcia, isn't it?" He leaned against the counter to stare at his wife for a long moment. "You know, Alice. You are worth more to me than anything or anyone else in this whole world."

"Well, thank you, dear. But I don't see what that has to do with what is happening in this town."

"It has everything to do with it. When I think of that poor woman out there on that ranch, and now the doctor, I don't know. You are the most beautiful and wonderful woman in the whole world, and if anything ever happened to you, it would simply kill me."

"I feel the same about you too," she said, putting her arms around him. "That's what frightens me. I'm afraid you'll go do something foolish and get yourself killed, and leave me all alone."

"No, I don't plan on getting myself killed. I know I'm not much of a fighter, at least not with guns or fists. But I just can't sit by and watch them get away with what they're doing."

"There's not much else we can do, is there?"

"Yes there is," he said walking to the back door.

"Arturo, come in here for a moment." He began writing a note as the boy joined him at the counter. "I want you to take a bag of flour and a bag of beans and put them in the wagon. Then, I want you to take them out to the Garcia Rancho. Give them to the maid, but I want you to give this note to Mrs. Garcia's father. You got that?"

"Si, Señor. But I just go there with Señora Carpenter."

"Yes, I know, but I want you to go again. Give them the flour and beans. But don't let anyone see the note but Mr. Flores. Understand?" Ike folded the paper and handed it to the boy.

"Si." He smiled broadly as he put the note inside his hat and pulled it down tight.

"What did that paper say?" Alice said after Arturo had gone.

"Nothing much. I simply promised Mr. Flores I would send word to him whenever I heard of anything that might help them stop the violence. I don't know if it will help, but at least it's something." He put his arms around his wife and held her.

~   ~   ~

"It is a letter from Judge Baines." Leonida tapped the letter opener nervously against the huge desk as she scanned the paper in her hand. "He offers his apology for all the difficulty we have been experiencing lately. And he is offering to buy our rancho for ten thousand American dollars. He says this is a generous offer since, in his opinion, we will lose title to the property and receive nothing once California becomes a State."

"He's got a lot of bark, I'll hand him that," Tex said as Juan and Paco muttered curses in Spanish.

"Well, if you don't mind me saying so, ma'am, I don't think that's quite fair. Seem's to me, you got a whole lot of land, and it should be worth a might more than ten thousand dollars." The young man in tattered clothing who had delivered the letter shifted nervously from foot to foot when he spoke. Paco and Juan had found him crossing the bridge and brought him straight to the hacienda.

"I'll say." Tex snickered.

"And what is your name, Señor?" Leonida folded her hands together like she was praying, and rested her chin on the tops of her fingers.

"Albert Johnson, ma'am. I didn't mean to make no ruckus," he said glancing around at the armed men in the room and those at the door. "I was just trying to bring this here message for you." He pointed toward the crumpled envelope lying on the desk.

"They are just trying to protect me." She lowered her eyes before leaning back in the chair to study him. "You are new around here, aren't you, Señor?"

"Yes, ma'am. I've only been here for a day and a half."

"I thought so. No one else would have accepted such a dangerous job."

"Dangerous? I don't quite follow you, ma'am. How can delivering a letter from the judge be dangerous?"

"Have you no idea what's happened here? What this man," she crumpled the letter in her fist and held it out to him, "has done to our family?"

He shook his head.

"This man....this Judge Henry Baines and his sheriff, murdered my husband and his brother. Now he sends this offer to buy our rancho? And tells me he is doing me a favor?"

"Oh, good God, ma'am. That can't be true, they're the law."

"It is, believe me. It is," Tex said as the boy glanced around at the nodding heads.

"I....I'm truly sorry. I....I didn't know. Honest."

"I believe you." She handed the letter to her father and slumped back in the chair to rub her forehead with her fingers. "How much money did they give you for bringing that letter to me?"

"A dollar. Well, you see," he let his eyes dart around the room once again, "I was hungry. I hadn't eaten in several days. And it was the only job I could find right away."

"Damn," Tex laughed, "almost got yerself kilt for a dollar."

"Killed?"

"You see, Señor Johnson, my vaqueros are very angry. You are lucky Juan and Paco found you first, or else one of the others might have harmed you indeed. Here," she said reaching into the desk and retrieving several gold coins, "take these and never work for those men again. They are evil, and you'll only get yourself killed."

"Aw, thank you, ma'am, but I can't...." she rose from the chair to look over her father's arm as he studied the letter. "Ma'am?" He tried once again to hand her the coins but she waved him away.

"Juan? Paco? Take this man to the kitchen and have

Maria give him something to eat. Then make sure he gets back across the river safely." They ushered him to the door, where he turned toward her once more.

"Ma'am? What should I tell Judge Baines when he asks what your answer is?"

"Papa?" She glanced toward her father.

Jose tossed the letter into the fireplace, then took time relighting his cigar. "Tell him my daughter and I shall never leave *Rancho Manantial Escondido*. Tell him that she is going to live to be an old woman and will be buried next to her husband and his brother. And my grandchildren and great-grandchildren are going to be buried there also. That is what you are to tell him."

"Yes, sir," he said with a smile. "I'll tell him. And God bless you." He glanced around the room and nodded. "All of you."

Chapter 16

Maria handed Sean the mirror. It had been two days since the beating. Two days of constant pain. Two days of hell. The only comfort Sean salvaged out of the ordeal was when Leonida came to bathe his wounds and change his bandages. He wanted out of Carlo's room badly. Not only was he occupying his dead friend's room, which added to the eerie feeling he had inside, but he wanted desperately to return the favor George Bidwell had given him.

"Holy Mother of God," he said, staring at his reflection. His face was a mass of cuts and bruises. His nose had been broken and his left eye still swollen. The miracle was that he had all his teeth. He closed his eyes and handed the mirror back to Maria.

"So, how is my patient this morning?"

Sean opened his eyes as Leonida glided silently to his side.

"Well, did my cat steal your tongue, as you gringos say?" She sat on the edge of the bed and began to gently touch the left side of his face with her fingertips.

"No, I'm not doing so well."

"And why not? My house doesn't feel comfortable?"

"Yes, it's just that Maria let me look at myself in the mirror."

"Ahhh," she said, glancing at her maid. "You shouldn't have done that, Maria. Didn't anyone tell you how proud and vain the Irish are?"

Sean started to laugh. "Oh!" The sharp pain in his side made him grimace instead.

"Leonida," her father's strong voice from the hallway made her jump.

Sean cursed himself for not knowing Spanish as the two exchanged heated words. He glanced toward Maria, who turned and began dusting the dresser with her apron. Sean grabbed for Leonida's hand as she rose to her feet, but she pulled away.

"Excuse me, but my father calls," she said and left the room with her maid at her heels.

"Waal, looks like he's gonna live," Tex said as he entered seconds later. "Got someone here who's been hangin' 'round for days tryin' to see you. Thought I'd better go ahead and bring him in, 'cause him and his pard's eatin' and drinkin' everything in sight."

"Come on in," he said, nodding toward the door.

Bear came in holding his hat in his hand and stood staring at the bed silently before shaking his massive head slowly as he spoke.

"Boy, they shore done a job on you. Thought you was dead when I run across you layin' in the middle of the road."

"You brought me here?"

"Didn't know nowhere else to take you. Besides, me and Charlie's blowing this hole."

"Leaving? Where?"

"Don't rightly know yet. Thought we'd move on up the Sacramento and get some mules. Maybe carry supplies over to Nevada. That's where the real gold is. Shore ain't none left in the ground."

"Bear, what's going on around here?"

"Hell, man, don't you know? You just about got yerself kilt. I thought you knew."

"We know some things. We know someone's trying to run these people off. But who, and why?"

His laughter hurt Sean's ears.

"He musta knocked yer brains out and I forgot to pick 'em up. Who's been hangin' and shootin' these Mexicans?"

"Pod Randell and Judge Henry Bains," Sean said as he rolled his head to look at the window. It was all coming back to him now. "What can we do about it?"

"Don't rightly know. Iffin' it was me, I'd get me a couple of real mean hombres and clean that burg up. Not that Tex here ain't mean. He could probably whup any three of them by hisself, but that sheriff and judge now, they got five or six gunmen hanging around causin' all sorts of trouble. So I'd get me someone like old Hanky. You remember him?"

"Yes, what about him?" Sean remembered the tall gray-headed, soft-spoken gentleman who only rode with them briefly on their journey to California. Sean hadn't thought much about him, for he stayed to himself and seldom spoke to anyone. He looked like a harmless old grandpa.

"Hanky? Josiah Russell?" Tex said, shifting his position.

"Yeah, old Hanky. Know him?"

"Heard of him down in the Panhandle. Good man." Tex studied the cigarette he was rolling.

"Anyways, I hear he's somewheres up the Sacramento. Iffin' I run across him, I'll send him your way."

"Why? And why would he come anyway? I didn't really know the man."

"Why would he come?" Tex snickered as he lit his smoke. "It'd be like shuffling a deck of cards in front of a gambler, or clinkin' some double eagles in front of one of them girls down at The Rusty Rail. That old Ranger lives for trouble."

"Ranger?"

"He was a Texas Ranger before comin' to Californy. Now he's lookin' for something else to do. Maybe you got it," Bear said gripping Sean's hand in a bone-breaking grip. "I got to rustle, son. You take it easy and stay outa that town, 'cause they'll kill you next time. And keep that girl here at home too, 'cause they'll shore kill her iffin' they see her."

Sean lay watching a silent Tex long after Bear had left the room. Finally, Tex threw his smoke into the fireplace and walked toward the door.

"Tell me what's bothering you before you leave."

"Nothin', just thinkin' that's all."

"Bear sending that man called Hanky back here worrying you? What's wrong with him?"

"Ain't nothing wrong with him. Like I done said, he's a good man. Better get well before he gets here, though. 'Cause you'll be diggin' lots of lead outa folks. Maybe even me."

Chapter 17

Leonida closed the door behind her with a bang. She was a grown woman and her father's words infuriated her. She took the veil from her head and threw it across the room.

"Put that back on," Jose said, opening the door. "You are acting like a...."

"A what, father? What have I done wrong?" She waited for him to close the door before continuing.

"I have done nothing to be ashamed of. I have conducted myself as a proper lady through everything. Look at me. I am a married woman, even if my husband is dead. And yet, you still treat me like a child."

"That is right. Rudolfo is dead, and you should conduct yourself as his widow."

"I have been doing exactly that."

"No, you haven't. You take your covering off whenever you feel like it. Like now, while you're angry. And you insist on going outside and playing with the children."

"I only sit and talk to them. I don't run and play with them like I used to."

"Si, but you still leave the house."

"And I shouldn't leave the house?"

"No, not unless you are going to the church to pray."

Leonida turned her back on him as she sat rigid on the edge of her bed. *Why won't he just leave me alone? Why does he insist on treating me like a child? Holy Mother, make him go away and let me be.*

"And this morning. You were jesting with that Irish doctor."

"What was wrong with my jesting? I did not laugh. I don't believe I even smiled. I conducted myself properly."

"No, it was a shame to have even been in his room."

"I was nursing a sick man, father. Remember, he was beaten very badly defending our honor?"

"Yes, and that was horrible. But you are a widow, and you should have let someone else care for him."

"And who would care for him? Father Franco? He is a kind old priest and I love him very much, but he sees nothing wrong with the sick children on this rancho. Rudolfo and Carlo knew they were sick, and asked the Doctor to come and treat them. Would Maria make him well? She believes you must prick a decaying tooth with a coffin nail to remove a toothache. And I doubt that you would mend his wounds. You used to have mother remove your splinters for you, remember? Tell me, father, who would care for him if I didn't. Besides, it is my responsibility. I am Doña Leonida."

"Si, you are the Doña," Jose said, kneeling in front of her and holding her hands. "And you must keep the proper appearance."

"For who? The children? They loved the old Leonida, not the one who dresses in black and cries in the church. For the vaqueros? They also loved the other Leonida. The one who sang and danced and rode like the wind. And who is left to keep the proper appearance for? Maria, or Father Franco? Don't forget, they were there when Paco brought the old Leonida who had been beaten and raped back to this house. No, father, there is no pretending anymore. They know all about me."

"It is only that I love you so much, my child, that I talk this way. You are all I have left."

"Yes, I know father. And I love you very much," she said, touching his cheek with the palm of her hand. "And I will be careful to hold appearances the best I can, but we owe Dr. Kilkenney much. He nursed my wounds when we needed him. He also cared much what happened to Rudolfo, and he was Carlo's friend."

Jose slipped his arms around her as she broke into sobs.

"Shhhh, it's okay, *niña*. Perhaps you should return to Mexico to visit your Aunt. I'll stay here and look after things for you."

She pulled away defiantly, holding her father at arm's length and looked at him momentarily before rising to her feet.

"Leave? Run away? Never. I am a Flores."

"Leonida, I never meant that you would be running."

"I am the daughter of General Flores, and both of my brothers died fighting for Mexico. I shall never run."

She glanced at the crow that had perched itself in the tree outside her window. *You understand, even if my father doesn't, don't you, beautiful bird?*

"They took my innocence from me, father, do you understand? I was to be for my husband only, and they beat me and took that away from me. I will never be the same again. Then they took my husband and his brother from me forever. Now, they've almost beaten our doctor friend to death, and you expect me to leave? You can't make me. I swear before the Mother of my God that I will some how see Rudolfo avenged or join him in his grave before I leave."

A long moment passed before Leonida noticed a grin creep across her father's lips.

"Spoken like a true Flores, my daughter. It was I, the general, whose heart had turned to water. I both apologize and salute you for reminding me." He clicked both heels and gave a gallant bow. "It was only because I feared for you, my child. But I can see now, that you are no longer a child, and I ask permission to serve you in your endeavor."

She silently held her father in her arms as she watched the bird through the window. *Perhaps his heart will return. I pray to God it will. But even if it doesn't, I'll feed their carcasses to you and your brothers soon, my friend.*

Chapter 18

"Y'all lookin' for some work?" Pod said, propping his foot on an empty chair. The two men seated at the table wouldn't be too particular where the money came from, just so long as they got their share of it.

"Who's askin?" drawled the one chewing on a matchstick, without looking up from his cards.

"I am. Name's Pod Randell, and I'm the sheriff of Dogtown."

"Hell, I wouldn't brag about it if I was you," the other said with a chuckle. "I ain't been here but a couple a days, but it shore ain't impressed me none."

"Well, you got me there," Pod said with a snicker as he pulled out the chair and sat down. "Yeah, it's kinda small and dirty, but the money's good. And there's more to be had for those who know how to go about gettin' it. Ya interested?"

"Might be. What's involved?" The first man laid the cards on the table and pushed his hat back on his head. He poured himself a drink and then filled an empty glass and shoved it toward Pod. "I'm Rusty Pardeen, and my partner here is called Montana."

"Just herdin' a little cattle."

"Why don't you do it if the money's so good?"

"Like I said, I'm the sheriff and I ain't got time."

He took a sip and freshened his glass before speaking. "What make's you think we'd be interested?"

"Just a hunch. I've been around this hole long enough to know y'all ain't miners. This feller here," Pod nodded toward Montana, "is more'n likely a puncher, guessin' from his garb and sunburnt face. And you're a slinger, if I'm not mistaken. Got yer iron all tied down, no chaps, or sunburn. And them hands of your'n ain't got no callouses either. So, ya ain't here to work no claims, and ya ain't got no money either, 'cause you're sharing the same bottle and there ain't no girls at your table."

"Pretty good, huh, Rusty?" the cowboy said with a laugh. His partner removed his matchstick and glared at him before speaking.

"Not bad. Where ya got your cattle at, and where ya want 'em moved to?"

"Well, they ain't really mine."

"Didn't think so." He turned toward his partner with a snicker. "Hell, this is the best one I've run across yet. The sheriff trying to get some one to rustle cattle so he can hang 'em."

"Business must be slow around here. Maybe he oughta go up to Bodie and catch a few bad men if he's that bored," Montana said pouring himself a drink.

"No, it ain't really been that slow. It's just that we got this here job to do, and I ain't suppose to get my hands dirty doin' it, me being the sheriff and all."

"Who's the *we* in this here project?" Rusty said, sticking the match back into the corner of his mouth.

"Don't guess he'd mind me tellin' you. Its Judge Henry Baines, he wants the job done."

"What? Hell Montana, am I drunk or what?" Rusty shook his head as he laughed. "I just thought the sheriff told me that the judge wants us to rustle someone else's cattle for him."

"No, you ain't drunk. I heard the same thing. Shore 'nuff sounds like a queer deal to me."

"Yeah, it's kinda queer at that," Pod said, pouring himself another drink. "But only because the judge and me's the only ones around here that got brains enough to make money without havin' to scratch around in that cold water in the creek looking fer gold. We let them do it, then they pay us fer keeping them safe. Well, we keep 'em safe by not lettin' some more fellers like us move in here.

"But, that's only the half of it. We also know how we can make a whole lot more money right across the river by herdin' some of that Mex's cattle off. Now, ifin' y'all ain't interested, I'll just have to find me some more boys. So, whadda ya' say?"

"Might be. What's the split? Fifty-fifty?" Montana said.

"Na, nothing that bad. You'll have to round 'em up, 'cause that Mex don't keep 'em no particular place. He just let's 'em run wherever. He's got somethin' like seventy-five square miles of land out there, ya know."

"Seventy-five square miles? Damn! How'd he get that much?" Rusty said.

"Inherited it, was what I was told. Anyway, like I was sayin', you'll have to round 'em up yerself. So, the judge and me, we was thinkin' more like we'd only take fifteen percent, and y'all could have the rest. How's that sound?"

"Fair," Rusty said looking toward Montana who nodded his agreement.

"Ya see, the judge ain't really interested in the cattle, he just wants to get 'em to move outa there. He wants the land."

"Well, it sounds like a sweet deal, sort of. But why doesn't he just run the Mex off and take the ranch over?"

"There's more to it than that. The Mex and his brother's already croaked. The judge hung one, and I shot the other right out there in the street. But the Mex had hisself a wife and she's holed-up out there with her daddy and a bunch of vaqueros and won't sell or leave. I'd plug her myself, if we could get her outa that house. And that's where you come in. If you can cause enough ruckus to get her into town, or even close to it, I'll finish it for you."

"Ah-huh," Rusty said as he took the makings out and started rolling a cigarette. "Knew it sounded too good to be true, Montana. All we was supposed to do was rustle a few cattle. What we didn't know was, we'd have to round 'em first from here to Hades and get 'em back across the river. But to do that, we got to keep an eye out for a bunch of angry Mexicans who's gettin' run off their land."

"Yep, sounds kinda like a combination land-grab and range war to me. Might get a little testy if you ask me," Montana said.

"You yellerin' on me?" Pod said, pouring another drink.

"No, just saying eighty-five percent of a few cattle might not be enough, especially seeing as we might get ourselves blowed all to hell trying to get it." Rusty lit his smoke.

"What do ya want then? A hundred percent?"

"No, just a piece of the action. We take care of the cattle and stir up as much trouble as you want. I'll even bore the old lady if you want, 'cause I done that sort of thing before. In return, we get ninety-five percent of the cattle and a couple hundred acres of river-front for ourselves when it's all done. And you'll also supply me with as many men as I think I'll need to get the job done. Agreed?"

Pod lifted his glass. "You drive a hard bargain, Rusty."

"It's a hard job, Pod." They toasted each other, sealing the pact.

"Here," Pod tossed several gold coins on the table as he got ready to leave. "Consider this a down-payment. The judge will more than likely want to meet y'all over in my office tomorrow."

"Hey, one more thing," Rusty said, stopping Pod in mid-stride. "Didn't you think it was kinda risky spillin' your guts like that? What if we didn't want the job, what then?"

"Na, it wasn't risky a'tall," Pod said with a laugh. "If'in ya didn't want it, I'd just had to kill you. That's all."

Chapter 19

Sean regarded the bowl of beef broth in front of him in disgust.

"What's the matter with you woman? Are you trying to starve me to death?"

"You are a stupid gringo," Maria said, snatching the bowl so quickly she spilled its contents. "You complain all the time. Never happy. Never.

"Go," she said, waving her apron as if she were herding a chicken. "Get out of my kitchen. Never come here again. I will not feed crazy gringos again."

"Whut about me?" Tex said, leaning in the doorway.

"You're okay. You're not crazy like he is."

"Looks like you got her plenty mad this mornin', Pard," Tex said, following Sean to the patio.

"I never thought I'd miss the beans and hard biscuits I got back at Dogtown, but I do. I'll bet no one on this ranch even knows what a potato or carrot looks like. It was bad enough getting beat half to death, but now they're trying to starve me."

"Well, how come you don't do something about it?"

"Like what?"

"Plant yerself a garden if you're so set on eatin' green stuff."

"Me, plant a garden? I'm a doctor, not a farmer."

"Hell, Pard, you're just as bad as them vaqueros. Afraid of gettin' a little dirt under them nails of your'n. My old pappy used to say if you ain't willing to get your hands dirty, don't complain if no one else does either. If I was you, and no one wanted to grow nothing I liked, and I wasn't willing to do it myself, why I'd find someone who was.

"Now, if you'll excuse me, I've gotta get to town, 'cause I got some serious spooning to catch up on." He slapped Sean on the shoulder and started walking toward the corral.

"Spooning nothing. I'll bet you're going to eat some hot bread with butter and honey, and maybe vegetable stew."

"Hadn't thought too much 'bout it 'til you opened yer mouth," he said, glancing over his shoulder. "But guess I probably will. Want me to bring you a biscuit?"

"You are indeed evil, you know that? May God have mercy on your soul."

Tex laughed at him and continued walking.

"Yes, bring me several biscuits."

~   ~   ~

Leonida sat at the window watching the doctor play with the children. He had carved a small wooden boat, which was now floating in the fountain. Every once in a while one of the boys would try to create waves large enough to sink it, and wind up getting everyone wet.

"Crazy gringo," the maid said, handing her a cup of tea. "May he catch cold."

"He didn't mean to insult you, Maria. He's just used to eating differently."

"He can eat snakes from now on." She turned quickly and walked back to her kitchen.

Although she'd never admit it in front of the woman, Leonida herself missed the spices, vegetables and pastries she had grown accustomed to in Mexico City. Most of the children playing out front had never heard of, let alone tasted the fruit-filled *empanadas* she grew up with. She sipped her tea and set the cup on the window sill, wishing it were *atole*, the hot thick chocolate with cinnamon she used to drink on cold evenings while the smell of freshly baked *pan* filled her nostrils. And when Lent came to the rancho, there would be no *capirotada*, the desert her mother always made with bread, cheese, fruit and raisins. She took another sip of her tea. *Perhaps when this is all over, I'll find someone who can teach them, Doctor. But, there are more important things right now.*

The children stopped their play and stood in silence as the rider slowly approached. The doctor tossed the boat back into the water and broke into a run toward the horse. It was Tex, and he was holding a girl in his arms.

~   ~   ~

Leonida held the door while Tex carried the girl inside and laid her on the sofa.

"It's Rosa. Found her this way this mornin'. One of them girls at The Rusty Rail said Pod Randell done it to her last night."

Leonida found herself shaking with rage as tears welled in her eyes. The girl was a mass of cuts and bruises.

"Did you see him?" Sean said, examining the girl.

"No, figured I'd better get her out here to you first. That horse-doctor in town said she was all right, outside of a couple of bruises. I'll take care of Pod later."

"You figured right. It's more than a couple of cuts and bruises."

Rosa moaned and tried to push Sean's hands away.

"She might have a concussion. We need to keep her awake. Maria," Sean said, glancing toward the maid. "Could you please fetch me my bag? And I'll need your help."

"Si."

Leonida felt her father's hands on her shoulders, gently pulling her aside while they worked on the broken girl in her parlor.

"Here," he said pouring her a glass of brandy. "I know it's early, but you need it."

She accepted the glass and sat stiffly on the edge of her chair as she sipped the fiery liquid. Everything seemed to stop. The laughter and play of the children outside had ceased, and Maria was no longer complaining about Sean Kilkenney's picky eating habits as she ran to fetch a pan of water. Leonida could not even hear the birds singing. The only sound came from the sofa as the doctor and Maria worked on the girl from town. She took another sip of brandy.

She wondered if she had ever known a prostitute before. *There were many women who came and visited my mother in Mexico City. Were any of them prostitutes?* She took another sip. *What would our Holy Mother think if she knew I let a woman like that lie on my sofa?* She glanced toward the sofa as the girl cried out in pain. *What does it matter? She's human, and she's hurt. I wonder if I looked like that when Paco found me?* She dropped the snifter on the floor as she covered her face with both hands and shook with huge sobs.

"When is it going to stop, father?" She laid her head on Jose's shoulder as he knelt in the spilled brandy and enveloped her in his arms.

"Soon, I hope."

"I pray and hope the men who did this burn in hell."

A mournful cry drew her attention to the window. Her black friend fluttered his wings and tilted his head, looking, wondering.

You know, don't you? It will be soon, won't it? Are you and your brothers hungry?

Chapter 20

"You think you can actually stop me from borin' that bastard?" Tex glared at a determined Sean Kilkenney blocking the front door. Rosa lay in one of the upstairs guest rooms, and with the doctor and Maria to look after her, there was no reason he should hang around. "He needs killin'."

"Perhaps you're right. But not now, not tonight."

"And why not?"

"Because that girl up there needs you. You're more than just a customer to her. She kept asking for you when I was trying to patch her wounds. Don't you understand? She's in love with you."

"No," he said thoughtfully. "Never thought of it that way. I knowed she sorta liked me a little more than the others. But hell, man, now you really done it."

Tex tried to step around the doctor, but he moved quickly to block his path.

"What have I done?"

"That's all the more reason I gotta kill him. My momma always told me I gotta stick up for the girls."

"And right she was. But not right now. Wait a little while."

"That's the problem. We've been waiting, and they've been rapin' and killin'. Maybe you can tell me who's gonna be next?"

"I don't know. I just don't want to see you buried beside
Carlo, that's all."

"Aw, hell now," Tex jerked his hat off and threw it on the floor. "Yuh shouldn't have said that, 'cause I've either got to whup, or bore you. Which one do yuh want?"

"Why? I'm your friend."

"Friend nothing. I thought you was, but you ain't no friend of mine, 'cause if you was, you wouldn't be insultin' me like that. First, you say that girl's in love with me, which means I gotta defend her. No Texan could do no less. But now you say I ain't man enough to do it without getting myself kilt. So which do you want? Want me to whup you, or shoot your leg off?"

A peel of girlish laughter caused both men to turn. Leonida stood beside Maria in the dining room.

"Shoot him outside," Maria said with an impish grin. "I don't want his blood on my floor."

"Whut's so funny?" Tex said, putting his hands on his hips.

"You, both of you. Standing there arguing like that. And both of you are willing to die for the honor of women you hardly know," Leonida said. "You're wonderful."

"I know Rosa. She's my girl."

"She might be your girl, Señor Texas gunfighter. But you don't know her. You didn't even know she was in love with you, did you?"

"And who am I supposed to be willing to die for? I don't have a girl like this Texas lunkhead."

"No, but you nearly got yourself beaten to death, Señor Kilkenney. And you did it for my family. For Rudolfo (who you hardly knew at all), and Carlo. For me."

"Aw, hell," Tex said, picking up his hat. All the fight had left him.

"But I think it's wonderful, and I love you both. We all do."

"I love Tex, but not him," Maria said with a nod toward Sean. She smiled and returned to the kitchen.

"I still got to kill that skunk."

"I know, and I hope you do," she said as the smile left her face. "But not tonight. We'll talk it over in the morning. All of us, as a family. *Buena noches, señors.*"

She turned and climbed the stairs gracefully, leaving both men standing silently at the front door.

"I'll be damned," Tex said as he unbuckled his gunbelt.

"I think we both are," Sean said.

Tex studied the doctor's expression as he gazed at the closed door at the top of the stairwell. "Yep, you probably are, pard. But then, most of us men are, one way or another."

"Come," Maria said, motioning them into the kitchen. "I make coffee."

~　　~　　~

"Dammit!" Pod flexed the bruised and swollen knuckles of his right hand. He hadn't meant to hit her that hard, or that often. But he'd lost his temper and it just happened. He tried pulling on a glove to hide the damage, but had to stop with a gasp of pain.

"Dirty whore. Hope she dies and rots in hell." He shoved his hand back in the pan of cold water. He was stupid for following her out to her tent in the first place. But the little Mexican bitch was pretty and he was drunk. *Yeah*, he nodded in agreement with himself. He had to be drunk out of his mind. There was no other reason he would have gone after a Mex. He'd hated the whole lot of them ever since his mother had run off, leaving them for that fancy card-playing greaser on The Lucky Lady. The river boat had been gone for a whole day and a half before they found out where she was. He could still hear the laughter and jeers of some of the dock-workers when their foreman explained what had happened. The whole thing just about ruined his father, and Pod swore that he'd kill a Mexican for every tear the old man shed. He didn't know if he could ever accomplish such a feat, but he had certainly tried. He would have killed her too, if the Mex card-player hadn't beat him to it. And it hadn't made much of a difference that the sheriff down in Mississippi hung him for the murder. He still hated Mexicans. But the problem right that minute was hiding the damage he'd caused to himself from the judge. Henry wouldn't like it none, and Pod was in no mood to listen to his griping. He gritted his teeth and tried once again pulling the glove over the swollen hand.

~   ~   ~

The rancho lay shrouded in a tule fog as Tex fed his horse barley from the bin, making it hard to see beyond twenty-five or thirty feet in front of him. He got an eerie feeling, thinking it would be a good time to sneak up on a person and do them in, like Henry Baines was hoping to do to Mrs. Garcia. He turned his collar up against the cool breeze. Winter was coming and it would bring more fog, a lot of it. But it would only last until the rain came. The rain always chased the fog away, you could count on it. But then, the rain made it virtually impossible to travel through the heavy mud. And when it dumped snow on the Sierra Nevadas and Mount Diablo, the temperature would drop to freezing in the valley below. Then the water in the Mokelumne River would rise, making it impossible to reach town. Tex hated winter. This was better than the blizzards he'd suffered on the Texas Panhandle, but he still loathed the idea of getting soaked in the freezing rain while trying to pull a calf out of a bog. If he was going to pay Pod Randell a visit, he'd have to do it before the rains came, or wait 'til next spring.

He'd looked in on Rosa earlier that morning and found her sleeping soundly. He took that to be a good sign. His mind was in a muddle about what Mrs. Garcia had said the night before. Not so much about Rosa's being in love with him, because he had already suspected that to be true, and had actually been making plans to take her away from there. But her wanting to have a "family" discussion about his killing Pod Randell bothered him. When was shooting a skunk a family matter? "Guess you could look at it that way," he said patting the beast on the rump. He continued talking to the horse as he washed his face and hands in the watering trough. "Pod and the judge are both behind killin' her husband and Carlo. They's probably behind her gettin' beat and raped too, if the truth was known. So, I guess it is sort of a family matter, so to speak anyway."

He dried on the soiled towel hanging from a rusty nail on the side of the shed, and walked toward the house. He was busy stamping his boots clean at the back door of the kitchen when the riders entered the courtyard. It was Paco and Juan, and they had Josiah Russell with them.

"Hell, guess I need to start totin' my iron with me wherever I go," Tex said as Hanky's eyes rested on him.

"Tommy? Texas Tommy?"

"Shore enough."

The door opened as the men dismounted and Leonida stepped outside followed by her father and Maria.

"We found this man camping by the river, Señora. What shall we do with him," Juan said, handing Jose Flores a Colt .44 butt first. Tex chuckled as he noticed the Ranger's empty holster.

"Hanky," Sean Kilkenney said, bounding through the door and grabbing the old man by the hand. "It's good to see you. How'd you get here so fast?"

"Do you know this man, Doctor Kilkenney?" Leonida said without a shred of emotion.

"Yes, he's an old friend of mine. We rode west together. I took the liberty of asking him to come help. I hope you don't mind."

"Josiah Russell, at your service, ma'am," he said,

removing his hat and bowing low like a true Southerner.

"Pleased to meet you, Señor," she said with a slight curtsy. "I don't mind your sending for your friends, Doctor. They are all welcome to visit as long as you are staying here. But how is Señor Russell supposed to help us?"

"Don't let that gray hair fool you none," Tex said rolling himself a smoke. "That old geezer's meaner than a caged mountain lion that's been starved half to death."

"Well, I see the miles ain't let none of the orneriness outa you," Hanky said. "You gave me one hell of a chase. Looked everywhere for you."

"It's a good thing you didn't catch me. I'da had to shoot you."

"You were chasing him?" Leonida said. "Why?"

"He was gonna lock me up."

"You needed locking up. You like to have shot that old man's arm off."

"He's lucky I didn't blow his damn head off. He came at me with that scatter-gun."

"He said he found you in the barn with his daughter."

"That's a damn lie. It weren't in no barn. She come to the bunkhouse of her own volition. I didn't force her none."

Tex felt his face flush as Leonida covered her mouth and giggled.

"Sorry, ma'am," he lowered his eyes.

"That's quite all right. I enjoyed learning something new about you. Doctor," she said turning to go back inside. "You may show your friend where to freshen himself, and then bring him into the kitchen. I'm sure he must be hungry."

Tex waited until he was alone before crushing his smoke with the toe of his boot and walked back toward the barn. He had suddenly lost his appetite. Josiah Russell showing up on the same rancho hundreds of miles from where he thought he'd lost him. It was like a bad dream. *I should've bored him. Might still have to, before this is over.*

Chapter 21

"Texas Tommy Burwell," Josiah Russell said with admiration as he watched the cowboy ascend the stairs two steps at a time.

Leonida waited until Tex had entered Rosa's room and closed the door before she spoke.

"All we've ever known him by is 'Tex'. I know you said his name is Thomas Burwell, but who is he?"

"Best puncher that ever forked a cayuse west of the Pecos."

She glanced at Sean and her father, but they only shrugged their shoulders.

"Cowboy, ma'am," he said, answering her question before it was asked. "Vaquero, like them boys what brung me in this morning."

"Oh," she nodded. "What else can you tell me about him?"

"He's a good boy. Don't let that stuff out front bother you none. He's a real Texan. Good as gold. Don't come no better."

"But he said you were trying to arrest him," Sean said, taking a sip of tea.

"It were my job. I was a Ranger, and he shot old man Jenkins in the arm. I was supposed to lock him up until the judge heered the case, but he taken off and ran. So, I chased him some, just to make it look good."

"You weren't really trying to catch him?" Leonida said, setting her cup on the table.

"Catch him? I might be old, ma'am, but I ain't crazy. He's quicker'n a sidewinder, and twice as pizen."

"But you said he was a good man."

"He shore 'nuff is, but we'd of wound up borin' one another just the same. You ain't gonna lock him up. No one is. Besides, that little filly of Jenkins was seein' every puncher west of the Pecos, so I figure it weren't much of a crime anyways. She up and married the Slade boy as soon as Tommy was out of sight, so her daddy was as happy as a fat puppy as it was. She liked to have drove Slade crazy last I heard. Tommy was lucky he got outa that bad deal when he did."

"You Americanos are a strange breed," Jose said with a laugh as he shook his head. "You vouchsafe loyalty to trivial matters such as the one you describe, and are willing to die for them, while you'll let larger matters go unnoticed."

"I don't think it was trivial at all," Leonida said. "He took a young girl to his bed and then shot her father."

"You've mistaken what I said, daughter. I simply meant that Señor Russell didn't seem to think it was much of a crime by his own admission, yet he was willing to chase a man who might have killed him if he had the chance. Doesn't that seem strange to you?"

"If you mean that he was willing to die for something that he didn't believe in, yes I guess that would seem strange. But not marrying someone he has violated and shooting her father is no small matter."

"No ma'am, I don't guess it was at that," Hanky said, studying the dark liquid inside his cup. "But the way I seen it, she more or less violated him. I knowed the girl, and she was plumb bad to the core. Now, that don't take no blame off'n Tommy none, 'cause he didn't run her off when she come to the bunkhouse that night. But he had to shoot that old man or he'd have been blowed clean full of holes, 'cause her daddy was crazier'n she was.

"Now, young Tommy here,' he nodded toward the upstairs room, "he's a good boy. Don't ride him too hard, 'cause when he tells you he'll do something, he'll stick with it or die trying. He'd be a good man to have around here, especially now."

"All right, he's forgiven." Leonida shifted uncomfortably in her seat. "For the time being, that is. I might have him horsewhipped later on, if he treats another girl that way. But it brings me to my earlier question, Señor. Why are you really here, and what makes you think you can help me and my father?"

"Well, 'cause ol' Bear, he done told me what they done to you and your family, and it made me plumb mad."

"Bear?"

"The big man who brought me here when I was beaten," Sean said.

"Oh, Señor Hanky. Your nick-names mix me up sometimes."

"They do us all, ma'am," Josiah said, placing his empty cup on the table.

"And how about your own? Why do they call you Hanky?"

"Got that from wearing these big bandannas all the time." He adjusted the one around his neck with pride. "They keep the dust outa your nose when you're stuck ridin' drag."

Leonida caught her breath, knowing the question she was about to ask would only raise another one. *Maybe I need Tex to interpret for me.*

"Anyways, I heered what happened, so I come as fast as that old cayuse could trot. 'Cause I run into Henry Baines when I was down Arizonie way, and he ain't no judge by no means. He was claiming to be a doctor back then, selling snake-oil to them poor folks what didn't have much money. He had to high-tail it outa Flag, 'cause when them punchers found out he was sellin' them white lightening instead of medicine, they were gonna tar and feather him."

"I thought as much," Sean said, handing Maria his cup for a refill. "That diploma on his wall doesn't have anything to do with law, it's a bachelor of arts degree."

Everyone in the room stared at him.

"Well, it simply means he went to college, and studied. But he's not a doctor or lawyer, or judge for that matter. He's been able to fool everyone up to now, because no one's able to read Latin."

"Do you understand Latin?" Leonida said.

"Yes, a little. Actually, quite a bit. They taught us in medical school."

"That is wonderful. I am surprised you haven't let us know before this. My husband has many books that were written in Latin." She got up and pulled one from the shelf and held it to her breast. "You're welcome to read them anytime you wish.

"Now, tell me, Señor Russell," she turned back to the old man.

"Hanky, ma'am. Just Hanky."

"All right, Hanky. What can you tell me about this sheriff?"

"Pod Randell? Now there's a bad one. Word is, he's not too smart. Kinda tetched, know what I mean?" He tapped the side of his head with a finger. "But he's fast with a gun, and likes to kill people."

"What do you mean, 'likes to kill people'?" Jose lit a cigar and threw the match into the fireplace.

"Exactly that. He likes to kill people. Some folks like to ride. Others like to eat. Pod likes killin'. Beggin' you pardon ma'am, but that's why he didn't mind killin' your men folks."

"How exactly do you plan on helping us?" Leonida said, studying the lined face with its shock of gray hair.

"Don't rightly know, yet. Plan on ridin' into town

tomorrie and havin' myself a talk with them two. Maybe remind Henry that I know him, and see ifin' I can't stir something up. You can't never tell what might roll down hill when you get things started."

Chapter 22

"I don't know. I just don't like it." Woodrow Black paced the floor. He had come to confront Ike Carpenter about frightening Susanna with all his talk about killing and claim-jumping. She was in tears by the time she reached their cabin. The thought had crossed his mind a time or two, but there was no reason to discuss such things with women. He began his verbal attack when the store owner turned the tables on him. He now paced the floor in their kitchen in the back of the store pondering Ike's proposal.

"All I'm asking is that you tell me if you hear anything that I can pass on to them."

"Yes, but if the judge or that sheriff get wind of what we're doing, they may hurt Susan, and she's all I got." Woodrow scratched his beard.

"There's absolutely nothing from stopping them doing that right now. When they get through destroying the Garcias, what makes you think they won't kill us all and take what we have?"

"Oh, I don't think they'll do that."

"How do you know, Woodrow? None of us would ever have thought we would have seen that horror down at the livery either. I still can't go to sleep without seeing Rudolfo's swollen face with his tongue hanging out," Ike checked the front of the store to make sure no one was listening. "You were there."

"Yes, and if I'd gotten there a few minutes earlier, I would have said something. But he's dead, and there's nothing I can do about it now. You're asking me to get involved in something that really isn't any of my business."

"You're already involved, don't you understand that? The same as I am. We were there and didn't stop them when they murdered an innocent man."

"How do you know he was innocent? Some of my own men heard him say he was going to kill Jake Teel. He could have done it."

"Yes, but he didn't, and you know it," Ike said as he poured a cup of coffee and handed it toward the miner who held up a hand. "Sorry. Forgot you people don't drink this or tea. Anyway, I talked to Dr. Kilkenney who examined the bodies over in the jail, and he says he firmly believes that Waylon Sunday killed Jake Teel, then Pod Randell killed both Waylon Sunday and Carlo Garcia."

"But why? Besides, how would he know? Did he see it happen?"

"No, but he said he can tell from the size of the bullets. He calls it ballistics, or something like that. He claims people have been studying such things since the days of the catapult."

"I still don't see what that's got to do with what's going on around here."

"According to him, the bullet that came from Jake matched Waylon's gun, and he says Carlo's gun was never even fired. Can you believe that? It's a fine sheriff and judge we got ourselves, I can tell you that. If anyone was going to get hung, it should have been Jake Teel for raping Mrs. Garcia. He did it, and every one in this town knows he did."

Woodrow quit his pacing and stood staring out the rear

window at the creek and row of oaks and sugar pines lining its banks. He had hoped not to get involved. He simply wanted to get what little gold he could out of the Dogtown Creek and take his wife on to Utah where people believed like they did. Prejudice wasn't anything new to him, because Mormons had been driven from nearly every place they settled in, including Europe. When they had to leave New York, he and his wife had taken a boat around the horn and landed in San Francisco, thinking it would be easier than making the long tedious trip across land. People were already flooding the countryside looking for gold, so it was easy for them to blend in and not be noticed.

"You know, Ike, it was a real miracle of God that I was the one to find gold here in Dogtown and stake the first claim. Susan and I had joined up with several other Mormon families traveling toward Utah and we'd only stopped here to make camp that night. I was drawing a bucket of water when I noticed the first nugget shining in the gravel. I called the others over to confirm my suspicions." He turned toward Ike with a weak grin. "We held a worship service that evening and dedicated the very ground on which the Three Mile Mine was located. I gave it that name because we were only able to travel three miles that day, because several of the group had become ill. I believe that too was an act of God, or else we would have passed that spot by.

"But," he turned back toward the window. "Like everyone else in town, I was willing to turn my back when the trouble first started, thinking it was just some more prejudice against the Mexicans. That isn't nothing new, you know. The miners ran them out of Columbia and several other gold strikes. Now, the Mexicans are congregated around Hornitos and they've let it be known that whites aren't too welcome there. It's gone on forever, Ike. Before this trouble with the Mexicans, there were the Indians who got pushed around. They still are,
for that matter. And now, the Chinese are getting treated badly by everyone, including the Indians." He glanced over his

shoulder and shrugged.

"I felt sorry enough for the Garcias to pray for them. But I really didn't think the treatment they were being given was anything new....up until a few weeks ago at the barn."

"I guess a lot of people felt the same way you did, Woodrow. But, when all is said and done, this is more than simple prejudice. It's plain murder."

"Yeah," Woodrow nodded and let go a deep sigh. "So, what do you want me to do?"

"Just listen, and tell me anything that might help them. You don't even have to tell anyone what you're doing. In fact, I think it would be better if you didn't. You might learn more that way. I'll write what information I get on a piece of paper and stuff it inside a bag of beans or flour, and have Arturo deliver it to them. I'm not going to put any names on it, that way even if they do find any of the notes, you won't be involved."

"You think it will help?"

"I don't know. But if they know something might happen before it actually does, they'll at least have a chance to stop it."

Woodrow groaned and scratched his beard thoughtfully.

"We've got to do something. The way I see it, we've already got the blood of two innocent men of our hands, and I don't want another. You're Mormon, and I'm Methodist, but I don't really think God's going to be impressed with either of our religions when we stand before Him if we continue to let this happen."

"You're probably right on that point. Okay, I'll do it. But you be real careful, Ike. Because if they do find one of those notes, or get wind of what you're doing, they'll make your wife a widow, don't forget that."

"I won't, Woodrow. Believe me, I won't."

"Fine. Now, I can't leave here without buying something. It might look funny if I start coming to your store and leaving empty-handed. Do you have any canned peaches? Susanna loves them."

They went to the front of the store where Ike pulled several jars from the shelf and handed them to the miner.

"How much?"

"Thirty cents for the lot."

"That's not enough and you know it." Woodrow laid fifty cents on the counter. "It costs money to run a business nowadays. Hear they're talking about some sort of property tax up in Bodie. They're going to build some sort of fancy courthouse or something. Wouldn't be surprised if they don't try something like that here one of these days."

"If the gold holds out, and the town continues to grow, they more than likely will, Woodrow."

"You'll have to start charging an honest price for your goods, then." Woodrow put two of the jars in his coat pockets and studied the other in his hands. "Price of labor's gone up too. Needed another man and had to hire myself a Gentile, only this man isn't like you and Alice. I don't think he has any religion at all. He's rather profane, if you know what I mean. I won't allow him to curse and use God's name in vain around the mine, but he goes to the saloon to drink every evening, and consorts with prostitutes. He never seems to have any money." He shook his head and walked to the door where he paused.

"He happened to mention this morning, that he overheard several men talking in The Rusty Rail about a cattle drive leaving the Garcia ranch in the next couple of days. One of the men was Pod Randell." He opened the door and tipped his hat. "Good day, Ike. Give Mrs. Carpenter my best."

"Give my best to your wife too, Woodrow."

Ike took up his pencil as the door closed and began to write.

Chapter 23

"Do you love her?"

Tex turned from where he was leaning on the porch railing. "Don't know. Guess I do."

Leonida pulled her black shawl tightly around her face and shoulders as she gazed at the silent courtyard. Even the crickets were quiet. The only sound was the trickling of the water in the fountain and the occasional distant mooing of cattle as they moved ghost-like across the moonlit hillside.

"She loves you deeply," she said after a long moment.

"Yeah, so you told me."

"Why don't you marry her, and take her away from that place?"

"Tried that once't. But Ambrose wouldn't let her go."

"Who's Ambrose?"

"Ambrose Brice. The man what owns The Rusty Rail. He's got a piece of paper that says her papa needed money real bad, so he gave him the money, and her papa gave him Rosa."

"He sold his daughter?" Her voice trembled as she leaned against the railing.

"That's how come she works there."

"*Madre de Dios*," Leonida crossed herself in a prayer. "Whatever became of him?"

"Who? Ambrose? He's still there."

"No, her papa. Where is he now?"

"Who knows? Gone somewhere. Nobody's seen him since."

"Where would you take Rosa if you had the chance?"

"Thought about Arizona. Get me a little land somewheres where nobody knows her or what she's done. Raise some beef, and maybe kids," he said with a grin.

"That would be nice. Rosa would like that, and I think you would make a fine father."

"Thanks."

She watched as he took his time rolling a cigarette.

"What's to become of us?"

"Who, you and your father?"

She nodded.

"Oh, my guess is you'll ride out this here bronc and everything will settle down and be fine. You more than likely won't keep much of the land, but it'll work out."

"Why won't I be able to keep *Rancho Manantial Escondido*? It's been in my husband's family for years, and now it's mine."

"It's too big. You only got about thirty vaqueros and some injuns working this place, and most of them aren't fighters. Only two of 'em know how to use a gun. Paco and Juan. The rest of 'em carry them old muzzle-loaders like yer husband's, if they got one at all. Fine gun in its day, but nothing like Pod and the rest of 'em's got. Naw, you'll never keep all the nesters off this place.

"Iffin' it were mine, I'd keep a big hunk for myself and sell the rest. Like say, keep this here house and everything down to the river over yonder," he said pointing toward the black row of trees. "Then, I'd keep everything out toward that wash headin' toward Diablo," he pointed the opposite direction toward the mountain. "That way you got more'n enough land to run beef on and won't have to cross no river or rough ground in order to chase someone off or keep yer critters in line.

"But I'd sell the rest to some sod-busters who's gonna plant wheat, taters, hay and corn. Things you don't grow yerself. Doc's right, you know. Beeves are mighty fine critters, but I shore do get a hankerin' for some biscuits and fried taters once in a while."

Leonida pursed her lips thoughtfully before speaking.

"You shall have your land, Tex. You and Rosa shall raise your beef critters and your children on your own land."

She left him on the porch and ascended the stairs to her own room. She could hear Sean talking softly to Rosa as she passed the opened door. *He sold her. His own daughter, and he sold her. Dear Holy Father, may he only find torment and not mercy through eternity.*

She closed and latched her bedroom door before grabbing the loose brick in the fireplace. It slid easily from its place and she removed one of several bags containing gold coins, and carefully shoved the brick back into position. The coins clink merrily as she poured them across her bed and began counting. How many would it take? She had no idea, but Paco and Juan would know. Guns and ammunition had to be expensive.

Chapter 24

Sean tapped on the open door before entering. "Good morning. How's my patient feeling this fine day?" The girl lying in bed pulled the blankets up tightly under her chin. He placed his bag on the bed near her feet and removed his jacket. "And how are you, Maria?" he said to the maid as she poured fresh water into the washbasin.

"*Bien, Señor*," she said with a nod.

"Now, let me look at those cuts, if I may." He reached toward Rosa's face but she pulled away as her eyes darted toward Maria who was about to close the door.

"Wait, Maria," he said, holding a hand out toward her without taking his eyes off the girl. "You may leave the door open, if you wish. But before you go, please tell her that I mean her no harm. I only want to help her."

"Si, I can tell her, but...." She shrugged her shoulders.

"But what, woman? Can't you see the girl is frightened?"

"Si, I talk to her before you come. I know she is frightened, Señor." She set her dark eyes on him for a moment before exhaling loudly. "*Bueno,* I tell her." She looked past him toward Rosa.

"*Señorita, Señor Kilkenney, el loco caballero medico desea curarla .*"

Rosa started to giggle at the maid's words, but quickly winced in pain and put a hand to her swollen lips. *Damn, I've got to learn that jabber. I think that woman just insulted me again.*

"*Permitir poss de considear tu.*" Maria looked at Sean and added, "*Bueno, Señor?*"

"I guess. I don't know what the hell you said, but I guess it's alright."

"I say you are a doctor, and you want to help. Then I tell her to let you look at her." She shrugged as Rosa giggled.

"Okay, fine. Thank you." He turned his attention back to the girl as Maria left, closing the door behind her.

"She could have left it open, like I asked. But then, it might be just as good. It'll give you a little privacy." He checked her pulse as he talked. "We don't want too many people poking their noses in on us while we see if we can't make you better, do we?

"Well, I think you're going to live as far as your heart's concerned." He laid her hand in her lap and leaned forward to gaze into her face. "Now let's see how these cuts and bruises are doing. Yes, I think they are going to heal fine. This one here might leave a little scar," he said gently touching a swollen cut above her left eye. He opened a jar and began applying more salve as he talked.

"You know, Mrs. Garcia went through much the same thing. Those bastards beat her up pretty bad too. I don't know if you've noticed it or not, but she's got a scar at the corner of her mouth, and one right by her left eye also. It's too bad that two beautiful women like yourselves had to suffer such horror from men." He put the salve back into the bag and wiped his hands on a clean towel.

"Now, let me see your teeth." She stared at him blankly, so he opened his mouth and pulled up his lip and pointed to his own teeth. "Like this. Teeth, see? I haven't looked at your teeth." She smiled slightly and gingerly opened her mouth a little.

"Yes, I know your lips are sore, aren't they? I'll be as gentle as I can." He continued talking as he gently ran a finger along her gums feeling for anything broken or loose.

"You can't understand a word I'm saying, can you? It's just as good. I guess I was blessed with the gift of blarney, you know. Sometimes I have a tendency to talk too much. Like with Maria. She's a fine woman, doing the best she can, but we just have a tendency to lock horns, as your Texas boyfriend would say. It's mostly because we're both hot tempered, I think. There," he said wiping his hands on the towel again. "Your teeth look in fine shape, which you should be thankful for. You'll find you're going to need every one of them if you stay at this house very long." He leaned close and spoke in a whisper. "The only thing Maria knows how to cook is dead cows, and she burns them until it's like trying to chew an old boot.

"Now we've got to get to the embarrassing part of this whole thing. You had taken such a beating around the head, that when your boyfriend brought you here I didn't really pay much attention to the rest of you. So, let's check and see if that beast broke any of your other body parts." He reached behind her neck and shoulders and began lifting. "Here, sit up now and let me see."

She kicked the blanket off and sat cross-legged on the bed, Indian-style. Her nightgown hiked up over her knees, revealing a shapely pair of brown limbs, and Sean cleared his throat as he pulled the blanket back over her lap and began feeling her arms. He rotated them at the shoulder and elbow to check the movement of the joints, first one, then the other.

"Well, nothing seems damaged here. He was probably more interested in trying to spoil your pretty face, wasn't he? We'd better check your back, though." Rosa closed her eyes and let her body relax as he began pushing and feeling the back of her neck. "That feels good, huh? Okay, we'll give you a little massage then." He began working her shoulders and neck. "Does anything hurt? No, I don't guess it does, or you'd let me know one way or the other, wouldn't you?

"You know, you and Mrs. Garcia are both extraordinarily beautiful women. Well, you might not know it, being treated by men like you have been. But you are. I can see why Tex likes you. If he wasn't around and we could understand each other, and if we had met under different circumstances, I would be interested in you myself. But that cowboy would probably shoot me if he heard me say that, so its just as well that you can't understand what I'm saying. And then, there's Mrs. Garcia." He stopped and lifted both of her arms up.

"Now, let me feel your ribs. I'll try not to tickle you," he said as she jumped and giggled at the feel of his fingers. "My, but you are a small one, aren't you? Now, what I was saying about Mrs. Garcia. She's just as beautiful as you are, and smart too. I find her fascinating. Those green eyes of her have damned my soul, if you know what I mean." She moaned with delight as he ran his thumbs up and down her spine, feeling each joint.

"I close my eyes at night and I still see them. Yes, I've more than likely fallen in love with that woman and her husband's not even cold in the grave yct. But then, what do I know about love or women? I've never really had a girlfriend of my own before. And I swore an oath on my own mother's grave the day I found her husband hanging from the livery, that I'd see Judge Baines and Sheriff Randell in their own graves before this was all over. I really liked her husband and Carlo too. They were fine men." He stopped and stared blankly at the wall for a moment. "Here, you can lay back down." Rosa laid back and Sean helped pull the blanket back over her chest and closed his bag.

"Well, I believe you are going to live, young lady. And, I might say you're a fine patient. You didn't yell and fight me like some of the others around here. And you didn't talk my ear off either. In fact, you're a mighty fine listener."

He stopped at the door and looked at her. "You know, Rosa, you really are a fine girl. I hope you never have to go back to that hell-hole you were working in. I'll tell Father Franco, and we'll both pray for you." He closed the door and was gone.

She lay quietly for a moment before the door opened again and Maria brought her a cup of broth for breakfast.

"So, what did you and the doctor talk about?" The maid sat at the foot of the bed as Rosa sipped the warm liquid.

"He talked and I listened. He doesn't believe I know how to speak English for some reason." She tried to smile, but held the corner of her mouth in pain instead. "I probably should have told him, but I was having too much fun listening."

"Oh? And what did the crazy horse-doctor say?"

"He's not crazy, Maria. In fact, he's very kind and gentle."

"Ha, he's got you fooled," she said, throwing her arms in the air. "Or, maybe he put a hex on you. The next time Julio Perez comes with his granddaughter I will have him say some chants over you."

"Stop it, please," Rosa said holding her mouth. "It hurts too much to laugh."

"All right, what did he say?"

"He said I was pretty and he would be interested in me if Tex wasn't around."

"Ah, so he isn't blind, then. That is good to know. It would be bad to have a blind doctor, no? Was there anything else?"

"Si, he said many good things about Señora Garcia. He thinks she is very pretty and he's afraid he might be falling in love with her."

"*Hoy, caramba.*" Maria leaned close. "He says that to you? Come on, tell me. Was there anything else?"

Rosa took another sip of the broth before speaking while the maid held her breath. "He says he's very sorry for Señor Rudolfo and Señor Carlo. They were good men, and he wishes their killers to die also." She took her time drinking more broth, knowing the suspense was killing the woman.

"Here, give me that." Maria snatched the cup from her hands, spilling some on the blanket. "You'll get no more until you tell me all he said."

"There's no more to tell, except he thinks you're a fine woman."

"Ah, now I know you lie. I am poison to the gringo. He wishes me dead."

"No, Maria. Before The Mother of God," she said crossing herself. "He says you are a fine woman who works hard. He does not like your food, but he likes you."

"Aha, see? I told you so. May he starve and eat coyote droppings if he does not like my food."

"Please, Señora, *por favor*." Rosa doubled over laughing, holding her mouth with both hands. "Oh, *Madre de Dios*, it hurts."

"*Que lastima, niña,*" Maria said, putting a hand on her shoulder. "You may finish your broth now, if you will tell me what else he said."

"There was nothing else, honest. But I should tell him next time he comes that I can understand what he says."

"No, don't you dare." Maria looked her in the eyes sternly for a long moment before a smile crept across her lips. "What else would there be for us to talk about, *niña*? We'll let this be our little secret, *correcto*?"

"*Si*, our secret."

"*Bueno,*" Maria touched her cheek with the palm of her hand. "Now, finish your broth."

Chapter 25

Hugh Zornes leaned against the hitching rail in front of the jail smoking a cheap cigar as the old man riding the dun stopped and dismounted.

"Is the sheriff in?"

"Might be. Who's askin'?"

"What about Judge Baines? He inside?"

"Could be, if the right person is askin'."

The old man tied the reins to the hitching post as Curly and Eb came from inside and stood silently watching. He started toward the door, but Hugh stepped in front of him.

"I said, who's askin'?"

The back-hand blow came so fast he had no chance to duck, and Hugh landed on the steps as Curly and Eb started laughing.

"You might've been askin', but I wasn't answerin'."

He jumped to his feet and grabbed for his gun only to have it taken from him by hands that latched onto him with a bone-crushing grip. The stranger let go and smashed Hugh's own gun into his cheekbone. He lay on the porch holding his bleeding face as he waited for the ringing inside his head to stop.

"Nice gun," the old man said, tossing the pistol in the air and catching it by the handle. He pointed it aimlessly, causing the two men standing behind Hugh to dive for cover.

"New Dragoon, ain't it? Keep it nice and clean." He worked the action several times and twirled it on his finger.

"Careful with that thing," Pod said, standing in the doorway. "You might shoot yourself."

"Hardly, but this here boy needs to learn some manners," he said, stepping over Hugh and handing the gun butt-first to the sheriff.

"Don't mind him. He's just got a lot of bark on him, that's all." Pod stuffed the gun in his belt and stepped out onto the porch. "Whut can I do for you, stranger?"

"Well, I come all the way from up Sacramento way to find someone's beat the hell outa' a pard of mine. And I was just wonderin' if you might know who would've done a cowardly deed such as that?"

"Don't know. Someone's always gettin' punched around a little every night here. Who did you say your pard was?"

"Didn't say. But it's Sean Kilkenney. Me and my other pards who come out West just call him Irish."

"Doctor Kilkenney?" Henry Baines said, coming to the open door. "Are you a friend of his?"

"Well hello, Hank. Thought you'd still be sellin' snake-oil somewheres. But they tell me you're the judge around these here parts."

"That's right, Hanky, I am. Now, what can I do for you? I'm busy."

Hugh started to get up, but a huge boot pushed him back to the rough board flooring.

"I didn't say you could get up yet, son. Just sit there until you learn some manners."

"Know this old coot?" Pod said with a smile.

"Yes, I know him. And you'd better do what he says,

Hugh. You're lucky you still have any brains left in your head."

"Well, was it these varmints here?" Hanky kicked Hugh with the side of his boot and nodded toward Curly and Eb.

"No, they didn't beat up your doctor friend. They're new in town, and I just hired them as deputies. We don't know who attacked Mr. Kilkenney. It could have been any number of people. He made a lot of enemies in Dogtown, you know."

Henry's hand trembled slightly as he packed his pipe.

"No, I didn't know. Me, Bear and Charlie all like him. So does Frank. And we don't take it too kindly a thing to do. So, ifin' you decide who might've done it, I'd appreciate you lettin' me know." He tipped the rim of his hat. "See you 'round Hank. You too sheriff."

He stopped beside his horse to nod at Hugh.

"You can get up now." He led the dun across the street and tied it in front of Carpenter's General Store.

"Who the hell is he?" Pod said, handing Hugh a scarf.

"Josiah Russell," Henry said, lighting his pipe with a shaking hand. "Retired Texas Ranger. They call him Hanky. He's going to become a real bother to us, so I want him out of the way in a hurry."

"I'll take care of him," Hugh said, holding a scarf to his bleeding cheek.

"You're not man enough. None of you are," Henry said turning to go back inside.

"What about me? Am I man enough?" Pod snickered as he tossed Hugh's gun in his lap.

"That, my boy would be real debatable. But I don't want to lose you trying to find out, so you just stay clear of him for now. We'll have to figure something out."

"Who the hell's he think he is?" Hugh said as the door closed. "Sayin' I'm not man enough? I'll kill that old man right now."

"No you won't," Pod said. "I need every one of you, and I don't want you gettin' yer brains splattered all over the street. You'll wait 'til I say you can before you go tangling with that ol' geezer."

"Besides, you didn't do so good a minute ago. What makes you think you can do any better now?" Curley said with a laugh.

""Cause I owe him, and I'll kill him if I got to shoot him in the back to do it."

Chapter 26

"Señor Flores, come quick. Ildefonso Baca wishes to see you behind the corrals." Juan's voice seemed urgent. Jose laid the quill aside and followed the vaquero out the door and across the patio.

"What is it, Papa? Is something wrong?" Leonida joined them as they passed the fountain.

"No, *niña*, it is nothing. Go back to the children. Juan and some of the men simply wish to discuss the cattle."

"No, Papa. You story to me. I watched Juan come to the house and it is more than that, isn't it?"

"*Niña*," Jose said as he paused to look his daughter in the eyes. "I will tell you if it is important. But for now, I want you to stay at the house."

"*Por que,* Papa? You know something is wrong. Why won't you let me come? I am the Doña, remember?"

He turned his back on her and followed the vaquero swiftly around the corral's perimeter and behind the tack house. He marveled at Juan's fluid-like movements as the boy quickly ate the distance with long strides. Most vaqueros hated to walk even a short distance, and when they did, they just sort of waddled, but not this one. His spurs clinked merrily with each step as the handle of the long-knife tucked inside his right boot wobbled with the movement. The pistol and holster that hung from the cartridge belt were tied low in the style of the gunfighter, and Jose had no doubt that the lad knew very well how to use the weapon. He was, in Jose's opinion, a fine specimen.

They rounded a small row of trees where they found Baca and two other Indians waiting beside three bodies slumped over the backs of horses. Two of them still had arrows sticking in them, while the third dripped blood from a gunshot wound in the head. It was exactly what Jose expected might happen.

"Where did you find them?"

"They were trying to take twenty-five head across the bridge toward town," Juan said, raising one of the heads by the hair and letting if fall again.

"Ever see them before?"

"No, never. But there are many new faces in town that one has never seen before."

"Si, I know what you mean. Were there any others?"

"No, and to make sure, Baca looks around and finds no one."

"Ah, then Judge Baines does not know this has happened. He will just think these men have simply taken his money and ridden away. But he must know if he is to be stopped, or he will keep sending men to plague our home. Baca?"

"Si, Señor?"

"Do you think you can get these men back to town without being seen?" The Indian smiled and nodded. "You and your men may keep the horses and anything else if you wish. But I want Judge Baines to know that if he continues to send men out here, we will in return send them back like this."

He turned and walked swiftly back toward the house. He had put Ildefonso Baca and Juan in charge of patrolling the border of the rancho facing town after receiving Ike Carpenter's note. Jose had thought it was a stupid idea. There were almost a hundred vaqueros on the rancho counting the Indians. And while it was true that most of them were not real fighters and gunmen, there were more than enough like Juan and Ildefonso

Baca, who loved to fight. And now there were white men who had joined them like Tex and the new man they called Hanky. There was the doctor, too. While Jose knew nothing of his fighting ability, a true medical man was a valuable item in any war. And this was what this was becoming, a war. He smiled to himself. It had been a long time indeed since the emotions had stirred inside him.

"It was *nada, mi niña*," he said and kissed Leonida's cheek. "There was a hungry peasant trying to steal a cow down by the river and Baca caught him."

"Did he hurt him, Papa?" She searched him with her emerald-green eyes.

"Goodness, no, *niña*. There is no need to hurt someone because they are hungry. Even Baca understands that." He adjusted the black veil on her head to hide more of her honey-colored hair.

"What did they do then? Why did they need you?"

"They just wanted to know what they should do. They've never run across this type of a problem before, but I'm afraid that it will become more frequent with all the new people coming to look for gold."

"What did you tell them?"

"I told them to give him one cow and let him go, and tell him not to steal from us again. That was okay, wasn't it, my child?"

"Si, Papa. But if it was simply a hungry person, why didn't Juan ask me? I would have taken the man inside and had Maria feed him, then given him food for his trip."

"Ah, but you see, there is the problem," he said with a smile and he touched the tip of her nose with his finger. "Juan eats at our table also, and he's tired of you giving away all the food in the house as it is. He says that man should have to kill his own beef and skin it himself. He says the rancho suffered too many years with no corn or flour before the ships started coming up the river, and before Señor Carpenter opened his store in town. He wants a chance to eat the *tortillas* himself."

"Is that all there is, *mi Papa*? You're not hiding something from me?"

"No, *niña*. That's all there is. Believe me." He kissed her and went inside.

Si, Señor Baines, send your men of war, and make them your best. I'll give you my best men in return, and we shall see who is the better, no?

~ ~ ~

It was after midnight when Rusty Pardeen staggered from The Rusty Rail and almost fell over the bodies lying in the middle of the street.

"Get up, you lousy drunk." He started to kick the one closest to him in the ribs when he noticed the arrows sticking in his back. "What the hell's this, some kind of joke?"

He wiped his face with a trembling hand and took another look. There were two arrows poking out of one of the other men. He carefully rolled one of them on his side.

"Aw, son of a bitch," he said, pulling his gun from its holster. He fired two shots into the air and waited. A few seconds later he was joined by Montana and several men from inside the bar.

"What the hell's this, Pard? Why'd you kill 'em fer?" Montana said with a slur.

"I didn't, you damn idgit. They got arrows stickin' in 'em. When was the last time you saw me shootin' a bow?"

"I'll be damned," one of the other men said poking one of the bodies with the toe of his boot. "Been quite a while since I seen someone get kilt with an arrow. Most Injuns nowadays got themselves guns."

Pod Randell walked up and squatted beside the dead

men. He lifted one of the heads by the hair to get a good look at it and let it fall. "These are your men, ain't they, Rusty?"

"Yeah, same ones I sent out to the ranch this morning."

"Well, you was wondering' what was takin' 'em so long. Now, I guess you know, don't you?"

"Yeah, hell of a way to go, ain't it?"

"Hell, being kilt by an arrow ain't so bad. I can think of a whole lot worse ways to go. At least they didn't scalp 'em," Pod said with a laugh. "Well, y'all can help me drag 'em down to the livery for the time being. I don't wanna sleep with a bunch of dead carcasses inside my office all night long."

~   ~   ~

Henry Baines paced the floor chewing on his pipestem. The death of the three rustlers was only a minor problem, and they could be replaced easily enough. What proved to be the major problem was when he had tried to organize a large militia and go after the murderers. There had been only a handful of men who were willing to go, and most of them were already in his employ. Woodrow Black, owner of the largest mining project in town had turned his back on him and hollered in a booming voice, "I ain't preventing any of you men in joining in Judge Baines' adventure here, hunting Indians on the Garcia Rancho. But I will say this, if any of you do, you'll be hunting another job when you get back, and you'll lose any shares you own in this mine."

"Now see here, Woodrow, we need every man we can get. I hear there's almost sixty or seventy Indians out there," Henry said.

"That's just the point, Judge. You stand to get a bunch of people killed, and I need every man I've got to keep this mine operating. Now if you went and got some of your men killed already, I'm real sorry for them and their families, if they had any. But they more than likely wouldn't have gotten killed if they would have stayed away from Mr. Garcia's property." He turned and waved one of his arms wildly at the idle men.

"Don't just stand there, get back to work."

"I don't know who told you those men worked for me, but that doesn't make any difference right this minute. What does matter is that some white people got killed by some Indians. We have to stop that right now, or we could have another war on our hands."

"No, you're wrong again, Judge. What matters is that you had Rudolfo Garcia hung for a crime most of us don't think he was guilty of, and that sheriff of yours killed his brother. And on top of that, that woman of his got mistreated by a couple of white men. Now, anyone in their right mind would know better than to go nosing around on that property, because if they did, they'd be asking for trouble. I don't know what those three men were doing out there, and I don't personally care, but I don't aim to see any of my Mormon brethren killed simply because you sent some white men to their death. Good day, Judge. Don't bother me or my men about this issue again."

He met with much of the same everywhere he went. Even Ambrose was against going, after all the money he had spent the past few months buying drinks for everyone at The Rusty Rail.

"Well hell, Henry, it ain't that I'm again' the idea. It's just that I got myself a business to run. Besides I hear there's more like a hundred and fifty Injuns out there, and you only got about twenty or thirty men rarin' to go. That ain't very good odds in my book. I'd say you'd be better off calling in the militia from up Columbia way. They's the ones what whupped the Injuns that was botherin' them."

"Yeah, maybe you're right," Henry said downing his drink. "Maybe you're right. I'll see what I can do."

He had no intention of calling in the Militia from Columbia or anybody else. The Columbian Militia had indeed beaten back a small Indian uprising over a dispute involving a missing ax, of all things. A miner had misplaced his chopping ax and accused the Indians who had been working near by of stealing it. A meeting was called and the Chief gave his solemn oath that he would get to the bottom of the crime, and if one of his men had taken the item, it would be returned and the guilty party punished. No one knew why, but when the Chief was riding his pony back up the hill toward his people, someone shot him in the back, and the Chief fell from his horse dead.

Stupid, Henry thought. *Real stupid.* That was the kind of stupidity he didn't need here in Dogtown. What followed was out and out war. The Indians did finally surrender after a surprise attack in the early morning hours killed a whole lot of women and children, but not before the white militia itself had suffered heavy losses. No, that would not do. And not simply because someone might get hurt or killed, because that was inevitable. But if outside help did get involved someone would surely start asking questions, and he simply couldn't have that. It had to be taken care of right here with the men he had and could trust.

Dammit, it would have all been over today if those men had ridden out there and destroyed her rag-tag vaquero army. How tough could it be? And why were they so upset over the hanging of the Mexican? Once he had control of the ranch he would spread enough of the money around to make them all rich. Why couldn't they see it? No, he'd take care of it himself, and then to hell with them and their town. He'd keep the money for himself.

"Pod," he said to the sheriff, who sat on the steps smoking a cigarette. "Get some of the men together and bring them here. I want to get this thing over with."

Chapter 27

Tex and Paco were checking on the cattle on the east range when they heard the shots. One heavy report that came from a buffalo gun, and two smaller ones from a hand gun. Without saying a word both riders spurred their mounts in the direction of the shots. Rounding a row of trees they saw the horse lying on the trail with its rider trying to find cover behind the dead animal. Another heavy report kicked up dirt very close to the wounded man.

"Hold on *Amigo*, they have a big gun over there." Paco grabbed Tex by the arm and gestured toward a rocky point by the river where gunsmoke hung in the air. "That gun, I think will reach us here."

They brought their mounts to a halt and Tex dismounted. He pulled the Prussian Needle Gun from its sheath.

"Well, let's just return the favor."

"*Caramba, amigo,* where'd you get such a big gun?"

"Won it from a buffalo hunter in a poker game in New Mexico. He had three Queens, but I had me four tens."

Kneeling beside his horse he took careful aim and squeezed the trigger. Paco had trouble holding the mounts steady as flame and smoke belched from the muzzle with an ear-splitting roar. The sound of small arms fire was quickly followed by another boom of the buffalo gun hidden behind the rocks. Tex flinched as the round kicked dust dangerously close.

"You wait here, *amigo*. I'll give chase," Paco said, and spurred his horse into a full run directly toward the rocks.

"Damn fool," Tex said, loading the Needle Gun as fast as he could.

The vaquero let out a pealing cry as he brandished his side arm and fired. Turning his horse broadside to the rocks, he slid from his saddle and hung on the opposite side of his horse, firing several shots from beneath its neck. One of the men stood to get a better aim and Tex quickly drew a bead. His round lifted the man from his feet and sent him sailing backward.

He was reloading as the vaquero pulled himself back into the saddle, turned his horse, and made a headlong charge. Tex watched as another man backed from his position behind the rock trying to get away from the crazy horseman. Tex fired again, but his bullet missed and sent a spray of rock and dust into the air. The buffalo gun boomed again and he heard the whine of the .50 caliber ball as it passed close to his head. He reloaded and placed the next round directly into the cloud of smoke above the rock as Paco sent his horse into a flying leap, firing his pistol at the same time.

"No!" he said as the vaquero spilled from the saddle and bounced on the soft earth. He fired the heavy gun one more time and drew his own pistols, firing as he charged.

It was over as quickly as it started. He reached the rocks to find a prostrate Paco firing at the fleeing riders.

"Thought they'd nailed you, Pard," he said, helping the vaquero to his feet.

"No, I fell when my horse turned," Paco said, holding his stomach. "*Caramba,* can't breathe."

"Just got the wind knocked outa you. Come on, let's see

whose hide we were trying to save."

"Bastards shot my hoss," Hanky said, looking up as the two men approached. He had a bullet hole in his right calf that was bleeding profusely, while his left leg was pinned under the dead animal.

"Me and this old cayuse has been friends a long time, and they kilt him."

"Looks like they nailed you too," Tex said, looking at the bloody leg.

"Damned mini-ball went right through and kilt my hoss."

"Come on, Paco, help me get him out from under here before the buzzards get him."

The two men struggled to get the old ranger free, and Tex knelt to feel for broken bones.

"Don't think nothing's busted. Yer lucky."

"Lucky? They kilt my hoss."

"*Madre mia.*" Paco shook his head and laughed. "Too bad they didn't shoot you in the head. It would have bounced off."

~   ~   ~

"He's been talkin' like that since we found him," Tex said. Leonida had been asking about the wounded ranger, but all Paco would tell her was that the old man was *loco*.

"All he can think of is that dead hoss of his. We brung the saddle and his grip in."

"I can't find any broken bones," Sean said, wiping his hands.

"Already told him that. Better check his head, though. I think the fall musta' shook somethin' loose."

"Yer the crazy one," Hanky said, trying to sit upright. "You ain't got no loyalty is whut yer problem is. Bet it wouldn't bother you none if yer hoss fell over dead right now."

"Shore it would. And I'd shoot any *hombre* who so much as touched him. But I wouldn't sit around cryin' about it."

"You lost your horse trying to help me, so you are welcome to have any horse you choose from my stock when you are able to ride. And I do offer my apology for the trouble you've had, Señor Russell."

"That ain't the point. It might be hard for you to understand, but me and that hoss was pards. We rode many a trail together, and he saved my neck more'n oncet from injuns. I thank you for givin' me another'n ma'am, but it won't be the same. With me, it was kinda' like when you lost yer husband. Do you understand?"

"Damn," Tex said, dropping the match that had just burnt his fingers. He couldn't believe what he'd been listening to.

"I guess I should be offended by your comparing my husband to a horse, but I will take it as a compliment. And I do thank you for at least trying."

"Well, I ain't done yet, ma'am." His voice stopped her at the door. "You don't honestly think a little scratch like this would slow me down, do you?"

"Well, yes I do. How bad is he, Doctor Kilkinney?"

"Not bad for a man who just got shot by a cannon," Sean said with a shrug. "It was a rather large bullet that went through your leg, you know."

"Hell, I been hurt lots worse'n this, and it ain't slowed me none. Besides, I can't quit now. I done got things stirred up back in town. Ol' Judge Henry recognized me, and I let him know I remember when he was sellin' snake-oil and got run out of Arizonie. And I seen where him and Pod's hired them some new gunslingers. One of them got riled at me, and I taken his gun away and whupped him with it. They want me dead real bad, that's why they tried to kill me out on the trail."

"And they almost succeeded," Leonida said as she turned away. "Paco, I want you to find Juan and bring him to my office as soon as possible. I want to talk to you both."

Tex lit another match as he watched the opened door the Señora had gone through. *What the hell's got into her? She don't sound or look the same. Still purdy, but colder'n rolled steel.* He quickly put the match to his cigarette as he listened to Hanky.

"Hell, I might've had 'em if you two hadn't of busted up my party."

"Didn't see as they was bringin' you no cake."

"No, but I'll bet ifin' you find out who it was, you'll find one of 'em has a busted cheekbone where I slapped him with his own iron."

Tex took a thoughtful puff on his smoke as he studied the old ranger.

"Paco said the one I nailed through the shoulder with the needle gun looked kinda buggered-up. Like he'd been in a fight or somethin'."

~   ~   ~

"Juan, Maria tells me you were a *bandido* and rode with the gringo Jack Slade."

The young vaquero with the youthful face shifted nervously under the intent gaze of the Doña.

"Don't be frightened. You're not in any trouble. I just need to know if this is true or not. Were you a bandido?"

"Si, for a short while. Jack was only here for a while, then went back to New Mexico."

"Then you know how to use your gun?"

"Si."

"Do you know where to buy guns? Good guns, real fast?"

He glanced at Paco who only shrugged.

"I need to know, Juan. I feel you and Paco are the only ones I can trust. My father doesn't even know about this, and would try to stop me if he did. Can you find me some guns and ammunition?"

"Si, Señora. But why?"

"You know there are gringos in Dogtown who are trying to take our land away. You saw what they did to my husband and Carlo. They've beaten our doctor friend and Rosa. And now, they have shot that old *anglo* who came to help us. I'm tired of my house looking like a hospital. They will try to kill me and my father if they can get away with it." She opened the desk drawer and removed the small bag of gold coins.

"Tex tells me my vaqueros are poorly armed for a fight with the *pistoleros*. I want you and Paco to take this and buy as many guns and ammunition as you can. I want good weapons for our people to defend themselves with. I am not going to give up without a fight. My blood will stain the earth beside my husband's before I leave. Do you understand?"

"Si, Señora." A broad smile crept across his face. "Chico Cruz has many guns in Hornitos. I will return with them in *cinco dias*."

"Go then. Both of you, and tell no one. *Vayan con Dios*."

Chapter 28

Hugh Zornes lay moaning on a table in The Rusty Rail as George Bidwell wrapped his wound with rags soaked with kerosene.

"Damn near shot his arm off. Can't tell if anything's busted up inside. Just have to wait and see."

"Who did it?" Henry Baines said, almost biting his pipestem in two.

"Hard to tell, but Eb and me think it was that Texas gunfighter that took Rosa off," Curly said.

"Why in the hell can't I send someone out to do a simple job like killing some old alkali-eaten buzzard and expect it to get done?"

"Well hell, Judge, no one expected Tex to be nowhere's around, let alone have that needle gun. And he had that crazy Mexican with him. That greaser was throwin' lead like you wouldn't believe." Eb's hand shook as he poured himself a drink. "Besides, don't forget ol' Hugh here did nail that old man for you before he got hisself shot."

"Yes, but you said he wasn't dead. I want him dead. Do you understand?" He turned and walked briskly back toward the sheriff's office.

"I'd say he's madder'n a hornet pinned inside a bonnet," Pod said with a smirk. "You boys better learn to do things right."

"Didn't see you out there dodging no lead," Curly said.

"No, but he didn't ask me to do the job, either. He asked you. And don't forget," he said, pointing a finger at Curly's head like a gun. "I kilt the two men he asked me to."

~　　~　　~

"How is she, Doctor?" Leonida said, entering the room.

Sean shifted his gaze from the young girl lying in the bed. "We're getting along fine, aren't we, Rosa?" he said with a smile and tweaked her nose. It was interesting to see him work with the young girl. It was much the same way he had treated her after her beating. "Right now, I'd say she's a much better patient than you were."

"And what, may I ask, do you mean by that?"

"Jumping and pulling away every time I wanted to examine you, or put some medicine on one of your wounds."

"Isn't that understandable?"

"Oh, yes, very understandable. I am just amazed that you have seemingly healed so completely this fast," he said.

His gaze made Leonida feel uncomfortable and she turned away to the window to watch the children chase one of the dogs around the fountain.

"Well, I'll leave you two ladies alone, ma'am. I have other patients I would like to check on, and I'm afraid I've talked Rosa's ear off," Sean said, shutting his bag with a loud snap.

"Good day, Doctor."

He squeezed the girl's hand with a smile and left, closing the door behind him.

Leonida glanced toward the girl and Rosa pulled the blanket tightly under her chin like a frightened child. She was ashamed to admit she hadn't been inside this room since Tex brought Rosa's broken and bruised body here four days earlier. She always had a good excuse as to why she hadn't looked in on her, when her father or Maria would ask how the patient was doing. She had to look after the children, or this happened or that happened. But they were all excuses and she knew it. She was the Doña, and Rosa was from The Rusty Rail. But now that she was finally in the room, she couldn't take her eyes off the girl. Her face was grossly contorted and swollen. The wild eyes that stared back at her were set in dark purple sockets that still bore the marks of the ring Pod Randell wore on his right hand. Her lips were a mass of scabs that made her speech slurred and difficult when she finally spoke.

"I am sorry, Señora. I shouldn't be here." The eyes darted away from Leonida.

"Nonsense. What are you talking about?"

"I am not worthy of your bed. I am a *prostituta*." A tear trickled from the corner of her eye when she spoke.

"You are a friend of Tex, so you are my friend," Leonida said, sitting on the edge of the bed. "You are welcome to stay here in this room until you are better."

"Why do you do this?"

"You're a woman who needs help. Besides, two men did much the same to me. Or, haven't you heard?" She rose quickly and walked back to the window.

"Si, I am sorry, Señora. You are so beautiful."

"Thank you. I return the compliment. I saw you the day of my wedding. You are very beautiful also, *chica*."

Sean's voice drifted through the open window as he talked with the padre on the patio below.

"The doctor, he is nice, no?" Rosa said in a timid voice.

"Yes, he is a very nice man."

"What is he saying? Does he talk to Tex?"

"No, I believe he is talking to Father Franco."

A smile swept across Leonidas lips as she listened

intently to the conversation below.

"He gave the padre some money and asked him to buy seeds so he can plant a garden for the children."

"Ahhh," Rosa said with a nod. "He talks much while he takes care of me. He does not know I understand English."

"Oh?"

"He likes Doña Leonida very much."

Leonida watched the two men below.

"Does Doña Leonida like him too?"

"I said he is a nice man." Leonida pulled her veil tightly under her chin and left the room.

Chapter 29

The barking dogs and distinctive sound of wagon wheels on the hard brick surface of the courtyard caused Leonida to lay her writing pad aside and walk to the doorway. Several vaqueros escorted the trail-weary prairie schooner close to the fountain, where the large, bearded man brought it to a halt and tied the reins to the break handle before standing upright and placing one foot on the front wheel. The woman beside him held a small girl in her lap. Leonida could also see a boy she guessed to be about ten, and a girl several years younger leaning out the back. All of them looked frightened except the man, who was red in the face with anger.

"Who's in charge here?" he said to Sean Kilkenney who just happened to be returning from the corral at that very moment.

"Mrs. Garcia is," he nodded toward the house. "My name's Sean Kilkenney," he said holding out a hand.

"Well, if you ain't in charge, then I don't need to speak to you at all do I, you damn Scotchman," he said, leaping from the wagon. He had taken a couple of steps toward the porch when Sean jerked his own hat from his head and flung it at the man's feet.

"Scotchman? Would ye insult me to my face now?" The man stopped to stare at the angry doctor. "I'm sorry that you had to hear such filthy talk coming from your own man, ma'am," he said to the woman in the wagon. "And I apologize for what I'm about to do, but me Irish mother, bless her soul, would turn over in her grave if I failed to defend her honor against such vulgar talk as that." He removed his coat and handed it to one of the small boys standing by, then spit on his palms and rubbed them together, then began prancing around the man with his fists doubled up.

"I ain't got no beef with you, son. So just go your own way before you get hurt."

"Vernon, get back into the wagon," the woman said as the little girl started crying.

"Hush your mouth, woman. This here's man's business."

"That's another lesson you've got to learn. A gentleman should never speak to a lady in such a tone. Come and get yours." Sean taunted him with a jab that fell a few inches short.

"Alright, sonny. You want to get hurt this morning? I aim to oblige," he said, removing his coat.

"Maria, go get the woman and her children and bring them here," Leonida said while the doctor continued his strange dance. The maid wove her way through the crowd that had begun to gather, mostly on the porch, all striving to get a better view.

"Got me a twenty-dollar gold piece that says the Doc's gonna whup him," Tex said, holding the coin up high as he perched himself on the railing.

"Oh, but Señor, he is so little, and the *hombre* is so big. I hate to take your money," Paco said, pulling a coin from his own pocket. They were immediately surrounded by noisy gamblers, all hoping to get a piece of the action. Leonida shook her head as her father placed a bet against the stranger.

"Come inside and let them make fools of themselves,"

she said as the woman joined her in the doorway. "I am Doña Leonida Garcia, and you and your children are welcome in my *hacienda*."

"I am Catherine Blackstone, and these are my children, Brian, Cynthia and Judith," she said in a shaky voice. "I'm terribly sorry for what's happening. We had really only wanted to talk things out, but Vernon, that's my husband, has such a bad temper."

"So does Doctor Kilkenney. But as of yet, neither of them has struck one another. They may dance out there all day long. Maria," she said turning to the maid. "Would you please see if we can't find something for these children to eat?"

"*Bueno.* Come, see what Maria has in the kitchen," she said, motioning for them to follow, but they stood transfixed on the two men pacing around in a large circle in the courtyard.

"And what brings you to *Rancho Manantial Escondido* in the first place?"

"Those men brought us," she said pointing toward the vaqueros standing beside their horses. "I was just starting to fix breakfast for my husband and children, when they came and told us we were trespassing on private property, and would have to come with them. Oh!" she said as Sean hit her husband with a jab to the nose.

"Aw, hell, I ain't got time for this," the man said and swung a looping right hand at Sean's head. Sean ducked under the blow and drove a fist into the man's mid-section, causing him to let out a groan and double over. Sean then stepped back and hit him with a short left jab and a right that landed on his chin. He fell on his backside, still holding his stomach.

"Now, perhaps you'll learn to address people in a more civil manner," Sean said, picking up his hat and dusting its brim. A rumble rolled through the crowd of vaqueros as they paid Tex and her father their debts.

"The big *gringo*, he's no *bueno*, eh, Señor Tex? That's a lot of money for such a short fight," Paco said with a shrug.

"Señor Kilkenney?" Leonida said, stepping to the edge of the porch. "Will you please show Señor Blackstone where to wash up, and bring him to the house when you're finished? I wish to talk to you both."

"Me?"

"Si, you are Sean Kilkenney, are you not? And you gentlemen," she said turning toward the crowd gathered on the porch. "As soon as you're finished paying your gambling debts, you may move the wagon and horses down to the corral where it belongs, and clean the courtyard." They glanced at each other, then back to her with a blank stare. "Children play around that fountain, and I, for one, am tired of having to step around and over the piles the horses leave. I don't understand why you think you must bring your horses right up to the front door of the *hacienda*."

"But Señora, that is where the hitching rail is," Juan said with a grin as he pointed to where his horse was tied.

"I'll have the Indians move it then. It belongs at the corral where the watering trough is. The fountain is to look at, not water horses." She turned and walked briskly inside, leaving the open-mouthed vaqueros standing in silence.

~   ~   ~

"Come, sit." She motioned toward two empty chairs as Sean and Vernon Blackstone entered the study. The man scowled as he glanced at everyone in the room before seating himself next to his wife.

"Where's the kids?"

"Your children are in the kitchen with Maria eating breakfast. We shall join them, but we must talk first." She stood behind the large desk with her palms pressed against its smooth surface as she spoke.

"Poor babies. Hope they have strong teeth," Sean said, sitting beside the man. "Just a private joke, ma'am," he added in response to Catherine Blackstone's look.

"Señor Blackstone, your wife tells me you purchased two hundred acres of land just across the Mokelumne River. Is that true?"

"Got the papers right here," he said. Reaching into his coat pocket, he retrieved a folded piece of paper which he handed to her. "Paid seventy-five dollars for that place, but it's good bottom land."

"Oh," Leonida raised her eyebrows, "I thought my land was worth more than that."

"It is, a might more," Tex said, striking a match and holding it to his cigarette.

"It was all the money we had ...." Catherine's voice trailed off at her husband's scowl.

"You purchased this land from Judge Henry Baines?" Leonida said lowering the paper to see their nodding heads. "I'm afraid you have been cheated out of your money. You see Judge Baines does not own that land, I do."

"But he said it was his, and he gave us that paper when we paid him." Vernon Blackstone stood to his feet.

"Can you imagine that?" Hanky said shaking his head as he laughed. "First he kills her husband and his brother, then he tries to sell her land right out from under her."

"He tells you the truth," she said as they glanced at the Ranger, then back to her. "Henry Baines did murder my husband and brother in law. He also did other things I do not wish to discuss with you right now, except to tell you he is an evil man. And now he has stolen your money." She turned to point at the map with her father's riding crop.

"The *vaqueros* told me the land you thought to purchase lies just over the river, right here. But as you can see, *Rancho Manantial Escondido* has its borders much farther than where you wished to build your farm. I'm afraid, Señor, that Judge Baines has sold you land he did not own."

"Oh, God, Vernon, what are we going to do? That was all the money we had," Catherine said, holding a shaking hand to her lips.

"I'll kill him with my bare hands," he said leaping from his chair.

"I'm afraid you'll have to wait yer turn. There's about a hundred *vaqueros* outside, and at least two or three right here in this room hopin' ta do the same thing, so just sit yerself down and let's work this thing out. No one, let alone this young lady, is gonna let y'all starve to death."

"Señor Hanky is right. Please, sit down," she said with a smile. "We shall discuss this matter and see if we can't get back at the judge. But first, we shall eat, and then I would like to ride out with you and see this land you wish to own."

"No, *niña*, it would not be safe," her father said, shaking his head.

"But, *Papa*, I must. These people have been cheated out of everything they own."

"Am I to be cheated out of my own daughter? No, I won't allow it."

"Oh, pooh. What can happen? You'll be there to protect me, and we'll take Baca and the *vaqueros*, so no one is going to hurt me."

~   ~   ~

Sean tied Cathy under a scrub oak and joined the others as they walked along the west bank on the Mokelumne. Baca was shaking his head and speaking quickly in Spanish.

"It is beautiful indeed, Señor. But Ildefonso Baca says that the whole area in which you wish to build your home is flooded every springtime by the river." The Doña pointed toward the flat grassy meadow on the opposite side of the river.

"I asked the judge about that, and he said it seldom ever flooded around here," Vernon Blackstone said matter-of-factly.

"If he would lie and try to sell us land that didn't belong to him, what makes you think he would be telling us the truth about the flooding?" Catherine said. This brought a scowl from her husband.

Sean worked his way through the small group to stand next to Leonida under a scrub oak as she interpreted for the *vaquero*. Something caught his eye and made him stop to concentrate on an area directly across the river from them. There it was again. A small flash of sunlight on something metal. "Down!" He yelled and gave Leonida's arm a jerk as a puff of smoke shot out of the clump of trees.

The tree seemed to explode and she crumpled at his feet with a whimper, covering her face with her hands as the men returned fire. The small arms they were carrying could not reach that far and Hanky cursed the fact as he reloaded his pistol. Sean started to drag Leonida behind the tree, but another round from the heavy gun across the river kicked up dust dangerously close to them, so he fell on top of the girl and pressed her to the ground instead.

"How is she? Did they hit her?" Jose Flores said, reaching from behind the tree toward his daughter.

"No, I think she's all right. Get back before they shoot you." Another bullet whined its way past and made a sick thud as it bit into flesh. One of the animals let out a cry and fell to the ground.

"Oh, damn! I don't believe it," Hanky said. "The murderin' bastards kilt the hoss I rode out here on. Tommy, get me that needle-gun of yourn'. I ain't taking anymore of this."

Sean brushed back the mass of golden hair to study the girl lying beneath him. There were scratches and welts on her left cheek and temple caused by flying bark as the bullet hit the tree close to her head. He gently brushed some chips of bark from her face as the eyelids fluttered and he found himself staring into the emerald pools only inches away. She closed them tight again and let out a cry as Hanky fired the heavy buffalo gun from behind the tree.

"Shhhhh, it's going to be all right. You're safe now," he whispered close to her ear. She opened her eyes for a second, and closed them tight as the gun boomed again. Sean covered her ears with his palms as the two men exchanged fire back and forth over the river for the next few minutes. He found himself wishing it would never end as he felt her warm body pressed against his and studied the eyes that were fixed upon him. Then as sudden as it began, the shooting stopped.

"I think you run him off, Hanky. We might as well mosey on back to the house and see if Maria ain't got dinner ready," Tex said. Sean could hear the striking of a match and smell tobacco as the cowboy spoke.

"Hope I didn't just scare 'em. I hope he's lying over there with a hole in his gut. He kilt another hoss. Murderin' son-of-a-bitch."

"I think you can let my daughter up now, doctor. I believe it's safe." Sean glanced up into the smiling face of Jose Flores. He rose and gently helped the girl to her feet.

"I guess I owe you a great debt for saving her life, don't I?" Sean didn't answer.

"*Caramba Señor*, look at this." Julio held up a lock of honey-colored hair. "The bullet, it cut Doña Leonida's hair from her head."

"Shore enough was close. Right where she was standing. Barked you pretty good too, didn't it?" Hanky said, looking at the scratches on her cheek.

Jose stuffed the lock of hair into his vest pocket and gave Sean a crooked grin before herding the crowd to where the horses were tied. Their conversation seemed to blend into one great noise as Sean leaned against the tree and fumbled with his pipe, spilling the tobacco he was trying to pack into the bowl.

"Here, take this, and don't burn yerself with the match," Hanky said, handing him a cigar. "Ya coming, or staying here awhile?"

"Yeah, I'll be along in a minute. Thanks."

Chapter 30

"You can't figure that one out? They sold you the land in an effort to get her outa the house and down to the river so they could kill her. And it almost worked, too." Hanky said, sawing at the meat on his plate. They were seated around the large dining room table eating their midday meal of beef steaks.

"You shall have your land, Señor, but under certain conditions." Leonida spoke over the glass of water in her hands before taking a drink.

"And what's that? You gonna give me the land? You know I ain't got any money," Vernon Blackstone said as his dark eyes darted to his wife and back to Leonida again.

"No, Señor, I can't give you the land. If I chose to do that, then the next person would want me to give them land also. I am willing to sell you the land with the condition that a portion of the produce goes to pay your debt. What is it that you *Anglos* call it?"

"Share-cropping," Catherine Blackstone said excitedly as she grabbed her husband's arm.

"Si, share-cropping. Would you be willing to such an agreement, Señor?"

"Well, yes, but why would you do such a thing? You don't know me, and you don't owe me a thing."

"For several reasons, the most important being, as you can see, we are eating beef. And we shall eat beef again for supper this evening. Tomorrow morning, Maria shall serve beef for breakfast. Doctor Kilkenney says we have a very poor diet, and he is right. I wish you to grow food for the people on this rancho. Is that agreeable to you?" He nodded. "By the way, where is Doctor Kilkenney? Why hasn't he come to dinner?"

"He eats with Rosa in the study," Maria said, filling several cups with hot tea.

"Why aren't they here with us? There is room."

"Don't know about him, but I couldn't get Rosa to come. She said it wouldn't be proper for her to sit at your table with company being present," Tex said over a mouthful of steak.

"Ahhhh," Leonida nodded.

"Back to what we were talking about, what's another reason you want to do this?" Vernon said.

"Simply that I do not wish the judge and his men to beat us. How shall I say this without sounding too sinful, Padre?" She glanced toward Father Franco and back again. "I hope to turn their evil into good. They sell you my land and take your money? Very well, you shall have your land, and we here at *Rancho Manantial Escondido* shall enjoy eating the food you raise. It is one of the ways we can take vengeance on them."

"Makes sense to me, Vernon. What do you think?" Catherine said.

"Yeah, but how do we know we can trust her? I mean, we've already been cheated out of everything we own."

"A very wise question, Señor," Leonida said placing her elbows on the table and folding her hands. She tapped her lips thoughtfully with her two index fingers as she continued talking. "Is it because we are Spanish, that you ask such a question?"

"Certainly not." He hit the table hard enough to make the tea in his cup slosh over the brim.

"Good, then we shall put the agreement in writing. That way, we will both be protected. You shall have your land, and we shall have our food. *Bueno*?" He nodded. "I don't blame you for being cautious, Señor, for you have been dealing with very evil men. Come, I will show you." She rose from the table and motioned with her hand as she led the way to the study.

"Oh, *me perdona, Señora*," Rosa said as she and Sean both jumped to their feet in unison. She had been seated in Rudolfo's chair behind the desk. Sean had pulled one of the other chairs up while they ate their dinner.

"Its all right, *chica*, sit back down. Both of you." They obeyed, slowly, while she walked behind the girl, placing her hands on her shoulders and leaning to kiss her cheek. Rosa dropped her chin to her chest, and the mass of curls seemed to fold around her, hiding most of her face from view.

"I brought them here to see you, Rosa. Not because I want to put you on display, and if I embarrass you, I beg your forgiveness. But I do this because I want them to know what kind of men Judge Baines and Pod Randell really are. And I also do this so you will know for certain that I am not ashamed of calling Señorita Rosa Carillo my friend." The girl snapped her head up to stare at her with large dark eyes. "Ah, there you are, *chica*," she said brushing back the curls.

"See, Señora Blackstone? You can still see some of the bruises, and the swelling at the corner of her mouth has not all disappeared." She caressed Rosa's cheek with her palm as she talked. "Rosa is only fifteen years old, but Ambrose Brice, another friend of the judge, claims her father sold her to him, and forced her to work in his saloon as a prostitute. Then, the sheriff in Dogtown did this to her. He almost beat her to death because she dared to laugh at him. Tex brought her here after the beating for safety. Doctor Kilkenney and Maria are nursing her back to health now. I have grown fond of her, and wish her to stay here with me after her Texas *vaquero* marries her." She kissed Rosa's cheek and walked back around the desk to face them.

"You wish to know why I would make such a deal with you, Señor? It is because they have not only done such a thing to this child, but they hurt me also. They hired men who tried to kill me while I rode my horse by the river. They murdered my husband and his brother and beat Doctor Kilkenney, simply because he was willing to stand up for what he believed was right. That is the kind of men they are, Señor, and they do these things because they wish to have my land. But I will not let them have it as long as there is one single breath left in my body. If I cannot keep it, I will give it to my people. I will give it to Señor Tex and Rosa. I will give part of it to you, Señor. But I must warn you first. If they find out that you have come to an agreement with me for part of the land, they will try to kill you too. Do you understand, Señor? Judge Henry Baines means to have all my land."

"Why doesn't one of you just ride into town and kill him? That would solve your problem, wouldn't it?"

"Vernon," Catherine said with a glare.

"Shore it would, and I aim to do that very thing, one of these days. But he's got hisself surrounded by hired gunmen and doesn't wander far enough away so's a feller can get to him," Hanky said.

"My father will take care of Judge Baines when the time comes, and I'm sure Tex would like to discuss Rosa's beating with Sheriff Randell," Leonida said, leaning against the desk. "But you still haven't answered my question, Señor. Are you willing to accept my offer, or shall I have to give the land to someone else?"

"Sure, I'll take the land."

"What if Judge Baines tries to harm you or your family?"

"I'll fight right beside you and your men. You can bank on that, Lady."

"*Bueno*. My father will draw up the agreement for you to sign, and I will have my *vaqueros* help you build your house," she said walking to the door, where she stopped and smiled. "But I would build your *hacienda* on this side of the river, if I were you. I've never heard where one of the Indians has been mistaken when it comes to the land, so it will probably get a little wet on the other side when spring comes."

~   ~   ~

Everyone had long since gone to bed when Sean sat in the darkness on the fountain's edge smoking his pipe. He had skipped supper, even though Catherine Blackstone had broken into her own private store of flour and had baked biscuits. Tempting as they were, facing Leonida this soon would have been too unsettling. He drew deeply on the pipe as a lonely dog pattered its way across the bricks toward the bunkhouse. That's where he should be. Perhaps he would move his few belongings there in the morning. Sleeping in the same house with her would never be the same again, even if there were two other bedrooms and thick oak doors separating them. The hand on his shoulder caused him to jump to his feet, dropping the pipe.

"I'm sorry, I didn't mean to frighten you," she said with a giggle as the moonlight danced in her dark green eyes.

"I just didn't hear you coming, that's all. I thought I was alone."

"I didn't see you at supper. It was very good. Señora Blackstone helped out in the kitchen. She baked some *pan*, little round things, what do you call them?"

"Biscuits."

"Si, biscuits. Here, I saved you one," she said handing him a napkin folded over and neatly tied with a bow.

"Thank you." Sean untied the bow and found a cold biscuit inside. "But you didn't have to go to all this trouble."

"I wanted to. Go ahead, you'll like it." He bit into the bread as she watched intently.

"Mmmm, it is good."

"See? I told you." She bent over and picked up his pipe,

wiping its stem clean on the hem of her skirt. She sat on the edge of the fountain and patted the bricks with her palm. "Here, come sit beside me. I want to talk to you."

"You shouldn't be out here alone, ma'am."

"But I'm not alone. You're here."

"That's not what I mean," he said glancing around.

"Oh, you mean for appearances? Don't worry, Ildefonso Baca is watching. You just don't see him, that's all."

"Yes, I'd almost forgotten about that devil," he said, choking down the last of the biscuit. What he really wanted now was a drink of water, or some of Maria's tea, but there wasn't any to be had.

"I'm sorry you feel that way about him. He's really a nice man, in his own way."

"You didn't get hit in the head by him either."

"No, but I scratched and hit you, and called you names. You don't think I'm a devil, do you?"

"I haven't made up my mind yet."

"Oh?"

"I thought you were an angel when I woke and you were nursing me. But there's been times since that have started me to wonder."

"You jest with me, Señor." Her laugh was intoxicating. They sat silently for a minute while she fingered the smooth wood of the pipe.

"Why did you come out here tonight? You said you wanted to talk to me."

"Yes, I was trying to find the words." Her eyes glistened and her voice trembled. "It is probably better to show you," she said, letting her veil drop to her shoulders. She turned her head slightly to the right and pulled her hair away from her ear to reveal a welt along her neck and a chunk of hair missing as though someone had chopped it off with scissors.

"I'm sorry. I didn't see that, or I would have put something on it," he said, touching the welt lightly.

"No, that is not why I show you. You don't understand, do you? You saved my life today. They would have killed me

if you were not there. And I don't know how to thank you. I could give you land, but I don't feel that is enough," she said shaking her head as she studied the bricks at their feet. "The only thing I
can do is tell you how I feel. Is that enough, Señor?"

"Yes, quite."

"I am very grateful that you are here, Señor. First, you doctor me when I am hurt. Then you doctor Rosa and all the others here at the rancho. And now you save my life. I owe you much, and I feel safe when you are near me." She leaned over and gave him a quick kiss on the cheek and jumped to her feet. "Oh," she paused she turned away, "I almost forgot. Here is your pipe."

He fingered the smooth burlwood as he watched her glide across the courtyard toward the house. Her feet made no sound on the bricks as her golden hair bounced in the moonlight, making him wonder if she had removed her slippers and made the visit in her stocking feet.

"Dammit, Sean Kilkenney," he said as she disappeared into the darkened house. "You'd better ride away from here soon, or you'll never be able to leave this place."

Chapter 31

"Mrs. Garcia?" Leonida placed her finger on the page to mark her spot before glancing toward the head poking through the doorway.

"*Hola*, Señor Kilkenney. What may I do for you?" She had not seen him for three days since thanking him for saving her life by the river. It was as though he had disappeared.

"I hate to disturb you, but I need your help real bad."

"Si?" she said after a long minute of them staring at each other. "What is it?"

"Well you see, I'm going to have to operate on Erasmo Gamarro. And I was wondering if you wouldn't mind telling him and his family what I'm about to do? They seem to trust you."

"Si." She used her hanky as a bookmark and laid the copy of Shakespeare aside. "What seems to be the problem?"

"Well, you see," he held the door open for her, "he got some sort of thorn stuck in the big toe of his left foot and let it get infected. And now it's so bad that gangrene has set in. I'm afraid that I'm going to have to remove it."

"Are you sure?" She paused in the middle of the hall to put a hand on his arm.

"Aye," he shrugged, "if I don't take it off now, I'll be taking his whole foot or even the leg in a few days. And if we don't do anything, he'll eventually die. But I don't want to start a war with the Yokuts, so I sure wish you'd explain everything to him."

"Well, most certainly." She followed Sean to the bunkhouse to find Erasmo lying on one of the beds with his foot elevated on several horse blankets. The sight of the swollen, oozing member caused her to wretch, and it took all the intestinal-fortitude she could muster to keep for vomiting.

"Sorry to ask you to do this, ma'am. But as you can see, it is an emergency."

"Yes....yes, I can see you're right, Doctor." She cleared her throat and gazed into the dark eyes of the Gamarro family a long moment before explaining what must be done. It was not easy convincing someone who believes he must have a complete and whole body in this life in order to have one in the next that he must give up one of his toes. He finally relented after she explained that his toe had been taken over by an evil spirit, but only if Doña Leonida would stay by his side during the entire operation. Her dinner that evening consisted of two glasses of wine, a dry corn tortilla and a little conversation with those gathered around the table. She then excused herself, saying she didn't feel too well and took a long-hot bath. She held Rudolfo's shirt while she sat on the edge of her bed and drank a glass of brandy. It was still several hours later before she was able to fall asleep.

~   ~   ~

"No, no, no. Just point the gun kinda like yer pointing yer finger. Like this," Tex said whipping his pistol from its holster and firing. Bark flew from the tree.

"*Caramba*," Pedro said stepping backward.

"If y'all took as much time aiming at a human as you

are at that tree you'd been dead long ago. A blind man could out-pull any of you. Now turn sideways and get ready like I done showed you." Tex stepped away as the four men stood flexing their fingers, with their gun arms facing the scrub oak.

"Ready, fire!"

Two of the shots went wide and completely missed the large tree while the third kicked up dust at the base of the trunk. The fourth man was struggling to get his gun out of the holster. Sean chuckled as Tex threw his hands in the air.

"Hold on. Yer gonna blow yer damn foot off," he said grabbing the man's arm.

"Ya don't really aim on taking this army up against the judge and Pod Randell, do ya Tommy?" Hanky said limping up to meet them on a home-made crutch.

"They volunteered. Every damn one of them on this ranch wants to go fight."

"Well, I hope so. I wouldn't give a plug-nickel fer any one who wouldn't. But don't forget, outside of Paco and Juan, these men ain't never had much use fer a handgun before. I think I'd try to get hold of some shotguns or rifles, if it was me. Then, I'd still rely more on the Injuns, unless these men are armed with something more than those old hoglegs they got stuffed in their belts. It's a wonder they even work. Where'd they find them?"

"They were stuffed in a box in the bunk house for a couple of years. Francisco said they got them off a couple of men who drowned in the river. Still know how to use that iron of yours?"

"A little," Hanky said and hobbled out to where the men were standing.

"Think you could hit something as big as that tree?"

"Hope to shout. Here, Doc," he said, handing Sean the crutch. "Hang on to my other leg fer me, while I show this young pup how to use a gun."

"Well, hold on now," Tex said as the Ranger turned his right shoulder toward the tree. "I know you ain't so old you couldn't hit a tree. What about that little knot stickin' out toward the left there? Think you could hit that?"

"More than likely."

"Well, then, how about the twig stickin' outa the knot?"

"Possibility," he said as the gun seemed to leap into his hand and fire. The twig disappeared.

"*Santa Maria, Señor*," Francisco said as they stepped back in amazement. "The old *gringo* is faster than you."

"Aw, now, I take that as an insult," Tex said standing beside the Ranger. "Come on, Doc. You do the counting, then tell us who's the fastest. On three."

Sean readied himself, then counted. "One, two, three!" The weapons sounded in unison as bark flew into the air.

"Okay. Tell us now. Who's the quickest?" Tex asked as he turned with a grin.

"My hell, man, I don't know. You both fired at the same time."

"Aw, you're either blind, or lying to protect this old coot's ego. Francisco," he said turning to the vaqueros. "You tell us the truth now. I'm faster now, ain't I?"

"On my mother's grave, Señor, I cannot tell. It is as the Doctor says."

"Hell, Tommy, they can't tell you nothing, 'cause they don't know nothin' about guns. Come on, let's try it again." What ensued was an exhibition of marksmanship that left the men speechless.

"Well, looks as though you might have learned how to use that iron a little since the last time I seen you," Hanky said, reloading his weapon.

"A might. You ain't seemed to slow down too much. I was beginning to wonder after that guy put that hole in your leg."

"Hell, he had to do it from a half a mile away. My .44 wouldn't reach that far, or I'd of returned the favor." He replaced the gun in its holster and took the crutch from Sean's hand. "Well, I'll go see what Maria's got cooking fer dinner."

"No sense in bothering," Sean said. "It's going to be burnt cow."

"Ya'all keep practicing, and try not to kill one another or shoot yer foot off," Tex said over his shoulder. "Think I'm gonna go see how Rosa's doing."

"I couldn't honestly tell who was the fastest, because I couldn't see either of your hands move," Sean said, walking beside him past the corral.

"It don't matter none, but he is."

"You think so?"

"Know so. Not by much, but still a little faster."

"How could you tell? I couldn't."

"Well, he taught me how to shoot in the first place, fer one thing." He paused by the hay stack to pluck a straw and stick it between his teeth. "And, when you use a gun like we do, you just know. That's all."

"Were you two friends back in Texas?"

"Hardly. He's my pa. But I still might have to kill him."

Chapter 32

Juan had just removed his saddle when they heard the gunshots. Paco glanced up from where he was building a campfire.

"Hey, *amigo,* looks like we find a place that's not quite friendly. Better put the saddles on the fresh ones. We might have to leave in a hurry."

They were camped at the base of a chaparral-covered hill about halfway to Hornitos. Paco doused the fire and both men checked the loads in their weapons and waited. They had wisely brought two extra horses just in case, for there were certain areas that were not too friendly to Mexicans, and they just happened to be in one at that very moment. Four more shots, followed by two more, farther up the hill.

Juan led the horses closer and held onto the reins. "Want me to go see who is celebrating?"

"No, I think we find out soon enough. Listen." They could hear the faint sounds of voices in the distance.

"*Gringos,* I think."

"Si, but they don't hunt food. They are using pistols,"

Paco said, lighting a cigarette and handing it to Juan, who took a puff and passed it back.

The sound of crashing brush from above made both men draw and cock their weapons.

"Wait until we see them, *amigo*."

"Si." Juan pulled the horses around behind them and held the reins tight as he crouched beside his friend.

"They come closer, but it is very hard," Paco said in a hoarse whisper.

"Si, they lose much skin on the chaparral, I think."

Juan wiped his palm on his pant-leg as Paco crushed the cigarette. Both men raised their weapons as three men stepped into the clearing.

"*Alto,*" Paco ordered.

"*Mexicanos?*" one of the men asked.

"Si, *Mexicanos.*"

"*Bueno, amigos,*" the man said with a laugh of relief and came forward. He was a good looking vaquero of medium height and build, but he was bleeding from a gunshot wound in the cheek. "Me and my compañeros are sorry to bother you, but we have need of your horses."

"Ah, *que lastima amigo,* but the horses are not for sale. Juan and I need them for our journey to Hornitos."

"*Bueno,* but who said anything about buying the horses?" one of the other men said with a crude laugh. He was a large man with two fingers missing from his right hand.

"*Pero hombre, La Doña Leonida Garcia* sends us to Hornitos. What shall we tell her if you take our horses?" Paco stepped away from the animals, turning his right side to the man as he spoke. Juan dropped the reins and took several steps in the opposite direction.

"*Amigos, por favor,*" the first man said. "There is no need for *Mexicanos* to kill one another while there are so many *gringos* wishing to do the same. Put your *pistola* away Manuel. We will not hurt these men." The man with missing fingers shoved his gun back into his belt as the leader stepped forward, palms outward.

"Forgive us, Señores, but you see we are in a bit of a hurry. The *gringos* on the other side of the hill have already killed one of our men, and want to kill us too. I wish to be gone when they get here." He removed his scarf and held it to his bleeding cheek as he spoke.

"Why they shoot at you, *hombre*?" Juan said adjusting his gunbelt.

"Because they are *gringos* and we are *Mexicanos*."

"Si, but not all *gringos* wish to kill us because of our skin. Why they shoot at you?"

"Joaquin, we waste our time. Kill them and take the horses," Manuel said.

"*Silencio,*" he said snapping his head toward the man. "Forgive him, my friends, but he hears the footsteps of the *gringos* and wishes to leave in a hurry." He stepped forward and offered Juan his hand. "I am Joaquin Murrieta, and the one you wish to kill is Manuel Garcia. The *gringos* call him *Three-Fingered Jack* because he loses two of his fingers when a *chica* comes at him with an ax. The other is Pedro Monzo. He does not talk much. The *gringos* catch him once and we get him back, but they cut his tongue out because he would not tell them where Joaquin hides.

"Joaquin does not hide, but they would not believe him," he said walking back to the center with animated expression. "You say you go to Hornitos, *amigo. Por que?*"

"To see Chico Cruz."

"You know Chico?" His eyes lit up as he smiled, showing a fine line of white teeth.

"Si, I ride with him for a while," Juan said.

"Ah, then you are my compañero. Chico Cruz and I are old friends. You wish to go to Hornitos? Hornitos sounds good. What do you say, Manuel? Shall we go to Hornitos with our friends?"

"Si, Hornitos is good." The bandit spoke without taking his eye off Juan.

"Then let's go, *amigos,* before the *gringos* try to stop us again."

They mounted the horses, two of the men riding bare-back and two more doubling-up on one horse. They rode silently into the night away from the hill with no sign of their pursuers. The tired animals plodded onward until the early morning hours when they finally stopped to rest.

"Hey, Joaquin, how much further, *hombre*?" Three-Fingered-Jack leaned back against a rock and rolling a cigarette.

"Not far. Maybe five or six miles."

Juan built a fire and started a pot of coffee before finding a grassy spot to lay down on. "Why were those *gringos* trying to kill you, man?" He rolled his head to look at the bandit leader.

"I think they did not like it when we took $600,000 from them," he said with a laugh. "It is good you came along, *amigo*. They killed our horses, but they would not follow us into the chaparral."

"They are probably still at the bottom of that hill waiting for us, Joaquin. Stupid *Americanos*," Three-Fingered-Jack said, lighting his cigarette. "They would have killed you too, *hombre*. They would have thought you were with us and hung you like they did Jesus at Mokelumne Hill."

"Did he ride with you?" Paco said pouring two cups of coffee and handing one to Joaquin.

"Jesus? No, Jesus was a miner like many others. His crime was being Mexican, but he is still dead."

They sat silently sharing the cups as they drank the coffee. After the pot was emptied, Three-Fingered-Jack, Pedro and Paco laid back and closed their eyes as Joaquin and Juan cleaned and loaded their weapons.

"Tell me, *amigo*, this Doña Leonida. Is she the one who owns the rancho on the other side of the Mokelumne River?"

"Si."

"Ah, her husband is the one who dies at the hand of the *gringo* judge, no?"

Juan nodded.

"Why do you not kill him, then? Why do you wait until

the white pigs own all our land?"

"He has many guns, and our people have none. That is why we go to see Chico Cruz. Doña Leonida wishes to buy many guns so our people can fight."

"*Bueno.*" Joaquin nodded in agreement. "We go to Hornitos, then. And you shall have your guns *mi compañero.* Then you can kill the *gringos* for Señora Garcia."

Chapter 33

"*Buenos, muchachos.*" Joaquin smiled and waved to people as they walked their horses down the street. Stopping at the livery, he tossed a gold coin to the man in charge.

"Take extra care of these horses, *amigo*. They served Joaquin and his compañeros well." Then he slapped Juan and Paco both on the back and draped his arms around their necks.

"Come, my friends. I buy you *tequila.*"

The streets were crowded and dirty with miners, merchants, gamblers and prostitutes all bumping elbows and hoping to get rich. Many of the small stone buildings had the same flat iron bars across the windows that Juan had seen on the buildings on his one and only trip to Mexico. Several of the residents patted Joaquin on the back, offering their greetings as they passed. They stopped at a small building with a sign that read, *La Bonito Mujer*, and Juan had to agree with its name as they pushed their way inside. It took a moment for his eyes to adjust to the light in the smoke-filled room with its low-hung ceiling, but there were plenty of girls and every one of them was indeed good to look at.

"Joaquin, *buenos dias, mi amor.*" The girl at the bar threw her arms around Joaquin and kissed him. Juan guessed her to be about fifteen years old. "Oh, you have been injured, *mi amante,*" she said, running her fingers over the bullet wound on his cheek. "You wait here, while I go get some medicine. Teresa will make it all better for you," she said, kissing him lightly on the lips.

Paco studied her backside as she swished away and turned to the bandit. "*Bueno?*"

"*Muy bueno.*" Both men laughed and lifted their glasses. "Salute."

An argument broke out at the card game near the door and two men jumped to their feet, brandishing knives.

"*Alto.*" The dealer pointed a pistol at them. "I don't give a damn if you kill each other, just do it somewhere else. You're bothering our game."

"*Puto.*" One of the men pointed a middle finger as the other man whipped his blade at him. They were surrounded by a cheering crowd who ushered them out the door. Juan couldn't see clearly past the crowded doorway, but the sounds of the struggle were clear enough to tell him what was happening. Seconds later, the larger of the two men staggered back inside with several wounds of his own and tossed down a glass of brandy. He retook his seat at the table, picked up his cards with a bloody hand, and fell over dead.

"Get the son-of-a-bitch outa here," the dealer said with a growl. "And someone get another deck of cards. The bastard got blood all over these."

Juan felt a pair of soft arms slip around his shoulders as warm lips touched the lobe of his right ear. "*Buenos dias, mi compañero.* You wish for Angela to keep you company?"

He couldn't help but grin as he returned his gaze to the glass in his hands. She couldn't have been much older than Teresa.

"Oh, you blush," she said with a squeal and kissed him on the cheek. "How sweet. I never see anyone blush in such a long time. I tell you what," she said tapping him on the chest with her index finger. "You buy me a drink, and Angela will take care of you for free."

Juan bowed his head laughing as he tried to avoid her eyes.

"You no like Angela?"

"Si, si. You are very pretty."

"Oh, then you are virgin?" The roar of laughter from the surrounding men seemed deafening. "I tell you what, pretty boy, I take special care of you." She kissed him on the cheek.

"Angela," Joaquin said putting his arms around them both. "This is Juan. He and Paco," he nodded toward the vaquero standing to the left, "are my compañeros. They lent me their horses and saved Joaquin's life when the *gringos* tried to shoot me."

"Ahhhh, you are a brave one then." She caressed his cheek with her warm palm. "You shall be Angela's special friend too."

"Here, *chica*," Joaquin said slipping a gold coin into her hand. "Show him a good time when he finishes his *tequila*."

"But, what about Chico?" Juan said.

"There's plenty of time to see Chico Cruz. You must learn to keep things in proper order, my friend."

Juan glanced at her smiling face from the corner of his eye. She was pretty. Almost as pretty as The Señora in a different way. He felt his heart racing as he wondered just how long he could make one glass of *tequila* last.

"Ah, Hornitos," Joaquin refilled his glass and raised it high. "You know, Paco? This town only exists because the *gringos* did not want us around. We *Mexicanos* were the ones who found the gold in Quartzburg, and then they ran us out and stole our claims. So, we came here and started our own town, and the *Americanos* are afraid to come, even though we find gold here too."

"I see a few *Anglos* on the street, *amigo*," Paco said as Teresa returned with another girl, who immediately attached herself to him.

"They are outcasts the same as we are. They come here

and are welcomed because the *Americanos* on the hill don't want them. They become the same as Joaquin and Manuel, even you my friend. Do you think you would be welcome there, Paco?"

"I don't know. I've never been to Quartzburg. I only go to Dogtown. Some of the *Americanos* are nice to me, like Señor Carpenter and Señor Hanky. But others, like Pod Randell and the judge I do not care for." Paco downed his drink and Joaquin refilled the glass.

"Si. And what about those who do not like you, my friend? What is your crime? It is because you are Mexican. No?"

"Si."

Teresa began applying some salve to Joaquin's wounded cheek as he talked.

"Now tell me, my friend, before Anita takes you away from me. What of this Señor Hanky? I hear this name before. Who is he?"

"Josiah Russell. He was a Texas Ranger, but now he is an old man. He is a friend to The Señora Garcia, and has been trying to help her. But he got shot in the leg by the *gringos* who wish to take her land away. Me and Tex save him, I think."

"Ah, that is where I hear of him before. He is supposed to be a famous fighter from Texas. I would like to meet this man some day."

The bandit turned to study Juan for a long moment.

"Señor, I think your glass is empty."

The girl leaned close and kissed him on the ear. "Come, *mi amor*. Angela will take you to paradise."

Chapter 34

The warm sun shining through the window felt good as Juan stretched his muscular frame. The mass of hair and soft skin beside him moaned as it moved and wiggled closer. His body tingled as he felt her lips caressing his skin from the side to the center of his chest.

"You like Angela?"

"Si, I like you very much."

"*Bueno,*" she said rolling her nude body on top of him and kissing his lips. Her breasts pressed against his chest as he ran a hand down her back and across her firm buttocks.

"Tell me what it's like on the rancho. Is it nice?" She ran her tongue along his neck and under his ear.

"It is very pretty. There is much water and grass, and more cattle than you can count. There is one big *hacienda* with many rooms where Señora Garcia lives. Then there are many small houses where all the vaqueros and their families live."

"Where do you live? Do you have your own *hacienda*?"

Juan laughed and kissed her lips. "No, Señorita, I don't have my own *hacienda.* The Señora only has them built for those who marry. I sleep in a large room with many other vaqueros who are not married."

"Ahhhh," she said raising on her elbows to study his face. "So *mi amante* has no wife then?"

"No, I was not so lucky as the others."

"But you are so handsome. I thought you would have a *chica* and many *bambinos.*"

Her smile intoxicated him and he found himself wanting to ask the ageless question, *why does a pretty chica like you do this*?, but he kissed her long and hard instead. She broke the kiss and patted him on the chest as she pursed her lips.

"Let me ask you a question, Juan Gonzalez. When you go back to your rancho and Señora Garcia, would you take Angela Vasquez with you?"

He didn't know what to say. He just lay there and stared at the pretty girl lying on top of him open-mouthed.

"No? It is because I'm a *prostituta*, right? Well, no matter," she said and patted him on the chest again before rolling over to sit up. "It was just a thought."

"No, *chica*," he said pulling her back down on him. "I'm sorry. I was surprised, that's all. I never dreamed you'd want to go with me. I thought you were just doing it because it was your job."

"*Bueno,* it is my job. Forget it."

"No, I won't forget it. Why do you ask me, then say 'forget it'?"

"It was a silly idea. You are a good boy, Juan Gonzalez. You don't need a *prostituta* dragging you down. Go back to your rancho and your Señora." She kissed him on the forehead and climbed out of bed.

"You could at least tell me why you asked the question."

"Why? Look around you. This," she said with a sweeping motion of her arm, "is my *hacienda.* This little room in the back of *La Bonito Mujer* with all its noise is my home. This is where I live, Juan. I bring men here who pay me to sleep in my bed." She slipped her arms into the sleeves of her dress and let it fall over her head.

"But why did you ask me?"

"Because I have no family." A tear trickled from the corner of her eye and mapped its way down her cheek as she glared at him. "My mother and father both were killed two winters ago in a snow storm in the mountains. I do not know where my brothers are. One of them used to ride for Joaquin, but he left six months ago and no one has seen him since."

"You still haven't answered my question, Angela. Why me?"

"Because you are a nice boy, and you live on that big rancho with all the cattle. Why else would I ask you?" She dropped to the edge of the bed and reached for her shoes.

"Ahhhh, foolish me. I thought perhaps you were asking me because you liked me. I don't know such things," he said crawling out the opposite side of the bed and pulling his pants on. "I even thought you might love me in some small way. That way, I might have taken you with me, Angela Vasquez."

He stopped buckling his belt long enough to glance at her. She suddenly looked lost standing open-mouthed as another tear fell. He wanted to take her in his arms but she hadn't said the right words.

"It doesn't matter to me if you are a *prostituta*. I'm a *arma guerrero* who rode with Jack Slade and Chico Cruz. I've used a gun and a knife since I was ten years old, so what does it matter what you've done. But just to run away, *chica*," he held his open palms toward her, "would be like leaving one burden for another. It wouldn't work." He slipped his boots on and grabbed his gunbelt.

"I must see Chico Cruz."

"Juan, *por favor*? Juan?"

"*Adios,* Señorita." He could still hear her pleading as he closed the door and walked away.

~   ~   ~

"Juan!" Chico Cruz grabbed him in a back-breaking hug. "It's good to see you again. I hear you came to town with Joaquin. Are you riding with him now?" The bandit nodded toward his competitor leaning by the door.

"No, Chico. I still ride for Doña Leonida. She treats me and Paco good, like family."

"Ah, then what brings you to Hornitos? You come just to say hello?"

"Si, among other things." He accepted the glass of brandy offered, and continued as Chico passed glasses to Joaquin and Paco.

"Señora Garcia has many troubles, Chico. There are some men who wish to run her off her land. They have already killed Don Rudolfo and his brother. They will kill her too, if they are not stopped."

"Why don't you and Paco kill them, then?"

"They are many, Señor."

"You wish me to take my men and kill them for you?" He looked indignant.

"No," Juan said with a laugh. "There is no need for that, Chico. The Señora has many men too, and we will kill them. But they are poorly armed, while the *gringos* have good weapons. The Señora wishes to buy many guns. She wishes to pay much for them. Will you sell?" He pulled the bag of gold coins from his vest pocket and dumped them on the table.

"*Chihuahua, amigo*," Joaquin said watching the coins bounce and wobble noisily in front of them. "You were carrying that around all the time you were with me? *Caramba*."

"How many guns does she need?"

Juan glanced toward Paco who answered for him. "Sixty, maybe seventy rifles, some *pistolas* and bullets."

"*Madra mia, amigos,* I do not have that many. That is a lot."

"Can you get them? There is more money if that is not enough," Juan said watching the man's expression intently.

"Si," Chico said thoughtfully. "What you think, Joaquin? We do not work together much, but the Señora Garcia needs help with the *gringos* who wish her harm. You know where we can get the guns?"

"Si, but it will take some work."

"The Armory near San Andreas?"

"Si. The *gringos* there do not know how to use the guns anyway. We shall take them and put them to good use for the Señora."

"Then it is settled. Come, we celebrate and ride out in the morning," Chico said putting an arm around Juan as they walked toward the door.

Chapter 35

"**Now I** wonder what the hell she's up to," Tex said as he leaned on the porch railing and watched Leonida in the courtyard.

"I would say she's talking to the padre," Sean said with a smirk. "What makes you think she's up to anything?"

"'Cause she stormed off like a buffalo in heat the day you patched ol' Hanky up. She said she wanted to see Juan and Paco both in her office. Now, we ain't seen neither of them since, and it's been almost a week now. And there's nesters movin' in all over the place, and she ain't done a blasted thing about it, even though I done told her so. She don't talk to no one but them vaqueros of hers, and she does that kinda' sneaky-like. So you tell me, what's she up to?"

"What are you talking about? She talks to each and every one of us every day. I heard her talking to you at the breakfast table this morning."

"That's not what I mean, and you know it, you lunkhead. She don't say nothin' worth a busted poker chip. Not like she used to, anyway," he said, chewing on a wooden match stem. "Remember how she used to sit and discuss things? She'd ask yer opinion on how she could hold on to this place. Now she don't even talk to her daddy about it, 'cause I done asked him, and he's plum worried about her. Say's he's ready to send her back to Mexico, but she don't want to go."

"Well, I hope he doesn't. I don't want her to go," Sean said, watching the figure dressed in black.

"I hope she don't neither, but not because I'm all moony over her like you are. I just want her to hang on to what's rightfully hers. And I'm dying to see Pod Randell and that damned judge get what's coming to them."

"I'm not 'moony' over her. What ever gave you that idea?"

"Hell, Pard, everyone knows yer stuck on the widder. Ya sit around watching her like an old dog waiting for a handout. Can't say as I blame you none. She's about as purdy as a newborn colt, and nice too."

"I suppose that's some sort of compliment to her, but back to what we were talking about. What makes you think anything is going to happen to Henry Baines and Pod Randell? They've surrounded themselves with a bunch of hired gunmen, and they've literally been getting away with murder. I was hoping that Hanky would be able to do something. Bear told me he was the best. But they even put him out of commission."

"Huh," Tex said as he rolled himself a cigarette. "You don't think they've really stopped him, do you?"

"Well yes, I do. That's a nasty wound he has in his leg."

"Hell, I fought right beside him once't when he had three arrows stickin' in him. Besides, he's got something to fight over now. They kilt his hoss."

"Damn, not you too? That's all I've heard the last four days, 'they kilt my hoss'. What is it with you Texans? You grieve over a dead horse more than most people grieve over a human being."

"Oh, I plum forgot," Tex said, lighting his smoke. "You're one of them funny-talkin' ferners. They prob'ly don't got no hosses where you come from. That's prob'ly why you ride that jackass of your'n."

"I'll have you know they had horses in Ireland long before they were ever here in America."

"So you say. If that's true, they were prob'ly little scrawny things, and it don't matter if they get blowed all to hell. Now you take a real Texas bred cayuse like mine, or that old roan of Hanky's. They's almost human to begin with. They think like a true hombre. You don't got to tell 'em what to do when it comes to herding cattle, 'cause it's already bred into 'em natural like. And they'll tell you when there's injuns or outlaws around too, 'cause they just know. They can smell a skunk a mile off. And they'll run their heart out for you, just like Hanky says, or die trying.

"Naw, I understand his grievin', 'cause that was a true Texas hoss. And I'll tell you what pard, its one thing to shoot a man, but it's down right high-lay-shoos to kill his hoss. Those men what done that deserve to be hung. And believe me, that little ol' hole in his leg ain't gonna stop him none. That's why he's been in there cleanin' and oiling them hoglegs of his. Those boys are gonna pay, even if he has to crawl to town."

"Even if he could get to town, what could one man do? You said yourself that they've hired a bunch of gunmen."

"You've never seen a riled Texas Ranger, have you Pard? That old geezer will make up for any three or four men Judge Henry Bances can find around here. Besides, who says he'll be alone? I plan on being there too. I got me a personal score to settle with Pod Randell, and she's lying in that bedroom upstairs. And I thought you'd kinda like to be along for the ride too. Ain't you got a little score of your own?" Tex said, slapping Sean's arm.

"Besides," he continued as they watched Paco and Juan ride in from the direction of the river leading several pack-mules, "when some of these Mexicans get angry enough, you're gonna see all hell break loose. I fought 'em down in Texas, and it weren't no picnic."

"Where do you suppose they were, and what do you think they are carrying?" Sean said as Leonida ran to meet the vaqueros at the bunkhouse.

"My guess is they're carrying pure hell."

Chapter 36

"**Aaaaah!**" Rosa gasped, and bolted for the door. They had been sitting together on the porch drinking their afternoon tea when the wagon pulled into the courtyard escorted by Juan and three other vaqueros.

"Rosa, what is it?" Leonida said, grabbing her arm.

"Nooo!" She yanked her arm away, but Leonida latched onto the girl's skirt and held it fast. "Let me go. *Por favor*," she cried, staring wide-eyed at the wagon.

"Maria, Señor Hanky, come quick," she called through the open door.

"What is it, Señora?" Maria said as they both appeared in the doorway at the same time. Leonida released her grasp on the girl and she darted past the maid in an effort to get inside, but the ranger caught her in his arms.

"Hold on now. No one's gonna hurt you," he said craning to see the wagon. Leonida turned and walked briskly toward the waiting men. "Watch yerself now, ma'am."

"You Mrs. Garcia?" the thin gray-headed man in the wagon spoke.

"Si."

"You speak English, or only Mex?"

"I speak several languages, Señor. Who are you, and what brings you to our Rancho?"

"I'm Ambrose Brice, and I come to get what belongs to me."

"I've heard much about you, Señor Brice, and I must say that your appearance has not disappointed me. Not only are you dirty, but the goats that Julio Perez raises have better manners." His jaw dropped as the *vaqueros* laughed and whistled.

"Now, wait a minute. I didn't come here to be insulted by no Mex, I only come to get what belongs to me."

"I am afraid you are mistaken, Señor. I have nothing that belongs to you, and you are not welcome. Be gone," she said with a wave of the back of her hand.

"Hold on now, that girl is my property. I got...." he stood to his feet inside the wagon and stuck a hand inside his coat only to freeze as Juan pulled a pistol and cocked the hammer.

"What do you have?"

"Just a piece of paper. It's signed by her pa, saying she's mine."

"Let me see it." She held out a gloved hand.

"All right, but can you read?"

She took the folded paper from his trembling hand and turned her back on him as she scanned the document. "I read French, English, Latin and Spanish, if it is any of your concern, Señor. And you must either think I am stupid, or you are awfully ignorant yourself." She folded the paper and handed it back to him. "It says nothing that is of any interest to anyone here on *Rancho Manantial Escondido*, now be gone."

"It says that I bought and paid for that girl over there. She's been here long enough. Any fool can see she's all healed up, now. And havin' her here's costing me money, so hand her over."

"It might say that, Señor, but it is only signed by an X,

and since Rosa's father is not here, you have no way of proving that the X was made by Señor Carillo, now do you?"

"It is his mark, and I can bring five or six witnesses, if you want me to."

"No, that won't be necessary. But, since slavery has never been legal in California, I am not letting you take Rosa Carillo back to work as a *prostituta* in your saloon, so don't ask me again."

"Now, hold on one minute. You can't do that."

"I wouldn't push it too hard if I was you, mister," Hanky said as he stepped forward and turned his right shoulder toward the wagon. He still held Rosa in his left arm. "This lady's been beaten, and seen her husband and his brother murdered. I'm surprised she's let you stand there jawin' this long. Take my advice and shut your mouth before one of these *vaqueros* does it for you permanently."

"But that girl belongs to me. She can't do that."

"Juan?" Leonida pulled her veil tight and tossed one end over her shoulder. "Show Señor Brice the road to town, and if he ever sets foot on *Rancho Manantial Escondido* again, shoot him."

"*Bueno, Señora. Muchacos, anda, pronto.*" One of the men snatched the reins from the stunned man standing inside the wagon, and spurred his horse. The vehicle lunged forward, throwing Ambrose backward over the seat and into the bed. With whoops and whistles, the *vaqueros* disappeared beyond the corrals and over the rise toward the river.

"*Señora, que te Dios bendiga,*" Rosa said, running to fall at her feet and grab her around the knees. "I will serve you for ever." She kissed her dress over and over.

"No, *chica*, you won't have to serve me. And you won't have to serve those dirty men at that *gringo's* saloon anymore. You are Señorita Rosa Carillo, and you will make a fine wife for your Texas *vaquero* one of these days.

~   ~   ~

Maria wiped the tears from her eyes with her apron before serving tea. Leonida could still feel the maid's strong arms around her as she held her and Rosa both in a bear-hug.

"Well, now I couldn't of done it no better, ma'am," Hanky said, leaning back and rolling himself a smoke. "Ceptin' maybe I'd a blowed a hole through that varmint. Don't know why Tommy ain't done it yet hisself."

"He didn't know about the paper for a long time," Rosa said, sipping her tea. "He kept talking about getting married. I was ashamed, so I never told him. I just kept telling him to wait a while."

"How did he find out?" Leonida said with a furrowed brow. "He told me the day he brought you here."

"Señor Brice told him after the Sheriff beat me. Tex said he was bringing me here to see Doctor Sean, but Señor Brice said he owns me and I must go back when I am well."

"What ever happened to your father, Rosa?" Leonida said. "I asked Tex, and he said no one has seen or heard from him since he left you at that horrible place."

"It is true. I don't know what happened to him. One night a dirty man who was drunk told me they found my papa dead in Hornitos. He said a man shot him because he was cheating at cards."

"Do you think he was telling the truth?" Hanky said, striking a match on his boot sole.

"I think no. *Papa* never played cards. Not even when I am small."

"Bastards. Excuse me, ma'am."

"Speaking of fathers," Maria said, banging an empty cup in front of the ranger. "Why don't you treat your own son like one?"

"Tommy? Who told you he was my boy?"

"He told Señor Kilkenney, and Señor Kilkenney told Señora Leonida. And Señora Leonida told me."

"And now everyone from here to New York knows he's my boy," Hanky said with a grin. "Well, pour that coffee and I'll tell you about that one." He shifted in the chair and stretched his legs as she poured the black liquid.

"It's like this. His mother and I settled down on the Panhandle and started ranchin'. We was just youngsters ourselves back then. It weren't too long after he was born that she took sick, and up and died of the fever. Something just seemed to die inside of me when I buried that woman. I sorta left the place to my foreman, George Burwell and his wife, and started kinda roamin' around. They was raising Tommy like he was one of their own, so I didn't never worry too much about him.

"Well, I joined up and fought along side of Sam Houston during the war. Guess I was sorta hopin' to get myself kilt, but it never happened. Then I joined up with the Rangers after the war and kept on moving. I always planned on going back and staying, when I got the hurt out, but I never did."

"You never returned to see your son at all?" Leonida said.

"Oh, sure I did. Once in a while I'd drop by and spend a few days here and there. See how he was doing and all. Taught him how to use a gun. But I'd never stay. Just couldn't get the move out of me. Guess it hurt the boy, 'cause he started calling hisself Burwell, instead of Russell. Can't say as I blame him none. And when he up and joined the Rangers hisself, I didn't tell no one his real name was Russell."

"He was a Texas Ranger?" Rosa said, wide-eyed.

"Sure. He didn't tell you?" She shook her head. "Well, he was, and a damned fine one, too. We rode together for a while, and fought side by side. Stood off some angry Caddo with me down by the Rio Grande a few years back. If it hadn't been for him, I might not be here today. Them screaming devils put three arrows in me that day."

"But you were trying to arrest him," Maria said shaking her head.

"Sure I was. He broke the law."

"*Caramba*, he makes no sense at all." The maid turned to the other women and threw up her hands.

"He shot a man, and that's agin the law."

"But, Señor, he says that man was trying to shoot him because of his daughter," she said, leaning across the table to stare him in the eye.

"And he was. But it's still agin the law. You just don't go around shooting people. It's not right, no matter who you are. If this here was a state instead of a territory, I'd be the first to call in a U. S. Marshall and let him handle the situation in Dogtown. But seeing as it ain't no state yet, we got to handle things a little different. But shooting folks just ain't right, and my boy broke the law when he done it."

"Are you telling me that you would have rather seen your son shot by an angry father than defend himself?" Leonida said.

"No, didn't say that atall. I woulda' probably done the same thing, except I wouldn't of run like he done. 'Cause I knowed ol' Judge Bates was gonna let him go. Like I done said awhile back, that little hussy was no good anyways, and up and married Slade the minute Tommy was outa sight. He wouldn't of spent no time in jail atall."

"Then why did you bother chasing him?" Maria said.

"Because it were my job. Don't you understand, woman? The law's the law, and he broke it."

"What would have happened if you caught him?" Rosa said.

"We would've had a tussle. He woulda tried to shoot my leg off, or I'd of had to bore him, one way or the other."

"You would have shot your own son? *Madre mia*, you are disgusting, *gringo*." Rosa pushed her chair away from the table.

"Didn't say I was trying to catch him too hard, did I? That Mustang of mine woulda caught that old cayuse of his one day out, ifin' I'd wanted him to. But if he was gonna run, I was gonna teach him a lesson. So, I follered him plumb outa Texas. And that's the way its gonna be 'til he's willing to stand before a judge and declare himself, 'cause he broke the law." Hanky finished by slamming his palm on the table.

Leonida spilled her tea laughing. "Have you told him

this?"

"Hell no. I ain't seen him in almost two years before I got here. Besides, I don't think he's sorry enough yet."

"Señor, it's a long way between Texas and California. Don't you think he's sorry, just a little?" Rosa said.

"Maybe, but he ain't showed it yet. That is, unless it's his standing by you and Mrs. Garcia here the way he does. I ain't never seen him stick by no woman too long before. Now, if he marries you like he says he's gonna do, I'll know he's sorry," he said, touching her cheek with his palm. "You've made quite a difference in his life, little lady."

"Well, Señor," Leonida said, standing to her feet. "You might as well get ready to forgive your son, because I know for a fact that this *chica* is going to be your daughter-in-law."

Chapter 37

Arturo crouched low and leaned his head against the wall to listen. If anyone saw him, he'd just say that his leg was hurting and he stopped to rest. It was believable, he thought. After all, what harm could a twelve-year-old Mexican boy who looked much younger do by sitting between two buildings and resting his head against the stone wall of the city jail. No one else knew of the missing mortar that left a gap between two stones allowing him to hear the conversation taking place inside.

"Hope ya don't mind me sayin' this, judge, but there is an easier way of goin' about it." The voice matched that of the new red-headed man called Rusty.

Someone struck a match against the wall and Arturo smelled the faint odor of tobacco. It was quiet except for the sound of someone drumming his fingers on the desk.

"Well, I'm waiting."

"There's only a couple of ways across that river as it is. That bridge and one boat further upstream. So, if it was me, I'd just put some men at each place and stop anyone coming or going out of there. She's bound to show up sooner or later."

"Well, Mr. Pardeen, I must admit that is more intelligent than anything else I've heard this evening, but it still isn't good enough. Winter's coming, and when the rains hit no one's going to be crossing that river until spring anyway."

"What do you wanna do then? Stealing their cattle didn't work. We only got some men killed doin' that." Arturo knew that voice well. It was Pod Randell's.

"I want you to go ahead and stake some men at those places and stop people like he said. But I also want some one inside the place causing all sorts of hell. Kill anything that moves. You hear me? I want that bitch outa there."

"Yes, sir." Arturo didn't recognize the voice.

"And one thing more. Someone's getting word to them about what we're doing. I'm as sure of it as anything I've ever been in my life. We've tried to rustle cattle three times and they've caught us three times, and killed four of our men and wounded another. If I find out it's one of you right here in this room, I'm personally going to kill you real slow. Got that?"

The door opened and he heard boots scrape on the wooden walk way out front. A shadow swept over him and Arturo found himself staring into the face of Shavers.

"Hey, Pod, come look what we have here."

"What are you doin' there, boy?" The Sheriff grabbed at his arm.

"*Por que?*"

"You heard me," he said dragging Arturo to his feet.

"Ow, Señor, *por favor*," he said hobbling and pointing toward the leg with the ragged splints.

"Aw, he's that crippled kid what limps around here all the time," Curley said.

"What's going on here?" Judge Baines said, blowing clouds of smoke from his pipe as he rounded the corner.

"Shavers found this Mex hiding here between the buildings." Pod gave Arutro a shove and he fell at the judge's feet.

"That right? What were you doing there, boy?"

"*Por que? No comprender, Señor.*"

"Don't give me that. You speak English. I've seen you hanging around Ike's store sweeping floors myself."

"Ike speaks Mex." The voice came from one of the men in back called Montana.

"What?"

"I said Ike speaks to the kid in Mex. I heard him jabbering away at him myself when I was in there this afternoon buying some chew."

"Alright," the judge said and gave Arturo's leg a kick. "Get the hell out of here and stay away."

Arturo was determined they wouldn't hear him cry as he limped away with his homemade crutch. The pain from the judge's boot made him light headed, but he was not going to give them the satisfaction. He never uttered a sound as tears streamed down his face. Not even when he heard one of the men behind him.

"Gutsy little son-of-a-bitch, ain't he?"

~   ~   ~

Alice Carpenter slapped the reins and urged the horse onward at a gentle lope as the buggy bounced and lurched toward the bridge crossing the Mokelumne River. Her heart began to pound in her chest like the hooves of the beast that pulled her onward. This would be the first time she had to make the crossing by herself, but Ike felt there was no time to have Arturo hitch the team to the lumbering wagon, and told her to go by herself using the much faster buggy. He wrote the note and hid it in the bottom of the basket she packed with goodies from their shelves. Now the hooves were pounding on the wooden planks with the swirling waters below. She closed her eyes and held her breath. *God, my Lord and Saviour, pleeeease save your child.* The roar of shod hooves on wood gave way to soft earth again and she opened her eyes the instant three men sprang from the bushes and grabbed for the reins. She yelled and tried to urge the beast onward but it was too late. The buggy ground to a halt.

"Where you goin' in such a hurry, little lady?" said a tall man with dirty blond hair, walking toward her. His face was covered with three day's growth of stubble and dirt.

"I'm going to see my friend. Now would you please let go of my horse?"

"Now, yer friend wouldn't happen ta be the widder Garcia, would it?"

"Yes, if it's any of your business. Now let me go." She tried slapping at him with the buggy whip but he caught it in his hand.

"Feisty little filly, ain't she Slinger?"

"Yeah," said the one off to her left. The man was almost as dirty as the one holding on to the whip. He had dark hair and was short and fat. "Don't suppose she's the one sneaking messages to them, do ya?"

"Wouldn't surprise me none. What's in the basket?"

"Just some things for Mrs. Garcia, and its none of your business."

"Oooeee, I told you she was a fiery one," he said with a laugh. "Guess I'll just have a look-see." He reached for the basket in the seat beside her but pulled back with a cry as an arrow imbedded itself in his forearm up to the feathers.

"Damn," Slinger said and drew his gun.

"I wouldn't do that if I was you." The voice came from behind a tree about twenty yards ahead. "There's a couple of dozen Injuns scattered all around you that's just hankerin' ta poke some holes in yer hide."

Slinger spun around in a circle with his gun cocked.

"Don't push it, mister. They wouldn't like anything better than to poke you so full of holes that you wouldn't float down the river. Better drop the gun."

He lowered the pistol and they were instantly surrounded by Indians. Baca came from the same clump of shrubs her would-be captors had been hiding in, carrying a lance. She recognized the tall man using a cane as the one who had introduced himself to her in the store a couple of weeks earlier. The man holding the horse tried to pull away from an Indian.

"Don't be a damn fool, let him have the gun," Hanky said as he approached the buggy. General Flores joined them from behind a clump of bushes to their left. "Y'all are pretty lucky, ya know that, don't you? These Yokuts really wanted to peel yer hide off and feed you to the varmints somewheres."

"They shot me, dammit. And we didn't do nothing to nobody," the one with the arrow in his arm said.

"Aw, quit yer cryin'. Yer actin' like a baby." He leaned his cane against the buggy and pulled a knife from his belt to cut the head off the arrow. The man fell to his knees with another cry of pain as Hanky gave the shaft a jerk.

"Told you you was a baby," he said tossing the bloody shaft to one of the Indians. "Whadda ya think, General? Whole different crop of bad men nowadays, ain't they? Not nearly as tough as them I used to tangle with when I was a young pup. How about you?"

"Si, they are stupid and cry when they get caught. These were not even worth bothering with. It is a good thing we rescued them from Señora Carpenter when we did, or she might have really hurt them."

Alice found herself wishing she had taken the time to learn Spanish as well as Ike, when Baca nudged one of the men with the blunt end of his lance and said something that made the General laugh.

"What'd he say?" the man backed against the buggy.

"Baca says your skin will make a fine pair of chaps when it is dried."

"Oh God, tell him no, mister. Please don't let him skin me."

"See, I told you he was yeller." Hanky spit and wiped his mouth with the back of his hand. The Indian said something else as he gave the man one more hefty shove with the lance and walked away laughing.

"I am sorry to tell you this, but Baca changes his mind. He thinks your skin might be cowardly like you are and would more than likely make poor chaps. You may keep your skin." The man slumped against the buggy in relief.

"Whadda ya think, General? The way I see it, these feller's hosses and guns, and whatever else they might have on them, is property of the rancho now, and Baca and his people are welcome to them." Hanky shoved his hat back on his head and leaned heavily on the cane.

"Si, but they are not such good horses as my daughters'. They will probably eat them."

"Now, wait a minute. You can't take our horses and guns." It was the man with the wounded arm who spoke.

"Mister, you're lucky to be gettin' away with your life. What Baca really wanted to do was take yer head and stick it on a pole somewheres to let coyotes like you know you ain't welcome here. Now if I was you, I'd get myself back across that bridge while I still had a head and high-tail it back into town. All of you." Hanky raised his voice and gave a sweeping motion with his arm. "And have that horse-doctor of yourn look at that arm before it festers up on ya."

All three men scrambled across the bridge and turned to look, but took off again as several Indians raised their weapons in the air and gave a piercing yell. Baca and his men broke out in laughter and pounded each other on the back as the men stumbled along with a clumsy gait in their heavy boots.

"General, how'd you like to escort Mrs. Carpenter to the house while I mosey on along with these Injuns?"

"It will be my pleasure." Jose removed his sombero and took a deep bow. "*Buenos dias, Señora* Carpenter. I am so sorry for the delay. My daughter will be happy you have come to visit her."

"Thank you, General Flores. And I do appreciate you and Mr. Hanky coming to my rescue. All of you," Alice said, glancing around at Baca and the Indians. "I must admit, I was pretty frightened."

He said something to one of the Indians, who ran to retrieve a horse which he tied to the back of the buggy. Alice picked up the basket as Jose climbed in beside her and took the reins. With a click of his tongue and a gentle shake of the reins, she was on her way again. She held her trembling hands in front of her and started laughing.

"I want you to know, I was really scared."

"We were too, Señora." He glanced at her from the corner of his eye. He was indeed a handsome man with his chiseled features and light brown skin. The flecks of gray in his moustache and around his temples made him look distinguished. "Those *gringos* might have hurt you."

"How did you know I was coming?"

"We didn't, Señora. One of the Indians saw those men hiding by the bridge and told Baca, and Baca told me. We were spying on them when we saw your buggy coming. I was very frightened that you might get hurt. But you did well, Señora." He turned and smiled. "The way you fought them was *muy bueno.*"

"Well, I didn't do that much."

"Oh, but you did. You hit at him with the whip, and you talked. All this was important, for it gave us time. And I have no doubt, Señora that if he had touched you, he would have grabbed hold of an angry *gato,* eh?"

"So, I'm a cat am I?" She held up her hands to examine her fingernails and they both laughed.

"Oh, I almost forgot," she said digging to the bottom of the basket to pull out the envelope. "My husband said to give you this. He said it was important."

He handed her the reins and opened the envelope. He frowned as he read the letter, then returned it to the envelope and stuffed it into his pocket.

"Si, it is just as I thought," he said taking back the reins. "Arturo listens to them say that they are going to block the bridge and ferry across the river. They do not wish us to get food and medicine from town while they try to attack us with small skirmishes here and there. They will be back at the bridge in the morning, and this time they will not be so easily taken."

"But, why? What do they hope to accomplish with all

this violence?"

"They try to get my daughter to leave the house so they can kill her. Señora," he said placing a gloved hand on her arm as he stopped the buggy in the courtyard. "Tell Arturo and your husband to be very careful. I am pleased they have chosen to help us, but if these men ever find out they have been spying for us, they will certainly kill them both."

<h1 style="text-align:center">Chapter 38</h1>

"Why do you feed the black birds? Most people don't like them. They eat the corn and cause much mess. They are also noisy."

"You could say the same about most people, couldn't you?" Leonida said as she threw another handful of meat scraps to the hungry crows.

"*Si.* I never thought of it that way before, but *si*, you are right." Rosa sat at the edge of the fountain with her head in her hands as she trailed her bare feet in the water. The visit from Alice Carpenter had been a short one and the men had disappeared, leaving them alone. It was the first day she had spent more than a few minutes outside and the warm sunshine felt good on her back.

"*Señora?*"

"*Si?*"

"Do you think *Señor* Tex really likes me?" There was a long pause and when she looked up, she saw the intent gaze of the Doña's green eyes bearing down on her. It made her uncomfortable and she quickly turned away. "*Perdonname, por favor, Señora.* I should not have asked such a stupid question."

"No, it is I who ask your forgiveness, Rosa."

She snapped her head around as Doña Leonida put her hands on her shoulders. *She called me by my given name.* She tried making her head a moving target, but Leonida took her chin and gently forced her to look at her.

"It was not a stupid question at all. What made you say that?"

"It is....it was...." She pulled from Leonida's grasp and turned her back on her. "You are Doña Leonida, and I am Rosa Carillo from The Rusty Rail. It is a shame for you to speak my name."

"And who told you that?"

"No one tells me." Her voice drew the attention of a group of children as she stood with both feet in the water and turned to face the young Doña. "No one had to tell me. I am not *tonta.*" She gestured flippantly with her hand and gave a slight curtsey with her hips.

"I never thought you were stupid, Rosa. Why are you acting like this?"

"It is custom that people of position like you don't mention those like me in public."

"Well, damn your customs."

She caught her breath as her hand leaped to her opened mouth. She had made Doña Leonida angry enough to use profanity.

"What have you to say to that, Rosa Carillo?"

What is there to say? The vaqueros will shoot at me and the women will throw rocks. They will say a prostituta has insulted the Señora, and I will have to leave this place and go back to town as soon as possible.

Leonida removed her shoes and hiked her black skirt, revealing white ankles as she stepped over the bricks into the water beside Rosa.

"Señora, you shouldn't...."

"Shouldn't what, Rosa? What is it that I shouldn't do? You and my father will get along very well. You both know what I should or should not do. 'Señora, do this,' and 'Señora do that.' Or, 'Leonida, it is not proper that you should act that way.'" The Doña lowered her voice and shook her index finger angrily. "Why, you two are so much alike, you should forget about Tex and marry my father."

Rosa sat on the bricks and held her sides laughing. "Ahhhhh, I'm sorry, Señora, but you are funny."

"I'm glad you think so. But you make me angry, *chica.* First, you ask me if I think your Texas vaquero likes you, then you insult me when I don't answer right away." Her kick sent a spray of water toward the center of the fountain.

"I thought you were offended by my asking such a question."

"And why would a question about love offend me?"

"I have no idea. I just thought that...."

"Well?" She stood with her hands on her hips as Rosa studied the bricks she was sitting on. "No, look at me, *chica.* Come on, look really closely. Am I so old and ugly that I cannot feel or think about love ever again?" Rosa lay back on the bricks with a giggle as several children edged toward the fountain to better hear and see the excitement.

"Yes, I think your Texas vaquero loves you very much," Leonida said as she scooped a double-handful of water and dumped it on Rosa.

"Ahhhhh," she came off the bricks wiping the wet hair out of her eyes. Doña Leonida was standing before her laughing as six or seven children jumped into the fountain with squeals and splashes. Leonida let out a peel of glee as she kicked water at one of them and instantly received a healthy dose in return. She lowered her head and glared at Rosa as a grin crept across her lips. The black veil hung dripping over her shoulders and her blond hair was nothing but a wet mass plastered to her cheeks.

"Señora, what are you going to do?"

"I am going to give you a bath, Rosa Carillo. I am going to wash some of that stuffiness out of you." She scooped another double handful and threw it in her face and called upon the children for help. Rosa was instantly engulfed in water from all sides as the children joined in on the fun. She gasped a deep breath as she closed her eyes and fought back, moving forward blindly. She felt the edge of the black skirt as she bent over to scoop more water and gave it a tug. The Señora squealed as she lost her footing and drug Rosa into the water with her.

"Aiiiieeee," she said with a laugh as she pulled from Leonida's grasp and pushed the hair out of her eyes. Something was wrong. The laughing and splashing had stopped, and except for the trickling of the fountain, it was deathly quiet. Leonida was sitting in the water and staring past her with a pale, frightened expression. The Señora stood to her feet and Rosa followed suit, afraid to turn and see what evil was waiting. Then she heard the familiar snort of a horse. They had been having so much fun that none of them had heard the riders enter the courtyard.

General Flores sat on the bay looking stern and disgusted at the spectacle before him. Tex sat with one leg draped across the pommel grinning while he calmly rolled a cigarette. She also recognized Paco and Juan, but there were three other men she had never seen before dressed in dark trousers and sweaters. Two of them had on stocking caps, while the older stocky one with the beard wore a black hat with a bill and a gold eagle on the front.

"Good afternoon, Mrs. Garcia." The man with the eagle nodded and tipped his cap. "I hope you remember me. We only met for a few minutes one time. I'm Jonathan MacDougal." He paused for a few seconds while the children scurried away.

"I pilot The North Star? The trading ship your husband has always done business with."

"Si, I remember Señor MacDougal," she said with a small curtsey. "We were just...." She tipped her head to one side and extended her palms.

"Having a little fun. I know, and I don't blame you one little bit, either." Rosa liked the man's smile. "Your father told us about Rudolfo and the trouble you've been having, and we really are sincerely sorry, ma'am."

"*Gracias.*"

"Well, if it isn't too much bother, ma'am, we'd like to take a little of your time and talk over some business. May we?"

"Si," she said with a nod. "My father will show you to the *hacienda* and I will join you shortly."

"Thank you. And I hope I didn't spoil your fun too much," he said with a grin as he turned the horse away. Her father followed, but only after one more stern look from his icy gray eyes. Paco, Juan and the two sailors followed closely behind, leaving Tex who sat calmly smoking his cigarette.

"*Compermiso, Señorita*, but I must go," Leonida said meekly as she stepped from the fountain and picked up her shoes. Rosa watched Doña Leonida patter across the brick courtyard in her bare feet and disappear into the house.

"Well, looks like y'all were havin' yerselves a passel of fun."

"I am sorry, Tex," Rosa said, watching her toes through the amber water.

"Na, don't be."

"But the Señora, she will get in trouble with her father. And the people will think badly of her."

"Think so?" She nodded. "I don't. That old coot loves her almost as much as I love you." She snapped her head up to see his smiling face.

"Know what?"

"*Que?*"

"I kinda like the way that dress clings to you when it's all wet." He turned his horse and trotted toward the corral.

~   ~   ~

"He'll be all right ifin' it don't fester up. We'll have to cut his arm off if it does," George Bidwell said, wiping his hands on a dirty towel.

"Well, dammit, make sure it doesn't fester then," Frank

Powell said. The grimy doctor had just bandaged the arrow wound without even washing it.

"Weren't much to do, boy. It'd already stopped bleeding
by the time ya got here. All a man could do was wrap it up and hope fer the best."

"You'd better make sure, 'cause I'll blow your damn head off if it does."

"What I would have liked to see was you blowing the damn head off that old Texas Ranger and that girl's father," Henry Baines said beating the ashes out of his pipe. "Why didn't you?"

"Hell, we told you already. There was a million Injuns 'round us. We couldn't do nothing."

"Oh, I doubt that. The way things have been going around here, there was more than likely only one broken down old Indian riding a jackass. Why in the hell can't I get one of you men to do what he's told?"

"Well, why don't you go shoot 'em yerself if its so easy?"

"I want him out of here this minute." Henry pointed his pipe stem at Frank while he glared at Pod Randell. "Do you understand me? I'm not going to take this any longer. I don't care how you do it, I want him out of here."

"Just calm down, judge," Pod said putting his hands on Henry's shoulders. "I don't blame ya fer gettin' riled. Ol' Frank here needs ta be taken down a notch or two, sure, but he's a good man. Sit down and let's put our hats together and see if we can't figure things out."

Henry sat at the desk while Pod went to the small cupboard in the corner of his office for a bottle and several glasses.

"Now, ya say that that there Carpenter woman was crossin' the bridge when all them showed up?" Pod said filling the glasses.

"Yeah. Pete caught hold of the bridle when the buggy first come over the bridge. I was reaching for the basket to see what was in it when that arrow stuck in my arm."

"Seems to be that they've been making all sorts of runs out to that Mex place, don't it?" Pod sat back and propped his feet on the desk and began rolling a cigarette. "Ol' Ike sent that buckboard of his out there twice last week with his wife and the young Mex boy with the crippled leg. Wonder what she was doin' out there today?"

Henry found himself almost holding his breath as the Sheriff lit his smoke. It wasn't often that Pod Randell had an idea of his own and this one was starting to make sense. He wondered why he hadn't thought of it himself.

"Whadda ya think, Rusty? Someone's been tellin' them everything we're doing, before we even do it."

"Sound's like ya might be on to something, Pod. Want me to check it out?"

"Na, I got somethin' else fer you to do. More important-like." He got up from his chair and refilled everyone's glass. "It's just that we need to be somewheres else when we do our cogitatin', 'cause these walls seems ta have ears. That is, unless it's somethin' we decide we want them to hear."

"Well, it's something that definitely needs to be checked out," Henry said filling his pipe.

"Shore, it do. And I aim to put someone on it real quick like. But I wanna take Rusty and a few others fishin' tomorrow. Never know, we might catch us something real big."

Chapter 39

"*Madre de Dios.*" Maria closed the door behind her.
"I never know why a grown woman, especially one like you,
the Doña Leonida Garcia, would choose to act like a child."

"Now, Maria, we have guests. You see to them, and tell
my father I will be down in a moment."

"But Señora."

"No, no, no," she said shooing the maid away. "I can
take care of myself. Send Rosa in if you wish. She's the one
who started this whole mess in the first place."

"*Bueno*, just let me help you with this," she said
unbuttoning the back of Leonida's dress. "*Niña*?" She took her
by the shoulders and turned her around to look her in the face.

"Si?"

"It was good to hear you laugh again." She kissed her
cheeks and left the room. Leonida had the wet dress off and
was in the process of removing the rest of her clothing when
her door opened and a dripping-wet Rosa entered.

"Oh, *perdon*," she said as she backed out into in the
hallway.

"Come on in." Rosa hesitated, her eyes downcast. Leonida held the top of her undergarments over her breasts and laughed. "Don't be silly, come inside and close the door."

Rosa meekly closed the door behind her without looking up. "It is not permitted to see one's naked body, Señora."

"Si, and I have been told since I was a child that I must wear undergarments when I bathe, for it is a sin to look at my own body, but I don't have time for such foolishness today."

"Señora." The girl gasped as her eyes darted upward.

"*Por que?* Come, we'll discuss this while you help me get dressed." Rosa gasped and covered her mouth as Leonida dropped her undergarments on the floor. "Grab another towel from the chest over in the corner and help dry my hair." She wrapped a towel around her body and sat bent forward as Rosa rubbed her head vigorously.

"Let me ask you, *chica*, do you think it is possible for me to actually bathe and change my clothes without seeing my body at least once in my life?"

"No, but one should try."

"Perhaps, but my mother saw my body many times when I was a child, and Señor Kilkenney saw my body after I had been beaten. And Paco saw me down by the river after the men fled. I had no clothes on then. Does that mean I am going to hell?" The girl stopped rubbing and studied her hard with her brown eyes.

"Look in the bottom drawer of the dresser and find me something to put on while I get a dress," Leonida said with a quick motion of her left hand. She tucked the edge of the towel under her arm and fumbled through the wardrobe.

"Rosa? Has your Texas vaquero ever seen your body?" Leonida glanced over her shoulder in time to see Rosa drop the undergarments on the bed and turn away stifling a sob. "*Chica,* come," she said taking her in her arms. "Come sit with me a moment."

"No," she said trying to pull away.

"But you must." Leonida pulled her close as she sat on

the edge of the bed. "I want to tell you of my husband. I know what they say, but I liked the feel of Rudolfo's hands on my body. I liked to snuggle close to him at night and listen to him snore." Rosa relaxed in her arms. "And I liked to run my fingers across his skin and feel the muscles there. I liked it when he kissed my breasts." Rosa pulled away with a catch of her breath.

"*Que?* Why does that shock you? I liked to kiss him on the chest too. Si. There was much hair to contend with, but I still liked it."

"But, Señora. That means he saw your body."

"Si, and I saw his body too. We were married, Rosa," she said in a whisper while knitting her eyebrows together. "They say when someone is married, they become one person, no?" She nodded. "So, I think that means my body belonged to Rudolfo, and Rudolfo's body belonged to me. I let him kiss my breasts and I kissed him back." She stood and dropped the towel. "Come, help me dress now.

"Does it surprise you to know I actually liked making love to my husband?"

"A little."

"I did. I loved the feel of his body as we lay together. I loved his smell and his caresses. He was a loving and gentle man, Rosa. We were one person. And there was nothing better than when he was inside me." She held the girl at arms length.

"*Chica,* the Holy Father made this body," she said patting herself on the hips and sides. "It is not something for everyone to see, that is for sure. But He sees it, for He sees everything, and He is not ashamed, nor am I. And it is not a sin for me to see my own body, or my husband to touch and feel, or kiss. Nor is it a sin for a young *chica* like you to see me when you help me dress. This I believe with all my heart. Here, help me pick a dress," she said going back to the wardrobe. "There is one good thing about being in mourning. You don't have to fuss over what you are going to wear. Everything is black."

Rosa pulled a dress from the rack and began pulling it

over Leonida's head.

"This is not what you've been told is it, *niña*?"

"No, Señora."

"I believe it to be true. I read it in the Holy Scriptures myself." Rosa's mouth dropped open. "My husband has a copy in his office. He kept it when the former priest died. Rudolfo could read Latin, and so can I. Oh, I know it's also been said that it is a sin for us to have much knowledge. But if the Holy Father didn't want us to think, then why did He give us a mind? If it is a sin, He can make me *tonta*."

"*Madre de Dios*," Rosa said, crossing herself.

"Ahhhhh," Leonida said, crossing her eyes and letting her tongue hang out of the side of her mouth.

"Oh, Holy Mother, please." Rosa clasped her hands together and stared at the ceiling.

"Ha, see?" Leonida said, laughing. "I still have enough mind left to fool you."

"*Caramba,* Señora," she said slapping at her playfully. "You have the heart of a pig."

"Si, but the Holy Father made me this way, Rosa, and He loves me, I am sure of that. Here, button me, please," she said dancing around and pointing to her back. "He loves you too, *chica*."

"Oh, but Señora, I am different."

"*Por que*?"

"I do bad things. You know, Señora. Many people, many men see my body and do things."

"So, does that mean the Holy Father does not love you any more?"

"Si."

Leonida shook her finger at the figure with the drooping head as she sat on the bed and began pulling on her slippers. "But that is where you are wrong, *chica*. How could a God who let *Jesus Cristo* die for you, not love you?" The corner of the girl's mouth drooped as she stared at her. "Stay with me, Rosa, and you will see." She got up and snatched a black scarf from the dresser drawer.

"This is another good thing about mourning." She tossed the scarf over her head and tied it under her chin with a silver clip. "It doesn't really make any difference what your hair looks like, for no one can see it anyway." She stopped at the door to study the silent figure standing in the middle of the bedroom.

"Think about it, Rosa. Go to the chapel and pray for me. And if I'm wrong, the Holy Father is wise enough to change my heart. But if I'm right, He is also wise enough to change your heart. *Bendiciones.*"

~   ~   ~

Her father refused to talk to her through the evening meal, so she addressed her conversation toward the guests seated at the table. Jonathan MacDougal proved to be a jovial, pleasant man, and he assured her that her husband and he had been more than just simple business partners.

"Check the records. I know that your husband kept a ledger. I think you'll find we have the only trading vessel that he would sell to."

"I already have. That is why we welcomed you here," Jose Flores said, studying the captain over his glass of wine.

"And why was that, Señor MacDougal?" Leonida said.

"Because he was a shrewd business man, Mrs. Garcia, and I happen to like that. While most of these people up and down the California coast can't even read and write, he could, and I hear you can too. And he also knew the value of a dollar. While the rest of them were buying on credit and going deeper and deeper into debt, he would only take what he needed, and he paid for it in advance. He also demanded top dollar for his hides and tallow, but on the other hand, most of them were cured when he delivered them. Anything you pick up from the other men are always green and have to be taken to San Diego to be cured.

"And in return, he also knew the quality of a good product. He wouldn't buy any junk, oh no, not Rudolfo," he said, leaning back in his chair and pulling a cigar from his vest pocket. "Mind?"

"No, go right ahead."

"Here, General, have one yourself." He passed one across the table to Jose before lighting his own. "All this furniture," he made a sweeping arc with his hand, "nearly everything you see inside this house, even the pots and pans Maria cooks with, came from my ship."

"Si," Maria said as she cleared the table. "And Señor MacDougal used to bring us corn and flour, chilis and chocolate. And he would bring cloth to make the pretty dresses with too."

"I know Carlo used to talk about you some, but I wanna know why you ain't been here for a while?" Tex said while he sat cross-legged rolling a cigarette. "Not that it's any of my business, ya know. It's just that I was wonderin', that's all."

"We were, Mr., ahhhh, what is your name?"

"Tex. Just Tex." He struck a match on the sole of his boot.

"I can see where you would be concerned, and believe me, I am too. We were here like we always have been for the past several years since finding out about this place. As you know, Mr. Tex, this place sits inland quite a ways. And in order to do trade, one has to take everything overland by wagon. Well, that's what we thought. But your husband, Mrs. Garcia, devised a plan where we would bring our longboats up the sloughs from the bay, and meet at the mouth of the Mokelumne, and it worked out very well. We would meet three times a year. Once in April, once in August, and again in late October just before the winter storms set in. I have to admit I was a little disappointed when nobody met us in August, but just figured that was business. But when we arrived the other day and still couldn't find anybody.... Well, that's when I decided we had better find out what had gone wrong. I was pleasantly surprised to find the weather still warm enough for people to play in the water." He smiled warmly at Leonida.

"Anyway, Rudolfo would tell us on a previous trip what

he wanted, and we would see that those items were on our boats the next time we made the journey. And, of course," he knocked the ash from his cigar in the empty saucer, "we'd always throw in a few extra items for the ladies here at the rancho like Maria. In return, he would meet us with the *carretas* loaded down with hides and tallow. It worked out fine, and we made a lasting friendship out of the business. I was really taken aback when I heard the news, Mrs. Garcia. I am honest when I say I am both deeply hurt and sorry that such a thing could happen."

"*Gracias.*"

"There's only been a few times in my life where I found myself wishing for a flood, and one of them was when your father told me what happened. I was thinking it would be nice if the water was deep enough to bring The North Star all the way inland right up to Dogtown. I'd turn her guns loose and blow them into eternity. Begging your pardon, ma'am."

"It's a nice thought, Señor MacDougal, and I have often found myself wishing for much the same thing. I did try once to slip into town myself and kill them, but our doctor friend was able to stop me. I wish he were here right now. I would like you to meet him. But, he is out visiting some of the people with Father Franco." She rose from the table. "Shall we go to the study? You say you wish to discuss business. I think it will be far more comfortable there."

The men seated themselves in the cowhide chairs and sofa as Maria placed a tray filled with glasses and a bottle of brandy on the desk.

"That will be all, Maria," Leonida said. "I will serve the gentlemen myself."

"Si, Señora," the maid said with a bow as she retreated toward the door.

"Oh, and Maria?"

"Si?"

"If you see the Doctor when he arrives, tell him to come. I would like him to meet our guests." The maid nodded and closed the door as Leonida handed each man a glass and then went back around the room filling them with the brandy.

"Now tell, me, Señor MacDougal. What is it you wish to
discuss?"

"I'll keep it plain and simple, ma'am. I'll make you the same proposition I made your husband. I'll pay top dollar for your cowhides and tallow, and provide you with the best products I can find from around the world."

"But you are docked at the mouth of the river right at this moment, no?" He nodded. "That would not leave us with much time to hold a *matanza*. A slaughter of the steers," she added after seeing his questioning look.

"Yes, I know that ma'am. But why don't you just send some people down to the boats and have them take what they need, and you can pay me on my next trip? I mean, just this one time now," he said with a grin as he held up his hands. "I wouldn't want you to do anything your husband wouldn't want you to."

"Have no fear of that, Señor. You will find I can be just as shrewd as my Rudolfo. I shall send some of the vaqueros with you in the morning, along with a few of the Señoritas to see what they can find. I wish to have a written statement of the items and what they cost. And I will warn you Señor, that I read very well in three different languages, so do not try to cheat me."

"Oh no, ma'am. I would never try to do that. You can ask any of these men with me."

"There is no need of that. I am sure they will vouch for you," Leonida said with a nod toward the sailors. "I only want there to be a good understanding between us before we start doing business together."

"There will be. I give you my word of honor."

"*Bueno*. But if you can keep your boats waiting for another week or so, we shall hold a small *matanza* immediately, and you will be able to take some hides and tallow with you. They will be green, and not worth as much as the ones that will be ready in the spring, but you shall have something for your efforts. *Bien*?"

"Good, it's a deal then," he said shaking her hand.

"Your vaqueros will find some interesting items in one of the boats, General," he added as he sat down and crossed his legs. "Things like powder, a little shot, maybe a rifle or two."

"It would depend on what type of shot, Señor. It seems that my daughter has already decided to make a purchase of arms from another source without discussing it with me first." Leonida's heart jumped to her throat as she glanced at her father's angry stare.

"*Papa*?"

"We shall discuss this matter at a later time, *hija*."

"Oh? What'd she get?" the Captain said, clearing his throat.

"Whole wagonload of Colt .36's," Hanky said, licking the paper on the cigarette he'd been rolling. "Revolving-cylinder percussion rifles. I seen 'em before, and they're pretty good guns. Got her a few revolvers too, but not near enough in my estimation."

"Unusual choice indeed," MacDougal said, stroking his beard. "But I might be able to help you out there. I believe I have a keg of .36 caliber shot on board." A knock drew their attention to the door.

"Excuse me, but Maria said you wanted to see me?" Sean Kilkenney poked his head through the door.

"Si, come in Señor, Kilkenney. I would like you to meet our guests. This is Señor MacDougal and some of his crew. They are from the ship my husband did business with." She waited as the two men shook hands and stood estimating each other. The Captain finally broke the silence, but only in a thick Scottish accent that had not been present previously.

"Kilkenney, is it? You wouldn't be Kilkenney from Dublin, now would ya?"

"Aye, me grandfather, bless his poor departed soul, was. But I myself am Kilkenney late from New York State."

Leonida glanced toward her father who only raised his eyebrows. The doctor continued speaking in his Irish brogue as he grasped the captain's hand.

"Now, you wouldn't be one of the MacDougals from Edinburgh, would you?"

"Aye, I would be at that. I took me own ship and set sail for America nigh onto twenty years ago, I did. And what be your first name, Kilkenney?"

"Sean. And what be yours?"

"My name's Jonathan, Sean Kilkenney. And I'll tell you that the MacDougals are a proud people, and we've fought the likes of you for a hundred long years, Sean Kilkenney."

"Aye, and we've found you to be an evil lot who'd make a pact with the Devil himself, Jonathan MacDougal."

"Here now, y'all just hold on," Hanky said pushing the men apart. "I don't know what ya got stuck in yer craw, but there ain't gonna be no fightin' inside this here lady's house. Ya hear?" The two men stood quietly scowling at each other. "Now, what's gnawin' at yer innards, Captain?"

"He's a Kilkenney."

"So? I'm a Russell, but that don't cut much of a shuck with most folks."

"I think what ya got here is a family feud kinda like the Mitchells and the Truits down at the Brazos," Tex said pulling the makings out of his shirt pocket. "Only these two *hombres* didn't just bring it from the hills. They brung it clean across the ocean with 'em."

"That right?" Hanky glared at them both, first one, then the other. Both men remained silent. "Waal, if ya don't straighten out, I'm gonna whup ya both right here and now. Got that?" Leonida's laughter caused all heads to turn her way.

"Oh, this is funny. Two grown men acting like *niños*."

"Now, wait a moment," Sean said, but she kept talking as though she didn't hear.

"I remember Sister Margaret DeVillanueva when I was attending school in Mexico City. When some of us girls would get into fights and refuse to forgive one another, she would make us hug and kiss. I tell you what, Señors, we did not have many fights."

The story brought a slight smile to Sean's lips as everyone else in the room excluding the Captain laughed.

"Well, since I would really hate it if I had to hug and kiss a Kilkenney, I'd better offer you the hand of peace instead."

"The feeling is mutual," Sean said, reluctantly taking the offered hand.

"Good evening, Madam. Hope to see you in the morning." MacDougal gave a quick bow at the hips and left with his men in close tow.

"Where're they bunkin' fer the night?" Hanky said refilling his glass.

"I thought they were sleeping upstairs in one of the guest rooms," Leonida said rising to her tip-toes to see over Tex's shoulder as he watched through the open door.

"Reckon they're headed toward the bunkhouse. Guess I got company t'night. Hope none of 'em snores too loud, 'cause I might be forced to shoot him if he does," he said closing the door. He glanced down at the Señora with a grin and added, "Just kiddin'."

"Excuse me," Sean said as he rushed by on his way to the kitchen. "Maria hurry, hand me some soap."

Leonida dashed to the kitchen wondering what could be wrong, and found him vigorously washing his hands in the basin. "What in the world are you doing?" she said watching over his shoulder.

"I'm washing the MacDougal off my hands, that's what I'm doing."

"You're what?" All of a sudden she exploded with laughter, and flopped in a chair, tears running down her cheeks.

"Well, I am," he said as she wiped her eyes on Maria's apron, and burst out in another fit of the giggles.

Sean stomped from the room scowling. "What's so damned funny, I want to know."

Chapter 40

She knew her smile was making him feel uncomfortable, but she couldn't help it. Captain MacDougal sat sullenly picking at the food on his plate while everyone else was engaged in jovial conversation about the trip to the longboats, and what they were going to buy. Leonida herself was not going to join them because her father thought she might be put too much at risk, so she decided to stay at the house with Rosa and a few others under the watchful eye of Ildefonso Baca. The doctor had not shown himself that morning, and after the way he stalked to his room the night before and slammed the door, she was not so sure he would leave the room at all, ever again. They were finishing the meal and about to rise from the table when he entered the room and nodded a solemn greeting.

"*Bueno,* Señor Kilkenney. I was afraid we would miss you this morning. The Captain is about to depart on his journey, and I'm sure you will wish to give him God's speed."

"Captain." Sean nodded.

"Doctor." MacDougal didn't look up from his plate.

"You would be interested to know what happened after you left last night Señor MacDougal."

"Leonida," her father said, but she held up her hand and continued.

"Right after you went out, Señor Kilkenney ran to the kitchen, and when I asked him what he was doing, do you know what he said? He said he was 'washing the MacDougal off his hands.'" She finished by clapping her palms and giggling.

"You'd say that about a MacDougal?" The Captain turned an angry face toward the doctor who took a half a step backward and readied himself for battle. Several of the men at the table started to rise but paused as she held her hands out. There was a pregnant moment while both men glared at each other before the Captain began a slow chuckle, which built gradually into a roar, with tears streaming down his face.

"You're all right by me, Sean Kilkenney," he said clasping the stunned doctor's hand. "Anyone with enough salt in his veins to say that about a MacDougal can raise his flag beside mine if he wants to. Besides, these men here kept me awake nearly all the night telling me how you've been trying to help these people. I just want you to know you're welcome aboard my ship any time."

"Thank you sir, the pleasure is all mine."

"*Niña,*" Jose said shaking his head with a sigh of relief. "You have more faith in these *gringos* than I have."

"She doesn't need to have any faith, Señor," Maria said pouring more coffee. "She was just seeing which way it would go, this way, or that," she tossed her head from side to side. "Because you can never tell what a *gringo* is going to do. They are all *loco en la cabeza*. All except Señor Hanky, that is." She smiled and patted the old man's cheek before going back to the kitchen.

Ah, mi companero, Leonida thought. *What have you been doing with my maid when my back is turned?*

~   ~   ~

Leonida lay on the bricks beside the fountain with her head in Rosa's lap while the warm sun soothed her body. They had said their goodbyes and her father had taken several men with him to the boats, including Hanky, Juan and Paco, and would be gone most of the day. Tex had accompanied the doctor and Father Franco on a visit to some of the Indians living at the opposite end of the rancho, and would not be back for a day or two. The rest of the *vaqueros*, with the exception of Ildefonsa Baca and a couple of Indians, had gone to spread word of the upcoming *Matanza*. She closed her eyes and listened while Rosa stroked her hair and forehead and told her of her own childhood. The barking dogs brought her from her near-slumber and she sat up as Rosa crossed herself. "*Madre de Dios.*" There were eight of them, seven men and one young girl, all covered with trail dust. They halted their exhausted horses at the fountain's edge.

"Doña Leonida?" The handsome young man smiled as he spoke. Leonida noticed a nasty scar across his right cheek.

"Si." She searched for Baca out of the corner of her eye.

"*Bueno.* You may tell your men we mean no harm, we only come to visit."

"They will not hurt you unless you touch my friend or myself."

"*Muy bien.* I am Joaquin Murrieta and these are my people." He swung his leg over the pommel and dropped to the ground gracefully. "*Rancho Manantial Escondido* is a beautiful place, Señora, you should be proud."

"*Gracias.*"

"Juan Gonzalez tells me much about you, Señora, but I think he exaggerates. Now I see he does not tell how really beautiful and gracious you are." He removed his sombero and bowed low. "*Mis complementos, Señora Garcia.*" She accepted the compliment with a nod of her head and a curtsey.

"May my people refresh themselves and water the horses here at your *hacienda*?"

"*Si, perdonames por favor.* They may water and feed

them at the corral," she said pointing. "And the señorita may come and sit beside us here at the fountain. After they have finished, I will have Baca, my vaquero, show the men where to freshen themselves. The señorita shall accompany Rosa and myself."

"*Muy bien.*" He turned and repeated the orders while the young girl slid stiffly from her saddle and limped to Leonida's side.

"*Gracias, Señora Garcia. Que Dios to bendigue.*" She eased herself to the water and splashed a handful on her dirty face, then scooped another which she gulped from cupped hands.

"*Señorita, no por favor.* The children and dogs play in this water."

The girl stopped to stare at her with large dark eyes. Pain and fatigue were apparent in them. "*Bien.*"

"*Perdoname, Señorita.* I did not know you were so thirsty and tired. Rosa? Why don't you take this girl to the kitchen and let her drink all the cool water she wants."

Rosa nodded and motioned for the girl to follow. When they were a few steps away Leonida added as an afterthought, "Then see if there is enough left for her to bathe in, and ask Maria to see if she can't find something for her to wear. *Por favor?*"

"*Bueno.*"

"That was kind of you Señora, Angela will like that."

"*Por que?* It is *nada.*" she said with a shrug. "Now tell me, Señor Murrieta. What brings you to *Rancho Manantial Escondido*? I can tell you and your men have ridden long and hard."

"I have come to see Juan Gonzalez. Is he around?"

"No, I am afraid that Juan is with my father, General Jose Flores. They have gone to the trading boats and won't be back until this evening."

"Ahhhh," he said with a nod of his head.

"You have mentioned Juan before. You know my vaquero?"

"Si, we met on the trail to Hornitos a few weeks ago. Juan and Paco saved my life, and the lives of Manuel and Romero."

"Oh?"

"Si, I owe them much. You see," he said softly with a shy smile, "we lose our horses when some *gringos* decide they would like to hang us from the tree. But we ran very hard and that is where we met your vaqueros, and they lend us their horses and we go with them to Hornitos."

"Ah, and why were the *gringos* trying to hang you, Señor?" She took him by the arm and led him toward the house as they talked.

"Oh, nothing much. It is just that we took some money they thought belonged to them, but I think they are mistaken."

"How so?"

"Oh, but Señora Garcia, if it was their money I took, that would mean Joaquin Murrieta is a thief. Now surely you would not believe that?"

"Never," she said with a laugh. She found him charming in an odd sort of a way. *Very much like Señor serpiente de cascabel, who rattles his tail before he bares his fangs to bite you.* She left him in Baca's care and went to check on the young girl. She found her asleep as she soaked in a tub of warm water in the upstairs chamber.

"Shhhh," Rosa said, placing a finger to her lips. "The señorita is very tired. They come all the way from Hornitos without stopping."

"What are they doing here, Rosa? That vaquero who brought her would only say they came to see Juan, but he would not tell me why."

"He is no vaquero, Señora. You do not know who Joaquin Murrieta is?"

"No." She shook her head.

"He is a very bad *bandito*, Señora. And he kills many men. The *hombre* with the crippled hand? That one is just as bad. They call him Three-Fingered-Jack. He kills many people too." Leonida felt a cold sensation flood over her as the girl spoke.

"What do they want? Is she one of them?" she said staring at the sleeping girl.

"Angela Vasquez? Na," she said making the dark mass of curls bounce with the shaking of her head. "She's a *prostituta* like me. She's here to see Juan Gonzalez."

"Juan? What does a *prostituta* want with Juan?"

"He's a man, Señora. What do all men want with *prostitutas*? Now go." She gently guided her to the door. "I will clean her up before your papa and the men return. I shall give her one of my dresses to wear. Go, Doña Leonida does not need to touch her."

She closed the door on her and Leonida stood silently in the hall listening while Rosa splashed water and talked to the girl in the tub. "*Doña Leonida does not need to touch her?*" *When did I ever need to touch anyone, chica? But what if I wanted to touch her? What if I wanted to listen to her words, and say words of my own? Wasn't it my choice?*" She raised a clenched fist to pound on the door but caught her breath and turned to walk slowly to her own room instead. She sat in her leather chair by the window with the curtains pulled shut until she could hear the clatter of hooves on the pavement below, and the familiar jingle of her father's spurs. They were home.

Chapter 41

"Oh, no, thank you. I couldn't eat another bite," Sean said, shaking his head at the basket of corn *tortillas*.

"*Por que?*" Lupe Perez glanced toward Father Franco. The dark eyes and long raven hair gave the young girl a wild look. The set of shapely legs showing from under her skirt, her small waist and brown arms only added to the excitement. She was beautiful.

"Tell her that the food tastes very good, but I am not hungry this morning, because I ate too much last night." She stared at him as the padre interrupted, and smiled as Sean patted his stomach. The home of Julio and Lupe Perez was the fourth and last visit of the Indian sheepherders on the rancho. It had been both educational and interesting for him, but Sean was now anxious to get back to the *hacienda* and more familiar surroundings. Sleeping on straw mats on hard-packed dirt floors was not his cup of tea. The one surprising element he had found on this journey was that both the diet and health of these Indians were somewhat better than those living in close proximity of the Garcia *hacienda*. He excused himself and went out to saddle Cathy for the journey home.

"I think ya got someone who's got a bad case of moonstruck on yer hands, Doc," Tex said as Sean began tying the roll behind the saddle. He glanced over his shoulder to see the young Indian girl standing beside her grandfather watching him with large, dark eyes. He smiled and turned back to his task. "Wouldn't do that too much, that is unless you're fixin' to settle down."

"Do what? What'd I do now?"

"Ya smiled at her, ya lunkhead. That's almost as much as sayin' ya like her."

"Well, I do like her. I think she's a very sweet girl, and pretty, too. But, she's only a child, so I don't know how you could even think of such a thing." He gave the leather straps a jerk.

"Julio says she's something like twelve years old. That's old enough to marry by Yokut standards," Tex glanced up from the makings as he rolled a cigarette. Sean stopped what he was doing and looked at the girl, who smiled broadly.

"Are you trying to see if you can get me angry on such a fine morning?"

"I ain't trying ta do nothing of the sort. It's just that you gave her that pocket mirror and those beads last night, and I been seein' the way she's been moonin' over you. Waal, I was just wondering, that's all."

"Those were just some trinkets I picked up before leaving the ranch. I gave things to the children everywhere we went, and you know it."

"Yeah, but ya saved the best for her, and she ain't no child."

"Well," Sean's eyes darted from Tex to Lupe and back again, "you have to make her understand."

"Understand what?" he said, putting his foot in the stirrup and pulling himself into the saddle. "I didn't make eyes at her, and I didn't give her no gifts either. Julio says you can have her ifin' ya want. She's yer woman, not mine."

"What? My God, man. I'm begging you, please say

something.”

“Like what? Want me to insult them fer you?”

“Certainly not, you damnable barbarian. Tell them I think she will make a fine wife some day, but I just can’t get married right now. Tell them I have other commitments. You know what to say.” He stood silently as the Texan spoke quickly in Spanish. Father Franco smiled and shook his head as he climbed on the back of his burro. The old Indian and girl both smiled and waved as Sean climbed into the saddle and started Cathy down the trail behind his two companions.

“Why is it that I get the strangest feeling that you just sold me to the devil?”

“I just told them what you said, honest Injun.”

“He’s lying, isn’t he Father? What did he say?”

“He said that you thought Lupe is most beautiful and will make a fine wife someday, but you simply can’t take her with you today. He said that you have other commitments you must attend to first.”

“Then, she thinks I might come back and marry her someday?”

“I’m afraid so, my son.”

“You bastard.”

“What’s got you all het-up?” Tex said with a laugh. “I told her what you said.”

“But you didn’t have to let her think I was coming back for her did you? I don’t want to marry her. I don’t love her.”

“Don’t make her no mind. She thinks you do.”

“Well, I don’t. What if I wanted to marry someone else?”

“Do you?”

“No, but what if I did and she found out?”

“Still wouldn’t make her no mind. Most of these Injuns got themselves more’n one woman.”

“That true, Father?”

“I’m afraid so,” he said with a sigh as he tapped the burrow on the rump with the riding crop.

“But don’t let that bother you none, ‘cause that little

filly can shore cook up a storm. Can't she?" Tex plucked a twig from a bush they were passing and stuck it between his teeth.

"Yes, I will admit that. I haven't eaten so well since I arrived in California. How'd she fix that meat last night? I've never tasted lamb like that before."

"Lamb?" Tex turned toward Father Franco. "Don't think that was lamb. Whatda ya think Padre? Sheepdog, or coyote?"

"Sheepdog. I believe the blue bitch had another batch of puppies." Sean felt his stomach churn.

"You're jesting, of course. Aren't you, Father?"

"I'm afraid not."

"Oh, Jesus," he said leaping from the mule and ran to the bushes where he began heaving.

"Hell, don't know why it's got you all tore up. If you was really in the Army like you said you was, you shore 'nuff ett things a might worse than dog." He let his eyes roll upward toward the Texan who sat side-saddle calmly rolling a smoke while he talked. "When Hanky and me was Injun fighting down along the Rio, there was plenty a time we ett skunk and bobcat. And there ain't nothing better than cougar if it's done up right."

"Shut up," he said turning back to the bush where he heaved again.

"Dog's just another varmint like any other. Different folks were brought up to eat different things. Some Injuns, like the Kickapoo, would rather eat a hoss than ride 'em. Now, I'll admit, I'd rather eat a beef-critter than a skunk, but dog's not really that bad when it's done up the way Lupe does. A man could get fat eatin' like that."

"I swear before Almighty God, that if I live through this, I'll beat the devil out of you." Sean could hear him laughing as he began another bought of heaving.

Chapter 42

"Daughter, who are those men, and why are they here?" Jose was pointing to the men scattered about the patio, some of them sleeping, while others were reclining and talking as they smoked.

"That is Joaquin Murrieta and his men."

"Who'd ya say it was?" Josiah Russell spun around to face them. He had been idly talking to Maria in the hallway.

"Joaquin Murrieta."

"That's who I thought you said. Ooooeeee."

"You know of this man, Señor Hanky?" Jose said.

"Know of him? I should shout. I'm surprised you don't."

"We haven't been here in California very long, and we've spent most of that time right here on the rancho."

"Yeah, I guess you have," he said thoughtfully. "Waal, where do I begin? He's a bandit and at last count I heard he's kilt himself ten, maybe twelve people, give or take a few. No one keeps much track of Injuns, Chinese or Niggers nowadays. Whut's he doin' here anyway?"

"He says he's here to see Juan, but I don't know why."

"My guess is you'll find out soon enough. They're jawing out there right now, and they seem mighty friendly."

Rosa came downstairs a few minutes later to say the girl was asleep in her bed and too tired to come to dinner. The meal was served in shifts with people eating everywhere, including the patio. Rosa was feeling lonely for Tex and opted to eat in the office with the door closed for added privacy. She asked Leonida to come and join her. "I would love to, *chica*, but my presence is expected in the main dining room because of my position."

"*Esta bien,*" she said and closed the door.

Later that evening, Rosa again excused herself and retreated upstairs as Jose led the after-dinner procession into the office for brandy, cigars and serious talk.

"Paco? Ask Juan to come and bring Joaquin and Manuel with him," Jose said, lighting his cigar. The vaquero stepped silently out to the patio, returning a moment later with the three men.

"Close the door, *por favor.*" The General blew a cloud of smoke. "Juan, why don't you give each of our guests a cigar?" He waited while this was done and then nodded toward Leonida who passed out glasses and filled them with brandy.

"Now, Señors, my daughter tells me that you have come to see Juan and Paco. Any particular reason?"

"Si, they are my *companeros*, Señor. They saved Joaquin's life, and the lives of his men." The man smiled broadly as he talked. "I love them like they are my brothers. They are good vaqueros."

"Si, I agree. They are very good vaqueros. That is why I am interested in what is going to happen to them. With all the trouble that has been happening, and with the threats to my daughter's life, I need every man I have, right here." He pounded the desk with his finger.

"Si, I agree also, General. And that is why Joaquin offers his service and that of his men. I will take care of this little problem you speak of for Señora Garcia myself."

"What?" Hanky said dropping his cigar on the floor.

"*Gracias,* but I will take care of it myself. I have good men right here," Jose said nodding toward Hanky. "I just want to make sure Juan and Paco are available also."

"Oh, *perdon,* General, but what can this old *gringo* do? He is too old to fight, and can't even run when the first shot is fired. He will just be in the way. Besides General, he will be fighting other *gringos,* and who can guarantee he will not try to kill you and the Señora himself?"

"Ya wouldn't care to step outside and repeat that remark, would you?" Josiah said, rising to his feet with surprising grace.

"But Señor, it would not be much fun in killing you. You are too old," Joaquin said and Manuel joined him in his laughter.

The Ranger opened the door and made a sweeping motion with his hand. "After you, jackass." The bandit's face fell and he started toward the open door, but Leonida's scream stopped him in mid-stride.

"Stop it! Stop it right now! Do you hear me? All of you!"

"But Señora, he called me...."

"*Silencio.* I will tell you when you can speak. Get back to the corner, both of you. *Pronto,*" she said to the bandits as she pointed a shaking finger.

"And you," she said glaring toward Hanky. "I am surprised and ashamed for you, Señor. I thought you better than this....this childish act."

"Aw now, Mrs...."

"*Silencio,* all of you," she said spinning around. "I do not wish to hear another word." Then holding her face only inches from the Ranger's and pointing toward the empty spot on the sofa she continued. "You sleep in my house and eat my food and make love to my maid behind my back and then talk about spilling blood on my floor?"

"But we was goin'...."

"*Silencio,* do you hear me? I did not give you

permission to speak. Sit down, now!" He did as he was told and the angry Doña turned toward her smiling father. "And you, General Flores are worse than all of them."

"But, *Niña*, what did I do?" he said with a shrug.

"Don't '*Niña*' me, *Papa*. I am not a child anymore. Look at me," she patted her breast, "I am Doña Leonida Garcia. You yourself have said so."

"Si, but...."

"I am not finished yet." She held up her index finger and moved it from side to side. "I want it understood by everyone, everyone in this house," she said in a loud voice sticking her head through the open door, then quickly coming back inside the office, "that I am in charge here, and that nothing is done from this moment on without my permission." Several of the men started to protest, but she held up her palms and shook her head while she continued talking.

"This is my *hacienda*. None of you here in this room were ever married to Rudolfo Garcia. I was the one married to him. But you *burros stupidos* come here to my house and treat me as though I am nothing. You say that Doña Leonida should do this, or that Doña Leonida should do that, but do you ever ask what Doña Leonida wants to do? No, none of you.

"And you, *Papa*," she leaned her hands on the desk to look him in the face. "You tell my *vaqueros* where they can go and what they can do, but they are my *vaqueros*. You even tell Maria and my guests what to do, but she is my maid, and they are guests in my *hacienda*. And all the time, not once do you come up to my room in the middle of the night to hold me while I cry for my Rudolfo. Not once do you ask me how I feel or try to mend my heart that is broken. You just pat my head and say 'poor *niña*' and then tell me and my people what they can and cannot do. Pooh." She flipped the back of her hand toward him as she turned away to the center of the room. Then turning back she quickly added, "Well no more. Do you hear me? Nothing is done here without Doña Leonida's permission. And that goes for everyone else." She spun around looking at the silent faces.

"You, Señor Hanky, you want to shoot this man? Go," she said pointing toward the door. "Go ahead. And you," she nodded toward Joaquin and made the same gesture. "Señor *bandito*, you want to shoot this old man? Well, go on, go ahead and shoot him. All of you. Go ahead and kill each other because I do not need you. Do you hear me? I don't want you any more. Just go outside because I do not want your stinking blood on my floor. I am sick of it. *Rancho Manantial Escondido* was meant to be a happy place with much singing and laughter, but you and those *gringos* in town have made it a place of many sorrows." She wiped her eyes on the back of her hand.

"Paco? Juan? You want to go with this man?" She pointed toward Joaquin. "Well go ahead and go. I don't want you anymore. Go and ride with him and get yourselves killed and see if Doña Leonida cares. I will not cry when you are gone." She took the scarf offered by Hanky and blew her nose.

"And you think you're such a big *bandito*, eh?" Joaquin sat silently watching her. "Pooh, I never hear of you before today. But I hear of my Rudolfo and *Rancho Manantial Escondido* when I was a child all the way to Mexico City." She patted her breast and bent her waist as she spoke. "I thank you for helping my vaqueros find guns, but I give you my gold for them, so they are my guns for my vaqueros and I do not need your help Señor *bandito*, do you hear me? What gives you the right to come into my *hacienda* and tell me you are going to defend the honor of *Rancho Manantial Escondido*? Did anyone ask you? No. You just come, bringing a *prostituta* for my vaquero and say you are taking my men away, and threaten to shoot one of my guests, and then tell me you are going to fight for me? I think not Señor *bandito*. Because I never asked you and I do not want you to fight for me.

"And that's another thing, Señores," she said glancing around the room. "I am tired of my house looking like a hospital or a *burdel*. Every time I come into my house there is someone bleeding on my floor, like Señor Hanky, or there is another *prostituta* sleeping in one of my beds. I want it stopped right this instant. No one comes to my *hacienda* without my permission.

"Now, you may all go," she said lowering her eyes for a quick second. "Go on, I don't need you. I have my guns and my vaqueros and I will take Ildefonso Baca and we will go to Dogtown and I will fight the judge and the sheriff myself. I don't need you, so go outside and shoot one another and see if I care." She spun around and walked to the doorway like a queen, where she stopped and glanced over her shoulder. "Well, what are you waiting for? Go on." She tossed the scarf toward Hanky, "*gracias.*"

She walked toward the dining room where she again paused in mid-stride. Maria stood in the middle of the floor holding a weeping Rosa Carillo in her arms. The girl turned her tear-streaked face toward her then fled up the stairs.

"Rosa." She started after her but Maria caught her by the arm.

"Not now, *niña*. It is not a good time. *Manana* is time enough."

"She heard everything?"

"Si."

Leonida could hear the ranger's voice drifting from the office as she stood watching the silent stairwell. "Waal, I guess she told us how the cow ate the cabbage."

Chapter 43

What the *hell's he want now*? Pod was seated at his favorite table in The Rusty Rail when Henry Baines stormed through the door red-faced.

"Do you know what's going on out there? They've built those damn farmers a house. She went ahead and gave them the land. What in God's name is going on, and why can't one of you shoot her? How hard can it be to shoot one widow woman?"

Pod hooked his toe in an empty chair and gave it a shove. "Sit yerself down and have a drink."

"No, dammit. I want some answers. We've been paying these men too much already with no results."

"No results?" he said, filling a glass and sliding it toward the judge. "Just shows you're not as observant as you think you are. Sit down, have your drink and listen." He waited until the judge had seated himself before continuing.

"Shore, I've known about that house for a couple of weeks now. Montana watched them build it. I also know she's got no need to come into town for supplies now, 'cause that ship's captain paid her a visit, and is bringing a boatload of goods right to her front door."

"So, you're telling me that there's absolutely no way of getting at her?"

"No, I ain't. I'm just telling you we've been going about this the wrong way. We've been thinking that she's been trying to hang on to that land all this time, and that's not it. She don't give a damn about it, or else she wouldn't have given a hunk of it to them sodbusters, now would she? And going after the cattle just got them Injuns riled and they kilt a couple of our men."

"Then what is it, if it isn't the land or cattle?"

"People, Judge. It's them people she's fighting for. The closest we've come to killing her was when she knew you'd cheated them sodbusters outa their money. She felt sorry for them and went right out to look things over, just like me and Rusty thought she would. And Rusty woulda kilt her right then, except for that doctor pulling her outa the way like he did. I hear he still got close enough to cut some of her hair with that shot."

"That doctor's another one I want taken care of. What do you propose to do?"

"Well, the way I see it, the straight-forward way is always the best. If she's all protective of them folks out on her ranch, we'll just start by picking them off, one" he turned an empty glass over, "by one," he said, turning another glass over with a grin. "That way, she'll get mad enough to come looking for us. It'll be easy."

~   ~   ~

Ildefonso Baca stood his watch as the black-clad figure carrying the large leather-bound book slipped into the chapel and lit the candles. Someone had told him long ago that the book contained holy words written by Gods many years ago, but this meant nothing to him, and he had no way of knowing if it were true, for he could not understand the white man's scribbles. Besides, he reasoned, what need would a God have of putting his words on paper in white man's scribbles? Is God a white man? He didn't think so. If he were really God, he would have no color at all and his language would be one that every man could understand. Such a God as this would be his, and he would tell his people about him. But a God who had to scratch things on paper to remember them would be like an old man and Baca would have to see his power before he could believe.

He watched as she knelt before the cross in the front of the building and started her prayers. Making sure the place was indeed safe, he took a position outside in the shadows and watched. No one would enter or leave without him knowing. Señora Garcia was indeed a brave and beautiful woman, but one with many sorrows, and this bothered Baca deeply. Rudolfo had been his friend as had his brother Carlo. They had given him food and shelter when he was hungry and understood the ways of Baca. But he would not go to the desert this winter. He would stay here at the rancho when the white mist came from the river and covered the land and the snows made the tops of the mountains white. He would watch over Señora Garcia to make sure no other sorrows came her way. He would also see to it that those who killed Rudolfo and Carlo paid with their own lives. This he decided was what Baca would do as he stood in the shadows motionless, watching the chapel door.

~   ~   ~

"Juan?" The vaquero straightened from where he had been leaning over the railing watching Joaquin Murrieta and his men ready their mounts for the journey. "You and Paco are not leaving with them?"

"No Doña Leonida, we stay here."

She placed her hands on the railing as she closed her eyes and arched her back. She had been up all night praying and had only taken time to wash and change her dress before coming to the porch. Her neck was stiff and painful and her head hurt. She wished Doctor Kilkenney were there to massage her shoulders like she had seen him do for Rosa.

"Why? They are your friends, aren't they?"

"No, Señora." The vaquero propped his boot on the bottom railing and leaned his elbows on the top as he began rolling a cigarette. "We were *companeros* while we rode to get the guns, but they are not my friends. This one I think has no real friends but himself." He licked the paper and, propping the cigarette in the corner of his mouth, started fishing for a match. "Maria says Señor Kilkenney is *loco en la cabeza*, but it is because he comes from a different place and does not understand our ways. But it is Joaquin who is the *loco* one. He is not like Paco and me. He is not even like Señor Tex or Señor Hanky. This one kills when there is no need to kill." He lit the cigarette and leaned on his elbows watching as Joaquin rode across the courtyard to stop before them.

"So we part ways, eh, Juan?"

"Si, Paco and I stay with Señora Garcia."

"*Bien*." The bandit removed his sombero and bowed from the hips from atop the horse. "It has been a pleasure, Señora. Until next time."

"*Buenos dias*, Señor." She nodded. Joaquin turned the horse and stopped where Josiah Russell sat on the steps smoking and drinking a cup of coffee.

"I will let you live for now, old man, because of Doña Leonida. But if I ever see you again, I will shoot you."

"Waal, I'll tell you what, son. Just as soon as this little fracas is over, I just might come and pay you a visit."

"*Bueno,* I will be looking forward to it. You will find me in Hornitos. Until then, *adios*." He turned his horse and galloped away, yelling for his companions to join him.

"What would have happened if I had not stopped those two last night?"

"Joaquin is like the fox. He is here, but when the *gringos* come to catch him, he is gone to where he kills again and takes more money. But he is not a real *pistolero*, and Señor

Hanky would have killed him and Manuel, and maybe even Romero.”

“Then?”

“Paco and I would have had to kill the rest,” he said with a shrug that made her shiver.

“Where is Angela? I did not see her with them.”

“She is upstairs in Rosa’s room, I think. Joaquin says she begged him to bring her to me. They do not want her, for a *chica* would only slow them down.”

“Why did she want to come here? Does she love you?”

“This, I do not know, Señora.” He tossed the butt into the flower bed.

“Do you love her?”

“Maybe,” he said with a shrug. “This I do not know either. How can one tell?”

“Si, it is hard to tell, isn’t it?” They were silent for a moment watching the riders disappear over the rise on their way to the Mokelumne.

“Juan, what makes a man like that?”

“Joaquin?”

She nodded.

“No one knows, Señora. It is said that Joaquin had a woman once. He and his brother had a small place near San Andreas where they found a little gold and raised a few chickens. Then one day some *gringos* came and said his brother had stolen a horse or committed other crimes. They hung him and beat Joaquin with a whip. They say these *gringos* raped his woman in front of him. Some say she died in his arms, but others say she still lives and rides with him sometimes. They did all this, Señora, to take his small place and get his gold. So now Joaquin swears vengeance and rides against the *gringo* settlements looking for the men who killed his brother and raped his woman. This is what they say, but I do not believe it.”

“*Por que?*”

“When we rode with him to get the guns, we found a camp of Chinese near Vallecito. Joaquin and his men rode into their camp and killed six men and took their money. I don't think these men raped his woman and hung his brother, Señora," he said shaking his head. "Paco says this Joaquin is a very bad one. He does not think like we do, or like Señores Hanky and Tex. This one likes to kill."

"Have you ever killed anyone, Juan?" She knew the answer before she asked the question, but wanted the boy's reaction more than any words. He studied her for a moment then sighed deeply as he picked a leaf from one of her rose bushes.

"Si, but I did not like it."

"Would you do it again?"

"For you, Señora, and to protect *Rancho Manantial Escondido*, si, but I would not like it."

There were riders coming. Leonida squinted as she shielded her eyes against the morning sun. One of the men rode a small gray burro.

"*Que bueno, vaquero mio*," she said kissing his cheek. "You are a good boy." She turned to go inside but paused at the door.

"Juan? When Father Franco arrives with the others, would you tell them that I want to talk to everyone in the office please?"

"Si."

"And Juan, I mean everybody. You, Paco, Señor Kilkenney, Tex and Hanky. Even Rosa and Angela. I have something important to say to them. *Bien*?"

"*Muy bien.*"

~   ~   ~

The room was quiet as she surveyed those seated at various spots along the walls.

"Juan, where are Rosa and Angela? I told you to tell them to come."

"Si, I tell them, Señora, they do not wish to come."

"*Por que*?" She glanced around the room once more

and everyone sat in stony silence. Her father simply shrugged and raised his eyebrows as he lit a cigar. "*Perdoname, un momento, por favor,*" she said and walked swiftly to the stairwell.

"Rosa, Rosa Carillo, come here and bring Angela with you." Silence. She climbed halfway up the stairs and called again, but received more silence. "Insolent child," she muttered as she walked briskly to the room and pounded on the door.

"Rosa Carillo, you answer me this instant or I will have Ildefonso Baca remove this door and carry you down stairs."

The girl jerked the door open and stood glaring defiantly at her. "*Por que?*" she leaned forward with her hand on her hip and wagged her head.

"Why aren't you and Angela downstairs like I asked?"

"Because we don't want to go. Any other questions?"

She glanced past Rosa's mass of hair to see a frightened Angela Vasquez sitting crouched on the bed looking back with large dark eyes.

"No, I have no further questions for you. But I will tell you this, Señorita Carillo, if you do not get downstairs this instant, I will call the vaqueros and have them carry you and tie you to a chair. You can be angry with me later on, if you want, but you will show me the respect to come to this one meeting. Do you understand me?"

"Uhhh," she stomped her foot.

"That's okay, I don't care. Now go." Leonida stepped back and pointed. "You too, Angela, go. Both of you, right now."

Rosa stomped every step of the way and, flopping onto the leather sofa, sat with her arms folded and head bowed as Angela meekly took her place beside her and sat with her hands folded in her lap.

"*Bueno,*" Leonida said, taking a position behind the empty desk. Then it dawned on her that for the first time since Rudolfo's death her father was not seated there. He had chosen to sit beside Father Franco against the opposite wall instead. *Ahhhh, so you are angry with me too, eh Papa?*

"I wish to thank all of you for coming here today, especially you Father Franco, and you too, Tex and Doctor Kilkenny. I know you are tired after your journey, and are probably anxious to wash and get some rest. I will not keep you long. As most of you know, we had some visitors here yesterday. Joaquin Murrieta and his riders were here and spent the night." Father Franco muttered a prayer and crossed himself. "Ah, I see you have heard of him, Father. I had not, until yesterday, but Juan tells me much about this *bandito*. Anyway, Señor Hanky and this *bandito* were about to go outside and shoot each other when I raised my voice and said some things in anger." Tex raised his eyebrows and turned toward the old man seated next to him. "Now, I wish to explain myself.

"I have spent most of the night in prayer. I say this not to make you think I am holy or better than any of you, for I'm not. I simply say this for you to know that I seek His guidance and forgiveness in what I do. I asked the Virgin Mother and her son, *Jesus Cristo* to forgive me, and I ask for your forgiveness too. I don't ask forgiveness for feeling angry, because I don't think this is sin. I think it is what you do when you are angry that is sin. I threatened to kill two people last night, and I still wish them dead. This, I think is sin, but they took my Rudolfo and his brother from me, and it hurts so bad inside." Her voice began to tremble as she placed a hand over her breast.

"I was happy when I heard that the two men who attacked me were dead, and I think it is bad to rejoice in such a thing. I also said some things last night that hurt many of you. For this I'm sorry, and hope you will forgive me. But I was hurt also, because many of you say I am Doña Leonida and yet do things behind my back. So, I tell you that I want to be informed of what is happening from now on, and to make the decisions, and for *this* I do not apologize. For if I am in charge of this rancho, then I shall be in charge of this rancho," she said tapping the desk with her finger. "And if this offends you, so be it. Now, I will tell you of my decisions.

"This *bandito*, Joaquin, said last night that he wishes to

ride to town and kill the judge and sheriff who wronged me, but I could not let this happen, for everyone would have thought he was one of us. Then the *gringos* chasing him would have come here and burnt the *hacienda* and killed all the vaqueros and taken the rancho from us. So I told him to go."

"Good thinkin', ma'am. That was real smart of you," Josiah said with a nod.

"*Gracias.* And *Papa,* I insulted you in front of people last night. This I should never have done. You are a great General and I love you very much. I wish you to take charge of organizing the vaqueros and these other men and protect the rancho. I only wish that you inform me of your decisions when you make them. '*Esta bien?*"

"*Muy bueno, Niña,*" he said nodding his head with a smile.

"Señores Hanky and Tex, will you help my father with this task?" Both men nodded their agreement.

"*Gracias.* Now, I come to the difficult part for which I prayed much." She turned to the two girls. "I said some things in anger which I did not mean. I did not know Rosa could hear me, and I hurt her deeply. I am sorry, *chica*, can you forgive me?" The girl was silent. "*Bien.* That is okay," she said with a nod.

"Angela Vasquez?"

"Si?" The girl's eyes darted upward then back to the hands in her lap.

"I did not know you before yesterday, and I do not know why Joaquin brought you here, except it is to be with Juan. Do you love this vaquero?"

"Si, I think so," she said twisting her skirt in her hands. "I think of him much, and I want to be with him."

"Juan?" He straightened and sat wide-eyed as she turned to him. "You said you do not know what love is and I believe you. But do you wish to be with her also?" He turned his attention toward the girl and studied her silently.

"Juan, please answer my question, for it is important. Do you want to be with her?"

"Si" he said with a nod.

"You will marry her then?" He nodded.

"*Muy bueno*," she said with a nod of satisfaction. "Father Franco will marry you in two weeks. That shall give us time to get one of the small *casas* ready for you and prepare a *fiesta*. It will also give us time for the *matanza*, and we shall use some of the cattle for our *fiesta*." She walked over to kneel before the open-mouthed girl.

"And *chica*, you will no longer be a *prostituta*, because you will become Señora Angela Gonzalez. *Esta bien*?" The girl grabbed her around the neck in a hug and quickly released her grip and pulled back.

"*Perdon*, Señora," she said lowering her head.

"Its okay, Señorita. I prayed much about this, and I feel that it is what *Jesus Cristo* would want." She smiled at Rosa as she stood to her feet. She paused at the door to gaze at those assembled. "Are there any questions?"

"Yeah, I got one," Tex said with a scowl. "If we have a wedding and a *fiesta* out here, you know good and well half these people got folks in town who are gonna want to come."

"Si, I expect that."

"Well, beggin' your pardon ma'am, but how in the hell are we gonna protect you with everyone in Dogtown crawling all over the place?"

"It will be up to *Jesus Cristo* and His angels to protect me, Señor. It is His will that these two should get married, no? With His help, we shall turn *Rancho Manantial Escondido* back into a place of singing and dancing, instead of a place of sorrows. Are there any further questions?" She glanced around the silent faces. "*Esta bien? Bueno.* I shall be up in my room resting if any of you need to see me. *Buenos dias.*" She could hear Tex's disgusted voice as she ascended the stairs.

"Jesus Christ."

"*Bueno,* Señor Tex. Remember, it is His will," Father Franco said.

Chapter 44

"Where in the hell's that man of yours, and what's he been doing?" Henry Baines said slamming the door behind him.

Pod looked up from the "Wanted" posters in his hands. He couldn't read but a couple of the words, but he did like to look at the pictures and the bounty offered on each individual. He always had the hope that one of them would point toward one of the judge's men so he could arrest the man, or shoot him, and collect the reward himself.

"Which one?"

"Rusty Pardeen. I want to know what's going on."

"I talked to him yesterday, and he's almost got the place all mapped out. Why, what's got you all het up?"

"In case you haven't heard, they're holding a wedding and a big party out there next week. They're not worried one little bit. They're holding a goddamn party."

"So, that'll make our job a little easier now, won't it?" Pod leaned back and propped his feet on the desk. "Maybe we won't have to kill everyone to get at her. Could be, we'll just sort of blend in with the crowd, and when we get close enough, knock her in the head."

"What are you talking about? I'm not going, and they wouldn't let you within five miles of that place."

"Aw now, judge, that just goes to show that you don't quite know as much as you think you do. Sit down and pour yourself a drink."

"Alright, you just tell me what I don't know, if you're so damned smart." Henry filled two semi-clean glasses from the bottle on the desk.

"Well, in the first place, no one's expecting you to show up, but they wouldn't croak you if you did, 'cause its a weddin'. And just to prove it to you, I'll go out there myself and pay my respects to the bride and groom. Got any idee who the happy couple might be?"

"No, just one of those vaqueros and some girl. I'll find out for you though."

"Don't bother. I'm sure Pete or Slinger knows by now. Them two likes to party. I'll find out when this here wingding is gonna come off, and I'll ride out there myself. Maybe even give them a little present."

"Then you're going to take a shot at that woman and get yourself killed," Henry said and Pod laughed so hard he spilled his drink.

"Damn, just how stupid do you think I am? Hell no, I ain't gonna do nothin' like that. But we do have a couple of numb-skulls who are just that stupid, and I aim to put 'em up to it. Then, after they've went and kilt that poor widder-woman, I'm gonna bore 'em real good right in front of them Mex's, and let 'em know Sheriff Pod Randell and Judge Henry Baines is on their side."

Henry paused before setting the bottle back on the desk and chuckled. "Damn fine idea, my boy, damn fine. I guess my genius has been rubbing off on you."

Pod took the drink and held it to his lips with a grin. *Not everyone's as dumb as you think, you fat tub of guts.*

~   ~   ~

Leonida closed the door behind her. She sat on the edge of the bed to remove her slippers, then began unbuttoning her dress. The cool darkness of her room with the curtains pulled tight felt good. She was exhausted after the frenzied activities of the day. The plans for Juan and Angela's wedding were going as scheduled. The vaqueros had rounded up several hundred fat beeves for the *matanza* to be held the day before the wedding. The Indians had brought goats and a pig to be cooked over open-pit fires when the time came. The land surrounding the *hacienda* began to resemble an Indian encampment. Miwoks and Yokuts alike had set up temporary housing of flat-framed sun-shades covered with brush. Dogs and children ran wild, raising the noise level to a fevered pitch. The only one who seemed not to enjoy the festivities was Tex, who always stood only a short distance from Doña Leonida with his arms folded and a frown on his face.

She laid her dress over the chair and crawled under the sheets in her undergarments, then felt around under her pillow for Rudolfo's shirt. She closed her eyes and inhaled deeply, letting her head sink into the soft down pillow. A knock at the door brought her from semi-consciousness.

"Si?"

"Señora, may I speak to you *por un momento*?" It was Rosa's voice. The girl had refused to talk or even look at her for the past several days.

"*Bueno*," she said with a deep sigh. The door opened slowly and a mass of dark brown curls poked its way through the opening.

"Oh, *perdon* Señora, I did not know you were sleeping. I shall come later."

"Nonsense, come on in and close the door."

"Angela wishes to speak also. May she come?"

"Si, both of you come and sit here beside me," she said patting the bed. The two girls closed the door and crept meekly toward the bed. "Sit," she patted the bed with her right hand first, "Angela, you sit over here," then her left. Both girls sat with their hands in their laps gazing at her in silence. Leonida sighed again before speaking.

"Well come, Rosa, I know you did not disturb my nap just to watch me in bed, did you? What is it you want?"

"Why do you do it?" she said with a trembling voice.

"Do what? What is it I do?"

"Have the *fiesta* and the wedding. It will take all the food you got from the boat and there will be no more corn for *tortillas* and flour for *pan*."

"Well, I do this because I want to. Captain MacDougal has not taken his boats away, and we can always buy more from the store in town before the rains come. Juan has been with the rancho longer than I and he deserves a big *fiesta*, and Angela is a very beautiful señorita who deserves a nice wedding. I shall do the same for you, when you marry your Texas *vaquero*. Besides, I want to see the children laugh and the señoritas sing and dance and hear the guitars again. Is that wrong?"

"No, and I'm happy for Angela, but I don't deserve such a *fiesta*, Señora, because I've treated you badly. Father Franco will marry us quietly when the time comes."

"Do you wish to disobey me again, Rosa?"

"No, Señora," she said shaking her head.

"Then when the time comes, you will have the same as Angela and I will hear no more about it. Is that all you wanted? You are worried about the food?"

"Si."

"Well don't. There are thousands of cattle on this rancho, and we can always eat them if there is nothing else. That will make Doctor Kilkenney happy anyway." The girl's laughter made her feel warm inside. "Now, Angela, what was it you wanted to see me about?"

"I just wanted to say, Señora, that I thank you for this that you are doing for me, and that I think you are a very fine woman."

"Thank you," she said reaching for the girl's hand. "I

believe that is one of the nicest compliments I've ever received. Oh," she said kicking back the cover. "I have something for you. Both of you." She ran to pull her wedding dress from the wardrobe. "I want you to wear this, and then give it to Rosa to wear at her wedding."

"Oh, Señora, it is beautiful," Angela said, touching the lace with her fingertips. "It is yours from your wedding?"

"Si, now I wish you to wear it."

"*Gracias,* but I cannot." She backed away and turned her head.

"Why not? I give it to you. To the both of you."

"It is white, the dress of a virgin, and we are *prostitutas*," Rosa said from the other side of the bed. "I shall wear a red dress when I marry."

"*Silencio*," Leonida said snapping her head around. Rosa sat open-mouthed as she approached the bed. "I never want to hear you speak that way again. Is that understood?"

"Si, but...."

"I see the both of you in the chapel praying every morning. Haven't you asked the Virgin Mother and her Son to forgive you?" Both girls nodded. "And if the Holy Father can make this world and everything that's in it, what makes you think He cannot make you a virgin again?"

"Nothing, Señora. It's just that I never thought...."

"Well, I did, Rosa. And I asked that He make you both virgins again, inside where it counts," she said patting her breast. "And He has, so you shall wear my dress."

"But the dress should be for your daughter, Señora. Not the wife of one of your *vaqueros*." Angela's smile made her look even younger than she was.

"You are my daughters, don't you understand?" The girls glanced at each other, then stared at her like she had lost her mind. "Oh, I know, I'm only a few years older than you, but I'm a widow and have no children." She held the dress up to Angela and smiled. "You are more than just girlfriends and future wives of my *vaqueros*. I don't even think of you as friends. You are my family and I love you."

"Señora," Angela's voice quivered as she kissed her hand.

"Hush. Stop that." Leonida pulled her hand free and laid the dress beside the one she had hung over the chair earlier. "Come, sit beside me," she said pulling the girl to the bed. She crawled to the middle to rest against the pillows and put her arms around both girls.

"Your husband's?" Rosa said, pulling Rudolfo's shirt from beneath the pillow.

"Si, I like to sleep with it. It reminds me of him."

Rosa held it to her nose and sniffed. "I remember seeing him at your wedding, and when you would come to town. He was *muy hombre*." She smelled the shirt again and passed it to Angela who held it to her nose.

"Si, my Rudolfo was big and strong, much like your Texas *vaquero*. But he was also gentle and kind, too. His lips were warm when we kissed, and his fingers were gentle as feathers when he caressed my body. He took his time when making love to me."

"Señora," Rosa said, jumping to her feet. "*Perdon,* I forgot this was your wedding bed, and it is holy." Angela tried struggling to her feet, but Leonida held her arm tightly.

"Don't be silly. Both of you, come back here, now. Come on," she nodded toward the pillow while keeping her green eyes fastened to the girl standing before her. "Don't argue with me. There's no way you can win, Rosa." The girls crawled back to her side and laid their heads on her shoulders.

"There, that is much better, don't you think?" They nodded. "The thoughts I share with you are good thoughts, and they are holy. There is nothing wrong with you being here. Rudolfo would be happy that you are here to share my memories of him. Besides, I am being selfish in a way."

"*Por que?*" Angela lifted her head to look her in the face.

"Si. I have no one else to talk to. Maria is my maid, and feels that she must agree with everything I say. And my papa will not listen. Besides, he is a man, and there are certain things he should not hear. There is Señora Carpenter, but she lives in town and we seldom see each other." She pulled them closer and kissed them both on the cheek. "So you see, *mi niñas*, I am being selfish. You are all the family I have. You are the only ones I can share these things with. Can you forgive me? *Esta bien?*"

"*Bien,*" Rosa said and kissed her cheek.

"You are my daughters, and your children shall be my grandchildren."

It was approximately two hours later when she woke with a stiff ache in her left arm and Rosa's massive hair tickling her nose. Angela had scooted lower and lay with her cheek pressed against Leonida's side and an arm draped across her waist, while Rosa lay much in the same position as she had fallen asleep, with her head against her left shoulder. Leonida rubbed her nose with her free hand and gently pressed Rosa's curls away from her cheek, then lay smiling at the ceiling.

"*Gracias, Señor*," she whispered. "You are indeed a good and holy Father."

~   ~   ~

"Is he dead?" Leonida watched as they laid Pablo on the kitchen table. The early morning mist still clung close to the ground and she pulled her cloak tightly against the chill coming from the open door. There was a gaping hole in his shirt and he was covered with blood.

"No, Señora," Paco said as he unbuttoned the man's shirt. "He only passed out. He lost much blood coming here. I think it was the same gun they shot Señor Hanky with."

"Wow," Sean said after removing the bloody shirt. "Dug a trough completely across his chest. He's lucky it's only a flesh wound, but he'll be sore for a while."

"Leonida," Jose said with a sterness that made everyone look. "I want to see you in the den. It is time for a family meeting. I want you to attend also Dr. Kilkenney, and bring Tex with you."

"You'll have to wait until I finish with Pablo."

"No, I will not wait. Maria is quite able to wash and bandage that type of wound. You may check on him later."

Silence fell on the room as they stared at one another.

"And Paco?"

"Si, Señor?"

"Find Juan and meet with us *pronto*."

The vaquero ran from the house without another word. Leonida stood frozen as her father marched to the other room and ordered the padre to join the meeting. Maria mumbled something about having to clean all the blood from her kitchen table as Sean paused at the doorway, watching Doña Leonida, who still had not moved.

"Leonida. Now."

She pulled her black veil tight and lowered her eyes as she walked timidly toward the door.

Chapter 45

"You must give up this idea of a large wedding and *fiesta.*"

Her father stood at the opposite wall in front of the crudely drawn map of the rancho. She let her eyes roam around the room. There was Tex leaning against the doorway smoking a cigarette. Josiah Russell sat in a chair with his leg propped on a footstool. Paco and Juan were both leaning against the wall opposite Tex. Sean Kilkenney sat stiffly on the sofa beside her, and Padre Franco sat in Rudolfo's chair holding his rosary.

"I can't Papa, I have given my word."

"But it is too dangerous, *niña.* There will be too many people here for us to watch at one time. My sources tell me that the entire town is planning on being here."

"Oh pooh," she made a shooing motion with the back of her hand, "you worry too much. I have Ildefonso Baca to watch after me. Nothing's going to happen."

"Will you talk to her?" Jose said, throwing up his hands. "She's my own daughter, but she won't listen to me. She never has."

"Better listen to him, ma'am. I've been plumb worried since you conjured up this idee of yourn," Tex said through a blue cloud of smoke.

"You're as bad as my papa, Señor." She couldn't help but giggle at his stern demeanor. "I will have over a hundred Indians watching after me, not counting the *vaqueros*. What could possible happen?"

"You could have the whole Yankee Army camped out front, ma'am, and it'd still take only one bullet to do you in. That Sharps they're using will bore you from a mile away if they know how to use it."

"I agree with Tommy," Hanky said. "I've taken a liking to you, and I'd shore hate it if anything bad happened to spoil yer plans. Why don't you just postpone this wedding fer awhile and let us clean things up first?"

"No, Señores. I appreciate your concern, but the wedding and *fiesta* will take place Monday morning as planned. I have prayed about it, and thought I made myself clear on the matter."

"Padre, why don't you say something and see if you can't talk some sense into her?" the Ranger said, tucking a chew in his cheek.

"Well, Señores," he said, clearing his throat. "If Señora Garcia has prayed and asked His guidance, who am I to question such things? Can I oppose *Dios*?"

"*Santa Maria*," Jose slammed his riding crop against the desk, causing Father Franco to jump. "I can't believe it. My own priest has turned against me! *Bueno*? That's the way you want it?" he said, walking to the door. "You want to go against my wishes and the advice of everyone who cares about you. Go ahead and hold your *fiesta* if you want. I will not try and stop you." He opened the door and turned to point the crop at her.

"But understand this one thing, Doña Leonida Garcia, you will do exactly what I say during your *fiesta*, or I will lock you in your room and have the *vaqueros* nail boards over the windows. Is that understood?"

"Si, Papa."

"*Bueno.*" He stormed from the house leaving both doors open.

"Well, don't guess there's any reason we should be hangin' 'round here no more," Hanky said, struggling to his feet. "Baca say's there's a pinto down at the corral that ain't never been forked by man or beast. Say's he's gonna try to ride her this afternoon, so I reckon I'll just mosey down there and see if he gets his neck busted."

Sean Kilkenney was the last to leave and paused at the door. "Mrs. Garcia?"

"Si?" He stared at her for a long minute. "What is it, Doctor?"

"Nothing, ma'am," he said shaking his head. "Nothing." He turned through the doorway leaving her alone. She walked to the window where she stood watching her father puff angrily on his cigar while ordering Ildefonso Baca to post a half dozen Indians around the *hacienda* for her safety. *Yes, my father. You are finally back, aren't you? After all these years of depression, you have found something worth fighting for, haven't you?* She smiled warmly as she turned to ascend the stairs to her room and change into her riding gear. *It is good to have you back, mi papa. I promise you will have many things to fight for, if that is what keeps you alive.*

<h1 style="text-align: center;">Chapter 46</h1>

"What the hell's he sayin'?"

Sean shrugged at the Ranger as they watched the Chemechuevi Indian limp around the dusty corral yelling at the pitching pinto that had thrown him. There were forty or fifty *vaqueros* crowded close to the railing laughing, whistling and giving cat-calls, which only seemed to infuriate him further.

"Beats me," Tex said, chewing on a straw. "I ain't never heered such talk before. Must be his own language. But I'll bet he's calling that mare every thing but a cayuse."

"The General's liable ta shoot his fool head off ifin he gets hisself all busted up. He's supposed to be watchin' after that girl of his."

"No need to worry none about Baca. He'll still do his job if he's got two busted legs and arms to boot."

"Well, would you look at that now," Sean said staring past the Texans toward the *hacienda*. The whoops and hollers ceased as Doña Leonida joined them dressed in full riding gear.

"Don't stop on my account, gentlemen. Please, carry on. I want to see the fun also."

"Ooooeee, ain't yer daddy gonna be angry when he sees you dressed up in that garb," Hanky said as he stepped back to allow her access to the railing.

"He already is, Señor. He saw me leaving the house without my veil, and stormed upstairs saying things I cannot repeat."

"Kinda like Baca there," Tex said as the Indian again jumped on the back of the horse, only to be bucked off immediately. He scrambled to his feet and threw a fistful of dust at the pitching demon and yelled.

"What did he say?"

"Probably something similar to what your daddy said when he saw you in that get-up, is my guess."

"I don't understand why men think they have to use profanity when they're angry."

"Ya don't?" Hanky turned toward her as if he were surprised. "Well it's a well known medical fact that swearing is good fer a man."

"Do tell?"

"Shore 'nuff. You tell her, Doc. It takes the strain off the liver."

"Well, how about it, Señor Kilkenney? Is there any truth in what this Texan's saying?"

"I've never read such in any medical journals, but it might be of some value....to Texans that is."

"Ah, I see. Next, I suspect that you will tell me that swearing is good for women also."

"Oh, no, Mrs. Garcia, I'd never say that," Hanky said, shaking his head gravely. "It's real bad fer them. It works just the opposite on a woman, 'cause the good Lord made them different."

"On that, Señor Hanky, we both can agree."

"Think we'd better rescue that Injun before he gets hisself kilt?" Tex said as the horse threw Baca for a fourth time.

"Yeah, why don't you go pull him outa there?"

"I don't understand it, Baca is an excellent horseman,"

Leonida said as Tex ran past the snorting mare and started pulling the Indian their way.

"Waal, it weren't just Baca. That mare's done throwed two others besides him. But, its like my old pappy used to say, 'no matter how big and tough you think you are, there's always someone else just a little better.' Now, that mare was just a little
tougher than yer Indian was today." Another *vaquero* stepped into the corral to take a turn, but Hanky waved his hat and whistled.

"Hold on there, son. It's my turn. I wanna show y'all how to ride that cayuse." He removed his gunbelt and hung it over the fence.

"You, Señor Hanky?" Leonida grabbed his arm. "With your bad leg?"

"Now, this I've gotta see," Sean said climbing up on the top rail.

"Tommy, come and hold this here varmint still long 'nuff fer me to fork her," the Ranger said, limping after the pitching horse while the onlookers hooted and hollered. Tex left the beaten and dejected Indian standing beside Leonida and ran to grab the horse's reins.

"I've got me a dollar that says that old man can ride that horse longer than Baca or anyone else has here today," Sean said, holding the coin high. He was immediately surrounded by takers and had to enlist the Señora's help in holding the bets.

"I hope you know what you're doing. Are you sure you have enough money to cover all these wagers?" She glanced from the pile of coins in her hands to the Doctor perched high on the fence.

"You don't have to worry, Mrs. Garcia. He will ride that horse, and then some."

"Check 'er out good, son. I don't want that riggin' to come loose while I'm on her back."

Tex ran his hands over and around the saddle and pulled tight on the cinch. He then held the horse's head low while the old man climbed into the saddle and readied himself.

Then, with a whoop, Tex let go and ran back to the railing while the mare jumped, heaved and twisted its way around the arena. The crowd went wild as the gray-headed Texan stuck like glue in the saddle. Then, as if by magic, the gyrations ceased and the mare came to a halt with a shudder and a snort. Hanky calmly walked the pinto around the corral in view of the disbelieving crowd and came to a halt in front of Doña Leonida.

"Waal, what do you think ma'am? She's a fine little mare, ain't she?" He climbed down and patted the horse's neck before handing the reins to one of the *vaqueros.*

"I wouldn't have believed it, if I were not here to see for myself, Señor Hanky." Ildefonso Baca jumped to his feet and threw more dust in the air before storming off angrily. "You are truly an amazing man."

"Thank you ma'am, but there ain't much in riding a hoss fer a Texan. It's true that most of these *vaqueros* of yourn are pretty good, and better'n most. But nearly every Texan I know of, that was truly born in Texas, was actually born on the back of a hoss. Their mommas were ridin' when they was born. Tell her if that ain't a fact, Tommy," he said as she started laughing.

"May all his hair fall out if it ain't, ma'am."

"My hair?"

"It was your yarn, not mine."

"But the fact is," Hanky continued as they walked back toward the hacienda, "that most Texans can ride better'n most folks I know. I knowed a feller down on the Brazos who'd roll and light cigarettes while he was bustin' mustangs, and that's a fact."

"Well, that ain't nothing atall. I've knowed several punchers who could do that," Tex said disgustedly. "Why don't you tell her something worth hearing? Like that puncher we seen down near Houston who was shaving while busting a bronc."

"What?" She came to a halt.

"Honest Injun, ma'am," Tex said holding up a palm as

they continued to walk. "He was holding a small mirror in one hand and the razor in the other, with a mug of hot water and some bay rum in a little basket tied to his arm."

"That is possibly the biggest lie I've ever heard," she said, stopping by the pond. "But I must say it was also the most amazing demonstration of horsemanship I've ever seen. I didn't think it was possible for anyone to out-ride Baca, unless it was one of the other Indians."

"It weren't really nothing atall, ma'am," Hanky said as a smiling Ildefonso Baca suddenly appeared from behind the house and joined them.

"Especially when you take the burr out from under the saddle." Tex held up a small thorny sticker and put it back in his shirt pocket. "Let's count our winnings, shall we?" Sean spread the gold coins out on the bricks and began dividing them into four equal piles.

"You cheated those men back there?"

"It weren't really cheating, ma'am. We just took advantage of their own greed before they lost it all during the *fiesta*," Hanky said, dropping his portion into a pocket.

"All of you were in on this? You Doctor, and Baca too?" Sean felt a tinge of guilt as he glanced up at her. "My own doctor and bodyguard cheat?"

"Aw, don't get so hct up about it. They would have cheated us if they got the chance," Tex said with a grin.

"Maybe so," she said and slapped the palm of her gloved hand across the pocket that held the burr.

"Ow, God, don't do that, lady."

Their attention was immediately drawn toward the open ground beyond the corral that was quickly filling with temporary Indian dwellings. A noisy crowd had gathered around a group of riders coming from the river and strange wild noises like Sean had never heard before were drifting their way.

"*El Oso*," Baca said stuffing his pockets with coins before running to meet them.

"*El Oso*? What's that?" Sean stepped up on the fountain

to get a better view.

"They caught themselves a grizzly," Hanky said. "Looks like we're gonna have us a bear and bull fight before this wedding's over."

He could see the bear, that was being held between three lassos, lunge at a *vaquero* on horseback as the crowd broke. The *vaquero* stopped his horse just out of reach and yelled as he waved a bright scarf. He spurred the horse forward as the angry bear lunged again. They were nearing a large pit behind the tackhouse.

"So, that's what the pit is for."

"Shore 'nuff. What'd ya think it was fer?"

"I had no idea."

"I hate these things. They had one at my wedding, and I hate them." The Señora turned briskly and headed toward the house.

~   ~   ~

"There's someone out there looking fer you." The doctor paused in the middle of the kitchen to turn toward the ranger, who sat sipping coffee behind the table.

"Oh? Who?"

"Lupe. They're camped out yonder near the bull-pit." The conversation at the breakfast table grew quiet as everyone turned their attention toward Sean.

"What does she want with me?" Leonida could see sweat bead up on his brow as he shifted from foot to foot.

"What they hell do you think she wants with you?" Tex broke into laughter, then quickly stopped and glanced at Leonida. "Beggin' yer pardon, ma'am."

"That's quite alright, but what is going on here? Is there something I should know?"

"Shore 'nuff is, ma'am," Hanky said, holding out his cup for Maria to refill. "Seem's that the Doc here has got himself an admirer. That little Yokut's got her brand set fer him awful bad. And she's kinda thinking that since there's gonna be one wedding tomorrie, why not make it two?"

Leonida sat motionless for a second while trying to decipher what had just been said. "You tell me, Señor Kilkenney. What is this man talking about?"

"Well, it's like this, Mrs. Garcia," he cleared his throat. "When I went with Father Franco and Tex to visit the Indians, the last place we went to was her house."

"Who's house? Are we talking about Julio and Lupe Perez?"

"Yes."

"And? Go on."

"Well, it seems, according to Tex and Father Franco, (because, as you know I can't speak much Spanish), that…that," he pointed a shaking finger toward the window, "little girl thinks I'm in love with her."

"I see. And did you give her any reason to believe such a thing?"

"Before the Mother of God, I swear I didn't," he said crossing himself.

"Now, that's not quite true and you know it," Tex said leaning back in his chair. "He done give that girl a mirror and a bead necklace."

"Yes, but I didn't mean anything by it. It was simply a gesture of kindness."

"But she didn't take it that way, Doc, and she wants to see you," Hanky said with a grin.

"Honest, Mrs. Garcia, you have to believe me. I didn't do anything wrong as far as she is concerned."

"I never thought you would have, Señor," she said stirring her tea. She took her time before placing the spoon on the saucer. Then she sat back to study him. "But one cannot control the feelings of someone else, can they? Is that why you haven't been eating, and have been spending so much time inside the Chapel praying?"

"Partly. But it has to do with some other things too. Things concerning my attitude toward people in general. Being with Father Franco among the Indians has caused me to change the way I see things."

"Oh?" she said lifting her eyebrows.

"Yes. Take Maria, here for instance." The maid set the pan down hard on the stove and turned to glare at him. "I've been real critical of her and the food she fixes, I'll admit that." He turned to face the woman beside the stove.

"Maria, I'm a proud, stubborn man, and will probably only say this one time, so everyone might as well hear it. I apologize to you, ma'am. I've treated you unfairly and criticized your labors without understanding why you do things the way you do. Now, I'm not saying I'll quit complaining, mind you. I'm simply saying I understand now, that you're a woman doing the best you possibly can, with what you have, and I want you to forgive me. Will you?" The maid's eyes darted from him then to Leonida and back again before answering.

"Si," she said, almost under her breath.

"Thank you. Now, if you'll please excuse me, I believe I will go to the church for my morning prayers."

"Señor?" He paused at the door. "I appreciate your honesty with my maid and everyone at the table, but you haven't addressed your problem. What about Lupe Perez? What are you going to do about her?"

"I don't know, ma'am. That is what I've been praying about. I don't want to hurt her, but I can't marry her either."

"Why not? She is rather pretty, I think."

"Yes, I'll admit that. But I don't love her, and she's way too young. And I just couldn't eat another dog if you paid me." He turned and bolted through the door.

"Dog? What is he talking about?" she said as Tex roared. "I've never known the Perezs to eat one of their dogs. They need them for the sheep." She listened intently while Father Franco explained what took place on the way home.

"You were in on this too, Father?" The padre nodded as he crossed himself. "*Madre de Dios*, you have been corrupted by these *gringo* pagans from Texas."

"Hold on there, I might take offense at such a remark,"

Tex said, trying to compose himself.

"I doubt that, Señor. But since you have caused my priest to fall from grace, please tell me why you conspired to commit such a gross sin."

"Waal, that Irishman is always actin' so high and mighty we, *I*, just thought he needed ta be taken down a notch or two. That's all."

"I thought you liked him. I thought you were friends."

"I do, and we are. But that don't stop me from teaching him a thing or two. Now, ya gotta admit, it was funny now, wasn't it?"

"Si," she started giggling, "but the poor man will probably never be able to eat again. And he'll always think of that nice young girl as someone who eats sheepdogs."

"Aw, he ain't gonna starve to death. And as far as Lupe's concerned, I know for a fact that Paco's kinda got his sights set on her."

"Paco? Interesting, but what if Señor Kilkenney really does in fact like this girl? Are you ever going to tell him the truth?"

"Shore we are. Probably sometime during this here wingding ya got going. But I wouldn't worry none about his being moonstruck over that little filly none. He's already got a thing for someone else around here."

"Really, who?"

"Better ask him yerself." Tex pushed his chair back. "Gotta check on the hosses. Wanna tag along, old man?"

"Old man yerself." Hanky rose from the table and retrieved his hat. "Didn't see you riskin' yer neck on that bronc yestiddy." They all filed out one by one leaving Leonida alone at the table while Maria washed dishes in the large pan sitting on the counter.

"They are a strange breed, aren't they, Maria?"

"Si, Señora. Especially the *gringo* doctor. Why should he apologize to Maria? Now I feel sorry because I have wished many bad things on him."

"You wished bad things on him? I wouldn't worry

about it. He is a good man in his heart. This I know, for I have watched him with the children, and I was present many times when he doctored Rosa."

"Si, and he doctored you."

"Si, and he was a gentleman at all times. I wonder who he 'has a thing for', as this Texas vaquero says?" Maria wadded the towel in her hands and, leaning back against the counter, studied her.

"Doña Leonida doesn't know?"

"No. Do you?" The maid nodded. "Tell me, who?"

"*Que lastima,* Señora," she said turning away. "You should ask him yourself."

"Maria, tell me who." The sloshing of dishwater was the only sound that returned to her ears.

~   ~   ~

"Here it is," Rusty Pardeen said, spreading the hand-drawn map out on the desk. "It's not the whole damned ranch, but it's every little outpost, cabin and Indian camp on the place. Anywhere people are living."

"Good," Pod said, leaning over the drawing before him. "Better make a copy of it, just in case this one gets lost."

"Already done that."

"That's a fine job, I must admit. But I still don't see what good it's going to do us." Henry's chair creaked as he moved to retrieve his tobacco pouch.

"Well, Judge, it's like this. If we can't take that woman out during this weddin' party of hers day after tomorrow, we'll start picking off folks living on her place one by one just like we planned. We know that's gonna bring her out of hidin' one way or the other. Now, to do that, we need to know where they are, don't we?"

"Yes, I can see your reasoning there." He struck a match and puffed several times on his pipe. "But I don't want you taking all year. We've wasted too much time as it is."

"No need to worry yerself none. I don't think she's

gonna live beyond Monday afternoon." Pod smiled as he filled
three glasses.

Chapter 47

"I wouldn't have missed this for the world," Jonathan MacDougal said as he seated himself in the back of the wagon beside Sean and Leonida. They made part of a huge circle of spectators comprised largely of people living on the rancho, a few sailors from *The North Star*, and a few from Dogtown who had gathered to watch the *matanza*. A cloud of dust rose from the herd of cattle that were being kept in a tightly packed circle by a dozen or so *vaqueros* on horseback.

"Will this be enough, Captain MacDougal? These are all my *vaqueros* could safely gather on such a short notice," Leonida said, leaning forward to speak to the Captain who was seated on the opposite side of Sean.

"Oh, I'm sure it will be. If we're a little short, we'll make it up come springtime. How many do you estimate there to be?"

"About a hundret and twenty-five," Tex said, chewing on a straw as he leaned against the wagon wheel. "Whadda ya say, Hanky?"

"Na, yer eyes must be getting bad, boy. There's got to

be at least a hundret and thirty if there's even one out there."

"It doesn't matter. I'm sure it will be enough, no matter what the final count is."

"Are you and your men going to stay for the wedding tomorrow?" Her cheek was only inches away from Sean's face as she talked to the Captain.

"You bet your life we are. I almost had a mutiny when I ordered several men to stay with the boats. As it is, I'm going to have to try and keep some of these men sober enough to go back and relieve them, so they can come and join in the fun."

Cheers rose as eight riders entered the area in shirtsleeves with red bandanas tied around their heads. Each carried large knives tucked into their belts.

"Oh, I see Juan has joined them this year. I hope he's careful. Angela will be so disappointed if he gets hurt. He's the one getting married, you know."

"Yes, I heard."

"I don't understand. How would he get hurt shooting and skinning a few cattle? And I don't know why everyone's so interested in watching such a thing in the first place," Sean said.

"You've never seen one of these, have you son?" MacDougal laughed and Sean shook his head. "Didn't think so. You're in for an experience, my boy."

"Them riders out there with the red bandanas are called *nuqueadores*," Tex said. "They're about to perform what they call a *nuquero*, or 'necking'. It's quite something to watch. I seen 'em do it last year, and there ain't no way this fool would try it."

The men with the bandanas began to circle the cattle at a slow trot. Sean watched as one of the *vaqueros* leaned in the saddle and drove the knife downward with a quick blow. He was close enough for Sean to see that the point of the knife had pierced the vertebrae at the nape of the neck. The cow dropped dead at the horse's feet without a kick or struggle. He sat open-mouthed as the others began to do the same.

"Holy Mother Of Christ, we came here to watch this?"

"Na, they're just gettin' started. The fun ain't begun yet." Tex struck a match on the metal rim of the wheel to light a cigarette.

Sean shook his head as they continued with the slaughter as methodically as a carpenter might drive nails into a board, still wondering what the attraction might be until one of the cattle bolted from the circle. One of the *vaqueros* gave chase, and drove him back with a flair of horsemanship Sean suspected was strictly for his audience. A moment later another steer bolted, then another. Soon all the *vaqueros* were busy with ropes and darting horses. The dust rose in great clouds and the crowd cheered them on until the *nuqueadores* themselves were chasing after the fleeing cattle and plunging their knives from horseback at a full gallop. Leonida stood to her feet and Angela screamed as Juan's horse fell and he rolled forward head-over-heels. But the *vaquero* bounced back into the saddle with a wave of his arm and continued with the *matanza*.

Soon after the herd diminished, the grounds began to crawl with Indians with sharp knives. These were the *peladores*, or skinners, as Leonida explained, who expertly relieved the victims of their hide coats in a matter of minutes. They were followed by another team called the *tasajeros*, or jerky-meat cutters, who butchered the cattle. When this chore was finished, another team that consisted largely of women took over. They cut and gathered the tallow and fat and piled it on the green hides. When they had finished, all this having taken place in an amazingly short amount of time, the hides were folded over and tied with thongs, then dragged in a cloud of dust to what Leonida called the trying-out fires.

Sean wove his way through the darting children and dogs, listening to the laughter and strange talk of the Indian women as they cooked the boiling fat in their great kettles over crackling fires. They were a happy folk, performing a simple task handed down from generation to generation. There was no thought that life around them would soon change. They accepted him, and he was beginning to understand their need for custom. But men would come after him who would have no regard for their way of life and they would have to change. He watched as Leonida laughed and talked to her father. Yes, some day she would change too. She would have trouble keeping her ranch and people. They would call it progress, but the day of the large rancho would soon end, and with it, a way of life he was learning to love.

~   ~   ~

"Ah, but Señor, you only have one coin. Where is the other?" Santiago said. Sean had been weaving in and out of the afternoon's proceedings when he found a red-faced Tex arguing with the *vaquero*.

"Hell, I don't know. It musta fallen out somewheres back yonder. I still got one. Don't that count for anything?"

"Si, but to beat Paco, you must have both coins." They were competing in a game called *Coraza*, or Housing. And as usual, the bets were running high.

"Dammit," he said, sliding from the saddle as the others laughed and whooped. Sean noticed a slight grin on his stern face as he joined him at the corral.

"What's wrong?"

"Nothing. It's just that I was supposed to have both coins and I lost one of them. Watch," he nodded toward another *vaquero* taking his place at the starting line. Santiago placed a coin between each knee and the saddle before stepping back to wave his sombrero. The object of the game was for the cowboy to guide his horse over, around and through a series of obstacles and return to the starting line with both coins still in place.

"Ha, see there?" Tex yelled triumphantly. "He lost 'em both right there on that jump."

"I don't think I could even stay in the saddle making those jumps. You kept one of them? How?"

"Just gotta keep yer knees squeezed nice and tight. That's all. I'd be in the lead too, if it weren't for Paco. That little Mex rides like the Devil hisself."

Sean felt a tug at his arm and turned to see the smiling face of Lupe Perez. "Good God," he breathed as she tugged on his arm and began speaking quickly in Spanish.

"Better go with her, Pard. She wants to show you off to all her friends."

"But I....what am I supposed to do? Tell me."

"Nothing. Just foller her around and smile. You don't got to say anything. And by the way," he heard him add as he reluctantly allowed himself to be led away, "you can eat anything yer offered today, 'cause it'll be beef critters from this mornin's kill."

"Well, at least you're not the type of woman who would talk her man half to death," he said as they wove their way through the crowded Indian camp. She smiled up at him and hugged his arm close to her body with both of hers. Lupe nodded as they passed a group of older women kneeling on a rug made of animal skins. They were playing a game of dice with eight split sticks of elder wood, burned with a pattern on the convex side. Evidently the betting here was also running high, for they only stopped long enough to smile and acknowledge their presence before one of the women gathered the sticks into a basket. She shook them violently, and sent them scattering across the skin. Lupe and Sean were both forgotten as the women argued over the score.

"*Carrera del gallo.*" Lupe pointed toward an open area lined with spectators before pulling him forward. Sean watched as two men buried a live rooster with only its head above the ground. The spectators let out a loud roar as a rider came at a full gallop and, leaning from his saddle, snatched the bird by the neck from its hole. He slowed the horse to a prancing walk as he held the flapping, squawking bird high and accepted the praises of the crowd. Then, it was another vaquero's turn to show off his riding skills. Only this time, the men burying the rooster must have packed the ground too tightly and the rider wound up holding only the head and neck instead of the whole bird. A woman ran out of the crowd to collect the victim as another live rooster took his place.

Lupe pulled him away toward a group sitting in a circle on blankets. He recognized Julio Perez and Paco from a distance, but smoke from one of the campfires stung his eyes, and it wasn't until they were standing on the blankets that he saw Baca and Doña Leonida. His heart skipped a beat as Leonida removed her veil and smiled at him.

"Sit here by me, Señor Kilkenney," she said, patting an empty spot next to her. "I asked Lupe to find you for me."

"Oh?"

"Si, we have important things to discuss." He sat Indian style as she continued. "I have already explained how your Texas friend and Father Franco played a prank on you, and Julio, being a compassionate man, has asked that I not punish them too severely."

"That's nice." Lupe took an empty seat beside a smiling Paco.

"I have also explained another predicament we have, Señor. It seems that Lupe has been quite taken with you, and pledged her love to you, whether you knew it or not."

"No, I didn't. Honest."

"I believe you. But you see, Paco has loved Lupe for quite awhile now, and was hoping to marry her next spring, and now he can't because of her pledge. So we wish for you to release her of her vow, and swear to Almighty God before her grandfather and these witnesses that she is still pure. Would you be willing to do that, Señor, or do you wish to make this *chica* your wife?"

"Well, certainly I would be willing release her, but what about her? How does she feel about this?"

"Careful, Señor," she said with a grin. "I will not rescue you again, and you just might find yourself married tomorrow afternoon. Will you release this girl from her vow and swear that you have not violated her?"

"Yes, yes I do." He nodded.

"*Bueno*?" she said looking at each and every one gathered and waiting for a nod of agreement. "*Muy bien.*" She rose to her feet. "Come, Señor, shake her grandfather's hand

and let's be gone."

She took him by the arm and led him away, waiting until they were out of sight before covering her head again with the black veil.

"I'm sorry, ma'am, but I just don't understand you women."

"*Por que*? What is it that you don't understand?"

"Well, for instance, how could Lupe Perez be so in love with me one minute, then ask to be released from a vow I knew nothing about, so she can marry another man next spring?"

"That is a good question, isn't it?" She paused near the corral to study him. "The women in California are not so different than the women in your Ireland, Doctor. Lupe is young and impressionable, and I suspect her infatuation with you was simply that. Besides, Paco is a good man and will make her a fine husband."

"I don't doubt any of what you say. I just don't understand how she could change her mind so quickly."

"Ah, do I detect some wounded Irish pride?" she said with a giggle. "Well, if it will make you feel better, Señor, I told her that you were a special person to me, and asked her and her grandfather to release you of any vows also." She jerked her head toward the open-pit area as loud growls and the bawling of a bull, mingled with cheering from human spectators, drifted their way. "I wish they wouldn't do that. I hate it."

"I'm sorry."

"It's quite alright, Doctor. You had nothing to do with the bear and bull fight."

"No, I mean about lying for me. You might have left them with the impression that there was some romantic interest between us."

"Oh?" she said tilting her head to one side. "And who said I lied?" Her skirts swished as she turned away quickly. "Come, Baca, we must visit our other guests."

~   ~   ~

Leonida yawned and laid the book of poetry aside. The clock downstairs had bonged eleven times quite awhile ago, but the first night of the fiesta was in full swing. She opened the shutters on her bedroom window to watch the dancers and musicians below. The party would last all night and would break only for the wedding, and then continue for two more days. She pulled her dressing-gown tightly around her neck and breathed in the cool evening air. A smile crept across her lips as Juan and Angela cleared an area for themselves and began to dance the *Jota*. A knock at her bedroom door caused her to jump.

"Si?"

"Mrs. Garcia, are you still awake, ma'am?" She pattered across the room in her bare feet to crack open the door. She smiled as she poked her head through the opening.

"If I wasn't, Señor Kilkenney, I would be now. Did you have to knock so loudly?"

"I'm sorry to disturb you, ma'am. But I've got to ask you a personal favor....just for me." The smell of wine was almost over-powering as the man gripped the doorjamb to steady himself.

"*Bueno*, what is it?"

"Please don't declare war on Dogtown because of what the judge might have done."

"*Por que*? What in the world are you talking about?" She opened the door wider.

"Well, I was just talking to some of the men, and they are sort of thinking that you bought all those guns so you could go and kill everyone in Dogtown. And I wouldn't want to see you do anything like that."

"Oh, I see. Well, you can rest assured, Señor, that I have no intention of doing such a thing. The guns are for protecting our *rancho* and nothing more. But regardless of what some of the men are saying, why should you think I would do such thing? I have friends in Dogtown."

"Well, I was listening to them talk, and then I

remembered the night in the corral when you had your husband's gun, and I just thought...." he left off speaking with a shrug and a grin.

"Yes, I would have gone that evening, had you not stopped me. And I cannot promise you that I would not try something like that again, given the same circumstances. But I was only trying to bring Judge Henry Baines to justice, not kill an entire village. And if I do go, I will take my *vaqueros* with me. The judge and his friends are the ones who are responsible for all the evil that has been happening, not the entire town. Does that answer your question, Doctor?"

"Yes, I guess so. But I wouldn't want you to go at all ma'am."

"*Que*? And why not, Señor? Shall I let them get away with the murders of my husband and brother-in-law? Am I to live like a prisoner in my own house to prevent these men from killing me and taking our land?"

"No, no, no. Nothing like that." He leaned his head against the doorjamb and blinked hard.

"Are you alright?" He nodded. "*Bien*, I thought you were going to faint. So, tell me why, Señor, that I shouldn't go to Dogtown."

"Because you're so pure and beautiful," his fingers brushed her cheek when he spoke. "I wouldn't ever want anyone to hurt you again." He paused and suddenly looked pale. "I'm sorry, but I need to go lay down. I must have drank a little too much." She stood in the doorway watching as he staggered down the hall toward his room. She waited until he had closed the door before she turned back inside.

"Yes, perhaps you did drink a little too much, Señor," she said touching the spot where his fingers had caressed her cheek. "But I didn't mind feeling your heart."

Chapter 48

"**Hell of** a way fer a champion to be treated, ain't it?" Tex chewed on a straw as they viewed the bear skin nailed to the shed wall.

"Hear he kilt three bulls before he died," Hanky said lighting his pipe.

"Yeah, but that last one gored him pretty good and he went ahead and croaked an hour or two later. Santiago says he's gonna make him a pair of chaps outa ol' *el oso*. Ain't much of a way to treat a champion. Havin' yer hide pull off so they can eat you and make a pair chaps and a rug outa yer skin."

"Hell, it's just a bar, Tommy. He weren't no human." The pealing of the church bells caused them to look toward the crowd filing into the chapel. A lone figure stood to one side looking their way as the wind whipped at the hem of her skirt and tousled her brown curls. "Looks like she's waiting fer you, boy. What's yer plans?"

"Nothing. I ain't gonna do nothing."

"Ain't ever gonna marry that girl and make an honest

woman outa her?"

"Hell yeah I am, just not today. Not until this whole thing is over. Come on, let's go see Juan nail the lid shut on his own coffin."

~   ~   ~

Leonida held Rosa Carillo in her arms while she cried all through the wedding. The girl had desperately wanted it to be a double ceremony, but Tex had refused, using the troubles at the rancho as an excuse.

"Naw, I ain't gonna get hitched to no girl, then turn right around and make her a widder." His eyes darted from Rosa to the Señora the moment the words left his lips. "I'm sorry, ma'am. I didn't mean nothing bad by it."

"I know you didn't, Señor. But this girl would rather be married to you for two minutes and become a widow, than never marry you at all. Don't you understand that?"

"Shore I do. And I want her too. But that ain't gonna make no difference, no matter what either of you say, 'cause I done made up my mind."

"You're lying to Doña Leonida, just like you lie to me." Rosa was almost hysterical. "You don't want to marry me because I'm a *prostituta.*"

"Aw, come on now," he said reaching for her shoulders, but received a resounding slap for his efforts.

"*Cerdo*," she said and ran from the house.

"I've been called lots of things, but I think that's the first time I've been called a pig," Tex said rubbing his cheek.

"She will get over being angry, Señor. But I do wish you would marry her now. She feels that you will abandon her like everyone else has."

"Now, that's not quite true. You ain't abandoned her, have you?"

"No, but I can't marry her either. She needs a man. Why don't you let Father Franco marry you and Rosa at the same time he does Juan and Angela?"

"Can't." He shook his head and turned away. He even refused to sit beside the girl during the wedding and stood like a statue at the door, glancing back over his shoulder at every little sound coming from outside, and quickly disappeared after the ceremony was finished. Rosa ran into the arms of Sean Kilkenney and buried her face in his chest, crying like a baby.

"She just needs a little understanding, Señor Kilkenney. She has a fragile heart that has been broken."

"But, I don't know what to say."

"Say nothing. It will be better that way."

Leonida hugged and kissed Angela, who looked stunning in the white gown, and left the Church to greet the guests who could not get inside. But she was met by her father at the doorsteps.

"But, *Papa*, it would not be right if I didn't. I must greet them properly."

"Nay, *Niña*, it would be worse for you to die. You may go outside, but only with an escort, and you will only go where they tell you." She started to protest, but he held up his palm. "Remember our agreement? If you do not obey me, I will have Ildfonso lock you in your room."

"He is my *vaquero*, and he will do as I tell him."

"No, Ildefonso Baca belongs to no one, and I already have him under an oath that no harm shall come to you, or he will kill himself."

"You didn't."

"I most certainly did. Now, behave yourself."

"Ugh," she gritted her teeth in anger, but her father only smiled and snapped his fingers. She was instantly surrounded by several Indian bodyguards, Ildefonso being one of them.

Her sulking only lasted for a few short moments though, for as soon as the music and singing started, she was lost in the atmosphere of the *fiesta*. Ildefonso must have sensed her frustration, for he gave her a surprising amount of freedom. She wandered through the crowd, greeting acquaintances and friends such as the Carpenters and the Blackstones. Woodrow and Susanna Black were present, and sought her out to give her a hug. And there were many miners who claimed to have danced with her at her wedding. They formed another line to offer their condolences and wish her well. At one point, she turned to find Ildefonso and his Indians standing a few feet behind her, guarding her every move, and watching very carefully those who might approach. The same group of girls who made her dance at her own wedding came begging her to join them in a dance by the fountain.

"No, Señoritas. It would not be proper," she said shaking her head. "I'm in mourning, remember?"

"*Por favor*," Juanita held on to her hand as she begged. Leonida glanced at her father, who stood talking to Woodrow Black a few feet away. He gave her a slight nod without breaking conversation.

"Alright, but only if you can get Angela and Rosa to join us." They squealed and darted through the crowd in search of the girls. Angela was easy to find, and even easier to convince. It was Rosa Carillo who proved to be the challenge, and it took Leonida herself to finally talk the sulking girl into joining them.

"Please, *chica*. This is the happiest day of Angela's life. Don't spoil it for her." Rosa glanced up at her with a pouty look on her face as she leaned against the kitchen doorpost. "If you will agree to dance for Angela, I promise that I will personally dance all by myself at your wedding. *Muy bien*?" She took her by the hand and gave a gentle tug. "Come, let's make Angela happy."

Rosa drug her feet in a defiant shuffle until they happened to pass Tex. Upon seeing him, the girl snapped her head upright smugly, and stepped lively to join the others. They waited expectantly for Leonida to join them. She stood beside Angela and looked at Juanita.

"I think you should save the *Bamba* for the bride to do alone. Shall we do the *Jarabe*?" The girl nodded. Leonida raised her hands high and clapped as she nodded toward the musicians. The girls swirled this way and that, stamping their feet to the beat of the strumming guitars and violins. One of the men started to sing a love song in a beautiful tenor voice. She closed her eyes, remembering the last time she danced here in the courtyard on her wedding day, when suddenly, the music stopped. Ildefonso Baca brushed pass her and she turned to see Pod Randell sitting on horseback, watching them.

"Ahhhhh," Rosa said and darted toward Tex who stood blocking the Sheriff's way.

"Somebody stop her," Leonida yelled as Rosa grabbed for the gun in his holster. Tex caught her wrist as she pulled the gun free and jerked it skyward. The gun boomed with a deafening roar.

"Dammit, stop that," he said as she kicked and scratched at him. "Somebody grab her."

"Let me go," she screamed as Sean caught her around the waist, lifting her from the ground. She began cursing in Spanish as Tex wrestled the gun from her grasp.

"Take her to her room, Señor Kilkenney. I'll be up there in a minute, after I settle this situation." He nodded and carried the angry girl toward the house as she flailed her arms and legs in an effort to get free.

"Not now, Tommy. Just take it easy," Hanky said stepping between the two men as Tex fingered the gun in his hand. The cowboy slowly returned the gun to its holster.

"What do you want here, Señor?" Leonida said coldly.

"Well, I understood that there was a wedding here today. I just brung the bride and groom a little present. I didn't mean to cause such a ruckus," Pod said bouncing a small leather pouch in his palm so the gold coins clinked loudly. "Couldn't really buy nothing at the store, 'cause it was closed. Probably better that way. I wouldn't know what to buy anyway."

He glanced toward Angela. "You the bride?" She nodded. "Here, catch," he tossed the bag. "My best wishes to you, ma'am."

"You are not welcome here, Señor. The memory of my husband and his brother are still strong."

"I can understand that, and I do apologize." He tipped

his hat. "Do you mind if I water my horse before I leave?"

"You may." She turned to a young boy standing nearby. "Antonio, take the Sheriff's horse to the corral and see that it is cared for." Then turning back toward Pod, she made a quick motion with her hand. "You, come with me. I shall have one of the girls fix you a plate of food and give you something to drink. Never let it be said that anyone, not even you, was turned away from *Rancho Manantial Escondido* hungry."

"Well, that's mighty kind of you, ma'am." He smiled as he dismounted and followed her through the murmuring crowd.

"Juanita, you and Angela finish the dance," she said, pausing by the fountain. "Come." She raised a hand and turned in a circle. "Play the music. Let's let nothing disturb Juan and Angela's wedding *fiesta*." The music and laughter seemed to pick up weakly at first, before escalating. She led the way to a long table at one end of the courtyard which had been set with all kinds of food.

"Here, Señor Randell," she said handing him a plate. "Gabrielle will see to your needs," she nodded toward a frightened young girl. "Then, after you've eaten and drunk your wine, I would suggest that you leave. There are over a hundred *vaqueros* on this rancho, Señor, and most of them want you dead, so I don't know how long I can keep you safe."

"I'm much obliged for your concern, ma'am."

"No, I don't think you understand. I would not cry if one of them killed you right this minute, but I don't want Angela's wedding to be spoiled with the spilling of blood. Now, if you will excuse me," she brushed past him before pausing by her father, who had been watching intently with Tex and Ildefonso Baca.

"Papa, I'll go now to check on Rosa. Please see that Señor Randell is able to leave the *fiesta* safely. After that, I don't care."

"*Bueno, Niña.*"

She walked past her own room and opened the door to Rosa's room without knocking. The girl's hair was a wild mess of curls that went every whichaway, and her eyes were red from crying as she sat on the edge of her bed. Sean Kilkenney stood by the window watching the proceedings below.

"Señora," the girl fell at her feet and grabbed her hands. "Paco tells me you bought many guns for the *vaqueros* to fight with. Is this true?" She nodded. "Let me have a gun, Señora. Just one, *por favor*."

"No, Rosa, those guns are for our men."

"Oh, please, *mi* Doña. I can pay you." She jumped to her feet and dug excitedly under her pillow to remove a neatly tied scarf. "See?" She opened it to reveal several gold coins. "I save them with my things that Tex brought from town. I will give them to you. All of them," she tried to hand her the money. "Take them, Señora. Just give me a gun. Any gun. *Por favor*?"

"No."

"But, Señora, they will not miss one gun. The *vaqueros* are *muy hombres*. They can fight with their knives and fists. I only need one little gun. Here," she tried putting the coins in her hand. "*Por favor*, Señora, one small gun."

"No, Rosa, I don't need your money. You keep it." The girl turned to fall across the bed sobbing.

"You don't care. You don't know what he did to me."

"*Chica*," she put a hand on her shoulder, but Rosa pulled away. "Look at me," she said, taking her cheeks in her palms to hold her still. "I do care. I was here when Tex brought you to me. I know what he did to you. They did the same to me, remember? Nearly every night I see them in my dreams and feel their hands tearing at my clothes. I've never told you everything they did to me, *Chica*." Leonida trembled with anger as she turned away. "But I know exactly how you feel. And I swear before *Jesus Cristo* and all the angels of heaven, that I'll die before I ever let anyone do that to me again." She rose from the bed and walked to the center of the room.

"And don't forget, Rosa, they also killed my Rudolfo and Carlo. I want him and that judge dead just as much as you do. But I cannot afford to lose you too, Rosa. Besides, Pod Randell is as good as dead anyway, without you getting yourself hurt trying to shoot him. Your Texas *vaquero* has vowed to kill him. Let him do it, *chica*." The girl clutched her pillow as she curled up in a ball in the middle of the bed.

"Thank you," Leonida said, turning to Sean. "Will you please stay with her awhile longer?" He nodded. "I think I will go lie down in my own room until I'm sure Pod Randell has left, or I might be tempted to do much the same thing myself." She paused at the door to smile at him.

"If either of you need me, you can open that door and call," she nodded toward the wardrobe. "There is another door in the back that opens into my room. Rudolfo said his father had it installed when he was small so he could slip into their room when he became frightened. Rosa uses it once in a while when she can't sleep. I think she is probably the only one besides myself who knows it exists. But," she tilted her head to one side, "now you do too."

She closed the door behind her, wondering why she had told him about the secret passage. This room belonged to Rosa until she was able to marry, and Leonida was not the type of woman who would have men slipping into her room in the middle of the night. She would have Paco nail it shut when Rosa vacated the room. She was still debating her actions when she entered her room only to be grabbed by two strong arms from behind. One hand covered her mouth and nose, while the other pressed her against the attacker.

"Got ya now, don't I, little woman?" he said in a hoarse whisper, kicking the door shut behind them. She could smell stale tobacco and whisky as he breathed heavily against her cheek. He removed his grip on her waist and she heard the bolt slide with a loud click, locking them inside the room. "Let's get it over with nice and quick-like." He jerked her away from the door as she struggled against him. "Ahhh, damn," he said as she sunk her teeth into the hand covering her mouth. She spun as he loosened his grip and raked her fingernails across his eyes. "Ow, goddammit," he said, letting her go as he covered the contorted face with both hands.

She bolted toward the center of the room only to freeze

again. There was a second man she hadn't seen standing in the shadows who slowly pulled a large knife from his belt as she backed toward the wall.

"Fiesty little bitch, ain't you?" He took a cautious step toward her as she slid along the wall feeling for something to fight with. "This is gonna hurt real bad." Leonida let out an ear-splitting scream as he raised the knife.

Chapter 49

Sean was standing by the window staring at the closed door when he heard the scream. There was really no reason for it, but instead of exiting through the door to the hallway, he jerked open the wardrobe and dove through, falling to the floor in Leonida's room in a tangle of clothing. Rosa bounded over him, let out a scream and started throwing everything she could get her hands on. Sean struggled to his feet to find the surprised assassin dodging flying projectiles while Leonida slid quietly along the wall in an effort to get further away from the knife. Sean bolted forward grabbing the knife hand in his own left and driving his right palm under his opponent's chin. His momentum lifted the assailant from his feet and slammed his head against the wall. The man let go of the knife and slid to the floor with a groan, where Sean kicked him once for good measure.

He turned his attention toward the other side of the room where Leonida was struggling with a second man. He had a gun drawn, but she had latched onto his wrist with her teeth and wouldn't let go. He was hitting at her and pulling her hair with his free hand. Sean's first blow caught the man across the temple and he sank to his knees. Leonida released her grip as the gun fell from his grasp. Sean's second blow landed flush on his nose and he fell back on the floor as someone started pounding on the locked door. Rosa ran to let them in.

"You son-of-a-bitch," Sean said hitting him again. "Why don't you bastards leave her alone?" His blows came like a hail storm until strong hands pulled him away and drug him to the center of the room.

"Easy now, boy. Easy." It was Leonida's father. Leonida bolted into Sean's arms and buried her face against his chest as she broke into a flood of tears.

"Well, looks like you had yerself a party, son," Hanky said, returning his gun to its holster as Baca and several Indians bound the men with ropes. "They musta snuck in here while we was keeping an eye on the Sheriff down there."

"Si, now we will take them outside and see what he has to say." The General gave orders to the men as Leonida seemed to calm herself somewhat, but refused to release her grip on the doctor. Rosa kicked at the man who held the knife and spit on him as Baca drug him from the room.

"Well, Señor Kilkenney, it seems you are making it a habit of saving my daughter's life. Again, I thank you." Jose bowed and glanced at the open wardrobe with its passage into the next room. "Convenient. Yes, very convenient indeed." He paused at the door to look back again. "You will stay with her for a while?" He nodded, and the General was gone.

Leonida sniffled, so he handed her his hanky and held her close to him. She felt good pressed against him. He could feel the swell of her breast with each breath, and the smell of her perfumed hair seemed to intoxicate him. It was as though she belonged there. She caught her breath with another sob.

"Shhhh, Nida, it's okay now," he said stroking her head. She stiffened and jerked up quickly. Just then the sound of two shots made them both jump.

Chapter 50

"**Well, now,** that's just about the slickest bottom-deal I've ever seen," Tex said, watching Pod Randell ride away toward town.

"I don't understand. What do you mean?" Jonathan MacDougal said, his eyes on the two dead men lying on the bricks with their hands still tied.

Pod had shot them both immediately after hearing that they had attacked Leonida in her bedroom. "Dammit, I won't stand fer anymore of this," he had said, then drew his gun and fired. "Tell the lady I'm sorry this all happened. Maybe this'll kinda make up fer all the trouble she's had."

"I'll agree that these men should have had a fair trial and maybe hung, or sent to prison at the very least," MacDougal continued. "But he was understandably upset at what they had done."

"Yeah, he was upset alright. He was upset that they didn't get the job done like he wanted, and even more upset that they got themselves caught. He bored 'em so they wouldn't talk. I coulda got 'em to confess right here in front of most of the town that he and the judge are behind this whole game, and we woulda went back to town and hung 'em both, except now, we ain't got no witnesses. I shoulda let Rosa go ahead and bore that bastard when she had my gun."

"Naw, she'd have to live with it the rest of her life, or he might of kilt her in the process," Hanky said.

"It's a damn shame, ruining a wedding party like this, regardless of the cause. I guess I'll take my men and go back to the longboats. Please give Mrs. Garcia my best, will you?" MacDougal placed his wine glass on the table.

"Ruining the party? I hope you don't think this wingding's over, do you?" Hanky said.

"Well, yes I do. For one thing, you have two dead men bleeding all over the patio. Just look at everybody."

"Well, I ain't gonna let it happen. That little girl deserves more of a wedding than this. Here," Hanky said with a sweeping motion of his hand to the Indians. "Y'all grab hold of them varments and haul them outa here. Throw 'em in the river if ya don't want to bury 'em. Then clean this here mess up. General? You come over here and interpret fer me," he said climbing up on the fountain.

"Y'all listen up," he raised an arm high as he shouted. "Some of you seem to think this wedding's tainted, but it ain't. Shore, the Devil's tried his best to bust it up and cause this young couple lots of grief. But the only thing he's succeeded in doing is killing two of his own men.

"Now, y'all know that Pod Randell and Henry Baines is behind all this killin' and hurtin' folks around here. And look at what they've done tried to do here today. While we was having us a good time, they slips these two coyotes inside to kill Mrs. Garcia. But did they get away with it? No, 'cause Mrs. Garcia is a Godly-type woman who's done talked to the good Lord 'bout these young-uns getting hitched. So God, He fixes it so all the Devil can do is shoot his own folks. So, instead of being grieved over what's come off today, we ought to be celebrating. Just look up at the winder over yonder," he said pointing toward Leonida and Sean standing above them in the open window. "Mrs. Garcia is fine, ain't you, ma'am?" Leonida waved, to the cheers of the crowd. "And these young folks," he held out a hand toward Juan and Angela, "They's starting a whole new life together. We ought to be celebrating the defeat of the Devil here today, instead of going around lower'n a lizard's belly."

"Damn," MacDougal said as the ranger jumped off the bricks and grabbed Angela in his arms. The crowd cheered as he held the bride loosely and danced her across the bricks to the center of the courtyard. It took only seconds until the music started and the place was again filled with laughter and dancing. "That man ought to run for Congress. He'd win hands-down over any other candidate."

"Hell, if that's the case, he ought to be President. You ain't seen him at his best yet." Tex licked the paper on a cigarette he'd just rolled. "Excuse me Captain, I got me something I should take care of." MacDougal watched as the young man wove himself through the crowd to where Rosa stood.

"Are we leaving, Captain?" He snapped his head around to see his men gathered in a group behind the table. Several Indians came with buckets of water and brooms and began scrubbing the blood from the bricks.

"Leaving? You heard the ranger, didn't you? Hell no. The party's just starting. Show those men how to swab a deck first, then get out there and teach those landlubbers how to dance."

~　　~　　~

The drummers stamped their feet on the hollow log which had been placed over the hole in the ground, while the dancers proceeded around the arena counter-clockwise, gradually increasing their motion as the drummers increased their tempo. The dancers carried wormwood branches in their hands and swung them in rhythm as they shuffled past. Another man entered draped in a bear hide, and grunted as he sniffed and scratched the ground, pretending to look for food. The children joined in the fun and chased him around the circle with willow switches. He scampered around frolicking with them until he lay down feigning exhaustion. Then the singers started as bouquets and garlands of wormwood were passed out. Everyone was invited to join in the dancing.

"It's called the *Wa-dom Buh-yee*, or the Bear Dance," Leonida said, placing a garland of wormwood on Sean's head. "The wormwood is a symbol of peace and friendship. We are all supposed to take part in the dancing." She pulled him to his feet.

"But I don't know how."

"You don't have to. Just shuffle around the fire a couple of times and we can sit back down. The older people are chanting prayers," she said as they shuffled and stomped their way past the drummers. "This is supposed to be a ceremony for giving thanks for having survived the year, and pleading that the grizzly bear will be friendly and will not molest them. They also pray that the rattlesnakes will treat them favorably. They are probably honoring the poor beast that died in that pit yesterday."

"Yes, it was rather ghastly," he said as he stumbled.

"Quit watching your feet. No one's going to notice what you're doing. They'll do this again in the spring, you know. But then, they will give thanks for surviving the winter, and pray for favor throughout the coming year."

They sat down and watched the others take a turn. The Indians laughed and joked as the clumsy miners stumbled past in their heavy boots. Then the Indian dancers started clapping hardwood sticks together in time to the sound of the drummers, as the last of the participants made their way around the fire.

"Come, it is time to leave," she said, jumping to her feet. "We'll follow the bear wherever he goes." They followed the lead dancer to the creek behind the corrals where everyone threw the garlands and greenery into the water.

"This will make you a true Yokut in their eyes," she said with a smile as she squatted to scoop up a handful of water and splash her face. "You're supposed to wash and say a prayer of peace and safety for the journey home."

"And which God shall we pray to?" he said, kneeling beside her.

"I'll pray to the same one I do in the chapel every morning, Señor. Which one are you going to pray to?"

"The same one, I'm sure." He crossed himself in the name of The Father, Son and Holy Spirit, then offered her his hand to help her back up the bank.

"*Buenas noches*," Lupe Perez said with a smile and a slight bow as they passed. Sean smiled and tipped his hat.

"Sweet child," Leonida said.

"Yes, indeed." She held onto his arm as they walked in silence, taking a roundabout way to the house. He had rehearsed many things in his mind earlier that day as to what he would say when they were alone, but he couldn't remember any of them to save his life at the moment. A lone vaquero strummed a guitar and sang as they paused under an oak tree within sight of the hacienda.

"I hope I didn't get you into trouble," he said, glancing around. "I know you're not supposed to be left alone without a chaperone."

"Don't worry, Señor. One of the *vaqueros* is close by, acting as *carabina*. Besides, you have saved my life twice now, so my *papa* is not too worried about leaving me in your care."

"He should be."

"Oh, how so?" She raised her eyebrows.

"Because, I'm afraid my feelings for you are probably stronger than they should be."

"I see." She pursed her lips while thoughtfully nodding her head. "And what is the limit one should place on their affection for another, Doctor?"

"You know what I mean. I've fallen in love with you, and I shouldn't have." He stuffed his hands in his pockets and studied the stars in the black sky.

"*Bueno*, I understand. But why shouldn't you have fallen in love with me?" The question caused him to stare at her. "Is it wrong for you to do so?" She removed her veil and shook her hair free.

"I don't know."

"Is it because I'm Mexican?"

"No, don't be ridiculous."

"I'm not trying to be, Señor. I am only asking because I have a right to know. You say you have fallen in love with me, yet you say it is wrong. When is it wrong for one person to love another? I would like to know."

"I love you for more than just a friend. Don't you understand? I think about you all the time." Sean felt his hand tremble as he wiped his mouth and turned away. "You're Rudolfo's wife. You're the daughter of a famous General, and owner of this huge ranch. And what am I? The son of an Irish immigrant."

"Oh, so I see." Her voice became a whisper as she lowered her head and turned away. "Because I'm Doña Leonida Garcia, it would be impossible for me to love such a lowly person as Sean Kilkenney. You insult me greatly, Señor."

"I didn't mean to." He took her by the shoulders, but she kept her head turned. "Leonida? Please?" He lifted her chin with his fingertips. Her green eyes glistened and her bottom lip trembled as she spoke.

"Am I such a small person that I cannot love someone who...." her voice broke and she bit her lip as a tear trickled down one cheek, "is from a different social background than my own? I love Rosa and Angela, who were *prostitutas*, and I love Tex and Señor Hanky too."

"Yes, but...."

"*Por que*?" She turned away with a shrug. "If I never choose to think of you as more than a friend, does that mean I cannot love you?"

"No, that's what I'm afraid of." She stared at him over her shoulder.

"That I will only think of you as a friend?" He nodded. "Señor?" She took a deep breath and turned to face him.

"Today, when you held me in my room, you called me by a name. Do you remember what it was?"

He thought for a moment. "I think I called you 'Nida'. That's just before we heard the shots."

"Si. There is only one other person who ever called me Nida. Do you know who it was?" He shook his head. "My husband, Rudolfo."

"Oh, God, I'm so sorry."

"Don't be. I'm not." She stood on her tiptoes and, quickly brushing his lips with her own, ran to the house.

"*Chihuahua, Amigo*," Paco said coming from behind the tree they had been standing under. "Doña Leonida thinks of you as *an amante*."

"Where in the hell did you come from?"

"From the tree. I was watching the moon and the stars the same as you." Sean heard a girlish giggle and turned to see Lupe duck back behind the trunk.

"Jesus Almighty God."

"*Esta bien*, Señor. He gives you the *amor* of Doña Leonida," he said slapping Sean's arm. "*Esta bien*."

~   ~   ~

Leonida lay clutching Rudolfo's shirt as her tears wet the pillow. She held it to her nose and breathed deeply, but his scent was almost gone. All that remained was the smell of her own perfume and the faint smell of Rosa who had spent several nights sleeping in her bed.

"Oh, my husband, my *amante*, what have I done? I didn't mean to kiss him. I feel so dirty. Forgive me, Rudolfo. You are my husband, and I love you, but I feel safe around him, and I've been frightened for such a long time. I've been scared every since they murdered you and Carlo. Even with Papa and Ildefonso to protect me, there's still no one but Rosa to hold me in the night, or to talk to like we used to. I miss you deeply, *mi esposo*.

"And I pray much every day. You see me in the chapel,

don't you? I talk to the Saints and to the Holy Virgin and her Son. I ask them for answers as I read the Holy Book, and I beg them to help me and to protect these people you left me with. And they do help, for the most part. They sent me the Texas *vaquero* and his father. And they sent me Rosa and Angela to love. But they also sent the Doctor, and that is the problem. You know, don't you, Rudolfo? He was here to help when you and Carlo were still alive. He is a good man, just like you said he was. He is kind and gentle, just like you. He reminds me a lot of you. And, as you know, he has saved me from these evil men twice now. And the last time, when he held me in his arms, forgive me my husband, but it felt so good. I didn't want him to let go.

"Oh, yes, I know he has a bad temper, but so did you and your brother. All men have bad tempers, *mi amor*. And at times he does act sort of crazy, like Maria says. But I find myself longing to hear his voice, and I make excuses to see him. I want him to touch me, Rudolfo. Do you understand? I hope so. I feel so dirty." Her voice broke into a sob as she curled up and buried her face against her knees.

"*Santa Maria, Madre de Dios*, please take these feelings away from me. I don't want to love another man when I'm still in mourning for my husband. I don't want to bring shame on my family. Please, Holy Mother, please help me."

Chapter 51

"**Now I** wonder what they're up to?" Tex said as the laughing men came out of the cabin.

"It is no good, *Hombre*." Paco pulled his revolver and checked the loads. "Domingo doesn't trust Anglos. These men from town would not be welcome here." They had ridden out to check on the Indian goat herder and his family whose house lay closest to the river, when they saw the horses tied out front.

"Don't think so either. Why don't you work your way over to that oak yonder while I make acquaintances?" Paco tied his horse to the juniper and removed his spurs before sprinting across the open area. Tex slid a round into the chamber of the needle-gun and stepped into the open.

"Hey, ya'all looking for someone in particular?"

The men stopped in their tracks and drew their guns. One of them fired but missed wildly. Tex dropped to one knee as Paco opened fire from behind the oak, causing the men to dive for cover behind the *carreta* which was parked in front of the house. Paco ducked back as a hail of gunfire sent bark flying. Tex shifted his position some and took careful aim at one leg sticking out from behind the large wooden wheel. He squeezed the trigger and the leg seemed to disappear with the recoil of the gun. The man fell to the ground with an anguished cry.

"Ya'all better give up," he yelled. "We got you in a cross-fire."

"Go to hell," one of the men said, and snapped off a couple of quick shots at him. The rounds fell short and to the left, but Paco's shot brought a yell from one of the men.

"God almighty, that Meskin son-of-a-bitch nicked me. Let's get the hell outa here." There was a quiet moment when Tex could hear them mumbling behind the cart, but he couldn't make out what they were saying. The wounded man cried out for help. Tex's heart jumped when one of the men behind the cart shot him dead.

"Damn, what'd you do that for, Rusty?" he could hear an excited voice.

"He was just gonna slow us down. Besides, the son-of-a-bitch was done for anyway."

Tex took aim and fired. Splinters and hay flew high as one of the boards gave way under the impact of the needle-gun. He fired again. Then, several more times. The *carreta* seemed to be falling apart under the assault of the heavy weapon. He had to stop and dig into his saddlebag for more ammunition and that was just the chance the men needed. One of them fired rapidly at the oak tree while the other ran to retrieve their horses. He was pulling the animals behind the cart as Tex threw another round into the chamber. He fired and the nearest horse fell. His next shot caused the *carreta* to lean lazily as one of the wheels broke apart. The men ran behind the house using the remaining horses as a shield. Paco stepped into the open and fired several rounds at the fleeing men before joining Tex as he slowly approached the open door to the cabin.

"Guess that answers my question as to why Domingo didn't poke his head out during all the shooting," he said looking at the mutilated bodies lying in the middle of the floor under a pile of dead animals.

"*Santa Maria, Madre de Dios*," Paco said, crossing himself. "Why did the *gringos* kill every one, *amigo*? Why did they kill even the goats and the dogs?"

"You know the answer to that one, my friend. Injuns believe that if their bodies get all tore up here in this life, they can't get into heaven. If some of the Injun *vaqueros* happened to come upon this, they'd think Domingo and his folks spirits would be mingled with those of the dogs and goats. They'd just sort of float around somewheres, lost. They did this to scare off all the Injuns on this place, so they can get at Mrs. Garcia. Dirty bastards."

"It almost works on me," he said wiping a shaking hand across his pale face. "What are we going to tell Doña Leonida, *amigo*? The Indians will find out and leave, when we bring the bodies back to the rancho."

"No they won't, 'cause we ain't gonna take them back."

"Eh? We can't leave them here like this. The coyote and the *gato* will come."

"We're gonna tell them the place got burnt up, and there weren't no bodies to bring back," Tex said, dumping the oil from one of the lamps across the bodies. "Come on, grab anything that will burn. Dry brush, hay, the boards from the *carreta*. We're gonna build a fire big enough to see all the way to Sacramento. Then, we're only going to tell the General and Baca what really come off here. Maybe a couple more. But as far as the rest of the Injuns are concerned, Domingo and his family are fishing and hunting with Jesus right this very minute."

"*Bueno*," Paco said, and ran to cut some dry shrubs with his machete. They found several gallons of lamp oil hidden in a lean-to shed out back and added that, cans and all to the pile. Then Tex calmly rolled two cigarettes, one for himself, and handed the other to Paco.

"Ready?" he said, striking a match on his boot and lighting Paco's smoke. The *vaquero* nodded. "Good." He lit his own cigarette and tossed the match inside. The flames crawled quickly to the opposite wall and licked through the open windows.

"What do we do with him?" Paco said with a nod toward the dead man lying by the *carreta*.

"First, we'll see if he's got anything on him," Tex said poking his fingers inside the dead man's vest pocket. "Then, we'll leave him for coyote bait. Nothing but a couple of double eagles," he said tossing the coins to Paco. "No papers, no nothing. Don't guess no one's gonna be writing home to tell Mama Junior's dead."

"*Caramba*," Paco said, shaking his head. "What should we do with this money? It is bad money from a bad man. I don't want it." He tried handing the coins back to Tex.

"Give 'em to the padre. Maybe, after he prays over 'em, they'll be fitting to give to some poor folks. Come on, let's get outa here. It's getting hotter'n hell," he said backing away from the burning building. They paused at the juniper where their horses were tied and watched as the roof caved in, sending a shower of sparks and smoke several hundred feet in the air.

~　　~　　~

Sean entered the study without knocking. The General looked up from the walnut desk where he had been talking to Tex and Paco. Juan and Hanky were seated on the sofa against the wall. All the men had somber expressions stamped on their faces. "Yes, what is it?" he said. "Come in, and close the door behind you." Sean shut the door and walked to the middle of the room and paused to glance around. "Well, come, Doctor. I'm a busy man."

Sean cleared his throat before speaking. "I didn't want to tell you in front of anyone else, but I'm afraid I'm going to have to leave."

"Oh, and why is that?" Jose pulled a cigar from the box on the desk and let the lid snap shut.

"It concerns you daughter."

"Leonida? What has she done now? Fired you?" He smelled the cigar and rolled it over several times in his fingers, watching Sean from the corner of his eye.

"No, nothing like that. I'd rather not say, sir."

"Well, come Doctor, there is nothing you can't say about my daughter that most of the men here in the room don't already know. Now, why is it that you feel you must leave us in the middle of a crisis?"

"It's just that I've fallen in love with her and," he dropped his head and let his eyes dart across the carpet. "I just can't stay here any longer."

"Oh, is that all? I thought you were going to tell me something that I didn't already know. Like her kissing you the other night under the oak tree." Sean caught his breath as the General continued. "The whole rancho knows these things, Señor, for this *vaquero* standing in front of me told some of his friends about that kiss, and they in turn told their friends. I have had men shot for less, do you understand me, Paco?"

"Si." The vaquero shifted nervously under the general's stern gaze.

"And your feelings for her are certainly no secret, Doctor. Everyone has seen the way you watch her every movement, like the mother hen watches after her chicks. Now, don't bother me with such foolishness as your leaving over feelings of love for my daughter. Most men would think you odd for not loving her, and would cut your throat to have her love in return. So, unless there is something else bothering you, we are busy men."

"My God, man, is that all you've got to say? We're talking about your daughter here."

"Yes, we are talking about her." Jose tapped the end of the cigar angerly against the desk top as he spoke. "And her actions the other night were very inappropriate. I shall discuss them with her when the time is right. Believe me, I am not taking this thing lightly, Doctor. Leonida knows it is not acceptable for a lady to kiss a man outside of the immediate family, unless she intends to marry that person. But," he shrugged, "her feelings for you must be stronger than I thought. We'll talk about this later."

"Begging you pardon, sir, there is nothing to discuss. I'm leaving this afternoon. I'm already packed, and my mule is tied at the corral. I just came to say goodbye."

Jose's jaw tightened and he surveyed the room before slamming his fist on the desk and crushing the cigar he'd never bothered to light.

"You are the stupid *gringo* Maria says you are, aren't you? You interrupt an important meeting in which these men are telling me of the murder of an entire family on this rancho, to tell me you're leaving us because you're lovesick over my daughter? What gives you the right to think that is more important than the lives of the people living here? Tell me that, Doctor."

"I'm sorry, I didn't know. Who was it?" Sean suddenly had a sick feeling in the pit of his stomach.

"Domingo, his wife and all the kids," Hanky said.

"Goddamit," he said wiping his face with a sweaty palm. "They've got to be stopped."

"Exactly," Jose rose to his feet. "We were in the process of discussing that very issue when you barged in here with your tales of woe." He pulled another cigar from the box and waved it in the air as he continued. "Tell me, Doctor, don't you think it would be foolish of me to let you leave when we are on the verge of war?"

"I'm sorry, I don't follow you."

"Certainly you do, Señor. A good doctor is just as valuable as powder and shot in any war. You know that. You were in the Army. And for me to let you leave would be downright foolish. It would be presuming that we would be able to go into battle without suffering any casualties at all, and that is highly unlikely. At last count, the judge had close to thirty armed men."

"I don't know what to say."

"There is nothing to say. You cannot leave this rancho until I say you can. Is that understood?"

"You can't do that."

"Like hell I can't. Just watch me. Paco?"

"Si?"

"As your punishment for acting like an old woman, you shall be Señor Kilkenney's escort, day and night. He is not to do anything or go anywhere without you being there. And he is most certainly not to leave the vicinity of this house and grounds without my permission. In fact, absolutely no one, not even one of you here in this room, is to leave without my permission. Is that understood?" He nodded. "It had better be, because I shall punish you severely if you disobey me." He turned to the others.

"Juan? Take Señor Kilkenney's mule out to one of the remote pastures where he cannot find her. And tell everyone that he is not to be given any beast, not even a cow to ride. Now that, Doctor," he said leaning on the desk with both palms, "Is my final decision. Is there anything else you would like to discuss with me?"

"No, I don't guess there is."

"Good. You may go now."

Chapter 52

"**May I** come in, Father?" Leonida poked her head through the partially open door.

"Yes, my child. By all means. Do come in." Father Franco held out both hands in greeting as he shuffled forward to greet her. "Come, sit here," he said, pulling out one of the two chairs at his small table. "I'll make us some tea." The living quarters located at the rear of the chapel matched the old priest, plain and modest. The only decoration adorning any of the four walls was the crucifix hanging at the foot of the small cot taking up space along one wall. The stone fireplace encompassed an entire wall by itself, and the small window and door took up another. The furniture consisted of the bed and one lamp sitting on top of the table with two chairs. The few books he owned were stacked inside a wooden box in one corner. She had repeatedly tried to move him into the hacienda but he had refused, saying the room was comfortable and humble, like it should be.

"I saw you inside the church praying." He set two mugs on the table and turned to retrieve the kettle from the fireplace.

"You seem to spend much time there. That is good." He filled the cups with steaming liquid then sat across from her and smiled as he rested his elbows on the table, tapping his fingers together. "Now, tell me, child. What brings you here? What is bothering you?"

"Couldn't I just be visiting a friend?" She dropped her tea fob in the water and bobbed it up and down.

"Si, but I visit you every day when I sit at your table. Do not lie to me, my child. Something is weighing on you heavily." He creased his brow and poked his bottom lip out. "What has Doña Leonida so troubled that she seeks me alone inside my dwelling?"

"I don't know what to do, Padre." She buried her face in her hands and the words came almost as fast as her tears. "I pray and I pray, but I still don't know what to do. I know it is wrong to hate those men who killed Rudolfo and Carlo and....and did this....evil to me. And I've wished many times to take my *vaqueros* into Dogtown and kill them all." She clenched her teeth and shook a fist at the air before covering her face again. "I even bought guns for the men to fight with. But I know such hate as I feel in my heart is wrong."

"Si, but they are evil men. And I have often wished the same thing myself."

"*Que?*" She looked up as the priest nodded thoughtfully.

"Oh, yes, my child. When I saw what they had done to you, then Rudolfo and Carlo, I wished many bad things on them. And don't forget the others they have hurt like Señores Kilkenney and Hanky. And when I heard about Domingo Rojas and his family," he lowered his head and crossed himself, "my heart has been broken many times by these beasts."

"I'm sorry Padre," she leaned across the table to place a hand on his arm. "In my own sorrow, I failed to realize that...."

"That a priest could have such feelings also?" She nodded. "Does not the shepherd get angry every time the wolf hurts one of the sheep?"

"Yes, I guess he does, doesn't he?" She leaned back

and tried to sip her tea, but it was too hot. "What shall we do, Padre? I thought that by arming the *vaqueros* and staying close to the *hacienda*, those men would leave us alone. But they keep on hurting my people. Tex says they will keep on doing these things until they get our land, or someone goes into town to stop them. Is that true, Father?"

"Yes, I'm afraid so."

"Then, what are we to do? I....I know that just going there to kill them would be wrong. And my *vaqueros*. Many of them have families of their own. It wouldn't be right to ask them to risk their lives over a piece of ground, would it? And yet, the longer I wait, those men hurt or kill some more of our people. What am I to do, Father?"

"I cannot tell you what to do, child. You are Doña Leonida and God has given you that responsibility. You have to seek His will and make that decision by yourself. I can only pray for you."

"Si," she nodded slowly.

"But let me answer one of your questions in this way." He took a thoughtful sip of tea before continuing. "When Señor Kilkenney operated on Erasmo Gamarro, did he cut the toe off because he hated the toe? Or did Señor Kilkenney cut the toe off because he loved Erasmo?" He shook a finger at her from across the table. "What ever you do, Señora, make sure it is done out of love for God first, then for His sheep, and you will be doing the right thing."

~   ~   ~

Ike Carpenter listened intently to the conversation as he wrapped the supplies in oil cloth and bound the package with heavy twine. He didn't really care for the two men who had been waiting when he unlocked the doors that morning. He'd only seen them a couple of times, but he did know they both worked for Pod Randell and Henry Baines, and that was enough to put the mark of Cain on them in his book.

"Why'd you get so much grub for, Shavers? Ain't like

Pod's askin' us to stay out there for a month."

"I don't like to get hungry, Bill. Besides, ya never know what's gonna happen. We might get stuck out there longer than you think."

"Here you are," Ike said shoving the pack forward on the counter. "That'll be $75.15."

"Hell of a lot for such a small package, ain't it?" Shavers said.

"It's all the .44 cartridges. You asked for twelve boxes, remember? You boys going hunting?"

"Yeah, huntin' Meskins and Injuns," Bill said with a laugh.

"Still say it's kinda high for a little coffee and beans," Shavers growled.

"Forty-fours have gone up the last few days."

"Yeah, I'll bet," he said digging into his pocket and tossing the gold coins on the counter. "The cost of doin' business around here must be a bugger." He grabbed the package and turned away. "Come on, let's go see the judge and get some of our money back. Ain't no Injun worth ten cents a slug."

Ike let the door slam shut before he grabbed his pad and began writing. He then folded the note and stuffed it in his apron pocket before asking his wife Alice to watch the front of the store while he left through the rear door to find Arturo. He found the boy in the grove of oaks lining the creek bank, watering the horses.

"Here," he said, stuffing the folded paper in the boy's pocket. "Make sure Jose Flores sees this as soon as possible."

"Well, well, Pod, would you look at this." Ike turned with a jerk to see Judge Henry Baines and Pod Randell emerging from behind a thick growth of bushes. "And to think I almost called Frank Powell a liar when he said it was our storekeeper. I didn't think such an outstanding citizen like Ike Carpenter would be spreading such vicious rumors about us."

"Just goes to show that you can't trust anyone, can you?" Pod said with a sneer.

"Someone's got to stop you." Ike licked his dry lips.

"Stop us? You haven't come close to stopping us. You might have hindered us, maybe slowed us down a little, but you certainly didn't stop us. I believe the only thing you really succeeded in doing was causing that pretty wife of yours a lot of pain. Now, tell me, what's in that note?" The judge took a step forward.

"You leave that boy alone. He had nothing to do with this."

"Would you listen to him, Henry? Still a liar till the end." Pod's hand was so quick Ike could hardly see it move. The bullet took him square in the chest, knocking him to the ground. A second shot sounded and Arturo fell across him with a gaping hole in his head. Ike had just enough time to see the judge dig around in the boy's pocket and remove the paper before the light seemed to fade. He could hear Pod's spurs jingle as they walked away. Then, nothing.

~   ~   ~

Father Franco's head flopped lazily with the movement of the burro as he dozed in the saddle. The warm midday sun felt good on his back and he more than likely would have fallen from his burro except for that pesky fly that kept landing on his cheek. He sat up with a start, realizing that he had been asleep.

"Thank you, Señor, for sending the fly to wake me," he said, glancing toward heaven. The fall from Pedro's back would not have been a great one, but a man of his age might have been injured, and that would not have been a good thing. And how would he explain to the General how and when the injury occurred, since he had purposely ignored his orders and left the vicinity of the main house to go visit Julio Perez? But it was needed. Julio was an old man like himself, and in ill health.

"Ah, but the General worries too much, doesn't he, Pedro?" he said with a laugh, patting the burro's neck. "We are God's servants, doing His work, so it is up to Him to protect us. And He does it right well. Just like sending the fly. Who knows if it wasn't really an angel? They have many forms, you know.

You're an angel, you know that, Pedro? You were at least given to me by God, for I prayed one day that I might have the means to go visit my flock of sheep, and the very next day, there you were, sent by the hand of a Miwok angel."

He arched his back, breathing deeply of the warm air and smiled as a cottontail darted across the trail in front of them.

"Yes, angels come in many different forms. I'm convinced of that fact. Take Señor Kilkenney for instance. Now, that is a strange one indeed, wouldn't you agree? He has a vile temper and the manners of a bear, but he has a good heart, and he does love the children. And anyone who loves these children, Pedro, is sent by God. It was a mean trick Señor Tex and I played on him, but I'm sure God has forgiven us. Besides, have you noticed how humble he has become since? Even Doña Leonida has taken notice of the change in him. And, I shouldn't be telling you this, but there's been talk of them having a romantic interest in each other." He brought the burro to a halt at the edge of the yard. "Hello, it seems they have company." There were three horses tied to a post in front of the house.

"That's strange, why isn't Chulo barking? He always greets us when we come." He studied the large black dog lying in the sun. He inched Pedro closer to have a better look. The dark spot on the ground he had thought was a shadow was actually blood. Chulo was dead. A girl's scream coming from the house made him jump.

"Lupe! *Madre de Dios, protégé su hija.* Mother of God, protect your daughter," he repeated as he leaped from the burro and raced toward the open door. Two strange men were standing in the middle of the room laughing, as a third with a bandaged arm wrestled on the bed with a partially nude Lupe Perez. She was kicking and biting, holding him off as best as she could. It only took one glance for the padre to see that Julio was dead. He was lying just inside the doorway with a hole in his forehead.

"Leave that child alone," he yelled in Spanish, lashing out with his riding crop.

"Goddamn, where'd you come from?" The man tried fending off the blows with his good arm as his companions laughed harder.

"Look out, Hugh, ya got two angry Meskins to deal with now."

"*Madre de Dios, protégé su hija.*" Father Franco brought the crop down over and over.

"What the hell's he saying?" one of the men behind him said.

"How should I know? I don't speak that jabber."

Lupe bolted upright only to receive a harsh backhand, sending her backward across the bed where her head hit the wall. She crumbled in a heap with a strange moan. The riding crop cut a welt across the assailant's cheek as the angry Priest pressed forward trying to drive him backward. "Dammit," the man in front of him said as his one good hand dropped to his side where a gun appeared. The crash from the bullet propelled Franco backward where he fell against the wall.

"Now you've done it, Hugh. You kilt their priest." The padre heard one of the men's voices echo from inside a tunnel. A huge weight was pressing down on his chest, making it difficult to breath.

"Well, what in the hell'd you expect me to do, let him keep hittin' me with that whip? Besides, you and Eb didn't plan on letting him walk outa here alive, did you?"

"I hadn't planned on killing no priest, that's for shore. Now, we'll have every Miskin from here to Mexico City after our hides."

"Aw, to hell with you both. I'm still gonna have my fun with the girl." Franco could see a shadow move toward the bed. Then, the room was suddenly filled with light as three more men entered the door. They wore sandals and were dressed in white ponchos and breeches, with white sombreros. One of them stopped to stare toward the bed, while another walked to where he lay against the wall.

"Hello Father, we've been waiting for you." The man had a warm smile, and Franco liked him. He let his eyes roll toward the others in the room. "Oh, don't worry about them. They can't see us."

"You're from Him?" He glanced up toward the ceiling.

"Si, He sent us here to escort you home. Come," he held out a hand, "Julio waits for us outside." Father Franco took his hand and the pain left as he stood to his feet.

"So, this is what it's like," he said looking back at his own body lying motionless on the floor. "I feel so young."

"You are. It's wonderful, isn't it?"

He paused in the middle of the room to glare at the beast pulling and tearing at Lupe's clothing.

"Don't worry about her, Father. She isn't feeling any pain, and Ramon will wait for her." He nodded toward the one dressed in white standing by the bed.

"Can't he stop them?"

"Another time, yes, but not now. The Señor has a better plan." They paused at the door where he said, "Ah, see? There she is now." He turned to see Lupe standing beside the one called Ramon, looking back toward the bed. "He has a *fiesta* planned in your honor this afternoon. You know, Padre, He is very proud of you, and He loves each of you very much."

Chapter 53

"Get out of here, you sons of Satan," Sean yelled and threw stones at the crows pecking away in the small garden. It wasn't much of a garden to begin with and he had his doubts as to what the harvest would be, having planted it so late in the year. But it had been a constant battle from the beginning. First, there was Pedro, Father Franco's burro, who insisted on wandering through the small patch of ground and eating all the fresh shoots. He received the padre's wrath on that one when the priest caught him throwing stones at the small beast and threatening to kill him if he ever caught him eating there again. And between the children and dogs, he'd almost given up hope of ever seeing any crop at all. But he wasn't in any kind of mood to put up with birds this morning. After being confined to the immediate area the day before, anything would have set him off. "I'll shoot you, if you ever come back again." He threw another stone at a particularly large bird who squawked angerly as he lifted heavenward.

"Stop that! You leave them alone!" He turned toward the second floor veranda to see Leonida glaring down at him.

"But they were eating the garden."

"I don't care. Yell at them, or flap your arms if you want to scare them, but don't throw rocks. You might hurt one of them."

"And if I did?" He put his hands on his hips. "They're not pets, Madam, they're scavengers. They eat dead things and carry disease. Besides, they are noisy pests."

"I like them, and they are too my pets. So you leave them alone." Her green eyes flashed back at him as she shook her finger.

"Aaaaa, you would make pets out of them, wouldn't you?" he said throwing up hands of defeat as he turned away. He then stopped and shook a finger of his own at her. "That's because you're as crazy as the rest of them around here. You know that? You're all crazy." He stooped to pick up a stone and heaved it at the last remaining bird, before stomping away amid a torrent of oaths flowing down from the balcony. He crossed the bricks and walked swiftly past the grinning vaqueros at the corral where he paused to shake a fist at Paco, who followed a few steps behind.

"You get away from me. Understand? I don't want you following me anymore."

"But, Señor, the General...."

"I don't give a damn what the General wants. I'm tired of being followed. I'm tired of hearing you jingle like a bunch of bells every time you take a step." He pointed toward the man's spurs. "And I'm damn tired of being a prisoner, do you understand me? If you don't get away from me right now, I'm going to beat you within an inch of your life." He swung a half-hearted right at the man's head, which Paco easily avoided, and scampered back a few paces to the hoots and calls of the men gathered at the corrals. Sean turned on his heel and walked briskly to the oak about a hundred yards distant from the bunkhouse, where he sat to smoke his pipe.

The General wasn't kidding. He'd searched everywhere for Cathy, but the mule was no where to be found. "If anything's happened to her," he almost bit the pipestem in two.

But nothing was wrong with the animal and he knew it. These people loved their horses and cattle too much to harm a mule. The vaqueros were just following orders when they hid her from him. He had considered simply walking away, but they had taken his clothes and medical bag also. Even his money was gone. He had nothing left but the clothes on his back, and they were in sorry shape. The more he thought about it, the angrier he got. Who did they think they were, keeping a man prisoner like that? He turned toward Paco who sat under the next tree about thirty yards to his left.

"You're a prisoner too, aren't you? That's okay, because you deserve it. It was your big mouth that started this whole mess. It's the General who needs a beating, and he's going to get one too. When this whole thing is over, I'm going to give that old man a pounding he'll never forget. Do you understand me?" He finished the last part by shaking his fist and yelling at Paco, who simply shrugged and calmly rolled a cigarette. "Na, you wouldn't understand." He lowered his head and closed his eyes.

Why should the little man understand? He was happy here with his horses and cattle. That's all he knew and cared about. How could he know the torment that plagued Sean's Irish heart? How she came to him in his dreams every night, to look at him with her green eyes and place her soft lips against his. He could even smell the scent of her hair and feel the swell of her breast against him. No, Paco wouldn't understand. All he loved was horses and guns....and Lupe. Yes, there was Lupe Perez. But he still couldn't understand even then, because he could hold Lupe in his arms and they were going to get married in the spring. All Sean could do was dream about Leonida. He'd never be able to have her. No one understood. He'd leave first chance he got without telling her goodbye.

The wagon coming up the road pulled him from his private hell. He could recognize Woodrow Black's huge frame even at that distance. He knocked the ashes from his pipe, as the wagon came to a halt in the courtyard and the large man jumped down. *Bet that'll make her happy. She doesn't like horses messing up the bricks. Didn't anyone tell you Woodrow?* The crowd that had gathered was listening intently, but it wasn't until he saw Leonida cover her face with her hands and lean against her father's chest that Sean rose to his feet. He walked silently past Paco, who waited patiently.

"Has to be no *bueno*, huh, Señor Sean?" He didn't answer, but kept on walking. It was Tex who stepped to the edge of the crowd and clasped a strong hand on his shoulder.

"It's Ike Carpenter and Arturo Horeno. They found them both shot to death down by the creek early this morning. Alice heard the shots and ran out. She found 'em dead, but never seen who done it, though."

"Ike, and Arturo?" Sean ran a shaking hand over his face. His knees suddenly felt weak. "Who'd want to kill that little boy?"

"Bet we all know who done it," Hanky said. "Woodrow says that Alice told him the boy was supposed to be bringing Jose a note from her husband. Seems they'd worked out a system where they was passing on information so's we'd know what was going on in town."

"You were using that lad as a spy?" His voice caused everyone to quiet down as he turned toward the General. "You bastard! What kind of a devil are you? Why didn't you just take your own gun and kill them yourself?"

"Easy boy." Hanky tried grabbing him, but he pulled away.

"I hope you rot in hell," he said as he lunged forward.

"Not this morning," Woodrow said, lifting him off the ground. "Some other time, alright? Here," the big man nodded toward the crowd. "Help hold him until he calms down." Sean was immediately dragged to the opposite side of the wagon.

"Okay, okay." He raised his hands in defeat.

"By the way," Woodrow said, turning toward Leonida. "Mrs. Horeno wants the padre to come to town and hold Mass for Arturo this afternoon. I'm going to say words over Ike myself. There isn't a Methodist minister within miles, as you well know."

"Si," she said with a sniff, daubing her damp eyes with a lace hanky as she glanced around her. "Where is Father Franco? Would one of you go find him for me?"

"You won't find him here," Sean said flatly.

"*Perdon?*"

"I said you won't find him around the ranch. I saw him ride away on that grey devil of his early this morning, from my prison window." He added the last part with a curt nod of his head toward the house.

"Where did he go?"

"Now, how in the hell would I know that? Ask your stable boy." Sean's heart pained him the moment the angry words left his lips but an apology was far from him at that moment. The Señora let out a long sigh before turning toward her father who was already interrogating the young lad.

"Where is Father Franco?" The boy only stood there shaking. "Did you hear me? Where is he? No one is supposed to leave this place without my permission. Do you understand that?" More silence. "Do you want me to punish you?"

"*Papa*, no," she said shaking her head. She took the boy's hands and squatted so he could look her in the eyes, and smiled. "Manuel, please, this is important. There's a boy about your age who has been killed, and his mother needs Father Franco to say Mass over him. Did he say where he was going?"

"Si, but he made me promise." The General started to say something, but she held up a hand.

"*Por favor*, Manuel, for me. No one is going to punish you. Where is Father Franco."

"Julio and Lupe. He says Julio Perez has been sick."

"*Bueno.*" She kissed his hand as her father paced around muttering curses.

"Tell Señora Horeno we shall send Father Franco as soon as we can reach him," she said rising to her feet. "And please tell Señora Carpenter I am deeply sorry to hear about her husband. Tell her I send her my heart and my prayers, but I cannot be there for her this afternoon. There has been too much trouble in Dogtown."

"I'm sure she will understand, ma'am," Woodrow said with a bow. "But if you folks will excuse me, I must be getting back to town. Those thieves will steal a man blind when his back is turned." Everyone silently watched the wagon leave before General Flores started barking orders.

"Juan, you and Tex come with me. We're going to find that padre and bring him back if I have to tie him to the back of that *burro*."

"But, Señor, I should be the one to go," Paco said.

"No, you just want to see the girl. You stay and keep an eye on him," he said pointing at Sean. "I don't want anyone wandering away from this house. Does everyone understand me?" He raised his voice as he turned in a circle. "My daughter included. The cattle will take care of themselves."

"I'd say the old boy's hoppin' mad," Hanky said placing a chew in his cheek. "Better do as he says or he might shoot yer leg off." He raised an eyebrow at Sean before turning away.

~   ~   ~

"*Santa Maria, Madre de Dios*," Juan fell to his knees beside Father Franco's lifeless body. "The padre, they kill the padre. Julio was old and the *chica* so small. They never hurt anyone. They killed the dog and goats too."

"Now, I've seen some mean sons-of-bitches in my time, but these skunks deserve all the hell they can get." Tex spit the match stem he'd been chewing on into the corner. "They raped that little girl. You know that? They raped her before killing her."

"Si, I know, Señor Tex." Jose ran a trembling hand across his face.

"And you couldn't find a nicer man than Julio. And the padre? Aw, hell." Tex turned away and leaned one hand against the wall as Juan rose to his feet trying to wipe the tears away with his dusty sleeve.

"Juan, go see if you can't find something to pull the

carreta with. We shall take them back to the rancho and bury them behind the chapel." Jose mopped his brow with his scarf.

"Ya know," Tex said after the vaquero had gone. "Yer not gonna be able to hold them *vaqueros* back after they see this, don't you? Some of 'em wanted to burn the town when they hurt your daughter and kilt her husband. And they was even more riled when Carlo got shot. And you haven't even told them about Domingo yet. What are you planning to do?"

"You misunderstand me, Señor. I don't plan on holding them back."

"Huh?" Tex looked up with a start from where he was wrapping a blanket around Lupe's nude body.

"It will be almost dark when we arrive at the *hacienda*, and we'll have to bury our dead first, of course. But the plan's all in order. I think tomorrow afternoon's a fine time to pay Dogtown a little visit, don't you?"

"Hell, I'll take Hanky, Juan and Paco, and we'll go tonight." Tex laid Lupe's body on the bed and began rolling a cigarette.

"Now, you sound like my daughter."

"What?"

"Si, she wanted to destroy the whole town after they killed Rudolfo. Remember her struggle with the doctor in the corral?" Tex nodded. "I had a hard time restraining her. There isn't a *vaquero* on this ranch that wouldn't have followed her to their death if she had gone then, and that is the problem. Our men are working *vaqueros*, Señor, not warriors like you and I. A lot of them would have died in such a battle. Some of them had never held a gun in their hands before now. That is why I had to ask you and Señor Hanky to teach them how to shoot. No," he said shaking his head. "But she was angry, Señor, and rightfully so. Just like you are now. We all are. I had to remind her, just as I do you now, that there are some good people in Dogtown. People like Señora Carpenter and Woodrow Black. It's important to get them to safety before the fighting starts. I'm afraid if we simply ride into town shooting, a lot of innocent people will get hurt."

"They might anyway, General."

"Si, but I've been able to make a list, and she has promised to send runners ahead to warn those friendly to us that we're coming. Perhaps that way, only the judge and his men will meet Leonida when we arrive in town."

"Leonida? Say, you're not gonna let her go, are you?"

"She is Doña Leonida, how will I stop her?"

"You're her father."

"Si, but she commands the respect of everyone on the rancho. Besides," he grinned, "would it be possible to prevent you from going, if you were in her position?"

"Hardly. You'd have to blow a hole in me to stop me."

"Si." The General inhaled deeply and smiled. "It is much the same with her. The only difference between you is, she believes that Judge Henry Baines and Pod Randell might surrender if she goes in first, by herself, and asks them." He shook his head and laughed. "You know as well as I do, Señor, that this will not happen."

"They'll kill her."

"Si, but my daughter cannot see this. Because the righteous can never understand evil, and neither can the evil understand righteousness. She doesn't understand that these men do not think like us. Our job will be to keep her from getting killed. I well let her go, but only after we have secured the village, and she will be surrounded by *vaqueros* from every angle. She will never be alone." He pulled a cigar out of his vest and grinned. "She doesn't know this yet, but that is what will happen. Even if I have to....how is it you say, 'hog-tie her to a post'?"

"You know there's gonna be a blood-bath, no matter what happens."

"Si, but we must try to control it the best we can."

"Don't plan on trying to slow me down when we get to town, do you?"

"No, Tex. You're a free spirit," Jose said, patting him on the arm. "Come, I hear the *carreta*. I think Juan found an ox.

~   ~   ~

"Where's Rusty?" Pod said leaning against the bar with one elbow as he took his time rolling a smoke.

"Out back with Ruby, that new girl of mine." Ambrose slid a bottle and a glass toward him.

"Hell, that'll mean he's tried every one of them."

"I ain't got no complaints, especially on a day like this. Keeps the money coming in."

"Yeah, where is everyone?" he said glancing around the almost empty saloon.

"The Mormons claim they found more color about a mile down the creek, so everyone's out climbing over one another trying to strike it rich."

"Hey, Ambrose," Rusty said, storming through the back door. "That new whore ain't no damn good. I want my money back."

"Well, I guess that answers my question," Pod said with a snicker as he struck a match against the side of the bar.

"Why, what's wrong with her? Yours is the first complaint I've had." Ambrose threw down his towel and walked around front to meet him.

"What's wrong with her? She don't know how to do nothing but lay there. And then she told me I need a bath. I want my money back, right now!"

"Why don't you just take the next girl for free? You can have your pick, anyone you want."

"Well, I guess that'd be okay. But I want you to have a talk with her, 'cause I don't put up with that kinda talk from no woman."

"Alright, I'll talk with her. In the meantime, pour yourself a drink. Ruby?" He left through the rear door, and a second later they heard a scream and the sound of several open-handed blows.

"Damn, I guess you got her into trouble," Pod said crushing his cigarette with the toe of his boot.

"Bitch deserves it. What'd you want to see me for, anyway?"

"Oh, yeah," he said refilling the glasses. "You believe in the wrath of God?"

"What?"

"I asked if you believe in the wrath of God?"

"Hell, I don't know. Never thought much about it. Why?"

"Well, I guess we're gonna find out about it real soon. You know what Hugh Zornes did?" Rusty shook his head. "He kilt that woman's priest that her and all them Mexicans go to."

"He what?" Rusty set his glass down and refilled it.

"Kilt him deader'n bleached bones."

"Why?"

"I told him to take Curley and Eb out there and kill that old Injun she likes so much. You know, the one raising sheep right across the river? Well, it just so happens the priest comes in while Hugh is trying to poke that little skinny granddaughter of his and starts causing a ruckus. So, Hugh shoots him right in the brisket."

"Damn, ain't never killed a man of the cloth before."

"Me neither. I don't believe in it. God's bound to get good and mad about something like that." Pod shook his head as he rolled another cigarette.

"You don't really believe that, do you?" Rusty said with a laugh.

"Damn right I do. I know better. My old pappy was a preacher once, before he got hisself kilt by one of them niggers working the fields. Damn slave wanted to run off and the old man tried to stop him. Nigger beat him to death with an ax handle." He paused to lick the paper.

"Anyway, what I want you to do is, get Montana and one of them new guys Henry's been hiring," he glanced upward thoughtfully, "take Bucky with you. And y'all go out there and hide along them rocks by the road coming in from their ranch, 'cause I gotta feeling she's coming to town right soon. And take that Sharps rifle with you too, 'cause I think you're only going to get one chance to nail her."

"Okay, but what makes you think she's coming?"

"Wouldn't you?" Pod said, refilling both glasses.

"Damn straight. I would've already been here. Here's to the wrath of God." He tossed off his drink and wiped his mouth with the back of his hand.

Chapter 54

It was the wailing and crying that caused him to sit upright. He had had his eyes closed when the squeaking and creaking of the *carreta* woke him from his troubled nap under the oak tree. He was used to that. Most of the time it was just one of the workers moving hay or something from one place to another. Sean blinked his eyes against the late afternoon sun as he watched Doña Leonida run from the house to join her father at the ox cart. His heart seemed to explode into a million pieces when she collapsed in his arms covering her face with both hands. Rosa and Angela were off to one side holding each other and weeping as Juan tried to comfort them. Others were coming from different points of the ranch, and all of them seemed to join the mournful song.

He rose to his feet and walked hesitantly to where a silent Paco stood watching, and clasped a strong arm around the vaquero's shoulder. "Come on, let's go see." The two of them timidly wove their way through the crowd, where Paco collapsed across the girl's body lying on the hay in the back of the crude wagon.

"Damn, oh damn, why wouldn't you listen?" Sean said, cradling Father Franco's head in his lap. "You must have some Irish in you, Father. You never listened to anything anyone said. And now look at you. You're dead, and what am I supposed to do without you? Answer me that, if you can." He fumbled around in the pockets of the priest's robe before turning to the ashen-faced stable boy.

"Manuel, I can't seem to find the cruet of holy-water he always carried. Could you please go to the church and bring the crucible? Someone needs to say last rites over them." He wiped his nose on the back of his sleeve before removing their sandals.

"Thank you," he said as the boy handed him the bowl. He carefully anointed each body and began the prayers. Father Franco first, then Julio, and finally Lupe. Paco started to lay the girl's body down, but Sean told him God wouldn't mind if he held her while he prayed. Paco nodded, and joined in the prayer. He was almost finished when he heard Leonida's voice from where she stood beside her father.

"Forget the water in the bowl, Señor. The true Holy Water is flowing from your heart. See how it falls from your eyes to anoint those you are praying for?"

~　　~　　~

Leonida rose from her desk and arched her back before rubbing both eyes with her knuckles. She was putting the finishing touches on the stack of letters which she had spent the last several days writing. It was her father's idea, and a good one too, she thought. But it was time to quit procrastinating and get the job done. No more *muy poco tiempo* concerning this matter. Although it would have already been settled a long time ago if it had been left up to her. Perhaps even months ago, but the doctor stopped her at the corral. She smiled, remembering the incident. But the smile quickly left as the sound of prayers and weeping from the chapel drifted in on the evening breeze. She called for a cup of tea and walked to the patio thinking that perhaps she should have allowed Joaquin Murrieta to take his men into Dogtown. Father Franco and the rest might still be alive. Sean, who had just finished the rosary, was sitting and talking with the men. They all rose in unison as she stepped through the door.

"No, sit back down." She tried smiling, but her bottom lip trembled. "They are almost finished, *Papa*."

"*Bueno, Niña.* We shall help you finish so we can all get some sleep."

"Thank you, but I doubt if I shall be getting much sleep tonight."

"Nor shall any of us, but you must try. You will be having a long day ahead of you." She nodded.

Rosa came running through the door to fall at Sean's knees, and grabbed the startled man's hands. "*Mi perdon, por favor.* Please forgive me," she said kissing his hands repeatedly.

"Stop that! What are you doing, young lady?" His eyes darted from her to Tex, who only shrugged.

"I did not know you were a holy man like Father Franco, and I've played jokes on you and treated you badly. Forgive me Father. Please?"

"No, I'm not a priest, Rosa," he said taking her face in both hands.

"But you say the rosary so well. And you gave them the last rites."

"That was because there was no one else. I'm sure when the new priest comes, he will say more prayers for them."

"How'd you learn to do that anyway?" Tex said tossing a match into one of Leonida's flower pots.

"An Irish priest taught me. He said it might be useful in the Army if we were ever in a battle and there was no priest near to minister to the wounded or dying. And he was right. I did have to do that once." He suddenly looked distant and sad.

"Well, I didn't understand much, but it was right purdy just the same."

"*Gracias Señor*, you are a great man," Rosa said,

kissing his hand one more time before rising to her feet.

"Oh, no. Thank you, but I'm not great," he said with a weak laugh. "Father Franco was the great one. I just try my best to mend a few bodies every now and then, but there wasn't a day that went by that he wasn't trying to save someone's soul. That's what being great really is." The distant look returned. "I loved that old man, and I never told him." There was a long moment where Leonida vaguely heard the bawling of a calf in one of the distant pastures before she spoke.

"You're wrong Señor. I believe we are all great in one way or another if we are trying to do God's will. Father Franco with his saving souls; you tending to the sick; Rosa and Angela loving the men He gave them to care for. Some day they both shall raise strong sons and daughters to carry on, and this is true greatness, Señor. To do God's will, no matter what He has given you to do."

She placed the empty cup on the small table and turned back toward the door. "Come, *Papa*, it is time to finish." Then, as an afterthought, she looked back over her shoulder.

"Sean?" Her use of his name in the familiar gave everyone a start. "Father Franco knew you loved him. We all did."

Chapter 55

Paco was leaning against the side of the bunkhouse checking the loads in his gun when Tex arrived with an armload of letters. "Is this the Post Office?" Paco returned the gun to his holster and folded his arms. "It was supposed to be a joke." Still more silence. "Well," he continued, "Mrs. Garcia wants to know if you and Juan would like to take a little ride into Dogtown tonight?"

"Por que?"

"Yeah, it seems she's got all this here mail she wants delivered tonight, announcing some sort of party she's giving in town tomorrie."

Paco shifted his feet as he reached for the envelopes. "Juan," he called for his friend who stood a few feet away.

"Mrs. Garcia says she knows it might be hard for you having to miss Lupe's funeral in the morning, but seeing as the doctor gave such a fine speech at the service tonight, it might not be too bad. Can ya'all read this here chicken-scratch?" He pointed to the names on the envelopes.

"Si, a little." Juan nodded.

"Good, cause ya'all got to rustle." He handed the neatly tied stack to Paco. "Now, I'm gonna make it real easy for you. If ya can't make out the names on the front, just shove one under every door in town, except for Judge Baines and Pod Randell and their friends. Understand? 'Cause the party she's giving is in their honor. Got that?"

Paco couldn't help the smile that crept across his face. The cowboy took out the makings and rolled a smoke as he continued.

"After ya get done, she wants you to wait down at the creek near Three Mile Mine where Baca's gonna join you. Then, when you hear the music start, come a running. Oh, I almost forgot," he said reaching inside his vest. "She says it's real important that Alice Carpenter gets this one." He handed the neatly written, scented envelope to Paco. "See you in town tomorrow."

"*Caramba, amigo*," Juan said grabbing his arm. "We go now? I get the horses."

"Si, we go." Paco patted his gun and turned toward the corral.

~   ~   ~

Ildefonso Baca chose to stand as the old man seated himself at the kitchen table and took a sip of coffee. He didn't feel comfortable inside Doña Leonida's hacienda. This house was too big and cold for a human. Indians were much more practical. They made their houses small enough to keep one warm in the winter, and the walls to be removed and allow the breezes to cool one off when summer came. Ildefonso liked the feel of the wind in his hair and one should see the stars and moon to remind them of who they were. Besides, those who served in the fields should remain outside the walls of the hacienda when at all possible.

"Señora Garcia is going to take the *vaqueros* to town tomorrow after they bury Father Franco and the others," Maria began interpreting for the ranger. "Señor Hanky has a very important job for you. He wants you to make sure she gets there safely. You are to check the roadway and see that there are no traps for her to fall in. He says he doesn't even want a rabbit or lizard to cross her path."

"Tell him that I already have, and there are three white mans with the big gun hiding in the rocks by the river. I have four *vaqueros* watching them now." A huge smile crossed the ranger's face and he nodded while Maria translated.

"He says you are *muy bueno hombre,* Baca. He says you are a great warrior and it will be a pleasure to ride with you." Ildefonso nodded as she kept on talking. "He wants you to remove the men and make the road safe for Doña Leonida."

"Does he want me to kill them?"

"He says he doesn't care what you do with them, so long as they're not anywhere around when Doña Leonida passes by." Maria waited while the ranger spoke, then continued translating. "He also says you are to meet with Juan and Paco and wait for Doña Leonida near Three Mile Mine after you take care of the men. He wants to know if you understand?"

Ildefonso nodded and stepped into the cool night air. A cold misty rain had started to fall and it was black as pitch outside. A perfect night for him to visit the men in the rocks and send a message to the judge. He grabbed his lance from where it leaned against the bunkhouse wall and leaped to the back of his horse. He motioned toward several dozen young Indians who were mounted and waiting patiently. The unshod horses hardly made a sound on the soft earth as they disappeared into the night.

~   ~   ~

Leonida listened to the rain patter against the window as she lay in bed. She rubbed the spot where Rudlolfo would lay with the palm of her hand. It was cold and empty, like the spot inside her heart. Part of her had died with him. And it seemed that a little bit more of her died each time she looked at another body. Soon, she would be nothing but a walking, breathing corpse. *Jesus Cristo, why didn't you take me this time? Why did you take Father Franco instead of me? I am so lonely and cold. I wish to be with my husband.* She buried her face in the pillow as the dam inside of her burst in a flood of tears.

My father is a leader of men, and Señor Kilkenney heals bodies, but what am I supposed to do? I wanted to be married and raise strong children for the Church, Holy Mother, but heaven has taken that away from me. Help me understand.

Maria and my father say it is wrong for me to have strong feelings for another man when I am mourning for my husband. You know, Madre de Dios, that I weep for Rudolfo daily. But you also know that when I am in the doctor's presence, he makes me feel happy. I think it is because he is both strong and gentle like my husband. If this is wrong, Holy Mother, please take these feelings away from me.

She turned and lay on her back, wiping her eyes with the sleeve of her gown. *I know what I must do tomorrow, Madre Maria. I don't know how it will end, but I do know that things will change, and never be the same again. If it is your wish that I should go home to you, I am ready. But, if it is your wish that I stay here, I will need to know what to do after tomorrow is over. I will be listening. Please tell Father Franco hello for me, and give Julio and Lupe a kiss.*

Chapter 56

"Why can't we have a fire? Its colder'n hell," Bucky said, rubbing his hands together. He'd hired on with the judge that morning, and he'd been told to go with Rusty Pardeen, and Montana. They were to watch a road eight miles from town, and that seemed like easy money. What he hadn't planned on was the rain.

"Well I guess it's colder than hell. From what I hear, hell's gotta be pretty hot," Montana said with a laugh.

"Already told you, can't have a fire 'cause they might see it," Rusty said. "So quit askin' and put yer gloves on."

"Who we looking for anyway? It don't make no sense sittin' out here freezing like this."

"The boogie man. Didn't they tell you anything?" Bucky was beginning to find Montana's humor irritating.

"The judge wants us to keep anyone from that rancho from comin' to town. Seems that they've been causing some trouble," Rusty said.

"What kind of trouble?"

"Don't know, didn't ask. Folks that ask too many

questions tend to get troubles of their own, if you get my drift." Rusty glared at him as he lit a cigarette.

"He didn't tell me there might be gun play. I don't know if I like that," Bucky said, turning his collar against the wind.

"What in the hell did you take this job fer if you're agin' guns," Montana said. "Think you was comin' out here on a picnic?"

"I ain't against guns. I know how to use mine. I just don't think two dollars a day's worth getting shot at."

"Two dollars a day? Hear that Rusty? Hell, he's paying him more'n I'm getting, and he don't wanna use his iron. I gotta tell Judge Henry I want more money."

"Well, the both of you can take that up with the judge when we get back to town. Right now I just wanna get some shut-eye. Montana, you can take the second watch and wake me when it's my turn. Our new friend here can be first," Rusty said, covering himself with his saddle blanket.

Bucky sat staring into the blackness as the wind whipped the fine mist around him. *Ain't worth two dollars a day to be freezin' like this. Ain't worth five dollars.* He rubbed his arms and legs. His feet felt numb inside his wet boots, so he stood and began stomping.

"Why in the hell don't you sit down?" Rusty rolled over to glare at him.

"I can't feel my feet."

"Well, if you gotta do that, go somewheres else and let us get some sleep."

Go to hell, you damn jackass. He stomped his feet again as he walked. They still felt numb. Bucky had gone almost twenty-five yards from the lookout point when he heard the screams. First one, then the other. He stood frozen for a second, trying to let what happened register in his cold-numbed mind. He drew his gun and ran back to where he had left his sleeping partners. Jumping the little mound of rocks that surrounded their camp, he was met with a searing pain in his stomach. The pistol dropped from his hand as he grabbed the lance sticking through him. He had just enough time to see the Indian's face before he fell.

~   ~   ~

Johnny Goodwin left The Rusty Rail at two-thirty in the morning. The rain had stopped and a few stars were starting to peek through the clouds. He pulled his coat tight around him as an icy gust of wind whipped his intoxicated body. He made his way toward the hotel, staggering from one hitching post to another, past the Nugget Saloon. He plodded onward, stumbling a time or two, but always able to catch his balance, until he felt he simply had to stop in front of the assay office in order for his mind to catch up with his body. That's when he saw them. Two dark shadows moving from building to building, stopping long enough to shove something under the door. *Now, what the hell's going on?* He straightened himself and moved forward, following the shadows down the street.

They moved silently, as though their feet didn't touch the ground. Pod Randell had told him to keep his eyes peeled for any *suspicious happenings* that very afternoon. Well, this was suspicious enough for Johnny Goodwin. He pulled his .44 and staggered forward. A gust of wind blew the hat from his head and he stumbled, knocking over a metal bucket as he tried to retrieve it. He brushed a string of blonde hair from his forehead and shoved the hat down tight. When he looked, one of the shadows was standing not twenty yards in front of him, staring. He leveled his gun, but the figure disappeared between two buildings to his right. *Sneaky son-of-a-bitch.*

Johnny tripped again as he turned the corner, but caught himself against one of the walls of Carpenter's General Store. He paused, allowing his eyes to adjust, hoping to pick them out of the darkness. There he was, slipping something under the back door of the store, but only one of them this time. Where was the other? The figure looked at him and darted to the left. Johnny ran without stumbling and paused at the corner. The cold wind was beginning to clear his head and he felt good. He held the gun out as he stepped forward and a sharp pain shot through his wrist. He stood staring at the young vaquero holding a machete.

"*Perdoname*, Señor, but you cannot shoot me. You have
no hand." Johnny stepped backward, but the vaquero followed. "Tell me, *gringo*, which way should the head fall? To the left, or the right?"

"Ahhhhh!" Johnny backed into the second vaquero who held a gun to his back.

"It would not be polite to leave, Señor. Juan asks you a question."

Johnny stood frozen, wondering why his legs refused to work.

"No answer? I think to the right, Juan."

"Si," the vaquero said and swung the machete.

~   ~   ~

"*Buenos dias, mi niña.*" Leonida squinted and blinked against the light as her father lit the lamp on the nightstand. The clock downstairs bonged four times. He perched himself on the edge of her bed, placing a walnut case in her lap as she scooted to a sitting position. "These are for you." She fumbled with the latch for a second or two before opening the lid.

"*Por que?*" She ran her fingers across the small, curious looking guns.

"The *gringos* call them pepper boxes. I bought them from Captain MacDougal when we visited the longboats. I should have given them to you long ago, but I was angry because you bought guns for the *vaqueros* without asking my advice. I'm sorry. If you had them with you the day of the *fiesta* when those *gringos* were hiding in you room, it might have been a different story, no?" He shrugged his shoulders and tilted his head to one side and grinned.

"But, it is a small matter. *Dios* has given you Señor Kilkenney for your protection." She glanced up at him, her mouth slightly open. "It's alright *niña*," he said brushing the hair from her forehead and kissing the smooth skin repeatedly. "He's a good man."

"Here," he removed one of the guns from its case and dropped it into her hands. "Be careful, they are loaded." She held it loosely in her open palm and tilted it back and forth. The tiny weapon had six barrels all molded together with only a ring where the trigger was supposed to be. The inscription read *Robbins & Lawerence Co., Windsor, VT.*

"Captain MacDougal said they are also known as the ladies' companion." He took the other from its case and held it up in the light. "See? They are small enough to hide in your pocket or handbag." He dropped the gun into his vest pocket and patted his side before pulling it back out. "The barrel is just over three inches long and rotates automatically every time it's fired. The gun is double-action, which means there is no need to cock the hammer before each shot. And you don't have to worry about finding the trigger if you're in a hurry. Just poke your finger through the ring and squeeze." He pointed the weapon toward the wall talking quickly like a true soldier training a new recruit. He paused and smiled at her before returning the gun to its case.

"I'm afraid they are not very accurate beyond eight or ten feet, but they shoot fast and will frighten most anyone having to look down their barrels. I want you to take them with you when we go to town."

"*Gracias, Papa.*"

"I love you, *hija*. Please be careful, and if there is any trouble, let your *vaqueros* do the fighting."

"I will, *Papa*. I love you too." She held him close and blinked hard against a stubborn tear in the corner of her eye. *Holy Father, send your Saints and Angels to protect my papa. This journey frightens me. If you must take one of us home to be with you today, please take me and let my father live.*

Chapter 57

Josiah Russell pulled his watch from his vest pocket and snapped the cover open. It was 7:15. He snapped it closed and returned the watch to his pocket. "Kinda early for a funeral, ain't it ma'am?"

The mourners who packed the small cemetery behind the chapel were waiting for Sean Kilkenney to say the final prayers over the padre and his companions before they laid them to rest.

"Perhaps, Señor Hanky, but I believe that Father Franco, Julio and Lupe are not really dead. I think they are living in the eternal light of our Holy Father. I will remember them every time the sun rises over the hills, such as it does now." She nodded toward Sean, who started praying.

Amen, sister, Josiah thought as he watched the crow flutter its wings in the tree above them. The first rays of the sun were beginning to turn the sky gold. *It's gonna be a good day. Let's go get the sons-of-bitches what kilt them.*

~ ~ ~

Pod Randell was awakened by a man screaming outside his office door. Leaping from bed, he grabbed his gun and ran forward, stubbing his toe on the doorpost. "Goddammit!" He found Charlie Shavers and Bill Codwell standing wide-eyed and ghostly white.

"What the hell's the matter with you two?" They pointed toward the sidewalk.

"Damn," Pod said jumping backward. It was Johnny Goodwin. He was leaning against the wall, holding his head in his lap. The hand laying beside him still held a pistol, but it wasn't attached to anything. "What the....? Son-of-a-bitch." He staggered backward against the door post.

"What happened to him?" Shavers said.

"How the hell should I know? I was in there asleep. You woke me up."

"Jesus, I'm sick," Bill said as he leaned over the hitching rail and vomited.

"Oh, Gawd," Pod said, holding his stomach as he turned back inside. "Go wake the judge, and tell him to get his ass down here, now."

Pod pulled his boots on and made coffee while they waited for Henry to show up. He had seen a lot of gore in his day, and even participated in quite a bit of it himself, but he'd never witnessed anything quite like this before. He listened to the exclamations of those congregating on the sidewalk as he poured the coffee. People were the same everywhere. And it didn't matter if the person was murdered or died by accident. They really didn't have to die, for that matter. Just so long as there was pain, and preferably some blood involved. People would come to gawk and offer their little expletives and fake pity, and say their meaningless prayers. Then they would leave, only to show up at the next tragedy. The only thing that surprised Pod this morning, as he stood in the doorway with his coffee, was how small the crowd was. It only consisted of a dozen of his own men.

He took time surveying the empty street. Dogtown was usually at a fast gallop by sun-up on any morning. He looked at his watch. 7:30. There were no noisy miners or Mexican laborers. There weren't even any mules or horses to be seen outside of the mounts belonging to his own men. Even stranger yet was the fact that all the stores and shops, excluding The Rusty Rail, were closed tight.

"What the devil is going on here?" Henry Baines said pushing his way through the crowd. "Holy Christ almighty, what happened to him?" He backed away from Johnny Goodwin's body.

"Why's everyone askin' me that question? I was in bed asleep," Pod said, rolling himself a smoke.

"You're the Sheriff. You're supposed to know these things."

"Well, okay, he got hisself kilt. Got his head and hand chopped off. And whoever done it, dumped his carcass right where you see it. Does that satisfy you, Judge?"

"I don't suppose you know who did it, do you?" Henry looked pale.

"No I don't. You keep telling me you're the brains behind this here operation. Suppose you tell us all who done it, 'cause I done told you what I know."

"I don't know who killed him. Send some of the men around town to ask some questions. Someone has to know if something is going on."

"Well hell, Judge, that carcass told me something's going on, and he can't even talk," Pod said with a laugh. "Besides, don't tell me you ain't noticed that this here town's locked up tighter'n a bank amongst a collection of thieves?"

"No, I hadn't noticed," he said, glancing around at the buildings. "It's still early, though. I don't see anything strange in that."

"Well, it might not be if it was just the general store or bank. But Dirty Ben's is closed, and you know how them miners like to eat before they go to work. All the shops are closed. Ain't nobody out walkin' round 'cept us." Pod stepped to the edge of the sidewalk and leaned against a post. "Haven't heard anything going on down at the mines, and there ain't none of them Mormon kids out playing with their dogs either. And one of yer men is right here at your feet, Judge, holding his head in his lap. Now, don't that seem just a little strange to you?"

"What are you driving at?" Henry said, backing away.

"I don't know. Thought you'd tell me. Maybe I'd better send some boys up and down the street like you said. Then, maybe they could go out to see how Montana and the boys are doing. They might know something." Pod smiled as he crushed his smoke with the heel of his boot.

"Yes, that's a good idea. Hugh, why don't you take Curley and Eb with you, and see what you can find out? I'll see you boys later. I have business to attend to." He hurried down the street as Pod broke into laughter.

"He's scared to death," Hugh said, while Pod held his sides laughing.

"I don't see what's so damn funny, Pod. That weren't no good way for Johnny to die," Eb said.

"You don't see what's funny?" he said trying to compose himself.

"No, 'cause it ain't funny atall."

"Well, I wasn't laughing at Johnny, but ya hafta admit it's kinda funny seeing him holding his head in his lap like that," Pod said as he closed and locked the door.

"What was you laughing at then?"

"You don't really know, do you? You can't see it?"

"No. See what?"

"You will soon enough. It'll probably scare the daylights outa you like ol' Henry there, but it's gonna be a hell of a lot of fun, too. Ya'all clean this mess up and go nose around like he said. If you find out anything, I'll be over at The Rusty Rail havin' myself a drink."

"Damn, how we gonna move him?" Hugh said looking pale.

"With your hands, I guess." Pod laughed and walked away.

He paid for a bottle of Red Eye and found a spot at a

table where he could watch the front door. He filled his glass and drained it in two swallows and filled it again. *It's coming, by God. I always knew it would, and here it is.* He leaned his head back and laughed until the tears ran down his face.

~   ~   ~

Josiah Russell sat on the fountain's edge and stretched out his bum leg. He leaned the cane against the bricks and watched the funeral procession wind its way into the courtyard. The watch in his pocket said it was 8:45. Tex propped his boot on the bricks next to him and began rolling a cigarette. Vernon Blackstone had arrived during the funeral armed with a ten-gauge shotgun and stood leaning against the house like a statue. They were ready.

"What now?"

"It's up to her, Tommy." He nodded toward the widow entering the house with her father. Sean sat beside them and began packing his pipe.

"It's a crying shame," he said, shaking his head. "The padre and that Indian were good men. And the little girl should have been allowed to grow up and have children of her own."

"If it's any consolation, Doc, you done a right good job out there praying over them," Josiah said as he took out his own pipe.

"Thanks."

"Now, would you look at that," Tex said, striking a match against the bricks. Several vaqueros were carrying armloads of rifles out of the bunkhouse and laying them in the center of the patio while others began loading them. A half-dozen Indians were driving a herd of horses into the corral where even more were waiting to throw saddles on their backs.

"Think the band's really gonna play?" Josiah said turning toward Tex.

"Yep, gonna strike up a real lively tune."

"What band?" Sean said, turning his head from side to side.

"You'll find out soon enough. Now, lookie here." He stretched his neck for a better view as Jose Flores came out of the house with a box tucked under his arm and began working his way through the crowd toward them. "He's totin' some heavy iron."

"Yep, .44 if I ain't mistaken. Hung kinda low for an army man," Tex said. "Wonder what he's got in the box?"

"Señor Kilkenney?" Jose said, stopping in front of them. "My daughter says to thank you for the fine rosary last night and the prayers you said this morning. Father Franco would have been proud of you." Sean nodded. "She would like you to have these as a token of her appreciation." Sean opened the case. It contained Rudolfo's dueling pistols.

"Aw, now that is awfully nice. But, tell her I can't take these. They were her husbands, and they should belong to her sons when she eventually has them."

"Si, she plans on them being handed down to my grandsons." The two men stood silent for a minute staring at each other. "You may argue that point with her later if you wish, Doctor. But for now, I would suggest that you make sure they are loaded, and collect your medical kit."

"Why?"

"I think you're gonna find out real quick," Josiah said, rising to his feet. Leonida was standing on the veranda dressed in her riding gear. The rancho was suddenly quiet.

"Romero?" she said in a loud voice.

"Si?" The young vaquero stepped forward.

"Make sure Rudolfo's black is saddled and bring it here. I want to ride it. And tell everyone to make ready. We are going to town."

"I'll be damned, Hanky. She's opened the ball," Tex said, tossing his cigarette away.

"Yer damned right she has. Let's dance," he said, pulling his pistol. Josiah let out a piercing rebel yell and fired into the air. Tex joined in the celebration, and in a matter of seconds the place broke into pandemonium as Indians and vaqueros alike yelled and fired. Someone rode a horse through the middle of the fountain as the extra guns and ammunition were being passed around. Hanky saw two boys he believed to be no older than twelve or thirteen loading pistols. As quick as it started, the festivity ceased as Doña Leonida mounted the huge black Arabian.

"Better grab us a couple of mounts, Tommy. I'd hate like hell to have to ride to town behind the doctor on that jackass of his."

"I'll see what's left."

He watched the widow sitting above the crowd as the cowboy ran toward the corral. She held her head erect and proud. The honey-colored hair danced in the breeze and her green eyes sparkled in the sun as she looked his way. He reloaded his gun and dropped it in the holster. She was waiting on her army. In a few short moments she would be leading them into battle.

Damn, she's purdy. Dangerous as a wounded cougar, but purdy.

Chapter 58

9:00 am. The *carreta* ground to a halt several hundred yards from the town limits, shielded by a row of oaks and sugar pines. Ildefonso Baca climbed in back and gave the bodies a push, where they fell in a heap in the middle of the roadway. He didn't know their names, and didn't care. They had been hiding alongside the road that Señora Leonida would be taking, and he knew they meant her harm. They may also have been the ones who killed Julio and Lupe and the others.

He got back up to the driver's seat, tapped the ox with his lance and drove to the creek bed, where he stopped. He tied the ox to a tree and ran silently in a semi-circle, skirting the edge of town. He stopped at a clump of trees lining the bank of the creek where he found Paco and Juan. Juan handed him a piece of dried beef and a tortilla. He ate while they sat silent, watching and waiting.

~   ~   ~

Alice Carpenter glanced at the clock on the wall and

then back to the letter in her hand. It was 9:10 am. She laid the letter on the table as her teapot began to whistle. She filled her cup and dropped the fob into the boiling water to steep, then sat back down to re-read the letter.

15 November, 1860

Señora Carpenter,

My heart was again broken when I heard of the loss of your beloved husband and our friend Arturo. May God judge those rightly who do such things. They are evil men who care nothing about His love and mercy. I pray that our Savior will heal your wounds while he comforts your husband and Arturo in heaven.

I am sorry to inform you of more sufferings, but this morning we buried our beloved priest beside a 12-year-old child and her grandfather. The child was abused in much the same way as I. I am sure the same men who took your husband from you did this evil deed. They also murdered another family living on our rancho. My heart is indeed heavy. But I will be coming to Dogtown with my vaqueros before noon today. I do not wish any harm to the good people of Dogtown like yourself, but I will require justice of Judge Henry Baines and Sheriff Pod Randell for the pain they have inflicted on me and my people.

I pray that we shall see each other when this matter is settled.

Doña Leonida Garcia

Alice carefully folded the letter and placed it in the pocket of her apron, then removed the fob from her tea. It was too hot to drink. She looked at the clock again and decided she had time for a casual breakfast even though she didn't feel like eating. Buttermilk biscuits would be nice. She would top them with honey just like she had done for Ike nearly every morning they had been married. She glanced toward her husband's picture on the mantle as she loaded his shotgun and laid it on the table. She missed him terribly. They'd never been able to have any children in fifteen years of marriage, and the chasm left by his murder would never be filled.

She sipped her tea and carefully loaded the .44. *Come, my dear Leonida, but please don't forget my hurt. Save one of them for me.*

~   ~   ~

Pod Randell laid the gold watch on the table. It was 9:12 and he was hungry.

"Hey, Ambrose, you got anything worth eatin' back there? I'm starvin' to death."

"Just some beans left over from yesterday. Don't know ifin' they're fit to eat."

"Hell, bring 'em on, I don't care." The bottle of Red Eye was half empty and Pod's lips felt numb. He laughed and poured himself another glass as Ambrose set the bowl in front of him.

"Found some biscuits out back. You're welcome to them too."

"Here's to you, Pard," Pod said, holding the glass up in a toast.

"Say, ain't you had enough of that?"

"Na, I ain't even started yet. Bring on another bottle."

"If you say so. But I'd slow down just a little if I was you. That stuff will kick your guts out."

"Yeah, but you ain't me, so just keep it coming 'til I tell you to quit."

George Bidwell stumbled through the door and stopped in mid-stride when he saw Pod.

"How can you sit there eatin' like that?"

"Simple. You fill yer spoon with beans and plop it in yer mouth like this." Pod laughed at the barber/doctor as he chewed the beans. "Then you wash it down with this." He took a swallow of Red Eye. George shook his head and staggered toward the bar.

"What's wrong with you? Look's as though you got caught cheatin' with another man's wife," Ambrose said as he wiped glasses with a dirty towel.

"Worse. I've been stuffin' Johnny Goodwin into a box. Give me a bottle."

"Johnny?" Ambrose said as he passed the bottle and a glass. "What happened?"

"Got hisself all cut to pieces. Didn't Pod tell you?"

"No. Is he dead?"

"Well, hell yes he's dead," Pod said, almost choking on a mouthful of beans as he laughed. "He ain't got no head."

"What the hell's he talking about?" Ambrose said.

"Just that. Someone cut Johnny's head and one of his hands clean off. Made me sicker'n a dog stuffin' all them parts into that coffin."

"No. You don't say." Ambrose's hand shook as he poured himself a drink.

"Why'd it make you sick, George? Johnny couldn't feel nothing. You coulda kept his head and kicked it around like a ball." Pod began laughing hysterically.

"You son of a bitch."

Hugh Zornes almost tore the swinging door off its hinges before falling across Pod's table and knocking over his bottle.

"Dammit," Pod jumped from his chair and slapped him across the face.

"They're dead. They're all dead."

It took a second to settle in his brain. "Dead? Who's dead?"

"Rusty, Montana and Bucky. They're all dead."

"He's telling the truth." Pod looked up as Curly came through the door smoking a cigarette. "Found 'em right outside town in the middle of the road where you couldn't miss 'em. Don't know why it's got him so shook up."

"They was gutted, that's why. Their innards was all hangin' out."

"Oh, shut the hell up," George said, wiping a huge hand across his face.

"Indian lances is what I'd say," Curly said. "I seen it before."

"Injuns? Well, that ain't no surprise. They already kilt three men trying to steal that woman's cattle and shot Frank in the arm with an arrow. Guess we got 'em real good and mad, now didn't we?" Pod refilled his glass.

"I just heard Montana and the boys with him got killed," Henry Baines said, bursting through the door. "Pod, what the hell's going on here?"

"Why, don't you know, Judge?" Pod leaned back in his chair and grinned. "You greedy bastard. Don't you know?"

"What's he talking about?" Henry's eyes darted around the room.

"Don't mind him, Judge. He's just drunk." Ambrose started to take the bottle, but Pod clamped a hand on it.

"I ain't drunk yet. And you do know what I'm talkin' about, don't you, Henry?"

"No, I'm afraid I don't."

"Sure you do. You should recognize it. It's judgment day, Your Honor. This jackass," he pointed toward Hugh, "Kilt the priest and now God's gonna get you. He's sending that woman to town and she's got a million Injuns and Mexicans and they're coming to get you." Pod leaned halfway across the table to stare Henry in the eye as the judge went pale. "You weren't satisfied with the little game we had going here in town, even though you were gettin' rich. You wanted it all, and now she's comin' to collect."

He couldn't contain himself and laughed until tears ran down his cheeks as Henry backed slowly toward the door.

"It's judgment day, Your Honor. And she's gonna get you."

Chapter 59

Woodrow Black stood by his office window at the far end of town. The clock on his wall chimed 9:30 am. His was the largest and richest claim in the area, but he hadn't even thought about the gold today. In fact, he hadn't even sent his men into the hole. He held the letter that had been shoved under his door in the middle of the night in his hand and read it again. The words were still the same.

15 November, 1860

Friends,

Many of you know of the sorrows we have suffered; the death of my husband and his brother, and the brutal attack on my own person. There have also been several vicious attacks on innocent people living at the rancho, which have resulted in the death of some. This morning, we buried our beloved priest beside a 12-year-old child and her grandfather. The child was abused in much the same way as I.

I will be coming to Dogtown with my vaqueros before noon today. I do not wish you harm. But I will require justice of Judge Henry Baines and Sheriff Pod Randell for the pain they have inflicted on me and my people.

Doña Leonida Garcia

It didn't matter that the name on the envelope wasn't his. He had already compared his letter with several others received by the miners and they all read the same. The conclusion was that it was too dark last night to see the names, or those delivering the letters couldn't read, which was all too common.

He crumbled the paper as he surveyed the street. Outside of a handful of men in front of the jail, the town seemed deserted. He had dismissed the letter as some sort of crude prank, but quickly changed his mind after passing the sheriff's office on the way to the mine early that morning. The letter was neat and precise, and carefully written. But the crude calling card left on the steps of the jail made him shudder at the implications it contained.

"Well, what's it gonna be? The boys want to know before that woman and her men get here," Carey Jones, his foreman closed the door behind him. Carey had helped gather everyone from all the neighboring claims to the Three Mile to discuss what should be done. Someone, Woodrow didn't know who, came up with the suggestion that the miners should help the woman. "After all," Cary said, "no one really likes being fleeced by the judge and his friends. And they like what's happened to that woman and her husband even less. They're asking you to make the decision."

"I just don't want anyone getting hurt."

"There's already been a lot of people hurt. Read that letter again. And what about Ike Carpenter and that little boy? Weren't they friends of yours?"

Woodrow turned his attention back to the empty street.

"They're gonna join in that fight whether you like it or

not."

"You're right," he said with a sigh. "Guess we've turned our heads too long already. Tell the men to sit tight until I give the signal. Then I only want them blocking the exits in case Henry Baines and his men try to run. I don't want them getting down in the middle of it. The Mexicans won't have any way of telling who is who out there, and some of them might get hurt. Besides, they're angry, and they'll probably be looking to kill every white man around. Couldn't say as I'd really blame them either."

~   ~   ~

Ildefonso Baca shaded his eyes to get the position of the sun. He had never owned a watch or clock, but he could have told you that it was two hours to midday almost to the minute. No one looking at the trees, brush and prairie grass from the buildings in Dogtown would have ever guessed there were thirty Indians waiting for his signal. Most of them were young and had never done battle before, but that did not worry him. They were good men, strong and skilled, and he had trained them personally. They were also patient like him. People might come into Dogtown that morning, but they would not leave unless Baca himself said so. Then, when the time came, certain men would never leave again.

~   ~   ~

Henry Baines looked at his watch and shook it, then looked at it again. 10:30 am. The Bank should have opened thirty minutes ago but the doors were still locked. He pounded impatiently and waited. There was still no answer. The stage would be there at noon and he needed the money he'd been hoarding away. True, some of it was Pod's, but Pod wouldn't miss it. Besides, he was so stupid, he probably didn't even know how much he had coming. He was over at The Rusty Rail at that very moment drinking himself into oblivion, talking some nonsense about a judgment day. Henry didn't believe in such things. True, four of his men had been brutally murdered in the past few hours, but they were also stupid. He might never get control of the Garcia Rancho like he wanted, but he'd leave Dogtown a wealthy man, and that's what really counted in his book. The others could stay and fight if they wanted. He already had his bag packed and he'd be gone when the shooting started. All he needed was the money. He pounded on the door again.

"Dammit, open up in there!"

~   ~   ~

Alice Carpenter finished her breakfast and stacked the dishes in the sink. There would be plenty of time to wash them later. She poured more boiling water in her cup, filled the fob with fresh tea and set the cup on the counter inside the store. She then opened all the window shades so she could see the street. There were approximately thirty or so men milling around in front of the sheriff's office. She recognized some of them as being employed by Judge Henry Baines and Pod Randell. Making sure the sign on her door read *Closed*, she returned to her kitchen and retrieved the shotgun and pistol, which she placed on the counter beside her tea. She perched herself on top of the stool behind the counter sipping her tea and watching the men across the street. The clock on the wall said 10:45 as the pans and canned goods on the shelves began to rattle, along with the sound of distant thunder. *That's strange. The sun is shining so bright, I didn't think there was a chance of rain.* The men in front of the jail were all turned toward the other end of town.

Chapter 60

Sean patted Cathy's neck as the mule drank deeply from the creek outside of town. It had been an exhilarating run to town. Doña Leonida had set the pace with her black, and outside of Cathy and a couple of horses, most of the animals were lathered and exhausted.

"She done it on purpose," Hanky said in answer to a complaint by Tex about abusing the mounts. This way, there ain't gonna be no runnin'. We're all gonna stay 'til it's over."

Leonida remained mounted while her horse drank. She sat, silent and regal, showing no outward sign of emotion. Over half of the vaqueros immediately disappeared on foot, skirting the town on both sides through the brush.

"Señor Russell," Jose Flores said as one of the remaining vaqueros led the *carreta* to the roadway. "I think perhaps you and I should go in first and show the young ones how to fight, no?"

"I reckon you're right," he said, and started to mount his horse.

"No, Señor. We take the *carreta*." He pointed to the ox-drawn cart.

"Now, why in God's name would I want to do that? That's a hell of a thing to ride into battle with. As tired as this old mustang is, he's still faster'n that contraption."

"Si, but they will know who you are the moment you get to town. The sheriff will not expect a couple of old peons in a *carreta* to come to fight." He handed Hanky a dirty serape and a battered sombero. "You will sit in back while I drive. We will be beside them when the vaqueros arrive. If there is trouble, you will have first choice."

"I'll be damned, but it just might work," Hanky said, slipping the serape over his head.

"Hey, old man, you'd better let me go in that thing," Tex said. "Ya might have to run when the ball opens up, and you'll have that bum leg of yours holdin' you back."

"Tommy, I ain't never run from a fight in my life. What makes you think I'm gonna start running now?"

"Nothing, and that's the problem. That girl of mine sorta likes you, and made me promise to look out after your onery hide."

"Huh, I'll tell you a real problem. I sorta like her too, and keeping you alive for her is gonna be the problem. Of course, if I was smart now, I'd let you take my place and get all blowed to hell. Then I'd marry her myself. But I ain't never done anything smart in my life, so I guess I'll just have to go instead. I don't want yer ma coming around hauntin' me 'cause I let you get kilt."

"Ready, Señor?" Jose said, climbing into the *carreta*.

"Shore am. Just let me get my ten gauge." Hanky climbed in back and hid the shotgun under the straw, then pulled his sombrero low over his eyes. "Let go huntin'."

"*Un momento, Papa,*" Leonida said. Pulling the black close the the carreta, she leaned over and kissed her father on the cheek. "*Buena suert, y que Dios lo bendiga.*"

"God bless you too, *niña*. Do as I say, and let the vaqueros secure the village before you enter."

"But, *Papa....*" He shook his head.

"I insist. I will call everyone back to the *hacienda* if you do not listen." She nodded, and Jose goaded the ox forward. Sean's hands trembled as he checked the loads in the dueling pistols and tucked them in his belt. He could hear Hanky's voice above the squealing of the wooden wheels as the cart rounded the curve in the road.

"Hey General, whaddaya you say about us throwin' a big *fiesta* when we get back? We can roast this here critter what's pullin' this contraption."

~   ~   ~

Jess McKain heard the squeaking of the carreta long before it came into view. It seemed to be crawling at a snail's pace. He saw Bart Lubker leaning against a post in front of the livery and joined him.

"Pard, I don't know what's going on, but I don't like it. We already got a pile of dead men and I don't wanna join them. I'm for getting the hell outa here."

"Just thinkin' the same thing myself," Bart said, crushing his smoke. "I been watching the judge pounding on the bank door. I'll bet you a month's wages that son of a bitch is planning on running out on us."

"Whaddaya wanna do?"

"I've been thinkin' about gettin' outa here myself. All hell's gonna break loose here any second. Got yer grip?"

"Already tied on the back of my horse."

"Good, but stay close to me. Them Mexicans will have the road covered, so we're gonna go across the creek and up behind the mines and catch the road farther down the way. The judge will take the stage and we'll wait for him down the Sacramento where it stops. Then, we can get our money and give him what's coming to him."

They led their mounts between the livery stable and blacksmith shop before climbing into the saddle. Bart urged his horse into a gallop with Jess close behind. They were nearing the row of oak trees before Jess saw them. Several Indians seemed to rise from the ground, swinging something around their heads. He was suddenly covered in a shower of blood as Bart's head seemed to explode and the man fell from his horse with a scream. The second stone caught Jess in the chest, knocking the wind from him. He fell and rolled several yards before coming to a halt. He lay staring stupidly at the Indian for several seconds before trying to draw his gun. The Indian plunged the lance downward.

~   ~   ~

Leonida waited until the *carreta* was out of sight before nudging her horse forward. "*Señora, alto, por favor.*" Romero tried cutting across her path, but she nudged the black forward, causing Romero's horse to shy away. "Señora," he grabbed the reins, "the General. He says...." he left off speaking as her eyes drifted from his hand on her horse to his face. A smile crept across her lips as she spoke.

"My father is worried that those men might hurt me. But you tell me, Romero, what could possibly happen? He already has *vaqueros* behind every building in town. And you and these fine men," she made a sweeping motion with her arm, "are going to be with me."

"But Señora, there will be shooting, and it only takes one little bullet."

"That is what I want to stop. My father is a warrior, and so is Señor Hanky. They will shoot before anything else. I want to see these men before the shooting starts, and ask them to surrender. I don't want anymore innocent people to die. Now, let go of my horse."

"Your *Papa* says I am to tie you to a tree."

"Romero, you are not going to tie me to any tree now, are you?" He studied her for a long minute before shaking his head.

"No."

"Good, now let go of my horse. You can follow close behind if you want. But I am going to see if I can stop the killing before it starts." She nudged the black to the middle of the road and toward town. Romero motioned with his head and the remaining vaqueros fell in behind. Each man held their rifles ready, eyes searching every tree, building and rock. But most of all, watching the woman in front of them.

~   ~   ~

Henry checked his watch and pounded impatiently on the door. It was 11:00 o'clock, and there was no reason on earth why he should not have his money. He paused for a moment. *Was that a scream?* No he had to be mistaken. It was more than likely the squealing of that damned Mexican's cart. Why couldn't they be like civilized people and make a wagon with spoked wheels and grease them like everyone else? He watched the *carreta* as it drew alongside. The driver sat slump-shouldered with his sombrero pulled low over his eyes. The man in back lay on the straw fast asleep. *Lazy sons of bitches will never amount to a thing.* He waited until they had passed and turned to pound on the door again.

"Come on, open up in there."

The familiar sound of prancing horses with silver trappings made him glance toward the street again. The sight of the girl sitting tall on the Arabian caused him to gasp. "Leonida! What's she doing in town?" His hand drifted toward the gun on his hip. "Like I said, Pod, it isn't that hard to kill a widow." He froze as the parade of armed vaqueros came into view. They hung a couple dozen yards back, taking up the whole street. "Dammit," he ducked behind a stack of empty barrels and watched through a crack as she passed. The woman looked straight ahead, proud, and beautiful.

Chapter 61

Ambrose Brice placed another bottle in front of Pod as George Bidwell staggered to the door and watched the carreta creep past. The barber weaved a little before leaning against the door post and wiping a grimy paw across his eyes.

"Now, why in God's name would they be taking that straw up to the mines?"

"I got no idee. Why don't you go ask em?" Ambrose said, walking back to the bar.

"Hey, Ambrose, come look at this," George said anxiously.

"Yeah, what is it?"

"No, come here. You ain't gonna believe it. Hurry." He was looking the opposite direction of the cart as he staggered onto the sidewalk. Ambrose tossed the dirty towel on the counter and grumbled as he went to the door. He stepped to the walkway as the black horse paused in front of them.

"See, what'd I tell you? It's that Mex woman," George said, grabbing her by the right wrist.

"George, don't...." Ambrose caught his breath as the

army of vaqueros stopped their horses at the corner of his saloon. The stupid drunk hadn't even seen them.

"Hell, might as well find out what them guys down by the river did for myself."

"No," the woman said and tried to pull away as her left hand dropped to her left vest pocket.

"Let her go, George." Ambrose backed toward the door as one of the men on horseback raised a rifle. The men eased their horses forward as the barber tried to pull Leonida from her horse. His laughter was cut short when the woman whipped her left hand out of her pocket to point the pepper box in his face and pulled the trigger quickly three times. George turned and fell toward the door with a groan. One of the three holes in his face was centered in his forehead. She swung the gun upward at Ambrose and fired again as he dove for the sidewalk. The bullet lodged in the door post where he had been standing.

"Oh, Jesus almighty God," he said, scrambling to the corner of the building. Another bullet crashed into the side of the restaurant next door as he turned the corner. He ran to the back of the store and dove under the raised porch as the sound of hooves rounded the building. He lay on his stomach, hardly breathing, watching the black horse prance back and forth not three feet from him. The whole town seemed to erupt in gunfire and screams as the vaqueros charged their horses down the street. The loud blast of the steam whistle from the Three Mile Mine was followed by even more yells and gunshots. Ambrose closed his eyes and covered his ears as he lay there, not realizing that the black horse had left soon after the fighting in the street began.

~   ~   ~

"Something familiar about that Mexican," Hugh Zornes said, watching the *carreta* squeak and squeal its way past the crowd in front of the sheriff's office. The sudden deaths of several of their cohorts had them trying to decide what they should do. Almost half wanted to simply ride off, while the others wanted the pay promised them by the judge.

"Would you forget about them and pay attention? Whaddaya wanna do?" Curly said.

"No, something's queer about him," Hugh said as he stepped into the middle of the street. He couldn't really get a clear look at the man's face as he lay in the back of the cart with his sombrero pulled low, but he could see his build, light skin and boots. That was it! The boots!

"Come on." Curly grabbed him by the arm.

"No, it's that ranger. I'd know them boots anywhere."

Eb joined them in the street.

"What ranger? Come on."

"The one what hit me that day."

"You sure?" Eb said.

"I know it is."

"Hey," Eb said, stepping forward as he drew his gun. Quick shots from a small gun accompanied by yells caused him to turn the other way.

"Hey yerself." Hugh looked back in time to see the ranger pull the trigger on the ten gauge. The first blast hit Eb square in the chest, while the second made half of Curly's head disappear. The driver of the carreta pulled a rifle from under the seat and began firing as the ranger dropped the shotgun and drew his pistol. Hugh ran for cover and threw himself against the front door of the general store. The lock gave with the weight of his body and he fell to the floor as three long blasts from the steam-whistle at the Three Mile Mine sounded. Scrambling to his feet, he saw the lady on the other side of the counter level the shotgun.

"Oh God, don't...." The blast propelled him back to the street.

~   ~   ~

"No, stop," Leonida said as the nervous horse pranced back and forth. All she had wanted was the surrender of Henry

Baines and Pod Randell, but Dogtown had instead become a war zone. She had stopped in front of the saloon to ask where she might find the judge when that man had grabbed her. Then, all she could see were the two men by the river dragging her into the bushes. The next thing she knew, she was firing the little pistol and chasing the man who had claimed to own Rosa around the corner of the building. The other one who had grabbed her lay dead on the steps to the saloon. Now everyone was shooting at each other.

"Wait....please stop!" She waived her arm in the air but no one heard her. This was not what she had wanted. Paco and Juan appeared from behind the store to grab the reins from her hand and lead her to safety.

"Juan....Paco? Please make them stop." The vaqueros stood silently with gun in hand, guarding their Doña.

~   ~   ~

Marvin Carson pressed himself tight against the wall. He'd only been hired yesterday and didn't understand what was happening. He had been out of work for several weeks and was cold and hungry when he rode into town, so the promise of steady work by the judge as a deputy seemed like a good thing. But the grizzly deaths of several men that morning had started him questioning the wisdom of his decision. And now all hell had broken loose. He just wanted out of there. Armed vaqueros appeared everywhere the moment the shooting started. They came from behind buildings shooting and yelling, while others fired from rooftops. A dozen or more charged down the middle of the street on horseback hooting and firing.

Several of the men standing in front of the jail bolted toward the other end of town, but they were met by a mob of angry miners who carried guns, picks and shovels. A couple more broke through the door in an attempt to make a stand inside the jail, but they were met with such a hail of gunfire from every angle that they stood no chance. Marvin fell to his knees and held his hands high in surrender, believing it was a miracle he had not been shot to pieces.

"Get down." A heavy boot pushed him to the boards. He glanced up at the tall man with the grey moustache. He was bleeding from a wound above his temple and another in his left arm. "I said, get down." He shoved the boot against the side of Marvin's neck and pinned him to the walkway.

"Don't even breath, boy," he said, removing Marvin's gun from its holster and dropping his empty one beside him. "If you so much as scratch an itch, one of them Mexicans will bore you fer shore." The man fired a couple of shots from the pistol and was gone. Marvin lay there as he was told long after the fighting died down.

~   ~   ~

Henry Baines sat behind the barrels, frozen in disbelief at what had taken place. He watched Leonida Garcia ride her black Arabian down the middle of the street, bold as brass. The horse halted in front of The Rusty Rail as George Bidwell came staggering through the doors, yelling for Ambrose, and grabbed her by the arm. Henry halfway expected her to slap the drunken barber when her left arm swung across the saddle toward his face, but the quick pop-pop-pop of the small gun turned his blood cold. George turned and fell face first on the sidewalk as Ambrose dove for cover. "Damn," Henry said as she spurred the horse after the fleeing bartender. The vaqueros charged their horses, and the streets were suddenly alive with gunfire. Mexicans appeared everywhere as if by magic. Henry drew his own gun and blew the lock off the bank door, pushing his way inside as someone appeared at the corner of the livery with a gun in each hand.

"You dirty bastard," he said, closing the door behind him. "You were in here the whole time." He pointed his gun at the frightened banker who backed against the open vault behind the counter.

"You've got to understand, judge. It's not my fault," Samuel Addington said, holding a folded paper in his hand. "I got this letter shoved under my door that...."

"I don't care if you got the whole Bible shoved under your door. You were still going to leave me out there in the street to rot, weren't you? You knew I had to leave, and you were going to keep all my money for yourself." Henry didn't flinch when a bullet crashed through the window only inches from where he was standing.

"No, it's not like that, really. Please, I've got a wife and children."

"Tell them goodbye." He fired twice and the banker crumbled to the floor. "Damn thief." He took a canvas bag from under the counter and began emptying the vault. "You were going to keep all my money, weren't you? So now, I'll just take all yours. How do you like that?"

Chapter 62

Alice Carpenter's arm was bruised by the kick of the shotgun, but she hardly felt the pain as she watched the scene unfolding before her. The driver of the *carreta* dropped his empty rifle as he leaped to the ground pulling a pistol from his belt. He aimed the gun and pulled the trigger, but nothing happened. He tried again and was met with the same results as a man named Shavers stepped in front of her window to point a gun at him. Another blast from her shotgun shattered the glass and knocked Shavers from the sidewalk into the street. She ran to the front door and tossed her husband's pistol to the driver. He scooped the gun from the dust and glanced up with a smile. It was Jose Flores. He disappeared to the other side of the cart firing Ike's pistol.

Alice walked back to the counter and reloaded the shotgun with trembling fingers. "That one was for you, Arturo," she said. Taking her seat on the stool, she sipped her tea and watched the action through her broken door and window.

~   ~   ~

Sean tied Cathy behind the barn in hopes the mule would not get hurt by a stray bullet. He had second thoughts about entering the street himself. He paused and doubled-checked the loads in the Coutys. The sound coming from the other side of the barn reminded him of the time his platoon had been pinned down by some Sioux. Beads of sweat collected on his brow as he dried his palms on his pant legs. "Aw, hell," he said and pulled both guns from his belt and darted to the corner where he stopped to look. He watched as Henry Baines shot the lock off the bank and went inside. He glanced around. The battle was moving toward the other end of town where a wave of miners was pouring out of the Three Mile Mine. Sean stepped around the corner and ran to the bank where he pressed himself against the wall. The judge was arguing with somebody, but the street was too noisy for him to hear what they were saying. Two shots rang out from inside. Sean caught his breath and counted to ten before kicking the door open. Henry looked up from the vault in panic. He had a canvas bag in one hand and a fistful of bills in the other.

"You killed him," Sean said, staring at the dead banker.

"Hell yeah, I killed him. He was a thief. He was trying to keep my money."

"So, what makes you think you're any different?"

"I'm simply taking what's mine, plus a little interest."

The shooting in the street stopped, with the exception of a scattered shot every once in awhile. Sweat began to bead on Henry's brow.

"Drop the money, Judge, and back against the wall. They'll be here any second now."

"Let 'em come." Henry's move caught Sean completely by surprise as he dropped the money, scooped the pistol from the floor and fired. The bullet caught Sean along the left ribcage and spun him sideways as he fired the gun in his right hand.

Sean fell against the wall, holding his side and waiting

for the smoke to clear and his ears to quit ringing. He saw the judge through the haze, leaning against the vault with the bone in his right arm shattered and poking through his sleeve.

"Don't," Sean said as Henry slowly stooped toward the fallen pistol. "It's over with."

"Not hardly," he said in a strained voice, grabbing the gun. Sean painfully leveled the other pistol while both men glared at each other. Henry dropped his gun, as Paco and two other men burst through the door with drawn weapons. The vaquero only glanced at Sean, then headed straight for the judge, whom he grabbed by the collar and drug toward the door.

"Wait, hold on. What do you think you're doing?" Henry said as one of the men slipped a lariat around his neck. The men didn't answer as they pulled him through the door. "You can't do this. I'm the judge. It's against the law. Wait, please."

Sean followed in a daze as they proceeded toward the livery stable where a crowd had begun to congregate. "Jesus," Sean said as Paco threw the end of the lariat over the same beam that had held Rudolfo's lifeless body. He started to step forward in an attempt to stop them, but Hanky's strong grip on his arm restrained him.

"Hold on, boy. Let justice have its way."

"Oh, God, pleased don't do this. I'm begging. Please don't." Tears ran freely down Henry's cheeks as he pleaded.

"Paco," Leonida said, edging her horse through the crowd. "Take the lariat off him."

"Thank you. Oh, God, thank you," Henry said, falling to his knees.

"But, Señora," Paco said glancing from her to the judge and back again. Several of the vaqueros began grumbling and shifting their feet.

"Take it off, Paco."

"Si, Señora," he said as he jerked the rope back over the beam.

"That is your leather lariat, isn't it Paco?"

"Si. I was going to hang this gringo with it." He pulled the noose from Henry's neck.

"Oh, thank you Mrs. Garcia. Thank you. I knew you'd understand." Henry ran to grab hold of her boot.

"*Silencio*," she said, kicking him in the chest. Henry fell with a stunned look on his face. "He is a *cerdo* and is not worth being hung with a good Mexican lariat, Paco." She spurred the horse to the corral to retrieve a hemp rope slung over one of the posts, and tossed it to the vaquero.

"Use this cheap American rope, and pull him up slowly like he did my husband. And leave him for the birds to eat." Paco smiled as he slipped the noose over Henry's neck and pulled it snug.

"No, oh God, no. Please don't. I'm beggin'. Please...." Henry's eyes were wide and his pants grew dark with urine as they tossed the rope over the beam. The vaqueros scrambled and pushed to find a hold on the rope as they hauled him upward. Henry kicked and jerked as the end of the rope was tied to the fence. Then it was over.

Sean felt numb as he watched Doña Leonida ride the prancing horse past the dead man. She looked at the judge without any outward sign of emotion, then turned her horse back toward the center of town. She glanced at Sean as she rode by and he felt a shiver pass through him.

"Come on, son." Hanky patted him on the back. "Let's see if we can find Tommy and see how he done."

Chapter 63

Tex was the last to enter town and headed straight for The Rusty Rail. He dismounted and calmly tied his horse to the hitching post as he surveyed the street. It was a war zone, with men running, shooting and screaming everywhere. He stepped over George Bidwell's body and drew his gun as he pushed through the swinging doors.

"Boy, am I sure glad to see you. Come on in," Pod said, pouring himself another drink. Tex let the doors swing shut as he glanced around. Except for Pod Randell, the place was empty.

"Lookin' for Ambrose?"

"Yeah, I wanna give him somethin'."

"Figures. But you ain't gonna find him around here none. That young Mex girl? She run him off after she kilt George out there. You shoulda seen it. Ol' Ambrose took off like a scared rabbit yellin' fer mercy, and her right behind him on that black horse tryin' to nail his ass with that pepper box. Funniest damn thing I ever seen," Pod said laughing.

"Did she kill him?"

"Hell if I know. But if she didn't, he's halfway to Los Angeles the way he was runnin'. Sit down and have a drink. We got time." He kicked a chair out for Tex as he filled an extra glass. Tex remained standing, glaring at him and still holding the gun in his hand. "Look, you can trust me. Here," he held up his left hand as he removed his revolver and laid it on the table. "There's my iron in plain sight where you can keep an eye on me, and you can still hang on to yours if you want. Plop yerself down and have your drink, then we'll settle this thing like we always knowed we would."

Tex turned the chair around and straddled it with the back in front of him before laying his own gun on the table. The fighting outside had calmed to just a few random shots here and there.

"That didn't take long," Pod said refilling his glass. His eyes were bloodshot and his speech was beginning to slur. "Knew them saddle bums wouldn't put up much of a fight when he hired them."

"Why'd you go along with it then?"

Pod looked up as if surprised by the question. "Weren't supposed to turn out like this. It was just gonna be me and him, and then he goes and hires all them yayhoos. Most of 'em needed killin'." He downed the drink and refilled both glasses. The doors swung open as Juan and two other vaqueros entered. Tex held up a hand and the men halted by the door.

"Don't suppose none of you boys are gonna let me walk outa here?" Pod said with a grin.

"Hardly."

"Didn't think so. Too bad its gotta turn out like this, Tex. I kinda like you. You and me woulda been great pards, you know."

"Na, it wouldn't of worked, Pod. You forked that devil-bronc of yours a long time ago, and you'll ride him straight to hell. Besides, you've been dyin' to know who's faster ever since I rode into town."

"Yer right there." He held up his drink in a final salute and downed it. "It's made me damn curious."

"Hell of a way to satisfy a man's curiosity, ain't it?"

"Why not? Ya gotta meet the devil sometime." Two shots rang out from inside the bank across the street. "What the hell was that, a damn cannon?"

"Paco goes to see," Juan said, looking out the door.

"Ready?" Pod said, checking the loads in his pistol.

"Just need to know one thing first. Why'd you beat Rosa that way?" Tex shrugged as he holstered his gun. The sound of a man screaming and begging for mercy drew both men's attention to the door.

"Paco is going to hang the judge, I think," Juan said as they joined him at the door. They watched the vaqueros drag the pleading man toward the livery.

"Hang him? Damn," Pod said shaking his head. "Well, can't say the greedy bastard don't deserve it." He walked back to the table and poured himself another drink. "It were all his idee, ya know."

"What was?"

"The raw deal with the Mex lady and her husband. I was happy with gettin' what money we was from the miners here. But the judge, he kept watchin' them come in here every week and starts wonderin' what it would be like to own that big ranch of theirs. So, he cooks up this here plan of his to kill 'em off, and then he'd just take over. But it didn't quite work that way. Then, he ups and hires that bunch lyin' dead out there in the street, thinkin' they'd be able to run 'em off, exceptin' that Mex lady don't run so easy. Now, he's gettin' hisself hung fer his trouble."

"*Caramba*," Juan said, doing the sign of the cross, still watching the proceeding at the livery.

"Done?" Pod said.

"Si, Doña Leonida see to it herself. Now, they come our way."

"Don't let them in, Juan. This is between Pod and myself." Tex adjusted his gunbelt.

"Right you are, Pard. But they wasn't gonna hang me no way. One way or the other, they wouldn't a hung me." Pod laughed as he walked to the other side of the room rolling a cigarette and leaned against the bar. He struck a match and drew deeply. "Better have yerself one, Tex. Never know, it might be yer last." Juan handed Tex the one he had just lit for himself and began rolling another as the men outside crowded to the door and windows to watch.

"Never answered my question, Pod." Tex walked around the table to give himself a clear view of the man he faced.

"What one was that?"

"About Rosa. Why'd ya have to hurt her?"

"She laughed at me," he said as his eyes darted from place to place before landing on Tex again. He took a deep breath and adjusted his own gunbelt. "I paid her, and when we got to the room, she laughed at me. You just don't laugh at someone's manhood like that, Pard. I don't care who ya are."

"She wasn't laughing at you, Pod. She said you reminded her of her younger brother when you got yer hat and shirt off. Ya got yeller hair and all that, but she says you look an awful lot like him. She laughed 'cause she thought fer a minute you was him."

"Damn," Pod said, taking his time crushing his cigarette. "Probably don't make much difference now, but tell her I'm sorry, that is if you make it through this."

"Someone will tell her."

"I don't cotton to women much, but I kinda liked her."

"Funny way to show a girl, ain't it?"

"Suppose so. Ready?"

Tex turned so his right arm pointed toward Pod as he stepped away from the bar. Both men stood motionless for a moment, then Pod's hand dropped to his holster. Tex had no way of knowing the reason, but his two bullets caught Pod in the chest and spun him against the bar before the little man could clear leather. Pod fell to his knees and raised his gun in an attempt to get off at least one shot, but the next bullet took him in the forehead.

"Game little bastard, wasn't he?" Hanky said, joining

Tex as he reloaded his gun.

"Yeah, real game." He had a bad taste in his mouth.

Chapter 64

Leonida Garcia dismounted and tied her horse in front of the general store before turning to face the group of miners. She felt exhausted and ill. The entire battle had only taken a few minutes. It wasn't supposed to turn out this way. She had only wanted to get the judge and Pod Randell, but dead and wounded men were lying everywhere. Woodrow Black stepped forward to greet her with a short bow.

"Mrs. Garcia, you know my foreman, Cary Jones, don't you?"

"Si," she said with a small curtsey. "My people appreciate your help, Señores, and offer our apologies if any of your men or property have been injured."

"I don't think any miners were hurt, were they, Cary?"

"No, not outside of a few bumps and scrapes. And they caused the most of them their selves trying to be the first out in the streets. But we did catch a couple of those varmints that were causing you all that trouble," the foreman said, pointing toward two frightened men being held by large miners. "We was wondering what you want done with them, ma'am?"

Leonida sighed deeply and glanced toward her father before answering.

"There has been way too much violence here today. Let them go, but tell them if I ever see them around here again, I will turn them over to Ildefonso Baca, and he will deal harshly with them."

"You hear that?" Cary said. "She says you can git. But if you ever come back here, she's gonna let that Paiute scalp you. Now, get on your horses and cut a shuck for somewhere else."

The two men glanced at her before running to the livery stable, where they stopped dead in their tracks upon seeing the body of Henry Baines swinging back and forth in the breeze. They glanced back a second time and dashed for the corral where their horses waited.

"I don't think they'll stop running until they cross the Arizona border," Woodrow said with a chuckle.

"I hope not. I never want to see any of them again," Leonida said. She turned as if to go, but stopped. "Señores, I know my people will want to hold a fiesta tomorrow to celebrate their victory. It would bring us much pleasure if you would come and bring your families with you."

"Thank you, ma'am. You can count on our being there," Woodrow said with a bow.

"*Niña*, come." Jose stood in the doorway of the store holding a hand out for her. The broken glass crunched under her boots as she stepped around the body lying at the steps and through the broken door. The general put an arm around her shoulders and pulled her close. "I wish to thank Señora Carpenter in front of you for saving my life."

"Oh?" Leonida raised her eyebrows.

"Si, my pistol had jammed and I was about to be killed when the Señora shot the man through her window. Then she gave me this gun to use." He held the Colt in his hand for her to see.

"Is this true, Señora?"

"They murdered our husbands and Arturo. I couldn't

stand by and see them kill someone else. I had no idea he was your father at the time. He looks so different dressed like that." Her lips trembled as she shrugged her shoulders. Leonida believed the lady didn't even know she was crying.

"I see," she said taking Alice by the shoulders and kissing her on each cheek. "I am greatly indebted to you, Señora. I wish you to come stay with me at my hacienda. We both have lost our husbands for the same cause, and we could comfort each other in our sorrow, and give each other joy."

"Thank you, Mrs. Garcia, but I'm afraid I can't. You see, I have this store and...."

"No, no," she said stopping her by placing her fingers on Alice's lips. "I will not hear of it. You must at least come and spend a few days with me. I insist."

"My folks will look after the store for you, ma'am," Woodrow Black said from the doorway. "Go ahead and go. It will be good for you."

"And if we decide it is too much trouble, I will buy the store from you. It would only cause you more pain to stay here and listen for your husband's voice and look for him in every corner. I know, Señora. My arms try to hold Rudolfo each night as I lay in bed, and I look for him every time my father lights a cigar." She turned to study the shelves lined with canned goods and boxes. "I long to hear happy voices again. I wish to love again someday, and you will too. You are still young."

"I'm forty, and that's old enough to be your mother, young lady," Alice said with a weak laugh.

"Si, but I ask you for me also, Señora."

"I'll think about it and let you know."

"*Gracias, Señora. Via con Dios*," Leonida said, kissing her again. "Do come to visit a few days, regardless. My people wish to celebrate, so you must come." She paused at the door and glanced around. "I'll ask some men to stay and fix your door and put some boards over the window, if you wish."

"That would be nice. Thank you Mrs. Garcia. And I will try to come tomorrow."

"*Gracias*. Papa, I will be leaving soon."

"Si, *Niña*. I'll be along in a moment, but I wish to talk with Señora Carpenter first."

Leonida untied her horse and led him to the middle of the street, then turned to see him kissing the woman's hand. *Have you found her interesting for another reason than saving your life, mi papa? She is pretty, isn't she?* She stopped as Josiah Russell came toward her dragging a young cowboy by the collar.

"Hate to bother you, ma'am, but I was wonderin' whut you wanted me to do with this here coyote?" She thought the dark wild eyes of the youth matched the hair poking out from under the tattered hat. His clothes were dirty and ragged.

"Was he one of them?"

"Don't rightly know. When the shootin' started, he just threw up his hands and fell like he was in some prayer meeting."

"I had no part in killin' your husband and them other people, ma'am, honest. I just got hired yesterday. I didn't know what was going on."

"He's telling the truth. He rode in here yesterday looking half-starved," Alice said from the sidewalk.

"What is you name?"

"Marvin Carson, ma'am. Are you gonna have 'em hang me? I don't wanna die."

"Why did you come to Dogtown, Señor Marvin?"

"Looking for a job. I come out looking for gold, but there ain't none. I was hungry."

"How old are you?"

"Seventeen, I reckon."

"Have you ever worked with cattle?"

"That's all I done back in Alabama, 'cept farming that is."

"Take him to Señor Blackstone and see that he's fed and clothed. Then tell him to put him to work on the farm. I will check on him later and pay Señor Blackstone whatever it costs."

"Come on, boy," Hanky smiled at her and started to leave.

"Señor Marvin?" They stopped. "We are a gentle and loving people by nature. What you see here today is what happens when we have our people murdered by those who wish to take our land away. You may find those on our rancho who do not like *gringos* too well at this moment. So if you find that you do not like working for us, you are free to go. That understood? There will be no hard feelings against you."

"Yes, thank you, ma'am." He managed a slight smile.

"How badly are you hurt, Señor Russell?"

"Been worse. Leg hurts worse'n anything. Hurt it jumpin' outa that damned contraption your pappy made us ride in on."

"See to it that you get Señor Kilkenney to look at your wounds."

"He's gotta get someone to look after him from what I seen. He let the judge bore a hole in him before he decided to fight back."

Leonida's heart skipped a beat. "I just saw him....I did not realize he was hurt. Is he alive?"

"Alive? Shore, it's just a little hole right 'bout here," he said, pointing to his side. "Mighta broke a rib, so he'll be sore fer a while. But he's a big strappin' boy, so he'll be fine. But say, I wanted Maria to look out after these here scratches of mine anyways, 'cause I kinda got my brand set fer her. Hope you don't mind."

"No, Señor, I don't mind at all, if you are speaking of *amor* and not a real branding iron." The ranger tilted back his head and laughed heartily.

She led her horse to the crowd of men waiting in front of The Rusty Rail. They were her men, her army. She had led them into battle, and now they waited for her next order. Her legs trembled and her stomach knotted in nauseating convulsions. *You must be strong. You must not let them see.* Hanky and Vernon Blackstone stood to one side of the crowd talking to the young man.

"Oh." Her hand jumped to her lips as she stifled the cry. Sean was leaning weakly against Tex as the cowboy helped him on the mule. His shirt and pants were soaked with blood. *I'm sorry mi companero. I did not know you were wounded.*

"He is not hurt badly, Señora." Paco leaned close to her ear as he spoke. She had failed to be strong, and now everyone knew.

~ ~ ~

Sean squirmed in the chair, trying in vain to find a position that didn't make his side hurt. He had come to a compromise with Maria in allowing her to become the administrating doctor while he supervised the medical treatment given to the wounded, including himself. And he had to admit that the maid had proven herself to be a capable nurse, and he told her so. This action left her speechless and Sean had almost decided to use the tactic more often, except for its reverse effect. She had become so attentive to him in her effort to show gratitude that she was now becoming a pest. She made sure he got the best chair on the patio and fluffed his pillow, and brought him tea. She even tried to bake him some biscuits like Catherine Blackstone had shown her, which she burnt. But Sean ate them anyway, believing the effort should be rewarded regardless of the results.

"I'll be damned. I get three holes blowed in me, countin' my leg, and you get that one little ol' scratch, and she's fussin' over you like you was somethin' special," Hanky said as Maria handed Sean another cup of tea.

"Señor Kilkenney is something special, Hanky. He makes me his nurse."

"Well, don't I need some nursin' too?"

"Si, but not his kind." She patted the Ranger on the cheek. "I nurse you in the moonlight after the others go to bed." She gave Sean a quick wink and went back to the kitchen.

"Oooeee, Pard. Guess I do get the special treatment."

"Oh, God. Oh, God," Sean said holding his side to keep it from hurting as he laughed. "I hope she doesn't do that again until this rib mends."

Leonida crossed the patio from where she had been talking with Tex and Rosa and paused at the door.

"*Buenas tardes*, Señores. I hope you both will be feeling better soon." She glanced a second time at Sean and ascended the stairs, where she paused to look at them again before entering her room.

"Don't be too hard on her Doc. She done what she had to do."

"She gave the order to hang that man. I saw her."

"I was there too, Pard. What'd ya want her to do, let him go?"

"No. I don't know, Hanky. It was the look in her eyes. I'd never seen it before. It gave me a chill."

"Oh, I see. Now you don't think she's the sweet innocent little thing you thought she was, is that it?" Sean glared at him. "Well, you are in love with her, ain't you? You might as well admit it, 'cause we've all knowed it fer a long time. She's kinda got her brand set fer you too, I think."

"Yes, I did love her, I guess."

"And now you don't, 'cause she had Paco hang a skunk. Well, hell, you tried to blow his arm off. What if you'd kilt him? Would that make you a bad man?"

"I wouldn't like it."

"What makes you think she liked it? None of us do, boy. And what gives you the right to judge that poor girl up there? You can't answer that one, can you? That woman's been through all kinds of hell and needs a little understanding. And you're sittin' here feelin' all outa sorts 'cause she told Paco to kill a hydrophobied skunk. Now, if she was one of them queens that live overseas, and someone kilt a bunch of folks, including the King, would you feel she was wrong having that murderin' coyote hung?"

"No, she would have every right to do so."

"Well, Doc, that's exactly what happened. She's a

queen, and she rules over these seventy-odd square miles. And she's got folks to look after. Ol' Judge Baines and Pod Randell raped and beat the hell outa her, then went about murderin' a bunch of her folks, includin' her king and his brother. Now, you can sit around feeling sorry 'cause she done it. But I ain't. Not in the least." He got up from his chair and limped to the door. "Think about it, Doc."

He stepped through the door and limped toward the kitchen. "Maria, I need some expert nursin'. I think my lips got plumb lonely out there today." He could hear Maria giggle as they scuffled playfully.

Sean sipped his tea as he watched the door at the top of the stairs. *Yes, you are a queen, aren't you? The most beautiful damned queen I've ever seen.*

End

The Rancho:

I don't remember a time when I enjoyed digging for information as much as I did during the writting of this novel. The living conditions on the ranchos I described are accurate, with the exception of Leonida's house itself. While hers seems elaborate, most ranch houses in early California were only single-story, with the cooking facilities located outdoors. And, strangely enough, nearly all of them were built without fireplaces so the occupants froze during winter months. But the diet and economic activity described in these pages stand on historical fact. The chief commercial products were hides and tallow for export. Even simple things that the missions made, such as wool blankets, shoes, saddles, candles and soap, were manufactured in Chile or Peru out of California tallow and hides, then brought back to California and sold at inflated prices. Their diet consisted largely of beef. Milk and butter were scarce even with millions of cattle roaming the grasslands. Very little flour could be found, and even brooms had to be imported.

There were about 20 land grants issued under Spanish rule, and another 500 during the Mexican period. The majority of the Mexican grants were made by Governors Alvarado, Micheltorena, and Pico after the closing of the missions. The government had set the maximum legal limit for a private rancho at 11 square leagues (about 50,000 acres, or 76 square miles). But as always, people found a way around even this generous limit. There were many instances where several different grants were given to the same individual.

The typical rancho had an Indian work force as small as twenty in some cases, and several hundred in others. They consisted largely of former mission Indians who spoke Spanish as well as their native tongue, along with a few new recruits who knew little, if any, Spanish. They usually received little more than food, shelter and some clothing for their labor. And even though they were thought of as being free, they were actually bound in a state of peonage for as long as the rancho cared to hold them. Rancho society was essentially feudal. The Dons ruled as lords on their estates, while the Indians worked in the fields and served as serfs.

Education:

It's hard for us who live in a society of free education, and where higher learning is thought of as a goal to reach, to grasp the idea of total ignorance. But the absence of education during that time period was incredible. There were only two Spanish governors, Borica and Sola, and only one Mexican governor, Figueroa, who made any real effort to establish schools of any kind, and they failed miserably. Then you'd have to realize that, with few exceptions, the missionaries themselves opposed education. They believed that knowledge and the ability to read would cause unruliness and discontentment among the working-class. And there was also a lack of qualified teachers. Every once in a while a retired soldier would try his hand at teaching in a school in Monterey or one of the other small towns, but that usually only lasted for a few days or weeks at the most.

To give an example, California's population in 1845 (not counting the full-blooded native Indians) was only about 7,000. Of these, less than 1,000 were adult males. If you took the ability to read or write anything at all as a standard of being educated, you could probably say that of 100 men. Many of the largest landholders could not even read or write their own names.

It's nice to see the romantic movies and read the books about this period of history. But the colorfulness of those days was only superficial, even for the ruling class. Their gay costumes were simply a desperate attempt to live the good life.

General Kearny:

General Kearny was at Fort Leavenworth when he received instructions from the secretary of war in June of 1846 to occupy New Mexico and then proceed to California to organize a military and civil government there. Kearny found Santa Fe quiet and peaceful, so he set out for California with 300 dragoons. Unfortunately, General Stockton had sent Kit Carson eastward in August to meet Kearny with the premature news that California was also peaceful and firmly in American hands. Upon hearning this, Kearny sent most of his force back to Santa Fe and continued onward with only 100 men, not knowing Los Angeles had fallen into rebel hands.

Kearny and his men set up camp just outside the Indian village of San Pascual, about 35 miles northeast of San Diego, on December 6 exhausted and half-starved. Many of their mounts had been lost along the treacherous journey, and some of the men were riding on mules or unbroken horses. Several hours before dawn, Kearny received word that a rebel detachment was hiding in the village. Kit Carson assured him the Californians he met were cowards who would not and could not fight. Hoping to capture the rebel's horses, Kearny attacked under the cover of the cold, dark fog. The rebels, under the leadership of Andres Pico, began to retreat, luring Kearny and his men into a pursuit that strung them out widely and unprotected. Suddenly, the rebels turned to attack.

The calvary sabers Kearny's men were carrying proved hopelessly ineffective against the Californian lances. Practically all the casualties were on the American side. 22 men were killed, including several officers, and another 16 wounded, including Kearny himself. The fight only lasted 10 minutes before Don Andres' men withdrew to go about their business. Because Kearny still had possession of the battlefield, he reported the battle as a victory. Army historians later certified it as (ahem) "not....a defeat." Kearny also noted in his report that the rebels were "admirably mounted and the very best riders in the world; hardly one that is not fit for the circus."

Treaty of Guadalupe Hidalgo:

The Mexican system for defining title of large land grants was a nightmare. The whole Pomona Valley, for example, was described as "the place being vacant which is known by the name of Rancho San Jose, distant some six leagues, more or less, from the Ex-Mission of San Gabriel, a map of which place we will lay before your Excellency as soon as possible." Since American laws require that land titles be defined exactly and clearly, you can imagine what happened when Americans gained control of California.

To make things worse, there were more than 500 ranchos in Alta California in 1846, but more than 800 claims were filed in the American courts, many of them overlapping portions of other ranchos. These claims covered nearly all the valleys of the coastal region as far north as the Russian River and a number of large tracts in the Sacramento and northern San Joaquin valleys.

The treaty of Guadalupe Hidalgo promised that "property of every kind" belonging to Mexicans in the ceded territories would be "inviolably respected." But American settlers generally believed that all the land was theirs by right of conquest. These settlers refused to believe that a few hundred Mexicans should be allowed to monopolize some 13 million acres of land, especially when little of it was visibly improved and remained entirely unoccupied. As a result, the Act of 1851 was introduced by Senator William M. Gwin, a chief political spokesman for the American settlers. This bill provided for the appointment of a board of three commissioners by the President. The board was to decide the validity of all the claims under Mexican titles. All the lands of the rejected claims were to be regarded as public lands. Both the claimant and the United States government had the right of appeal to the federal court and then to the United States Supreme Court. Critics argued that this would have the effect of confiscating the lands and violate the treaty with Mexico. Every title was to be treated as a fraud against the United States until its holder had established it in three different courts, one of them being the Supreme Court, some 3,000 miles away.

The commission held its hearings from January 1852 to March 1856. All sessions were held in San Francisco except for one brief term held in Los Angeles. Nearly all of the 800 cases presented were appealed to the district court, and 99 cases were appealed to the Supreme Court. 604 claims, involving nearly 9 million acres were confirmed. Another 209 claims, involving about 4 million acres were rejected. Some of these cases dragged on in the courts for several decades, with the average length of time required to secure ownership being 17 years.

By the time a grant was confirmed, the original owner was more than likely bankrupt. Jokes about lawyers' fees are often exaggerated, but history tells us of dozens of cases where the grantees were ruined while their attorneys became rich. Because the landowners were usually cash-poor to begin with, they willingly gave away part of their land as payment of legal fees. Lawyers held on to the land and let their cases drag out in court while land prices sky-rocketed, then ultimately won the case. It was virtually impossible for these land owners to secure a loan to pay off rising debts, because they did not yet have a secure title. Many sold large portions of land at a reduced price while others had mortgages with rates as high as 8 percent per month in the early 1850s. As a result, I couldn't find one grant that ultimately wound up in the hands of its intended owner or descendants.

Dogtown:

There are four different locations in our area claiming the title, but seeing as the 49ers had a habit of calling their camps by whatever name they chose as descriptive and fitting, there very well could have been many different Dogtowns. The term was used mainly as a derogatory description of the deplorable living conditions in the camp, but it stuck in some cases. The Dogtown we chose is still known by that name, and was founded in 1857 by Mormons, and helped to start the mining excitement in that area. We were hard-pressed finding its actual location (relying on neighbors living in the area) and found little more than a few buildings still standing and piles of sand and rock placered in the creek.

Hornitos:

Hornitos was founded by outcasts who were run out of the neighboring town of Quartzburg for the crime of being Mexicans. They joined a handful of settlers already located in the area and formed their own community, which soon outgrew Quartzburg. Today Hornitos lives as one of the best preserved ghost towns in the Mother Lode. The knife fight mentioned was based on an actual account, and was only one of many such events that earned Hornitos the toughest reputation in the Mariposa district.

Bodie:

It was also known as "Badman's Roost. The references to Bodie in this book are taken from actual accounts, and I would not have time nor space here to list more. Let it suffice to note the Western phrase, "Bad man from Bodie" was a real one. As one little girl, whose family was leaving the neighboring town of Aurora for Bodie said in her nightly prayer, "Goodbye, God; we're going to Bodie!"

In July 1859, Waterman "Bill" Body, a Duchman from New York State, shot and wounded a rabbit. While trying to dig it out of a hole, he discovered gold. But Body never lived to reap the rewards of his find. He died in a snowstorm while trying to reach his cabin a few months later. In August 1860, a painter from the rousing town of Aurora is said to have changed Body's name in putting up the sign *Bodie Public Stables*. In any case, it has been Bodie since the early 1860s.

In its heyday between 1878 and 1881, Bodie ran full blast around the clock. The Standard, the Bodie, and nearly thirty other mines, uncovered $25,000,000 in gold and silver ore. It boasted of the hell-roaring Bonanza, the Rifle Club, the Champion and a dozen or so other saloons. It had two banks, three breweries, half-a-dozen hotels, a sizable red light district, four daily newspapers, a well-populated Boot Hill, a volunteer fire brigade, and a Chinatown second only to San Francisco's.

Miwoks and Yokuts:

The name Miwok is the native word for people, plural of miwu, *person.* It is pronounced Mee'-wock. The Plains Miwok in San Joaquin County were in the area from the Calaveras River north. Those Indians living in the southern part of the county were Yokuts. The word Yokut is also the native word for person or people. It is pronounced Yo'-cut, or Yo'-koot. As these names were often descriptive, the translation might also mean people of the rush marshes. The Yokuts were different from the Miwoks and most other California natives in one respect. Like the Comanche, there was no Yokuts tribe, but rather, dozens of small nations, each with its own territory and leaders. They differed from the Comanche in that the Yokuts could have customs and beliefs that were widely divergent from band to band. They were divided into true tribes, with their territory extending to the southern end of the San Joaquin.

Both Miwoks and Yokuts were fine weavers and could make baskets that were water-tight for cooking. Although they were often referred to as "Digger Indians," there were no Digger Indians as a group. This was an expression of contempt given to them by early settlers who saw them digging for the root of the Piñon Pine which they used in some of their baskets.

The descriptions of Indian housing, traditions, religion and *Wa-dom Buh-yee* (Bear Dance) are all taken from actual customs relating to the Miwok, Yokut and Maidu tribes. And while one can still find information and documents regarding the Miwok and Maidu, I found it distressing that very little has been written about the Yokuts. (I actually found only one book concerning them in the County Library where they lived) and very few people are familiar with their name. The name Yokut is not mentioned in the current B. I. A. list of California Indians. The best and most extensive description of this people I found to be in *Indian Summer* by Thomas Jefferson Mayfield, from Heyday Books, which tells of traditional life among the Yokuts in the mid 1800's through the eyes of one who lived with them.

California Grizzly Bear:

This of all the animals was the most feared by the Indians. This bear often weighed one thousand pounds and roamed over much of the lowlands. The bear was seen in great bands in the early spring eating the tender clover and digging for the same bulbs and roots the Indians prized as part of their diet. The Indians not only feared the Grizzly, but respected his cunning. It is said that when they did hunt him, it was from the safety of trees. The California Indians didn't considered him a fit item for their diet, for there was a chance, they thought, they might be eating human flesh. It was commonly believed among these tribes that the shaman, or bear doctor, as described in this book, could actually on occasion become a bear. The last known California Grizzly Bear was reported shot in 1922.

Joaquin Murrieta:

Joaquin Murrieta was living near town when a gang of Americans descended on his place. They hung his brother for a crime he didn't commit, ravished his sweetheart and horse-whipped Joaquin for good measure. Swearing vengeance, the proud youth took to the outlaw trail and formed a band of cutthroats to prey on white settlements up and down the Mother Lode. All twenty-one murderers of his brother were brought to justice, nineteen by Joaquin's own hand. Between 1851 and 1853 he was in and out of nearly every mining camp in the southern Mother Lode, robbing where he chose, laughing at the law, taking from the rich and giving to the poor in true Robin Hood fashion. At least this is how the popular version of Joaquin goes. Now, are you ready for some facts?

Probably no American bandit, not even Jesse James or Black Bart, has been more widely chronicled. Joaquin has been the subject of more than two dozen biographies, eleven of them in Spanish; several novels; two epic poems; one play; several motions pictures; and almost countless newspaper serials, magazine articles, and separate book chapters (including this novel). And it would be hard to find a town in the southern end of the Mother Lode that doesn't lay some claim to having been a favorite haunt of Joaquin.

What we have endeavored to accomplish in this book is a gleaning out of fables and sticking to what is known about this bandit. We have clung largely to newspaper accounts for this purpose. The attack on the Chinese camp, the hanging of Jesus, and the battle at Mokelumne Hill (excluding meeting our fictional characters Poco and Juan) were actual events. After all that has been written and put on the silver screen, newspapers simply report that a bandit called Joaquin terrorized Amador, Calaveras, and probably Mariposa Counties for two months - January to early March, 1848. During that time, he was involved in at least 6 gun battles that left 3 white men dead; 3 separate robberies against whites; rustled cattle at least once; and stole horses at least two times. Robbing Chinamen seemed to be his favorite pastime. He is credited with at least 4 robberies against Chinese camps that left 8 persons dead and a take of approximately $40,000. Like Jesse James and other contemporaries of his time, Joaquin Murrieta was not a nice guy. And that is the end of the story.

But, not being one to throw a wet blanket on romantic dreams, let me add a little fuel to the fire. On July 25, 1848, Captain Harry Love, a former Mexican War express rider and California peace officer, and twenty rangers came upon a band of Mexicans in the San Joaquin Valley near the mouth of Arroyo Cantua, north of the present town of Coalinga. In the fight that followed the rangers killed the leader (supposedly Joaquin) and also a man identified as Manuel "Three-Fingered Jack" Garcia, well known in California as a thief and cutthroat. Court records exist showing one Charles Francis Bludworth, soon to become Sheriff of Merced County, rode with Captain Love, and was listed as a second lieutenant of the official muster. The men were paid $150.00 a month for their trouble. The records also state the deputies happened on Joaquin and his men, and Bludworth was listed among those who pumped nine bullets into Three Fingered Jack, after Jack shot at Love several times, narrowly missing him. Joaquin's horse was shot, and the bandit was killed while trying to escape on foot.

Regardless of which account is accurate, to prove he had actually killed Joaquin, Love brought back the leader's head and Three-Fingered Jack's hand preserved in a keg of brandy. In Mariposa County and other parts of the state, Love sought out seventeen persons who supposedly knew the bandit in an effort to secured affidavits that this was indeed the head of Joaquin. The grisly trophies were put on display at Stockton, then in San Francisco, where the curious paid $1.00 admission.

No sooner had the head been placed on exhibit than some persons claiming to have known the bandit said it was not Joaquin's. Curiously, the head was never taken to Calaveras County, the one area where a number of people had actually seen the outlaw. One caretaker of an Angel's Camp museum who we interviewed claims her grandfather knew Joaquin and his sister personally, and that the bandit was a frequent visitor to their farm. Her grandfather (like many others) said that Joaquin was a true gentleman while in their presence.

Joaquin's sister claimed to be one of the seventeen persons who were called upon to identify the head. She said she affirmed it as Joaquin's, but only did so in order that her brother might be able to flee to Mexico and safety. The caretaker also said her grandfather knew of at least eight bandits in and around the Mother Lode at that time, all claiming to be Joaquin Murrieta. If this is true, that might explain some of the exaggerations concerning his exploits. Or, it just might add more fuel to the fire. You decide.

Terms:

Rancho Manantial Escondido: Ranch of the hidden springs, or Hidden Springs Ranch.
Señora: Madam; mistress; Mrs.
Señor: Mister; gentleman; master; lord.
Cayuse: Horse trained and broken by Indians.
Vaquero: Spanish or Indian cowboy.

Niña: Girl child, baby.
Niño: Boy child, baby.
Chica: Teenage girl.
Chico: Teenage boy.
Adios: Goodbye.
Señorita: Maiden.
Gracias: Thank you.
Anglo: White person.
Companero: Friend, companion.
Dias: Days.
Arma guerrero de pistola: A gunfighter who uses a
    pistol.
Buenos Noches: Good evening.
Amor: Love.
Amante: Lover.
Cabeza: Head.
Silencio: Silence.
Perdon: Pardon.
Don: Lord; master; landowner.
Doña: Mrs.: madam; landowner.
Hija: Daughter
La Bonito Mujer: The Pretty Woman

About The Author

MAJOR MITCHELL is the author of five published novels and two children's books, and currently has two full-length novels in the publishing process. He lives with his wife, Judy, in Northern California. A member of The Western Writers of America and a frequent guest speaker at historical meetings and schools on the west coast, he has also written several songs, and takes the stage on rare occasions as a singer.

More about the author, his books and photo gallery may be found at www.majormitchell.net.

Correspondence should be addressed to:

Shalako Press
P.O. Box 371
Oakdale, CA 95361-0371

For your reading pleasure, we invite you to visit our Trading Post bookstore.

Shalako Press

http://www.shalakopress.com